BEYOND THE BRIGHTENING SEA

A NOVEL

TRUDY J. MORGAN-COLE

BREAKWATER BOOKS LIMITED
www.breakwaterbooks.com
P O Box 2188 · St. John's · NL · Canada · A1C 6E6

CERTIFIED CANADIAN PUBLISHER

LIBRARY AND ARCHIVES CANADA CATALOGUING IN PUBLICATION
Beyond the brightening sea / Trudy J. Morgan-Cole.
Morgan-Cole, Trudy J., 1965- author.
Canadiana (print) 20260218758 | Canadiana (ebook) 20260218804 |
ISBN 9781778531040 (softcover) | ISBN 9781778531057 (EPUB)
LCGFT Historical fiction. | LCGFT: Novels.
LCC PS8626.O747 B49 2026 | DDC C813/.6—dc23

COVER DESIGN Juliane Van Huizen
COVER IMAGE Cannon Rock by Winslow Homer, 1895
PAGE DESIGN AND TYPESETTING Julianna Smith
AUTHOR PHOTO Kate Clow
THE PUBLISHER GRATEFULLY ACKNOWLEDGES THE SUPPORT OF
The Canada Council for the Arts;
The Government of Canada through the Department of Heritage; and
The Government of Newfoundland and Labrador through the Department of Tourism, Culture, Arts and Recreation

Canada Council for the Arts · Conseil des arts du Canada · Canada · Newfoundland Labrador

PRINTED AND BOUND IN CANADA
Breakwater Books is committed to choosing papers and materials for our books that help to protect our environment. To this end, this book is made of certified and other controlled material.

FSC www.fsc.org MIX Paper | Supporting responsible forestry FSC® C103567

PRAISE FOR TRUDY J. MORGAN-COLE

THE CUPIDS TRILOGY

A Company of Rogues

"This is not a dry rendering of history—Morgan-Cole creates convincing characters, dialogue-rich prose, and tension in the narrative." – *Atlantic Books Today*

"It's the finest form of time travel I know."

– *Guylaine Spencer*

Such Miracles and Mischiefs

"A delicious book, full of adventure . . ." – *Consumed by Ink*

"*Such Miracles and Mischiefs* is a wonderful read, presenting Newfoundland history as we've not seen it before . . ."

– *Atlantic Books Today*

A Roll of the Bones

- *The Miramichi Reader's* "The Very Best!" Book Award, Silver Medal, Cover Art/Design Category
- Canada Book Award Winner

"Morgan-Cole is a detail-oriented writer who clearly has all of her characters firmly fleshed out in her imagination, and the consummate skill she uses to have them interact in ways and means we might never have imagined will keep the reader entranced from the first word to the final full stop."

– *The Miramichi Reader*

"The prose in *A Roll of the Bones* is flowing and sensuous."

– *Paul Butler*

"Morgan-Cole is skilled not just with historical fiction but that of several different periods . . ." – *Joan Sullivan*

"Morgan-Cole cracks open the past and lights it up."

– *Michelle Butler Hallett*

MOST ANYTHING YOU PLEASE

". . . a wonderful achievement." – *Kevin Major*

"[Morgan-Cole's] characters are vivid and nuanced . . ."

– *Michelle Butler Hallett*

A SUDDEN SUN

- Heritage and History Book Award finalist, 2015

"Trudy Morgan-Cole is building a reputation as a writer of compelling fiction, and *A Sudden Sun* . . . can do nothing but enhance that reputation." – *The Northeast Avalon Times*

"*A Sudden Sun* is not just an absorbing book, but an important one. It is a page-turner with heart." – *Ed Kavanagh*

THAT FORGETFUL SHORE

- IPPY Awards, Gold Medal, Best Regional Fiction, Canada–East, 2012
- Heritage and History Book Award Winner, 2012
- Best Atlantic-Published Book Award Finalist, 2012

". . . uncovers the hidden lives and untold stories of women and girls with great precision and care, building a gripping novel of love, loss, and ambition . . ." – *Kate Pullinger*

BY THE RIVERS OF BROOKLYN

- IPPY Awards, Silver Medal, Best Regional Fiction, Canada–East, 2010
- Best Atlantic-Published Book Award Finalist, 2010

"Trudy Morgan-Cole has broken new ground . . . a finely nuanced novel that is a pleasure to read." – *Joan Clark*

EPIGRAPH

The barrèd east beyond the brightening sea,
Thick with portentous wraiths of phantom fear,
Is flushed with triumph, stirred with melody . . .

The mystic Four their solemn vigil keep
Until day break, and eastward silently,
Over the kingless land and wailing deep,
The sacrificial symbol fire the sky;
Then they arise, no more to watch and weep.

– From J. Arthur Blaikie, "Arthur in Avalon"

PROLOGUE

January 1649: England has been torn apart by civil war for six years. The king, Charles I, is at war with his own Parliament, and Parliament's forces are winning. Some of the rebels want only to limit royal power, while others flirt with the unprecedented idea of forming a republic—a country with no king at all. Many of them are Puritan religious reformers, who question not only the authority of the Anglican Church, but the authority of the monarchy itself.

King Charles has been Parliament's prisoner for the last two years, kept under house arrest in a series of castles and stately homes. As he is moved from one household to another, he constantly hatches escape plots while trying to negotiate a peace treaty with his captors. But his time is running out.

Meanwhile, across the Atlantic, English colonists spend another long, cold winter on the shores of Newfoundland, waiting for news from home.

CHAPTER ONE

Spring 1649

"The king is dead."

Frances had heard those words many years ago, when she was still a young woman in London. Old King James had died, and his son, the good, ill-fated Charles, had ascended the throne. No one had known then that Charles was ill-fated; it had been a sunny, golden day full of promise. "The king is dead; long live the king," people said all over London that day. And long before then, she thought, in a nearly unbroken line stretching back to the days of William the Conqueror. "The king is dead" was like a line in a church service, always followed by the people's response: "Long live the king."

But not today. *The king is dead* was the end of a sentence.

The king is dead; we have no king.

"When?" said her sister, and it was only then that Frances knew she had spoken aloud.

She looked up from the paper in her hand at Sara's stricken face. *How can she be shocked?* Frances thought. *We knew this would happen. I told her it would happen.*

"In January."

"Four months, nearly," Sara Kirke said.

Four months they had been without a king, citizens of a kingdom that no longer existed, cast away and forgotten here on the outer edge of England's domains. When King James died, Frances had heard the news immediately in the streets of London. But if anything happened in England in January, even something as momentous as the murder of a monarch, nobody in Newfoundland would hear of it until winter ended. News came when ships began crossing the ocean again in spring.

Not even Frances Hopkins, she who had slept under the same roof as King Charles and spent evenings reading poetry and playing chess with him, who had helped plan his last, thwarted escape attempt before she and her sons left England in November, not even she could defy the tyranny of the winter ocean to learn of events when they happened.

She had known ever since she fled England that the king might be dead. When she left—when her husband had told her she must leave—King Charles had been negotiating with Parliament, one last attempt to forge a treaty that all sides knew would likely fail. That was why William had sent Frances and the boys away: If the treaty failed, England would not be safe for King Charles's most ardent supporters.

Even so, Frances had held out hope all winter that there might be a last-minute reprieve. And all the time she had fretted about it, thinking that even men like Fairfax and Cromwell could not be so wicked as to murder God's anointed, all this time, the deed had been done.

"What will happen now?" Sara said. There was something in her voice Frances had never heard: uncertainty. Strong, sensible Sara, who had a plantation to run and a husband by her side, always knew what to do next. But what certainty could anyone have when the world had turned upside down?

"The ship's captain had a whole packet of letters for David," Frances said. "I am sure your husband has his orders, along with far more information than I have."

"Orders? Will we be taking orders from Parliament, now? Do we hold this land at the pleasure of the Puritan rabble?"

"I cannot say," said Frances, still scanning the letter. She knew her sister's concerns were real, and important. What would become of this colony of Avalon, this New Found Land, in a strange new world without a king? What would become of David's governorship—David Kirke, known to be the King's man?

But those fears seemed faint and distant; all she saw in her mind's eye was King Charles in the sitting room of the big house in Newport, smiling at Frances's son Richard as they read a poem together. How kind he had been. How very like an ordinary man, and yet how unlike.

"The king is dead," Meg Taylor said to her husband.

"Aye, and about time, too," said Peter.

"That's shocking for you to say—you can't mean it." She laid her dinner on the table and sat down across from him. He had already said grace and was tucking into his meal with gusto, though it was the tail end of last year's salt fish and not near as tasty as it had been in the fall.

"Who's to be king now?" Peter wondered aloud, not troubling to say whether he meant the shocking words or not. "The queen and the Prince of Wales are in exile, last I heard—are they going to put the Duke of Gloucester on the throne? A child king? Or is it really rule by the people, at last?"

"Lord ha' mercy, Peter, I know naught of such things. All I know is I was up at the big house when the letters came in off that ship, and I heard Lady Frances say, 'The king is dead, murdered by those wicked Puritans.'"

Peter laughed. "That's what the likes of her ladyship would say. I had the same news off the sailors—everyone was buzzing with it as soon as they came into port. Happened back in the winter, it seems, but we're only getting the news now."

"So, what are you asking me all them questions for, if you got the same news I did?"

"'Twas all jumbled up, the news the sailors passed on. Seems things are still in quite a state over in England. I thought mayhap the folks at the big house might know more of what's going on."

"Happen they do, but Lady Frances wouldn't be telling that to me when I'm there picking up her wash."

"And if she had, you'd ha' paid no mind to it. Women!" Peter said, with an exasperated shake of his head.

Meg thought the difference between herself and her husband was not only the difference between women and men, considerable though that was, but the difference between someone like Peter who had been born in England and fought in the wars there, and someone like herself who had never set foot in the home country. Meg had been brought up to pride herself on being one of the first English children born in the

New Found Land. Peter had come out to the colony from a world that seemed as far off as a fairy tale, a land ruled by a real flesh-and-blood king whom Peter had once seen passing by in a carriage. A king who could be imprisoned, put on trial, and put to death.

Meg was loyal to the dead king without ever having seen him. But Peter had not just seen the king, he had taken up arms and fought against the king's army in the taking of Bristol. Peter's sentiments were firmly on the side of Parliament, which Meg understood to be the party of men who wanted to pull the king from his throne.

"There must be someone to rule, mustn't there?" she said now, tucking into her turnip and parsnips. Like the fish, the vegetables were last year's crop; everything tasted old at this time of year.

"What if the people rule themselves?" Peter countered.

"But that would be madness! There must be some order. Does not God anoint the king, and the king names governors and lords and all that?"

Peter laughed again. "So, David Kirke, yon man there in the big house, he's put there by God to rule over us, is he? And yet up in Bristol's Hope where your mam and da are, they never see his face but once every year or two. There might as well be no governor, and everyone gets by well enough."

"But we all know we are subjects of the king."

"Not any longer." He pushed back his empty trencher, and she took it from him, passing him the ale jug. He waved it away. "Nay, no more for me now—I'm off to work repairing the stage. Belike I can talk to the sailors and find out more of the news from England."

"Like a bunch of old women gossiping," Meg said.

"Like a bunch of men who mean to change the world," said Peter, getting up from the table. "A world without lords and kings, Meg—think about it! That's the world we will raise our children in."

Perhaps he meant it as a word of hope, she thought as the door closed behind her husband. It did not seem so to Meg. She had always meant to raise her children in a land far from lords and kings, in the New Found Land, where every planter-fisherman looked to his own land and his own family, and all pulled together to help one another in time of need. Where a ship's captain or a merchant was the loftiest man she would ever clap eyes on, yet somewhere far away in shadowy England there was a king in charge of it all. A king who made sure the ships crossed the ocean with trade goods aboard and took away their fish in the fall. Who made the world, the world she knew, run smoothly as a spinning top.

To say that this king no longer existed and that no other would be put in his place was like going to services on a Sunday and being told by the minister that God had died the night before. What would be the point, then, of all the kneeling and praying and preaching? What anchor would hold them in place if the seabed was gone? God and king were the same: distant, unseen, but necessary.

"Enough of that," Meg said aloud. Today was washday, not for her own and Peter's clothes, which could wait, but for the baskets of garments she had brought down from the big house. She had an afternoon's work ahead of her. The linen undergarments had been soaking in the bucking-tub and were now ready for scrubbing. The day was fair and sunny, though cold—a good day for washing clothes and drying them in the sun.

With the remnants of her own and Peter's dinner cleared away, she hefted the big pot of water off the hearth and carried it carefully out into the yard. The smell of the bucking-tub, left warming over a smaller fire in the yard, hit her as she approached it: a mix of urine and ashes to bleach the white linens. Meg had been brought up to do this kind of thorough cleaning only twice a year, when it was time for the Great Wash; otherwise, she scrubbed her own clothes and Peter's with the soap she made herself. But Lady Sara and Lady Frances at Kirke House insisted on having their wash soaked in the bucking-tub and then scrubbed once a month.

The ways of a big house, of people like the Kirkes, were almost as foreign to Meg as the poor old king in England. As Peter had rightly said, Meg had grown up in a place that knew no governor and no lords and ladies. Her father's plantation in Musketto Cove, tucked between Carbonear and Harbour Grace, was part of the colony of Bristol's Hope. There on the shores of Conception Bay, some planters tended more land, hired more fishing servants, and lived in bigger houses than others. Meg's parents were not as well off as the Guys in Carbonear, who owned half the shore, but her family had a fair-sized house, a nice piece of land, two fishing boats, and six men to work for them in the fishing season.

Meg had been twenty-two, content in her parents' house with no particular inclination to marry any of the young men she had known all her life, until Peter Taylor had come to fish out of Harbour Grace the summer before last. When he made an offer for her hand, her father had said a house and boat would be her marriage portion. The land on which the house was located was not in Conception Bay where they lived, but down the shore in Ferryland. Her father had been a planter, fisherman, and sailor in the New Found Land for nigh on forty years and had acquired odd bits of property all around the coast, which he passed on to his children. One of them was this planter's house in Ferryland, which some of the older folks called Avalon, nestled in the shadow of Sir David Kirke's Pool Plantation.

So, Meg and Peter had married six months ago and arrived in Ferryland as owners of a house, a boat, and a piece of land. All three were modest, but being a planter was a considerable step up for Peter, who had come to the New Found Land as a hired crewman on a fishing vessel.

Meg often felt she did not know her husband very well; he thought and talked about things she did not understand. But they both wanted the same things, she thought. She had married because she wanted to be the wife of a prosperous planter like her father, and having already brought a house and boat into the marriage, she was determined to do whatever she could to improve their fortunes. When Lady Frances Hopkins's servant Hannah had told Meg that Kirke House was looking for a woman to take in their laundry for a little extra coin, Meg leapt at the chance.

"I have come too late, you are started already," said Hannah Peake as she opened the gate to Meg's yard.

"Nay, I have barely begun. Here, take these." She handed Hannah a pile of reeking petticoats to plunge into the hot water. "Is her ladyship still in a swivet over the news from England?"

"*Both* their ladyships," Hannah said, "and Sir David too, and the lads. They all talk of nothing else but how the poor king died and what this will all mean for them." She looked down at the garment she was scrubbing, then up at Meg with a sly half-smile. "I washed out his underclothes too, you know."

"The king's? Truly?"

"Acourse I did. I worked for Lady Hopkins back when they were at Newport, when the king was kept prisoner in their house."

"Mercy me. Washing out the king's underbreeches—strange to think of it."

"Seems his last laundry maid was spying for him, passing secret letters and all that business. So, when they put him in Sir William and Lady Frances's house, they wanted none of the king's own servants about him, only the ones already working in the house. After awhile it seemed like nothing special—a king wears underclothes like any ordinary man, and they need washing. And I surely wasn't going to be doing any spying for him."

"Did you ever see him? Up close?"

"I never waited on him. I was a scullery maid and laundry maid. I'd see him across a room, like, as I might be carrying something in or out."

"How long were you . . . with Lady Hopkins?"

Meg hesitated a bit before "with"; she had been about to say "working for" but realized she was not certain what exactly Hannah's station in life was. Meg had only met one Negro other than Hannah, a sailor named Omar who had sometimes sailed with her father and once or twice visited their house when his ship was in port. She had occasionally glimpsed other dark-skinned sailors who came and went on ships, but never a woman of that complexion and never anyone who lived here in the New Found Land. Her father's friend Omar was a free man, but she knew that not all Africans were so. And was Hannah even African? Her dark skin suggested it, but her speech was purely English.

"Two years. Before that I was maid to another woman, Mistress Hill. That was my first position. Went to her when I was fifteen and stayed four years, then Sir William hired me. My father works for a blacksmith, and my mother is a washerwoman, so they were pleased to see me in good service." She paused a moment, scrubbing at a stubborn stain. "My father is a free man, born in Africa but raised up in London, and my mother is an Englishwoman, born in Devonshire." Answering the question Meg had not asked.

"You chose to come here with Lady Frances, then? Instead of quitting to find another position?"

"I gave thought to leaving her service," Hannah said. "She could only afford to take one servant; her husband had no great fortune and had spent a good deal of what he had in housing the king. Sir William was determined to get her ladyship and the boys away from England, for he thought the king had little chance of being restored, and anyone who had helped him might be in sore trouble. When he put Lady Frances on a ship to come over here, none of the other maids would even consider making the crossing. But I thought . . . I suppose I thought 'twould be an adventure." She laughed. "And here I am, fishing clothes out the bucking-tub, same as I did back in Newport."

Meg laughed, too, and thought, *She made her choice.* The same choice Meg's parents had made long ago, to come out here to the New Found Land, to break from home and all that was familiar, to start an entirely new kind of life. The choice Peter had made, to come and settle here instead of staying in Bristol. Meg could not even imagine choosing such a vast, strange venture.

"It changes nothing, for us," David Kirke insisted. He stood with his back to the fire in the main hall of his house, his hands clasped behind his back, swaying a little on the balls of his feet as he spoke to his wife, his sister-in-law, his sons and nephews. "The murder of the King is a terrible crime, but 'twill not affect our trade. Business at the Pool Plantation will go on in the accustomed fashion."

"In the accustomed fashion?" his wife, Sara, echoed. "How can it not have an effect on us, when everyone back in England knows you for a royalist? We know nothing about what kind of government Parliament may have in place now, nor what contracts they will honour."

"And we are already deep into this dispute with the Calvert family over ownership of the land here," David and Sara's eldest son, George, pointed out.

David waved his hand as if brushing away flies from his meat at dinner. "That is no matter. The Parliament men may be a crowd of ignorant Puritans, but they understand good business, and this plantation is good business for them."

"How can *anything* go on in the accustomed fashion?" Frances had not meant to speak, but the words burst from her. "This is . . . this is the end of everything, of life as we know it. How can any of us continue with our business as usual?"

David looked at her with the condescending smile she had already learned to hate. "My dear sister Hopkins, the death of King Charles is a terrible blow for all of us, and I know 'tis all the more so for you, who knew him so well in his last days. It is indeed unthinkable that England should continue without a king. I pray that situation will be soon rectified and the Prince of Wales come back from exile to take the throne. But, business? How should we not continue with business? Will the codfish cease to swim about the ocean? Will men cease to drink wine, or make rope, or build ships? It is for women to rend their clothes and weep, and for men to plan and prepare how things shall go forward."

"Well said, Father!" said young George. *Dreadful little lickspittle*, Frances thought, and then reprimanded herself silently. It was fitting and good that a young man of fourteen should admire his father, follow his father's lead. When she had been at home with William, she had expected Richard and Nicholas to do the same.

William. In the grief and shock at the king's death, she had pushed aside her fear for her husband. When they had parted in November, the king was still staying at their house in Newport, but William had sent Frances and the boys on a late-autumn ship going to the New Found Land, with a letter from the king commending Frances and her sons to the care of her brother-in-law David Kirke. Their plan was that if the king's cause succeeded, she would return to England in the spring. If it failed, William would follow her to the colony.

When the ship had come in this morning with news and letters from England, Frances had first hoped William might be aboard. When he was not, she had asked if there was a letter for her. But there was nothing.

The weight of her losses—husband, country, home, king, all gone in a matter of months—pressed on her suddenly. She had been standing, as they all were except Sara, to hear

David's speech, but now she stumbled backward as if she had lost her footing and sank onto the bench by the wall.

The rest were all talking, a chatter of male voices, with Sara's clear, womanly tones ringing in among them. No rending of garments and weeping for Sara Kirke!

Frances closed her eyes, let the voices wash over her. She thought of those last months in England. The king's failed attempt to escape from Carisbrooke Castle and the news that he would be moved into her husband's care in Newport. The negotiations between Parliament and the prisoner-king, to make what they called the Treaty of Newport. Their house suddenly filled both with the king's own men and the soldiers sent to guard him. The coded letters, the frantic plotting in corridors, the sense of a noose drawing tighter around all their necks.

She had hated the thought that she was running away—abandoning William, abandoning the king—at such a crucial time. But William had begged her to think of the boys' safety, if not of her own. She knew then that he believed the king would lose—his throne, at least, if not his life.

So, she went to her sister, her strange, hard, decisive sister Sara, who had pulled up the stakes of her life to follow David Kirke to a plantation in the colonies. Frances had no more desire to throw herself on the mercy of Sara and David than she did to cross the ocean at the very end of autumn, when the November gales threatened danger. But she had done both.

"Mama?" Richard's small voice was almost lost in the clamour of the Kirke clan. He had crept onto the bench next to her and put his hand on her arm.

Frances forced her eyes open. "Yes, my dear?"

"'Tis terrible evil, is't not, about the king?"

"It is, indeed, the greatest sin any of us has ever heard of." She thought again of those evenings at Newport, King Charles reading aloud with Richard, teaching him to play chess. Nicholas was too young to benefit much from the king's company, but King Charles had insisted she bring Nicholas before him to say hello when the nurse brought him in to see his parents. It was plain that the king missed his wife and children, the large family that had once been the centre of court life, now scattered and exiled. "He was a good man, and God's anointed king."

"Does this mean we can never go home?"

"Ah, sweet lad, I know not. None of us knows what the future will hold." But at the very least, she thought, it would be much longer than she had anticipated, for they could not return to a kingless England, to a land ruled by Puritans and parliamentarians who defied the divine order. The winter she had just spent in this bleak country, cut off from all news and trade with England and the Continent, had seemed to last forever. Could she and her sons be stranded here for a year? Two years? It did not bear thinking.

Sara and her husband and sons stayed in the hall for over an hour, wrangling about what the news from England would mean to their business. Frances thought it almost indecent that in the wake of such tidings, Sara and David could think of nothing but profit.

"It is as if they do not even think about the horror of it, the terrible loss," she said later to her maid, Hannah.

"'Tis true, my lady. But then, they did not know His Majesty as you did," Hannah replied. She was putting away clean linens in Frances's trunk; the larger items were still drying by the hearth in the washerwoman's cottage. "To you he was more than just the sovereign, he was—"

"I would not be so presumptuous as to call the king a friend," Frances said, cutting off the disrespectful suggestion.

"Acourse not, my lady."

"In happier circumstances, I would have thought of myself and my husband as the king's devoted servants. And yet we were expected to act as his jailers! It makes my heart ache, to think how that good man was treated."

"Indeed, my lady. Is there anything I can bring upstairs for you? A little supper? Or will you go down to the hall?"

"Nay, I'll not go down again tonight. Send my boys up to me when they are ready for bed, and bring me—oh, a little bread and cheese, and some ale, that will be more than enough. I can hardly eat at all today."

"As you like, my lady." Hannah bobbed her head respectfully and left, closing the door behind her.

Among the many indignities of exile, Frances had been reduced to confiding in her servant—and not only a servant, but the Negro maid. She had never so much as spoken to Hannah back in Newport, when she had worked under the housekeeper's guidance. But when Frances's own maids and Nicholas's nursemaid had refused to make the journey across the ocean with her, she had been left with Hannah. To her surprise, she had found the maid intelligent, capable, and quick.

Chattering to servants was beneath her, but to whom else could she speak? Richard and Nicholas were too young, and there were no women of any social standing in Ferryland save Sara. And there had never been anything in their relation as sisters that led Frances to think of confiding in Sara.

Settling herself in the chair by the window, Frances took out her prayer book and turned to the evening prayer. *"Lighten our darkness, we beseech Thee, O Lord . . ."* Words as familiar as her own name. Four years ago, the Parliament, stuffed with Puritan heretics, had outlawed the use of the prayer book in churches. Frances's household had continued to use it in their private devotions; she remembered now sitting in the little chapel at Newport, their chaplain reading the forbidden words of devotion in the king's presence.

"That it may please Thee, to keep and strengthen in the true worshipping of Thee in righteousness and holiness of life, thy servant Charles, our most gracious king and governor . . ."

Well, it had not pleased God to keep his servant Charles safe. Or rather, it had pleased God, but wicked men had defied the will of God, and what would happen now?

CHAPTER TWO

Summer 1649

"You see? Papa was right," young Davey Kirke said, looking out at the fishing flakes from the front step of the Kirke House. "Naught has changed in the colony, and naught ever will. What does it matter that the old king got his head chopped off?" He drew a finger across his throat and made an unpleasant slicing noise.

"Davey! You must not speak so of His Majesty!" Frances sat sewing by the open window as her nephews and sons idled on the steps outside.

He turned back with a grin that was in no way contrite. "Forgive me, Aunt Frances."

"Watch your tongue, Davey," his brother George said. "Our father *is* right, of course, but 'tis only because he manages the colony so well even when all is chaos over in England. The fishermen still catch fish, the fishwives and their brats still make the fish on shore, and when the sack ships come, we shall sell the fish as we always do. Even so, you must speak of the king with respect."

George, now fifteen, was the eldest among the brood of cousins. Frances's Nicholas, at nine, was the youngest. In between them ranged young Jarvis Kirke, a year older than Nicholas, Davey Kirke and Richard Hopkins, both twelve, and Philip Kirke, thirteen and teetering on the brink of manhood. While the governor kept a tight rein on all the boys and allowed little idling, they had easy lives compared to the handful of other boys their age in the settlement. Lads of ten were out in boats with their fathers, and children younger than that helped their mothers in salting and turning the fish on the flakes.

Governor Kirke's sons had, of course, never caught a fish or split and gutted one, though they were taken to watch the work so that they might know it well. A tutor instructed them in reading, writing, and enough mathematics to know where the money came from and where it went. Sometimes there were more exacting lessons in history, geography, and politics, but that depended on the tutor. The one who had been with them throughout the winter had taken the first ship back to England in the spring, and the lads currently had more idle time than usual while the rest of the harbour was busy with the summer fishery.

"Is Harry Thomas a fisherman's brat?" Jarvis asked. "He's my friend."

Harry Thomas's father was the largest planter in the settlement after the Kirkes themselves; he tended a good-sized piece of land, had three fishing boats, and employed fifteen servants during the fishing season. Still, Frances knew what George's answer would be.

"Yes, he is, and you ought not to be too familiar with him," said George airily, laying down the law, "for you will be his master someday. Or rather, I will."

"Why cannot I be his master?" Jarvis asked.

"I am oldest, so I shall be governor. I will be master over all the fisherman, whether they are servants or planters or sharemen. The governor rules all."

"I want to be governor!" That was Davey, always quick to claim a privilege.

"And I!" little Nicholas chimed in.

"There can be only one governor, you ignorant knaves!" George's voice betrayed the irritation of a young man bedevilled by the folly of children.

"Only one g-governor, perhaps, but P-papa says we *can* all be masters," said Philip. He spoke with a slight stammer, far less confident than his bolder brothers.

"That is true." George, as he often did, jumped in to finish Philip's thought. "He says there is land enough for us all to have our own plantations along the shore, and there will never be a lack of poor men coming out from England to fish."

All the more so now, Frances thought, now that Cromwell's army had made sure its conquest of England and turned to conquering Ireland. There were still Levellers and Diggers, the most extreme of the reformers, who believed that England could be an Eden where every man was equal and there was no longer any rich or poor, but the news from England made it clear that no such thing was happening. Men were men, after all. The Parliament men wanted wealth and power just as surely as the king and nobles did. The supply of fishing servants and settlers was unlikely to dry up.

"I've no wish to own a fishing plantation," another voice, silent until now, piped up. It was Frances's son Richard. "I do not like this place. I want to go back to England and be a schoolmaster like my Papa."

"'Tis not likely my father meant that you and Nicholas would have lands of your own, Dickon," George told Richard. "The colony is for us, the Kirkes. We will make a great dynasty here. Even if your father still lives, he owns no land here."

"Look not so downcast, Cousin Dickon," Davey said. "When I have my plantation, you may come and work as my steward. Or mayhap, if we all have enough sons, you may be a schoolmaster after all, head of the first school in the New Found Land."

The Kirke boys all laughed at the prospect of a school in this wild place. Frances bit her tongue. She wanted to reprimand Davey for speaking so to Richard, as she had reprimanded him for speaking lightly of the king. But she said nothing. Though Richard was Davey's elder, he was her son—she, Frances, the poor exile. All the lads were well aware of the distinctions in fortune between the governor's sons and their Hopkins cousins.

And indeed, the very question the boys had raised in jest was one that worried Frances when she thought about William's promise to follow her to the New Found Land. What would they do if he did arrive? Would the Kirkes grant them a piece of land? Could William become a planter? He could not be a schoolmaster here, unless David and Sara hired him to tutor their boys. Perhaps he could do bookkeeping for the Kirkes' enterprise. She prayed every night that William was still alive and would make his way to her, but his arrival here would not lessen their dependence on the Kirkes.

She was not surprised to see Richard come into the house a few moments later, as the torrent of young voices and laughter indicated that the other boys had run off together. Head down, heels dragging, Richard looked the very picture of unhappiness.

"Is Nicky with you?"

"No, he has gone off with the rest of them. They don't lord it over him as—"

"As they do with you."

"Why are they so . . . so full of their own importance, Mother?"

"Boys can be unkind," Frances said, minding her words carefully. Criticism of Sara's four golden princelings would not win her any favour with her sister and brother-in-law. "Even if the words are unkind, the truth is in them. Davey and George and Jarvis and Philip are better off than you, for their father is wealthy and has a good position. You must remember that and not be saucy or rude to your cousins, for you need their goodwill."

"I had much rather *not* need it." Richard kicked at the leg of her chair, his eyes fixed on the ground.

Frances laid down her sewing and put a finger under Richard's chin. Oh, that this lad of hers—he who had played chess with a king, who had carried whispers and secrets from one adult to another as the king planned his escape—that this boy should have to touch his cap and bend the knee to her sister's sons, just because they were stranded on this rocky shore a thousand miles from home!

"We all must do many things in this life we would rather not do," she said, putting some steel in her tone. He must not see that she pitied him. "Do you think good King Charles *wanted* to lay his head on the executioner's block? Do you think our Lord Jesus *wanted* to be nailed to the cross? Compared to the sufferings of the saints and martyrs, our own troubles are small. Yes, we are exiled from home, and we know not if your father is alive or dead. But even if he is gone, he left you a good example of honour. This is what you must show every day, no matter how—" she caught herself, "no matter how anyone tries to make little of you. Do you understand me?"

"Yes, Mother." He did not say it reluctantly or churlishly as another lad his age might; his shoulders straightened and there was a light in his eyes. He had taken her examples to heart, she thought.

She laid down her needlework and drew from her basket the little book called *Eikon Basilike*, already well worn from the weeks it had been her possession. "Let me read you a prayer from our good king." She cleared her throat and put on her most solemn tone as she read the blessed martyr's prayer: "*To thee therefore, O my God, do I direct my now solitary Prayers; what I want of others' help, supply with the more immediate assistance of thy Spirit, which alone can both enlighten my darknesse and quicken my dulnesse*. So, you see," she added, "a truly faithful person knows that even when we have no help from others, God Himself will come to our aid."

"I will try to remember that, Mother."

"It will not always be so," she reminded him. "Time will be when these wicked Parliament men will be overthrown and the true king, the young king in exile, will come back to England. Then we shall go home too, and the new king will reward us for your father's loyalty to him, and you shall have what is yours by right."

"When will that be?"

"It cannot be long; God would not allow such wickedness to continue. A year, perhaps."

Davey Kirke put his head around the door. "Come, Dickon, a ship is coming into the Pool! Make haste, so we can see where it be from!"

Richard followed his cousin, Davey's unkind words apparently forgiven. Oh, to have the reckless generosity of youth, to let go so easily of slights and insults! Frances found herself cherishing her small grudges almost as much as she cherished her little book of King Charles's prayers, given to her by the captain of one of the royalist ships her brother-in-law had engaged to patrol the waters near the colony.

All summer she had eagerly met every English ship, hoping for letters from William or, better yet, William himself. Perhaps it was because she was so downcast at the lack of news that one of the captains had given her this precious copy of the late king's book of thoughts and prayers. The mere fact that this book had been widely circulated gave her courage, for it meant that back in England, King Charles's words and deeds would stand as a beacon of hope until good times came again.

In the meantime, here she was in her sister's house, in her brother-in-law's colony, a dependent woman with no portion or inheritance to give her sons. They had been here half a year already, and she had only tolerated her situation, not done anything to change it.

Frances did not, at this moment, see how she could change anything. Her fingers traced the frontispiece of the *Eikon Basilike,* the revered features of the martyred king. He had fought the rebels for nearly a decade, fought to hold the crown for himself and for his son, for the good of the country. What did it matter that his striving had, in the end, been for naught? He was a model of how to accept defeat with grace, but also a model for how to fight even when one's cause seemed lost. *And I,* Frances thought, *must learn how to fight for myself.*

The dim twilight that came through the open windows of David Kirke's tavern was brightened only by a single smoky lamp; the room had a hearth, but this summer evening was too warm for a fire. Hannah Peake brought a jug of beer from the keg and filled the cups of the two fishermen standing before her: Meg Taylor's husband, Peter, and one of the summer fishermen whose name she did not know.

The workdays were long at this time of year, everyone busy either catching fish or making fish. Most folks tumbled into bed as soon as the work was done, but there were always a few men who took advantage of the tavern that Governor Kirke had set up next to his brewhouse for a little recreation before sleep.

If Hannah had had her choice, she would have been among those to go straight to bed at sunset. Since the fish had come in, she was doing her regular work about Kirke House—cleaning, laundering, caring for the younger lads, and helping Mistress Durdle with the cooking—and then spending several hours each afternoon at the flakes, splitting, salting, and turning fish along with the other women. Lady Frances had told Hannah at the beginning of the fishing season that "all hands" would be needed to make fish. Not Lady Frances's own hands, of course.

Then, a fortnight ago, the governor had informed Hannah that he needed her for an hour or two after the evening meal, several nights a week, to serve in the tavern. Some question must have shown on her face, for Sir David had said, "'Tis all arranged with your mistress. She has agreed to lend me your labour for a time. With all the planters and their families busy with the fish, I've not been able to find anyone to tend to the tavern save George, and I do not want him in there every day."

No mention, Hannah noted, of any of her other duties being reduced. But what could she say? Like her mistress, she was entirely dependent on the goodwill of the Kirke family.

"Say what you will about the governor, he brews good beer and sells it cheap enough," said Peter's drinking companion. "Fill it up again, maid—I've a powerful thirst on me this night."

"Any man would, the day's work we have put in," said Peter.

"I had rather be doing your day's work than mine," the other man said. "For at the end of the season, when 'tis all counted out, your work will go to your own account, and mine goes to make the merchant richer."

Hannah knew that Peter's friend was one of the men who came out on ships from England in May, fished through the season, and returned home in October. Each man was paid a wage out of the final tally of what the summer's catch was worth.

"Aye, but I'll not get rich from it," Peter said. "'Tis a wicked world, where some men drape themselves in silk and velvet, while others barely scratch out a living. And do we see sign of it changing? Do you, from what you have seen back in Bristol?"

The two men moved away with their mugs to stand by the window in the fresh evening breeze, while other men came to have their cups filled. Hannah's muscles ached as she filled the jug and poured from it again and again. She had started life as a scullery maid and hoped to rise through the ranks of service but had never imagined herself a tavern wench.

"Hey now, my dusky maid, pour us another cup full!" shouted old Abel Goode, who was drinking at a table with three other men. "Bring it here!" he added. The room had a long table in front of the beer kegs where the men could bring up their cups to be served, a couple of smaller tables for those who wanted to settle in and drink for a long time, and standing room for the rest. Sighing, Hannah brought the jug around to the rowdy table.

"'Twill be another farthing for all of you if I fill you up again," she said, not pouring until the coins were put into her hand.

"I'll give you an extra farthing for a good peek at those duckies o' yours," said old Abel, leering at the front of Hannah's well-laced kirtle. "I've never seen brown ones before. 'Twould be worth the farthing, and you need not pay that one to Governor Kirke."

The other men laughed, one adding, "Doubt you've seen any duckies at all, black, brown, pink, nor white, these ten years or more, Abe!" Abel Goode's wife had been dead a long time; he was a fairly well-off planter, by the standards of the colony, but he had not had any success at luring a woman to come and keep his big, ramshackle house for him, and serving maids hired to cook and clean for him rarely stayed long. Now that Hannah was in the tavern, she had a good idea why that was.

"I am not in that much need of a farthing, my good man," she said now, filling Abel's cup and stepping away before he decided to take for free what she would not sell him. She had a fine line to walk here—she would not let these men take advantage, but she could not be too pert in answering them, or they would complain of her to Sir David. If he gave the task of serving in the tavern to someone else, she knew not what that might mean for his agreement with Lady Frances and how that might fall out for herself. Better to smile, give a soft answer, and keep well clear of roving hands.

As she wound her way through the press of men back to her station by the kegs, she heard voices raised by the window. Peter and his friend were in an argument with some other men. "You know not what you talk of, ye crowd of settlers out here," Peter's friend was saying. "Ask any of us who have come out from England. The country is far better off with the king gone. We'll have a true commonwealth now, every man as good as the next."

"That's Leveller talk," said another man, "and you know what happened to Lockyer and the other Levellers at Bishopsgate. No matter what them Parliament men say, they don't want every man the same. They want to rule the roost, same as the king did."

"Levellers had the right idea!" Peter shouted. "Kings and lords and governors—what makes any of 'em better than the rest of us? 'Twasn't so in Scripture! When Adam delved and Eve span, who was then the gentleman? Ain't that the gospel truth, there?"

"Hush up, before them words gets back to him as owns this tavern," said yet another man, "or you'll lose your rights to drink here, and more rights than that."

Peter slammed down his cup. "Come, Simon," he said to his friend, "we'll no more of this. 'Tis one thing to drink a healthy cup of good beer at your own table, but this place is no more than a den of iniquity." He threw a glance of contempt at Abel Goode's table.

"Aye, turn tail and run, Leveller coward!" said the fisherman who had been arguing. Before Peter or his companion could answer, Hannah said, "Remember, fellows, there's to be no fighting in here. Take it outside, if you've quarrels with each other. 'Tis soon closing time, now, so if anyone has a last order, this is the time for it."

In the warmth of the summer evening, as sunset turned to twilight, Frances watched the fishermen wend their way home from the tavern. There was no reeling and stumbling; David did not keep the tavern open long enough to allow for much drunkenness, which meant there was little brawling and violence. But the tavern, which he had just started operating this season, was a great success, and when her brother-in-law had approached her about Hannah serving there, Frances had readily agreed. Much like Hannah's work on the flakes, it fit well with Frances's plans for the future.

"No trouble with the men tonight, was there?" she asked when Hannah came to her room to help her undress and brush out her hair.

Hannah paused for a moment, then said, "Nothing I could not deal with. A few saucy old fellows, like Abel Goode, but he knows I'll brook no foolishness from the likes of him."

"Very well." She heard the clink of metal as Hannah drew

coins from the pocket of her kirtle. “Go give that money to my sister when you have finished here. She is still up, doing the household accounts by candlelight.”

“I will.” Another pause as Hannah pulled the brush through Frances’s long hair. “Sometimes, the men give me a farthing more, here and there, and say ’tis for me to keep myself. But I think your sister and brother-in-law know where every coin in this settlement goes, so I know not if ’tis right to keep them.”

“I am sure they do know. ’Tis their own coin, and neither of them is the sort to lose track of even a farthing. You are right to give it all over to them.” Sara had explained to Frances when she first arrived in Ferryland that much of the business in the colony was done on credit; everyone from the small fishermen with single boats, to those who operated larger plantations with several servants, traded the value of their fish for goods sent out from England at the end of the season. Grain, molasses, and other foodstuffs the land could not provide; fishing gear, glazed windows, iron nails; bolts of fabric, horn buttons, boots and shoes; pewter dishes and fine pottery; wine and spirits—anything that could not be grown or made in the colony could be traded for fish. Those who had servants often paid them in goods for anything they were owed beyond their room and board, and very little money was exchanged.

But David Kirke had begun to mint his own coins, tokens with the initials DK on them, and these could be used by anyone in the settlement who wanted to buy some of the goods that the Kirkes had in abundance, including beer at the governor’s tavern.

“Yes, my lady. I will give it all over to your sister.”

Frances hesitated a moment. She would never thank or apologize to a servant, of course, but she knew that she and the Kirkes had piled many extra burdens on Hannah this summer. "It is a long day for you," she said, "working here around the house, and at the fish, and serving in the tavern. You are a hard worker, Hannah."

"I have always had to be, my lady."

"I do not mean to always use you as a fishing servant nor a tavern maid. But just now, I am trying to better my position, to have something for myself and my sons. And I have very little to bargain with."

"So . . . you are selling my labour to your brother-in-law?"

"Yes. In return for a share of the profit, when the fish is in. Right now, you are all I have to sell." Hannah nodded, her hands busy now putting Frances's hair in its nighttime plait. "Of course, you will benefit as well. You are part of my household. Indeed, apart from myself and my sons, you are my whole household, right now. Whatever I can earn will be for the good of us all."

At first, Hannah said nothing, and Frances wondered if she had even heard. After a moment Hannah said, "Of course, my lady. Is there anything else you need tonight?"

"No, you may go. Leave the candle."

Hannah dropped a half-curtsey and went out, shutting the door behind her. Frances wondered if she ought to have taken the coins from Hannah, paid them to Sara herself. But no, Hannah could be trusted entirely.

The position would be an uneasy one if Hannah were a different sort of servant. Back in England she had received a small wage along with her room and board. There had been no talk of that, of wages or terms or indentures, when Hannah had agreed to cross the ocean with Frances and her sons. Simply an understanding between them that Hannah would continue to serve in whatever way Frances needed, and in return, Frances would make sure that Hannah was looked after.

When the fishing season was over and the value of the fish tallied up, Frances would see what was due her. Then she would know whether her plan to build something of her own had a chance of succeeding.

She took the *Eikon Basilike* and her prayer book from the table before her, pulled the candle closer, and turned the pages, selecting a prayer to carry her into the night.

"There's a boat coming into the Pool," said Abigail Bullard as she passed Meg. The women were bringing armloads of salted and dried fish in from the flakes to stack in the storehouse against the day when the merchant ships would load it for the voyage across the ocean. The short summer had flown by; the fishing season was nearing its end, and all the work now was bent toward making sure the cured catch was ready for shipping to market.

"A sack ship?" Meg straightened up and rubbed her lower back, sore from all the lifting, bending, and carrying. Ships carrying trade goods were always a welcome sight.

"Nay, 'tis only a pinnace, like as not from one of the other fishing stations."

Meg stepped outside, blinking in the brilliant September sunshine. Sure enough, the pinnace was far too small a vessel to have made the voyage across the ocean, but what mattered more, she recognized it. A year ago, she and Peter had sailed here on that same boat to begin their married life in Ferryland. It was the *Kathryn,* Master Nicholas Guy's pinnace out of Carbonear, and Meg's heart leapt at the sight. Her father often sailed aboard that vessel, and even if he were not on it, someone aboard would certainly have news of home.

Fortune smiled on her today. The pinnace dropped anchor, and in a little while, she saw the sailors, some of them familiar to her, off-loading boxes and barrels. Among the men coming ashore, she spied her father Ned's broad-shouldered form and sandy, greying hair. Meg left her place at the splitting table to greet him.

"Aye, there's my grand girl, my lovely Meg! What good cheer 'tis to see you! How are you keeping?" He lowered his voice a little. "Is that husband of yours treating you well?"

"Yes, Papa." What else could she say? She had seen women whose husbands beat them for disobedience or a too-quick tongue and was grateful not to be wed to such a man. She had chosen Peter freely and must make the best of her choice.

Meg's mother, had she been there, might have sized things up with a keener eye and probed more deeply. Mama readily saw through a lie, even the pleasant lies people told to make life easier. Papa was a simpler soul, Meg thought. He wanted people, especially his children, to be happy and therefore was quick to believe that they were.

As Meg gladly accepted her father's embrace, she felt a twinge of sadness that her mother was not also there. Men travelled back and forth often on the ships that linked the handful of English settlements in the New Found Land, but women rarely did. Meg had not left Ferryland since her marriage and did not know when she might ever return to Musketto Cove. It seemed very hard, suddenly, not to be able to go home again, especially now that she did have news to share.

The pinnace was staying at Ferryland for the night and returning the next day. After Meg had finished carrying fish to the storehouse, Ned accompanied her home to eat the evening meal at his daughter's house. Peter grumbled that the salted pork should be saved for Sunday, but Meg made bold to talk back to him. "'Tis a special occasion, after all. Rare enough for me to see any of my family. 'Tis worth a little celebration."

Peter shrugged. "Not as if I will ever see any of my kin again, and you do not hear any complaint from me, do you?"

"I missed my family sorely when I came out here," Ned said, "but I know there are men who travel to these shores who are glad to have an ocean between themselves and their families."

"I suppose I am such a fellow, then," said Peter. "My father and I never saw eye to eye, and he turned me out of the house for fighting on the Parliament side when Bristol was taken, even though his side lost and mine won."

Meg caught her father's eye and tried to warn him with a look. She did not want any discussion that touched on the war, the king, or any other business out of England. She had news to deliver tonight.

Ned Perry was not the most subtle of men, but he caught that look and said only, "Well, things are often uneasy between fathers and sons. But I am sure your mother misses you, like all the mothers in England who have sons out here in the colony."

"Aye, she took my going hard," Peter admitted.

"'Tis only natural," Meg said, "for what on earth is stronger than a mother's love?" Here, she thought, was a nice opportunity to share her news.

But Peter's thoughts ran, as they so often did, along another course. "That is a woman's sentiment," he said. "The bond a man has for his fellow man, a soldier for his comrades, and all of us toward Almighty God, all those are stronger by far than the tenderness a woman has for her youngsters. A woman's love do be but a weak thing compared to a man's honour and duty."

"You may say so," countered Meg, "but for a woman, especially one who is in that way that leads to motherhood, well, 'tis hard to imagine any passion stronger. Even if the babe be not yet born."

"That is exactly what a woman *would* say—" Peter began, but Ned was quicker to understand.

"That is what a woman would say if she had some happy news to share," he said. "Meg, my girl, is there something us two hard-headed fellows ought to know? Out with it!"

And so she told them both—told them that she was sure now, a good five months along, and that the babe might be born about the New Year. When her father took her in his arms and said how glad he was, tears came to her eyes.

Ned's joy seemed to rouse Peter to a sense of what was expected of him. "'Tis grand news indeed," he said, "not even a year married, and I will be a father. Aye, grand news. Mayhap we'd best celebrate aright, with a cup of wine. I can get some from the tavern, and if I see Simon there, I might ask him to stop over and share a drink with us."

"Go and get the wine—'tisn't every day I will be giving you

such news," Meg said. Peter had been much cheered when Simon, an old friend and comrade-in-arms from Bristol, had come out for the summer fishery. Meg was not overly fond of Simon, but on such a glad night she would not begrudge Peter the company of a friend. And while Peter was off hunting for Simon and a jug of wine, she would have some time alone to talk with her father.

"'Tis a great pity the babe will be born in winter," Ned said when Peter was gone, "else we might be able to send your mother and Aunt Kat down to help you with the birthing."

"I wish they could both be here, but there's no knowing when a child will come, and neither of them could be away for so long. We've a good woman here: Granny Love. She's a widow woman whose daughter is married to a planter, Sam Thomas. Granny Love has tended dozens of childbeds. Tell Mother she need not fret."

While it might be a comfort to have her mother in attendance, the person Meg would most like to have in the birthing chamber was her Aunt Kathryn. Properly Mistress Nicholas Guy, Aunt Kathryn was not only the wife of the biggest landowner in Conception Bay, but also the most experienced midwife. She and Meg's mother Nancy had been among the first English women to come out to the New Found Land nigh on forty years earlier, and Aunt Kathryn had been catching babies, binding wounds, and making compounds to cure illness for all those years. Meg did not think Granny Love, though older, had as much skill as Aunt Kathryn, but she would not say so to her father; she wanted him to leave thinking all was well.

After Ned left the next day, Peter did not mention the baby, and Meg was once again alone with her secret. A few days later, she told the news to Hannah when they were working together in the Kirke House garden. Meg had made an effort to grow her own little garden, but there was not enough to keep herself and Peter all through the winter, and Lady Sara had promised to pay Meg in turnips, parsnips, and cabbage if she helped Hannah weed and harvest the garden for the big house.

"How far along are you?" Hannah asked.

"Five months," Meg said, digging her spade into the rocky soil. "I said nothing for a long time, because . . ."

"I know . . . too soon. You've not lost one before, have you?"

"No. My sister lost two in a year, afore she had her first one that lived."

"Not every babe is meant to be born. Some never take root in the womb. But when 'tis meant to be, it quickens."

"Yes, the quickening. I have felt it now. 'Tis so strange!"

"Your man, what does he think of it?"

"I only told him a few nights ago, when my father was here. I told him I had quickened, asked did he want to feel the baby in my belly. But he said 'twas women's business."

Hannah raised her eyebrows but said only, "A breeding woman needs care. Gentleness. I hope he knows that." She took the spade from Meg. "Let me dig that spot—'tis heavier work."

Meg looked for it from then on, that gentleness. "Will you make a cradle for the babe?" she asked Peter, as the crisp cold of October gave way to the chilly winds of November.

"Why? Any wooden crate will do."

"'Twouldn't be hard, you know, to make a cradle. Just a simple one, not fine work."

"When would I find time for the likes of that? Now that the fishing is done, I'm cutting wood all day. We'll need every stick of that to burn through the winter; can't be sparing any of it to go making cradles. Use a crate. Line it with one of them quilts you do be always sewing."

Wood and time, she thought. Two things that surrounded them in seemingly endless supply. In winter the hours stretched long. The women sewed and knitted, while the men turned to hunting, trapping, and cutting wood. There was time in that cold, dark season for a man to make or mend the few pieces of furniture a family needed. She remembered the cradle that she and all of her brothers and sisters had slept in as babies; her mother told her how her father had made it in winter, planing and shaping the wood in front of the fire in their little house.

She could not change Peter. His interest was kindled far more by news from across the ocean than it was by the prospect of fatherhood. The ships that had brought salt, molasses, grain, and the rest of their winter supplies had brought news also. Peter had been roused to learn that Oliver Cromwell's army was conquering Ireland; sometimes he said that he wished he had stayed in England that he might join the New Model Army and be fighting there now, forcing Irish papists to bend the knee to Parliament and to true religion.

So far as Peter was interested in their own future here in the New Found Land, his thoughts were all focused on the fishery and how to improve his catch. This summer he had hired Alf Bullard's fourteen-year-old son Rafe to fish with him: the Bullards had so many sons fishing with their father that they could afford to hire out the youngest and least useful in exchange for a small share of Peter's earnings.

But when the fish was in and traded for their winter supplies and the fishing fleet had returned to England, Peter told Meg that he had contracted Simon to come back next summer and work for him directly.

"Then we will have to house and feed him," Meg had pointed out. "How is that better than hiring Rafe, who can live with his parents?"

"I mean to hire Rafe, or some other young fellow, as well as Simon. What I lose by giving Simon board for the season, I will more than earn back with the added fish I can catch if I have the labour of another grown man in the boat and onshore. Any planter who hopes to prosper along this shore hires his own fishing servants for the season, and 'tis best I start with Simon, for I already know him to be a steady man, a good worker, and a sincere Christian."

All true, and it was not as if Peter were asking Meg's opinion: such decisions were his to make. She could not help thinking of how tiny their house was, and how there would be a baby in the winter and Simon in the summer crowded into that space. Her father always had men hired for the season, but her parents' house was larger and had a separate space where the fishing servants could sleep apart from the family.

She sighed. Peter was right: they were on this shore to fish and make fish, and to prosper as best they could. A little inconvenience was nothing against the prospect of a better fishing season. "Very well, if you think 'tis best," she said. And to the list of baby's clothes and blankets and all else she would make over the winter, she added a set of curtains for their bed, so they might have at least a little privacy.

CHAPTER THREE

Spring 1650

Meg was already in bed, baby Mary curled asleep at her breast, when Peter and Simon came into the house, talking loudly. It was the third time this week that they had gone to Kirke's tavern in the evening. Meg pulled the curtains closer around the bed. If the men were going to sit by the fire talking about politics and religion while Meg tried to get the baby and herself to sleep, she was grateful to have a few yards of cloth around her to block out the noise.

The men's loud voices caused the baby to stir, and Meg hushed her back to sleep; she would lay her in her little wooden crate on the floor later, after Peter had come to bed. That could be an hour or more yet.

"Those pirate ships have a ring around this colony tight as a dog's collar," Simon grumbled as the men sat at the table. "Governor Kirke's private navy, so he calls it." She heard the slap of Peter laying out cups for them, and the sound of ale being poured.

"Aye, some of 'em are pirates," Peter said, "and the rest are navy men loyal to the late tyrant. Cavaliers, every man jack of 'em. Got the place barricaded so no ships loyal to Parliament can enter the harbour here,"

"Did you see yon ship that came in today, all flags blazing?" Simon asked.

"Aye, and among those flags was the banner of Charles, the old tyrant," Peter said. "They do say Prince Rupert himself is aboard her, though what business that rogue has with Kirke or this colony is a mystery to me."

Meg had no idea who Prince Rupert was, but clearly Peter did not approve of him. Simon, like Peter, had fought against the king in the wars, and they now settled comfortably to grumbling about the royalists, and the Kirkes, and anyone who was not of the true religion.

Since Simon had arrived a fortnight ago and moved into their house, Meg had recognized something she had not understood before: how lonely Peter was, far from his friends in England, with no men here who shared his interests and his way of thinking. Knowing this, she did not mind these late nights when the men wrangled through their strange arguments, even though she begrudged her lost sleep and how difficult it was to settle the baby.

On the evenings when they were not too weary from the day's fishing, Peter and Simon would go for a few cups of beer at the tavern and continue the conversation with a cup of ale at Peter's table. They did not get drunk—Peter prided himself on being a temperate man—but all the same, the drink and the late hour loosened their tongues. Meg tried to sleep, and listened to talk she did not understand, and worried about those loose tongues.

She was lonely too, of course. She was friendly with the wives and daughters of the other small planters, but the only woman she felt genuinely at ease with was Hannah Peake. Hannah had been a steady companion throughout the long months of autumn and winter while Meg prepared for the baby to come, and she had been by Meg's bedside along with the midwife when Mary was born. Meg knew it was not entirely right, at least in Peter's eyes, that a Negro maid should be her closest friend, but there was no one else she trusted as she did Hannah. In truth, Meg and Peter were both lonely, and after nearly two years of marriage, they had not managed to find solace in each other's company.

It was Hannah, who served in the governor's tavern, who had warned Meg about Peter's habit of airing his opinions too freely. "Anything said in this place makes its way back to the Kirkes," Hannah had told her, "and your husband takes no care with his words. I'd not want any trouble to come to you because of it."

"What I heard on the ship on the way over here," Simon said now as he laid down his cup heavily on the table, "is that all the colonies are supposed to swear their loyalty to Parliament instead of to the king. If they will not, their governors will be replaced with Parliament men."

"And right enough they should," Peter said. "Kirke is an old-fashioned man with old-fashioned ways. He belongs to the past."

"Aye, but they'll have no chance to get near the place to question him, nor ask him to take any vows neither, not with this blockade he's got put in place."

"Especially if Prince Rupert himself is taking an interest in the business," Peter added. "I'd not be surprised if we see shots fired before the fishing season is done."

Meg shivered in her bed. She knew that pirate vessels were always a threat to the fishing fleet, but this talk of barricades and princes and ships sent out by Parliament seemed like a new and more dangerous business. Unlike Peter, she had never seen or heard guns fired in anger.

"Governor Kirke is setting himself up for trouble," said Simon.

"Pride goeth before destruction, and a haughty spirit before a fall," Peter quoted solemnly. "We'll ne'er have peace and prosperity here till David Kirke is pulled down and a godly man put in his place."

"Or no man at all," Simon suggested. "Have none to rule over us, but every man before God and his own conscience."

When the men had drunk their ale and Simon gone to the makeshift pallet by the hearth where he slept, Meg bundled the baby into her crate and settled herself back to try to rest, resenting the lost hour of sleep. It must be near ten of the clock now, and they would be up before dawn. When Peter parted the bed curtains and lay down beside her in his nightshirt, she hoped he would not be in the mood for swiving, for she had no energy for that. And that hope was granted, for he only said, "You are still awake? Goodnight, wife," and turned his back to her.

That should have been that, but she was too much worried. "'Twas hard to sleep with all your talk."

"'Tis good for me to have someone to talk to, someone who understands the way of the world."

"Good for you, mayhap, but dangerous. 'Tis dangerous

talk—traitorous, even."

He snorted and turned to face her. "What do you know about treason? If anyone is a traitor, 'tis yon man David Kirke, still holding true to the old king, still saying prayers from the prayer book and leading his household in idolatrous worship. 'Twould not be allowed in England."

"But the government in England knows not what we do here. Governor Kirke knows for certain sure what men are saying in his tavern—aye, and likely in their own houses."

"What have you heard?"

"Hannah has told me—more than once. She said the governor has asked her to tell him if there be any rebellious talk among the men in the alehouse, any men he ought to watch."

"And she will tittle-tattle on me and my friends, will she? A blackamoor tavern wench?"

"She would not! But she warned me. If the governor is asking questions, you ought to be more careful what you say—at least where others can hear you."

"Be careful yourself, talking of things a woman knows nothing about. 'Tis not your business to take care of what I do or say."

With that, he rolled over again, his back to Meg, and was soon snoring while she lay staring at the darkness, unable to sleep.

Ship's captains and merchants, some of them very wealthy men, took their supper at the Kirke House table often during the summer season. But to have an actual prince of the blood—the dashing Prince Rupert of the Rhine, the late king's nephew and his greatest general—actually in their house was a tremendous honour. Even Sara seemed daunted by it.

"I suppose you'll tell me if I'm doing aught wrong," she said to Frances, a little snappishly. "You having lived so cozy with King Charles, and all."

Prince Rupert spent much of his time and fortune on the seas harrying Parliament's ships, fighting the royalist cause that had been defeated in England itself. Now he had arrived in Ferryland in all his glory. When his ship sailed to the waters around the colony, he was pleased to find that Governor Kirke had hired a small fleet of royalist vessels to protect the New Found Land from Parliament ships that might try to seize control of the fishing trade and the colony itself. Prince Rupert and his ship's captain had spent the day with David, first aboard the ship, then walking along the shore inspecting the colony's defences, then closeted in the governor's private chamber for further discussions.

Mistress Durdle and Hannah were hard at work in the kitchen, for the prince had said he would sup with them. The boys were agog with excitement, and for once, Richard was earning some respect from his cousins. With the arrival of a real prince, they were suddenly eager to hear his stories about what the king had been like. In honour of the special occasion, Sara had decreed that they all might be presented to Prince Rupert and eat at the table, rather than in the kitchen with the servants as the younger boys usually did when there was distinguished company.

Frances had never seen Prince Rupert before, but he had been a figure of legend throughout the course of the war, dearer to King Charles than anyone save his own wife and children, and more relied on than any other commander.

King and prince had quarrelled over Rupert's decision to surrender the city of Bristol, but they had made up the quarrel; the king had been heartbroken when Parliament exiled Prince Rupert from England. He was a striking young man, and there was a look of his uncle about him—the Stuart looks, Frances thought.

As they ate the finest supper Sara's kitchen could produce, Prince Rupert regaled the table with tales of Portugal, where his ships had been at anchor since last autumn. They'd long been prevented from leaving by a fleet sent by the English Commonwealth, who had declared the prince a pirate and sent men to capture him.

"But those halfwit Roundheads, they could not capture you, could they?" young Davey burst out as the prince told how his sailors and the Commonwealth sailors had brawled in the streets of Lisbon.

The prince laughed. "Indeed they could not, lad, though they made a damnably good attempt—even tried to kill me while I was out hunting. But I slipped away from their grasp, and then escaped altogether, aboard a good merchant ship whose captain is loyal to the true King of England." He nodded towards the captain, who had accompanied him to supper.

"It is my honour to serve Your Highness," the captain said.

None of the young lads could take their eyes from the dashing prince who had survived so many battles and evaded so many attempts at capture. "'Tis grateful we are," the governor said, "that that ship was headed for our shores."

"Oh, 'tis no mere accident," the prince said. "I have long had an interest in this country, and in a governor who remains true to the Crown when it would be profitable to bow to Parliament. I honour the effort you have made to protect your shores, and if I can see my way to it, I will be of help to you in the future. A royalist colony here in the New World might be a valuable foothold indeed."

Frances could see that her brother-in-law was near to bursting with pride at these words of royal favour. Sara, though she smiled, had a more guarded look, and Frances knew just what she was thinking: all very well for a prince to make such promises, but had he any means of keeping them, when he had had to sneak away from Portugal without even his own ship? The prince spoke bravely, but all other news they heard from England hinted that hopes of returning a Stuart monarch to the throne were growing faint.

When supper ended and the younger lads were being sent off to bed, the prince approached Frances. "Lady Frances, I have been told that you once gave good service to my uncle, King Charles."

She dropped her deepest curtsey. "I was honoured to serve His Majesty of blessed memory, Your Highness."

He put out his hand, and she took it and let him raise her to stand before him. "So many Englishmen and women were so brave and loyal. Your sacrifices will not be in vain."

"I pray not, Your Highness."

"The captain of our ship was given a letter for you before he left England," the prince said, nodding towards his companion, "but I asked him if I might hand it to you myself, that I might thank you for your past service." He took a sealed letter from an inner pocket and gave it to her.

"Oh, thank you, Your Highness! Is it—do you know if it contains word of my husband?" She saw his polite expression replaced by confusion and added, "Sir William Hopkins, Your Highness. I've not heard word of him since I left the Isle of Wight."

"Ah, the Isle of Wight! You were at Carisbrooke, then?"

He does not know who we are, Frances realized. *Someone has told him, "This woman Frances Hopkins did some service for the late king"; that is all.* The weeks that the king had lived in her house had been the most momentous and important of her life, but to others they were only a small incident in the final tumultuous years of King Charles's life.

"Newport, Your Highness. My husband was master of the school there and was knighted by the late King for his service. We were honoured to have King Charles stay in our house for a time." That he had been placed there by his captors, for Frances and William to watch over him like jailers, need not be said; the prince would understand the circumstances.

"Ah, yes, of course. I had heard of the name Hopkins, but I have been so long out of England, I forget. Perhaps this letter holds the news you seek." He glanced at the ship's captain. "Captain Wells, do you know who gave you the letter? Was it this man Walter Hopkins?"

She did not correct him to *William*. The captain shook his head. "No, Your Highness, 'twas a lady gave it me. She did not give her name, but she was well known to be one who had been close in the counsels of King Charles."

"Jane Whorwood," said Frances. Now that she was looking at the letter, she did not even need to see how it was signed. She knew that writing, knew it from dozens of coded letters.

Clever Jane: spymistress, founder of plots, intimate friend of King Charles. Some said she was the king's lover, but though Frances had arranged to bring Jane into the king's private chamber more than once, she could not believe that anything immoral had happened there. The king was not only too devoted to his wife, but too upright a Christian to carry on in such a way. The intimacy Jane had enjoyed with him was, she was sure, one of the spirit only, an intimacy Frances had envied.

The letter was not long; Jane still used the number codes the king had used in his letters, addressing Frances as "my dear 47" and telling her "I bear news of 48." She signed herself not Jane but "Helen," one of her many aliases.

The meat of the letter was in three sentences: *It grieves me to tell you that after 48 escaped England and made his way to Ireland, intending there to seek a way to travel to you, hee took ill and died of a fever. All this is some months gone now, for hee dyed in April, foure months after our good lord was killed. As soon as I learnt of it, I penned this letter and will look for one who can send it to you.*

Frances stared at the paper much longer than it took to read the words. "I fear it is bad news," the prince said gently.

"Aye, 'tis what I'd feared." She looked up, first at Prince Rupert, then past him to David and Sara. "He is dead." Not at the end of a hangman's rope or at sword point, but dead of a fever. William had been driven into debt by the cost of maintaining the king and his retinue and feared that if the king was not restored and able to repay him, they would lose the house in Newport. All that trial and worry, and the flight to Ireland . . . well, perhaps he was a martyr after all. She would think of him in that way.

Frances folded the paper and put it in her reticule. "Thank you for bringing me this, Your Highness. 'Tis better to know." To Sara she added, "I will wait until tomorrow to give this news to my sons, so that they may fall asleep thinking only of His Highness's visit. 'Twill be a good memory before they swallow this bitter pill."

"I am sorry for your loss, Lady Frances," said Prince Rupert. "Your husband was a faithful servant of the king."

"He was a good man, Your Highness," said Frances.

"I fear your husband is not a good man," said Hannah, as the two women sewed side by side by Meg's hearth.

"What, because he sits up late talking to his friend while I try to get Mary to sleep?" Meg had just been complaining about this very thing, but she was shocked by the bareness of Hannah's statement. She shook out the small petticoat she was sewing for her little daughter, who had just gone down to sleep. "Many a man does far worse than that."

In these weeks before the fishing began, while the men were busy readying boats, nets, and stages for the season, the women took what hours they could steal from their other work to do some extra sewing and mending; there would be little time for those tasks once the fish struck in and all hands were needed on the flakes. At five months old, Mary was growing quickly, and Meg had cut up some of her own petticoats to make garments that the baby could wear in the months ahead. She was grateful that Hannah had taken a few of her busy hours to come work alongside her.

When Hannah did not reply, Meg pressed her point. "Peter is a good man. He be hard-working and godly—he prays all the time and quotes Scripture. He has whole chapters off by heart."

"That makes him a good Puritan—it hardly makes him a good man."

"He mislikes being called a Puritan." Peter called himself a Dissenter, or sometimes a Leveller, but most often said he was simply a true Christian and that no man could order his conscience, only God.

"Puritans never want to be clept by that name," said Hannah. She looked down at the baby in her makeshift cradle before shooting a quick, measuring glance at Meg. "Did you tell him what I said about the governor and Lady Sara, that he ought to mind his words when others are about? They call that kind of talk treason. My own ladyship asked me had I ever heard any such talk here at your house and said that it might be better to have someone else do the wash."

Meg felt a wave of fear. She did not want to lose the extra coin she earned for taking in the Kirke family's washing. "He will mind his tongue," she said, though Peter had agreed to no such thing.

"I told her I never heard nothing bad here in your house. Indeed, I doubt your husband has spoken four words in front of me." Peter always made himself scarce when Hannah visited, saying he did not like women's prattle. "The loose talk in the tavern is easy enough to blame on his companions." She nodded toward Simon's bed in the corner.

"Simon is Peter's servant," Meg said, "and if Peter tells him he should mind his words, Simon will be bound to agree. And Peter is not a bad man," she repeated.

"A decent man may still be a bad husband."

"A bad husband beats his wife for no reason, or fails to provide for her," Meg said.

"Can you say he is a good one?"

"Oh, what is a good husband?"

Hannah paused to think. "Your mother and father, would you say they are well married?"

"Indeed, they are." Meg smiled. She remembered cozy winter days by the fire at home. Her mother and Aunt Kat talked as they sewed, just as she and Hannah were doing now, their conversation punctuated by the laughter her mother and father shared as he came in and out of the house. He still stole kisses from her, even now that they were both growing old. "But 'tis not as if most folk are like my parents," she hastened to explain. "Sure, theirs is a famous romance, folk all over Conception Bay know of it. When they were young, my mother was taken captive by pirates, and my father sailed all round the world to rescue her. There's not many marriages could compare to that."

"True enough. My father and mother were famous in their village too, though 'twas not so pretty a tale." Hannah's fingers went to a little tin brooch in the shape of an owl that she sometimes wore pinned to her kirtle; she had told Meg once that it was the only thing she had from her mother. "Mama married a Negro, and her family and all the neighbours said 'twas a disgrace, and her family turned their backs on her. My parents moved to London, where people were not so much in one another's business. I think they were happy there—still are happy, for aught I know."

"So, we both grew up in happy homes, with parents who were well matched," Meg said. "But not all couples marry for love the way our parents did."

"True enough. My mistress and her husband were no great love match, but they seemed content, and now that she knows for certes he is dead, she grieves for him."

"My sister Lizzie married a neighbour she'd known since they were children. His land lay alongside a piece of our land that my father gave her as a marriage portion, and he had a good fishing room, so 'twas convenient for them to wed. But they get along well enough and seem merry together. They laugh a good deal, as my mother and father do."

"Your husband is not such a merry fellow."

Meg tried to remember when she had last heard Peter laugh. Just then, she heard Mary stirring in the cradle, followed by a lusty cry. She moved to pick up her daughter, but Hannah said, "Let me pick her up. She is not hungry, is she?"

"Nay, she was on the teat just over an hour ago—she only wants to be held, or mayhap she needs her clouts changed."

Hannah picked up the baby, cradling her while humming a soft melody Meg did not recognize. Hard on the heels of wondering when she had last heard Peter laugh, Meg tried to recall if she had ever seen her husband pick up their daughter, cradle Mary like this, rock her and sing to her. Peter had, of course, hoped for a son—it was natural for a man to wish that. Would he have been more tender with a baby boy, paid more heed to him? Meg could not know, and in any case there was nothing she could do about it. Mary settled easily, her curious fingers exploring the owl brooch on Hannah's kirtle as Hannah rocked her in time to that strange, faraway tune.

CHAPTER FOUR

Autumn and Winter 1650-51

Frances sat in the chair across from Sara, on the other side of the large desk that both David and Sara used for keeping accounts. In theory, the household accounts were Sara's responsibility, as the accounts of the colony and Kirke Enterprises were David's. But Frances was well aware that Sara knew as much as her husband did about what was shipped out and received in trade. Now that the trading ships were headed back to Europe or to the New England colonies for another winter season, the business of keeping accounts took up much of Sara's day.

"Why do you make so much of this?" Sara demanded. "You know we will keep you in room and board here until you can return to England. 'Tis to be hoped that by the time that happens, your husband's fortune, such as it is, will have been restored to you. Why trouble yourself about counting pennies?"

Frances knotted her hands in the satin fabric of her gown, keeping her face and voice calm. "I have told you before. We have no way of knowing when my sons and I may be able to return to England, nor any guarantee that I will recover what small fortune is owing to me."

"Many royalists have had their lands and wealth returned to them," Sara pointed out. All through the fishing season, ships had brought news of the latest developments in England, including stories of men who had been pardoned by Parliament for their loyalty to the late king.

"Yes, men have been pardoned if they bent the knee to Parliament and renounced any fealty to the king," Frances said. "And even then, some have made that shameful abasement and still gone penniless. I cannot rely on what may be mine someday. I must begin to build something for myself now. No, not for myself, but for Richard and Nicholas. If 'twere only me, I should be glad to play the part of the widowed sister in your household. But I have my sons to think of."

"Well, I have kept a careful accounting, as you asked. I only want you to know that 'tis not needful."

"Say it is needful to me. Humour me."

"Very well." Sara pulled her account book toward her. "We agreed when you came that your servant, Hannah, would work as part of my household in return for the room and board we give to yourself, your sons, and the maid herself. Food and living space for four people in return for the labour of one housemaid is generous." She looked up, cocking one eyebrow in a glance Frances remembered from their childhood. "One might even call it sisterly."

"Generous, indeed. Of course, I have not been idle myself."

"Indeed not. You mend and sew and embroider, as I do, to keep us all clothed and covered. Of course, with more bodies to clothe, there is more cloth to purchase and more laundering to do. The cost of your garments, and the coin we pay the washerwoman, must also be a part of the accounting."

"As must the extra tasks I have given you leave to use Hannah for."

"Yes. Your servant's work making fish and serving in the tavern goes over and above your contribution to the household, so I have credited it as a separate item. See?" Sara turned the book, knowing full well that Frances had not her experience with understanding figures. Though both women had received a good education for their sex, Sara had spent years honing the skills of bookkeeping in her husband's business.

I have to trust her entirely, Frances thought with regret. *If she cheats me, I would not know it.*

"And so, when we tally the takings from this summer season, as I am doing this week, you can see there is a credit to your account. Once I have accounted for feeding, clothing, and housing you, your sons, and your servant, we—that is, my husband's enterprise—owe you a small amount. I did the same last fishing season, and again, there is a balance in your favour. You can take what is owed you in money or in goods."

This was the difficulty. Frances was selling the only thing of value she had—Hannah's labour—but how could she be paid for it? Frances wished she knew more of business; she wished she had a man to advise her. A husband, ideally, but if she had a husband she would not need to worry about any of this.

"I want neither, for this year or last," she found herself saying, "for I know the amount is small. I do not want to take any additional luxuries from the trade goods, and I have little use for money in this place. I want you to keep this accounting, to keep count each season of what is due to me, whether from Hannah's work or any other means I may find to add to my earnings."

Sara smiled. "And when the time is right, you will tell me in what form you would take your payment?"

"Yes. For much depends on things that are out of my hands. If the young king is successful in his fight to take the throne, I can take my sons back to England and would buy fine clothing and some household goods with my portion, so that we would not return as penniless beggars. And if this wicked state of affairs in England lingers and we must stay here in the colony, then . . ."

"Then what, sister? For aught we hear, there is little chance of success for the royalists. Even Prince Rupert, for all the fine promises he made when he visited here, is back across the sea fighting Parliament's forces, and most like he has not given us a second thought. No, we must all trim our sails to suit the wind, even if it be a Puritan wind, so you'd best not count on going home anytime soon. If you must stay here, how will you take your payment?"

"Land," said Frances. "Land, and a house, and a boat of my own."

"You mean to become a planter, then?"

"I mean my sons to be planters. 'Twould not be my first choice, as well you know. But if this is where I must stay, there is only one way to earn a portion for my sons in this country. I know I will not be able to set myself up in my own establishment in a year, or even two. Only keep the accounting, and when the time is right, I shall take what is due to me."

Sara nodded, making a few notes on the page of her account book. "It shall be so," she said. "And in time we will talk of what is due to you and how we might pay it out."

"In time," said Frances. "The one thing I am very good at is waiting."

"Indeed." And for the first time in many years, perhaps in all Frances's memory, there was something like respect in the look Sara gave her.

The October wind howled like a forlorn ghost around Meg and Peter's house, battering at the shutters and chilling the room despite the sail canvas Peter had nailed up to cover the window. The fire needed more wood, the baby was crying, and Meg had given up her attempt to finish mending Peter's shirts. She picked up baby Mary from the wooden crate.

"Ah, there, my poppet, Mama has you, all is well. Hush, hush." Meg paced the floor, trying to settle the child. She could not be hungry—Meg had nursed her not an hour ago and put her down to sleep, but here she was crying again. *Must have a tooth coming in*, Meg thought. Mary was nine months old, and Meg knew that each new tooth made her fussy. She poked a finger around Mary's mouth looking for evidence and found none, but Mary suckled her mother's finger with as much enthusiasm as if it had been a teat. It seemed to soothe her, so Meg left her finger where it was.

She would have liked to put another log on the fire, but the woodbox was empty. There was more wood stacked outside the house, but to get that she would have to put down the baby, and she was not willing to sacrifice these brief moments of peace and quiet.

For the first year and a half of their marriage, the little house had seemed too quiet with only Meg and Peter in it, compared to the lively, busy home Meg had grown up in. Now with baby Mary, and with Simon whom they had hired and housed for the fishing season, it felt crowded.

She knew Peter had been right to hire a man for the season. With both Simon and young Rafe Bullard fishing in Peter's boat with him, their catch had been far better than the previous year. Even with Rafe's and Simon's wages and Simon's board taken out of the accounting, Peter had finished the season with credit to spare. "You see?" Peter had gloated when the catch was tallied and exchanged for trade goods. "I know how to get ahead in this country."

There were other costs, beyond the cost of filling an extra bowl of pottage or making another loaf of bread; the crowding in the little house was one of them. The other was that the evenings Peter and Simon spent talking over the news from England and discussing religion and politics went on even longer than they had the summer before.

A like-minded friend improved Peter's mood, for which Meg was happy, but that friend being under their own roof wore on her nerves, especially now that she had the baby to care for along with all her other work. Also, the presence of a fellow believer had led Peter to begin instituting lengthy family prayers and placing numerous restrictions on what Meg was allowed to do on a Sunday.

But the last English ship of the season was bound out for Bristol on the morrow, and Simon would be aboard it. Though he planned to return next spring, for the cold, closed-in months of winter when so much time must be spent indoors, Meg would have only her own husband to contend with. Peter alone seemed like a blessing.

Today the two men were off in the woods cutting and hauling firewood. She heard them coming back now, and as Mary had settled to the point where Meg could put her down on a blanket by the fire with a rag ball to play with, she went outside to take a few more sticks from the woodbox that would shortly be replenished.

After it was, she was generous with her thanks for the wood: Men, she knew, liked to be praised when they did even the simplest things for the good of the household. "What a grand load of wood Papa and Uncle Simon have cut for us!" she cooed to Mary, whom she had gathered up in her arms. "This will keep us warm until Christmastide."

"Less talk of pagan festivals, wife. But 'tis a good load of wood, far more than I could have managed on my own," said Peter. "In the woods as in the boat, two men are better than one."

"True, indeed! We will miss that extra pair of hands when you go, Simon," Meg said, trying to fill her voice with warmth. "Does the ship sail at first light?"

As soon as Simon glanced at Peter, she knew. Her heart sank. Perhaps she had known for days, as one ship after another left the harbour and Peter continued to tell her that Simon had booked passage on a later vessel. "You will be glad, then, at our news," Peter said. "We'd a good talk today, going and coming in the woods, and 'tis all settled. Simon is to overwinter with us here."

"Here? In . . . in the house?" Meg's glance went to the pallet by the fire where Simon's bedding had been taking up limited floor space since May.

"Aye, where else should he stay? Not on the floor, of course—we will build him a proper bed here by the hearth, and he will help me put up a wall to partition off our own bedchamber. Mayhap next year we will even be able to add another chamber on to the house. In faith, wife, we are doing well. Our own manservant!"

"'Tis a great boon to me as well," said Simon, "and most grateful I am for your offer. This way I need not spend any of my earnings on passage back to Bristol. 'Tis glad I am, indeed, Meg, that you will put me up for the winter. And come spring we will be back fishing again."

But what will you do till then, to earn your keep? Meg wanted to shout. *And how am I to bear six or seven long, dark months pent up in this house with the two of ye prating Scripture at each other—and at me?*

She said none of this to Simon's face, of course. Whether he was their servant or their guest—the situation was unclear—she could not say openly that he was unwelcome, any more than she could question her husband's decision in front of another man. But later, when Simon had gone up to the tavern to purchase some beer to bring home, she turned on Peter.

"What kind of sense d'you make of this? 'Tis one thing to have Simon here in the fishing season—I'll allow you were right about that. But in winter there is not enough work to keep one man busy, much less two. Well enough for him to talk of saving the money for his fare, but who's to pay his keep for more than half the year while he eats our bread?"

"Hush, woman!" Peter raised his hand in a warning gesture, and Meg stepped back. He had never yet struck her, but she was careful not to give him reason to. "D'you think I would take such a step without careful thought? There's work indeed both of us can do over the winter. If you can scrub petticoats for them two fine ladies up in Kirke House, you're not the only one can earn a few extra pennies. Old Abel Goode has already promised us a nanny goat if we cut and haul his wood all winter, for he's too old to be at it."

"A goat? That's generous, indeed, for a winter's worth of wood."

"Not the wood only; he's other jobs he wants done. Leaks in his roof repaired and broken boards in his wall, that sort of thing. I could not do it all on my own, but with Simon here, I can take on more work. 'Twill be all to our good."

"Very well, if you think 'tis best."

"More of that out of you, and less of your saucy questions and answers in future," Peter said. "For the husband shall be head of the wife, as Christ is head of the church. You're not to question my decisions, no more than I would question God about the workings of his providence, d'you see?"

Meg saw. Her eyes drifted again to Simon's pile of bedclothes. Could they at least find a more out-of-the-way corner to put his bed, she wondered, so she need not always be tripping over it? The promise of their own bedchamber was appealing, but spring seemed a long time away.

Snow came in the middle of the Twelve Days of Christmas, not the light skiff of frost and dust of white that had traced the ground for much of December but a true, heavy snowfall, the first of the season. It cloaked everything so that the trees looked like old beggar women bent low and swaddled up in shawls. "This is the proper kind of weather for

Christmas," said young Davey Kirke, looking out through the small diamond-shaped panes of green glass that made up the big window of Kirke House. "Should we go out and make snowballs?"

The younger lads all fell into line behind Davey, as they generally did, and tumbled outside. Being too mature for throwing snowballs, George and Philip remained in the great hall, sipping on cups of warm spiced ale. Richard hesitated in the doorway, as if torn between the two worlds, but Frances gave him a nod. "Go on out and enjoy the snow," she said, which was all the encouragement he needed to run after his brother and younger cousins.

"All their clothes will be soaking wet," said Sara.

"They'll be dressing up in their mummering get-up before long," George pointed out.

In England, Parliament continued to strip away all kinds of entertainment from the people. If snow as heavy as this were on the ground in England today, Frances wondered if the sad little Puritan children would even be permitted to make snowballs. Christmas services in the churches had been forbidden in those last years of the war when Parliament was ascendant over the king, even before Frances had left England. Since the king's death, things had, apparently, become even stricter.

An English merchant had told her this past summer that not only were the churches not allowed to have Christmas services, and shops and markets forced to remain open for the holiday, but people had been fined for feasting, for holding a private Christmas service, and for decorating their homes with holly and mistletoe. "'Tis forbidden even to sing a carol," he had said, "or make any kind of holiday. Old Noll

Cromwell decrees that the Twelve Days are to be the same as any other working day, though of course a good many people still do as they wish behind the privacy of their own doors and hope no one will inform against them."

With not only the privacy of doors but the width of an ocean between themselves and Cromwell's harsh government, the Kirke family was keeping Christmas. They had gathered for church services on Christmas Eve and Christmas Day, the governor reading from the prayer book as he always did if no priest was about. They could not, of course, celebrate Christ's mass in the absence of a priest, but the prayers and readings honoured the holiday.

Apart from the worship services, the Kirke family continued the customs Sara and David had established since coming out to the colony: There were little gifts for the servants and plans for a Twelfth Night celebration with music and dancing. The tavern, closed since the end of the fishing season, was open again for the Twelve Days so men could enjoy beer, wine, and company. And the Kirke lads were insistent that there must be mummering.

Frances was not sure about her sons going mummering. It was an entertainment for the common folk; on her first two Christmases in the colony, the Kirkes had remained in their home while the villagers and servants, mostly the young men, had dressed up in outlandish costumes that hid their faces and gone about banging on doors, demanding cake and ale. Finally they had come to Kirke House and put on a little play of St. George and the dragon, with singing and dancing, in exchange for mince pies and a cup of wine each. A colourful entertainment, but there was an edge to it that reminded the wealthy folk that if any number of the poor battered at their door and demanded to be fed, they could not hold out against them.

But that was the way of these things, whether the local tradition was mummering, or wassailing, or whatever it might be. Christmas was always a time to turn things topsy-turvy and to be generous to the common folk. She had expected this Christmastide to be the same.

This year, however, something had gotten into the elder Kirke boys. Perhaps it was defiance of the news from England. George had organized a game of football for all the young men in the settlement on St. Stephen's Day. There was no village green to play on, but they found an open space beyond the gardens that was almost flat. Plans for more sports throughout the holiday had been concocted, as well as the Twelfth Night celebration.

George, Philip, and Davey were determined to make up a party of mummers from Kirke House to join up with the village mummers. Molly Thomas, a planter's daughter of fourteen whom Sara had recently hired as a maid, was eager to go with them, so Frances had told Hannah she must go also, to safeguard Molly's virtue and keep an eye on the exuberant lads.

She had expected some reluctance, but the usually reserved Hannah seemed quite willing to dress both herself and Molly up in men's breeches and coats and cover her face with a lace veil, while the lads squeezed themselves into petticoats and kirtles. Davey, back inside and dried out from the snowball exploits of earlier in the day, produced from dusty old trunks a collection of outlandish hats in the styles of several decades past and went about dropping them onto various heads. And Frances decided that, as all the Kirke lads were going, along with the two maids and Caleb the manservant, she might safely let Richard and Nicholas join in the fun. It was an entertainment for adults, not for children, but if Jarvis was joining in, Nicholas insisted he must go also.

"Come, we'll go to the tavern and from there see where the village folk are heading," George said, rounding up his crew.

"They'll only be heading to each other's houses. 'Tis not as if they're going to tramp all the way to Renews," Sara pointed out.

"No riots now, no fighting," David Kirke warned his sons. "You chose to take the maids and the young lads with you, so get them home if the revelry gets out of hand. You may have masks on, but everyone will know you are Kirkes. Behave accordingly."

Hannah could not have said why she agreed so willingly to go with the mummers. Of course, the presence of another, steadier woman would protect Molly, the young maidservant. And once the little fellows, Nicholas and Jarvis, were permitted to go, there was no question that she must go along. But if she had dug in her heels at the start, said mummering around a rough fishing village was an entertainment for grown men only, then Molly and the younger lads would perforce have had to stay at home also. Hannah had the power to stop the whole foolishness.

And yet she had not done so. Hannah had memories of Christmas seasons in the Hopkins's old house on the Isle of Wight and in the household where she had served before that. She and the other servants and some of the village folk would have dances and drinks and cakes in the great hall on Twelfth Night. They had not got themselves up in fancy dress as mummers did, but that upside-down nature of the holiday, the low folks crowding into the fine halls of the wealthy and demanding food and gifts and merriment, was much the same thing as the mummering.

She suddenly wanted to do it again, to do something freeing and strange, to wear a kerchief over her face so that no one would say, "Look, 'tis Lady Frances's blackamoor maid!" For one night she would lay aside the novelty of having the only dark face in the colony, with the stares and comments that so often aroused. She would be no one and yet part of a crowd.

And so she found herself in the little party led by the three oldest Kirke boys, all having had more wine than was good for them, prancing up the path to the tavern and opening the doors, and the barrels of beer, for a larger group of mummers from the fishermen's houses. These, too, were nearly all young men, though she heard a few womanly voices from some shorter and slighter mummers.

Bessy Thomas, Molly's elder sister, must be one of them, for she and Molly linked arms at once. With her was another young woman got up in a fisherman's breeches and tunic, whose high giggling voice gave her away. That must have been young Clara Kean, who stuck close to George Kirke's side in a way Lady Sara certainly would not have approved. Hannah could not identify several of the mummers with their faces shrouded.

Abel Goode's large, ramshackle house was the first place they stopped, everyone crowding into his dingy hall. Someone struck up singing "Come bring the noise, my merry,

merry boys," and all stamped their feet or thumped their sticks on the dirt floor as they joined the song. Though the song promised "rare mince pie" and "white loaf," there were no such treats at Abel's house. He passed around a jug of some home-brewed liquor that several of the men swigged from, coughing and wiping their mouths after they drank.

They fared better at the big and comfortable house of Samuel Thomas, father of Molly and Bessy. The Thomases were the most prosperous planters in Ferryland apart from the Kirkes themselves, and there was room by their hearth for all. Nell Thomas had baked some tarts, filled with the preserves of the autumn berries, and her small ale was good. The mummers stayed in that comfortable hall for some time; Hannah thought it likely that the Thomas girls and their elder brother had led the crew to their mother's table knowing she would be well prepared. Old Samuel brought out his fiddle, and the singing and dancing went on until the mummers were hot and had to stumble back into the chilly evening.

By now everyone in the settlement knew that the mummering was going on, and doors were flung open as they passed. Some of these houses were far too small for a group of twelve or fifteen mummers, so they stayed in the yard, dancing and singing there, and such small treats or drinks as each family could manage to provide were passed around outside.

An hour later the party had grown merry to the point of disarray: The men had drunk very freely, the women were giggly and flirtatious, and the children so excited they were almost falling into ditches. Hannah made Nicholas hold one of her hands and Jarvis the other. Bits of costume fell off or were discarded, despite the chill of the evening. Hannah saw a high-crowned, feathered hat that her mistress had brought out from England tumbling into the road, and snapped at Molly to put it back on her head before somebody trampled on it. "Christmas or no Christmas, she'll not forgive you if that hat don't come back in good shape," Hannah warned.

They had looped around and doubled back, coming up the path that led along by the wharves and stages. George Kirke was leading the party toward his parents' house, where the mummering would end with everyone invited into the hall. *Nearly there*, Hannah thought with a sigh of relief, *and no trouble at all.*

She had enjoyed the mummering, though she would have enjoyed it more if she had not had to keep the lads in her care. She had given up looking out for Molly, who was still clinging to her sister's side, the both of them chattering freely with the young men. Bessy Thomas could look after her own sister, Hannah decided. Clara Kean was openly clinging to George Kirke's arm now, but that was none of Hannah's worry.

The last small house they passed was the Taylors', and the Kirke lads marched on past, making no effort to turn in at the gate. Hannah breathed another sigh of relief—she did not want any trouble for Meg. Soon they would all be back by the warmth of the Kirke House fire.

But in the crush of revellers along the road between the Kirke sons up front and Hannah's little charges at the back, one of the men—she thought it was Johnny Pike, the Thomases' manservant, or perhaps Alfie Bullard, both of whom had had a good deal to drink—stopped. Grabbing a couple of his fellows, he turned and went into the yard of the Taylor house. "We cannot pass these good folk by! They must have some Christmas cheer!"

A few of the other men whooped agreement and followed him into the yard. "Nay, leave them be," said Philip Kirke. Quiet and hesitant as always, he still had his wits about him, but had little chance of prevailing over the boisterous crowd. "They are P-puritans, they don't keep Christmas."

"Don't keep Christmas?" called another. "Then we must bring 'em Christmas, whether they like it or no. Aye, Christmas, in the king's name!"

"No, no," Hannah said, almost under her breath, but little Nicholas, a perceptive child, said, "Why no, Hannah? Why should we not bring them Christmas?"

"Because they will not like it."

"Everyone likes Christmas!" his cousin Jarvis put in.

Hardly, Hannah thought. If they were back in England now, the mummers might find themselves hauled before the magistrate, fined or even beaten. Here in Ferryland, with the Kirkes ruling, things were quite different: The dour Puritans were in the minority, while the Anglicans who celebrated the holiday had the upper hand. She well knew that Peter Taylor would not take kindly to the confrontation that was about to unfold.

But it was too late; the men were battering at the door. There was no response, and Hannah hoped there would be none, that Peter would barricade himself in his house, ignore the mummers, and they would tire of the sport.

Instead, two or three more men began banging on the door. "The mummers are here! Let the mummers in!" they shouted, and suddenly the door opened.

Peter stood in his doorway, his face ghostly in the glow of a torch one of the mummers carried. Next to him stood a second man: his servant, Simon Tolliver.

"Get out of my yard with your pagan foolery and be gone!" Peter shouted.

Hannah, drawing the lads to the back of the crowd as mummers surged forward, looked to see if she could make out anyone behind the men. The little house showed only a dim glow, likely from the hearth fire, and she hoped Meg and baby Mary were well away from any trouble. What if the mummers pushed into the house?

But as the mummers kept shouting and cajoling, Peter showed at least some sense. He and Simon came out onto the step, closing the door behind them. Hannah imagined Meg running to put the latch on as Peter raised his voice again above the clamour. "This is a sinful racket! If ye were in England, I'd see every man jack of you whipped before the magistrate. 'Tis against the law. Get ye gone!"

"Aye, but we're not in England, are we, Roundhead?" The voice that rose above the rest was surprisingly young, and Hannah knew at once the only fellow in that crowd so saucy and so bold was no servant or fisherman's son but young Davey Kirke. "This is the New Found Land, and Governor Kirke rules here. He has no truck with your Puritan holiness!"

"You said true enough there—no holiness in this place!" Simon shot back, and Peter, now in a fine fury, began shouting epithets at the mummers. "Cursed heathens, filthy scum, sucking at the Roman teat! Satan's minions, ye're no better than a crowd of Spaniards or Frenchmen. No better than the Indians in the woods—"

"Shut your mouth, Peter Taylor!" A man—Hannah thought it was one of the Bullard boys—reached forward, grabbed the front of Peter's shirt, and hauled him down into the yard, then let go of him and stumbled back as Simon's fist hit the reveller's jaw.

Hannah knew that any time one man hit another in the middle of a crowd of drunk, angry men, they had only seconds before the scene turned into a brawl. In this case it would be a very one-sided brawl, with the mummers far outnumbering the two Puritans. Oliver Cromwell was far away in England; here, numbers and fists were what mattered.

She was still holding the little lads' hands, about to start running—Molly and the other women were already backing away from the Taylors' house—when she had a thought. "Molly! Take these lads home," she said, grabbing the young woman's arm and transferring care of the children to her. Hannah surged toward the crowd of men, several of whom were now throwing punches, and took Philip Kirke by the shoulder.

"Get your brothers out of here," she said in his ear. "A fight among fishermen is one thing, but if someone should hit you or George or David, your father will look on things differently. 'Twill turn a small matter into a great one."

Philip nodded. "I thought the same," he said, grabbing George and Davey and pulling them toward the road. Peter and Simon, outnumbered though they were, were still fighting the men nearest them. Of course, they were likely sober, where all the other men were worse for drink.

Philip and George joined Hannah in retreat, but Davey was stubborn, planting his feet. "I'd like to give one of them a smack. And if he hit me back, he should suffer whatever my father has to say about it."

"Be not such a fool," Hannah said, for Davey was not that much of a man yet that she could not chide him as she did the younger lads. He was tall for his years but spindly, and

George and Philip between them had no trouble dragging him out of the yard. "If yon Puritan laid hands on you and left a mark, your father'd have him hanged, and this whole harbour would be up in arms."

"She has it right, Davey," said George. "Leave this to the common folk to fight among themselves." And then the four of them were running, following the women and children up the path to Kirke House, away from the mummers and the brawl. Hannah bent as she ran to pick up Lady Frances's old hat, once again dropped in the snow and trodden on, and clutched it to her chest until they were through the doors and into the welcoming warmth of Kirke House.

CHAPTER FIVE

Spring 1651

"Josiah! Get into the house! 'Tis the Lord's Day, not a time to be frolicking and climbing trees!"

Her small son, engrossed in scaling the maple tree, ignored his mother's cries. Patience Treworgy raised her voice. "In here, now! Or I shall call your father to come get you!"

As Josiah jumped to the ground, Patience sighed. Her own parents had named their children for the virtues they hoped to see in them, but her mother had often commented that, all unknowing, they had named their eldest daughter after the virtue she most lacked. If she and John had named their sons on the same principle, Josiah ought to be called Obedience, and baby Matthew, currently howling at his inability to follow his brother up the tree, should be named Silence.

"Hush, Matthew." She stood Josiah in front of her on the step and brushed the leaves and grass from his petticoat. "Shame on you, Josiah. And you asked me only yesterday when you might put on breeches. Here you are showing yourself to be a baby still."

"But Mama, I want breeches so I can climb trees!"

Patience stifled the laugh that rose to her lips and hoped Josiah could see no hint of it in her eyes. "That is very wicked of you. When a lad puts on breeches, he is on his way to becoming a man. You should be breeched on your next birthday, when you are five, but if you do not show yourself better behaved than this, Papa may wait until you are six, and that is a very long time."

"No, I must be breeched when I am five!"

"Mama! Beeches! Five!" howled Matthew. At two years old, his conversation consisted mainly of echoing things he heard other people say and loudly demanding what he wanted. Last Sunday in meeting, he had grabbed the front of Patience's gown and shouted, "Titty!" in a voice twice as loud as the minister's.

That was the moment, Patience thought, when she was most glad that she had married John Treworgy, instead of the young minister back home who had been showing interest. If she had been a minister's wife, her child's bad behaviour would have been the talk of the colony for weeks afterward. But as she was the wife of a prosperous merchant, tongues might wag, but the congregation's disapproval mattered less to her husband than it would to a clergyman. John had only laughed at Matthew's misdeed. "You might have tried putting a hand over his mouth. I've no idea what else might still that child," he said. "Perhaps he will be the preacher in the family, for he's a powerful set of lungs on him."

John could be stern when the occasion called for it, and when she sent Josiah in to him, John gave the appropriate lecture about respecting the Lord's Day. The whole family was presentable in time to go to Sunday meeting.

The meeting house was small. Most of the English settlers here in Maine were Anglican and worshipped by the prayer book as people had done before the war in England. To Patience, raised in godly Massachusetts, the Anglican way of worship seemed almost as pagan as the rituals of the native Abenaki people. This would all change, John had assured her. The Massachusetts Bay Colony was expanding its influence north into Maine, with right-thinking planters and merchants like John leading the way. Soon, they would convert both Anglicans and Abenaki, and the meeting house would be full of people who were truly devout. Patience looked forward to that time; since marrying John and moving here to Kittery, she longed for the familiar world of her childhood.

After the service, she chatted to some of the other wives while their children, unhappily confined to Sunday-best clothes, squirmed in their mothers' arms or at their sides. Patience was glad to see other children squirming; she was ever eyeing other women's youngsters, hoping hers were not the only ones to be ill-behaved betimes.

When the knot of men around the preacher finally dispersed and John collected her and the children, his mood was buoyant. "I have had some interesting news," he said. "Josiah, no, you must not run—'tis Sunday. Hold my hand and walk beside me. There's a good lad."

"What news?" Patience asked.

"I know we ought not to talk of business on a Sunday," he said, "but what I heard this morning only confirmed what has been said on the weekdays. Parliament is looking to send a party of commissioners to the Pool Plantation—or the Colony of Avalon, as 'tis sometimes called—in the New Found Land. 'Tis likely they will put the governor, who is a notorious royalist and a very dishonest dealer, out of his office. And I have been asked to be one of the commissioners."

"The New Found Land!" She knew little about that wild island, even farther to the north than Maine, save that it was part of the great fishing trade from which men like her father and husband drew their wealth. "How long would you be away?" Trading voyages were part of a merchant's life. Since their marriage, John had already been to the New Found Land once, had voyaged up and down the New England coast, and had twice gone all the way to England.

"The commission will travel there within the next few weeks and, I suppose, stay as long as it takes to investigate Governor Kirke's dealings. The business will have to be concluded back in England, and I may have to travel there as well."

"'Tis an honour to be asked."

"Indeed, but there is more than that in it," John said. "Most likely one of the commissioners will be appointed governor, once they have removed Kirke, and I have been asked if I would be willing to be considered for the task."

"Governor? Of the New Found Land?"

"Yes. Kirke's enterprise is based in his plantation, but he has rule over the whole coast—a huge territory, with much opportunity for wealth. And if it came to pass that I were to govern there, you could join me and be the governor's wife." He glanced at her as if waiting to see how she might respond to this plan.

Governor's wife. Patience liked the sound of those words but liked the sound of *New Found Land* less. Kittery, Maine, already seemed like an isolated wilderness to her. She knew little of the wider world; she had come out to the colonies with her parents as a small child. Unlike John, who had already been a man grown when he left England, she had never known any home but Massachusetts until moving to Maine with her husband.

"Is't not all fishing stations and rough fishermen up there? Is there a church, even an Anglican church, never mind a true Christian meeting house?"

They were approaching the little hill before their house now, and when Josiah began to drag his feet, John took the lad up in his arms before answering. "There be a scattering of women and homes and villages—no churches, so far as I know," he said. "I doubt there are many of the faithful up there, if any at all. This is an opportunity to place a man of true religion there as governor instead of Kirke and bring enlightenment to the people, as well as to keep the fish trade growing. The fisherfolk are rough and unlettered, but they have very little trouble with the native folk as we have here. The natives keep to themselves in the forest and do not come near the English habitations. Kirke has a great plantation there, and it will all be run by the new governor once he is replaced. Would you not like that, to be governor's wife and mistress of a grand plantation?"

He smiled at her, and Patience saw the hope in that smile—he truly wanted her to join him, even though he must have known that moving to such a remote place was a great deal to ask of any woman. She knew what she ought to say—that if it was God's will, she would go, even if her own selfish heart rebelled. But after all, it might never happen. "Go first with the commissioners, and trust God for the outcome," she said.

"Of course. And if God were to grant me the post, you know, I might go alone. I could spend summers there; the place may not need a year-round governor. You might keep the house here against my return," John added.

"No! I mean, I should not like that, for us to be apart for so long." It was not that she was so very much in love with her husband. He treated her kindly, was not too old and certainly not ill-looking, but Patience had never expected to marry for love. She simply did not want to be left alone in Maine with the children for half the year. If John could bring her back home to Boston, to be near her mother and father, she would not mind him going off to the New Found Land, but it seemed unlikely he would do that.

John Treworgy took his wife's arm, the one that was not cradling Matthew, and tucked his own free hand into it. "Then I shall go with the commissioners and seek God's will for the next steps."

"Hannah!" Frances had called for her maid twice already with no reply. She let a sharp edge hone her voice now as she called a third time. After two years in this wild place, had Hannah grown slack in her ways? Or perhaps the fault was not with the place but with the maid herself. Hannah was, after all, half-African, and Frances, who had not had much to do with Africans, had a vague sense that Hannah's people were best suited to field work such as they did in the southern colonies. Likely as not the change in their circumstances here had brought out the coarser side of Hannah's nature.

Sara walked into the room on the heels of Frances's call.

"Hannah is busy. I set her and Molly to dress the boys in their best clothes; Molly does not know enough to do it herself."

"Well enough, but I need Hannah to sweep out my chamber."

"That can wait. The lads—your sons as well as mine—must be dressed now, ready for these . . . whoever they are. Emissaries, I suppose."

"Very good. The governor's wife has spoken." Frances paused. "I wonder how much longer you will be able to enjoy that title—governor's wife?"

Sara settled herself on the bench with a rustle of skirts. "What, are you turned Leveller and would pull my husband down from his position? Who would you see in his place—a parliament of fishermen?"

"Do not speak nonsense. I want your husband to keep his post as much as you do, for my position depends on his."

"You will do well to remember it."

Frances was used to her sister's moods. It had not taken long, after coming out to the New Found Land, to remember what Sara's temper had been like when they were growing up. As the younger of the two sisters, she ought to have deferred to Frances. But Frances was the deferring sort; Sara never had been.

Prince Rupert's one visit to the colony had conferred a kind of royal authority to David Kirke's ragtag navy of vessels blockading the waters around the colony during the first two years of Cromwell's rule in England. While the blockade held, no ship representing the new government of England was allowed through. But paying the privateers had proved costly, and the blockade was impossible to maintain, especially as Parliament's grip on England and the seas grew firmer.

Now, as another spring had brought the fishing fleet and merchant ships back into their waters, Frances knew that David and Sara were braced for Parliament's latest move in an increasingly tense game. The English ship that had anchored offshore the evening before, flying the Commonwealth flag rather than the old royal standard, boded no good.

David Kirke and his two eldest sons were already waiting at the dock. Sara moved to the large front window that gave a commanding view of the harbour. "These are no strangers," she said as the men from the ship drew nearer.

"Friends, then?"

"Nay, hardly. They are all merchants we have had dealings with before, but a good many are ones my husband has had disputes with over trade."

This was hardly surprising, Frances thought, as David Kirke seemed to be ever engaged in lawsuits and conflicts with one merchant or another.

"There is Captain Pyle, and that rascal Sikes who took us to court, and that man Redwood," Sara elaborated. "The younger fellow, John Treworgy, has lands down in the Maine colony. Every one of them has some grudge against us."

Frances joined her at the window just as the two maids appeared, ushering in the two youngest boys. Their rarely worn hose, shoes, and doublets had been well brushed, and their long hair freshly washed and combed. A few steps behind them came Davey and Richard, who had managed their own grooming. They generally ran about in breeches and tunics, attired like the fishermen's lads they played with, but anyone arriving at the house today would know them for gentlemen's sons.

"Very fine. Stand straight, like little soldiers," said Sara.

The youngest lads had never seen any soldiers save the tin ones they played with, and they looked like so many little toys as they lined up by the far wall of the great hall, getting into place just as the men arrived at the door.

"Gentlemen, my wife, Lady Sara. Some of you have met her before," Governor Kirke said as Sara gave the men her hand and inclined her head a few careful degrees. "My younger sons and my nephews—" A sweeping gesture included the four lads, who bowed. "And my wife's sister, Lady Frances."

The men were introduced, the names flying past Frances's ears. Judging by their dress of sober but expensive blacks and greys, if they were not all Puritans, they were at least the sort of men who trimmed their sails to Parliament's wind and would do well under the new Commonwealth.

"Ladies, you may take the little lads and leave us. George and Philip, you stay with me," the governor said, having invited the visitors to sit. Frances herded the children out before her, noting the looks of mutiny on two faces: Sara's and young Davey's. Davey thought himself as much a man as his elder brothers, and Sara, of course, wanted to sit with the men and hear their talk, perhaps even contribute to it. She would listen with her ear at the keyhole if she could, Frances thought.

Instead, Sara went to the kitchen, where Frances heard her sister ordering Mistress Durdle to prepare a dinner for the visitors. Beef, she decreed, would be on the table, "for we must show ourselves to good advantage before these fellows." Frances thought that if the commissioners were claiming that David had diverted tax money to enrich himself and his family, it might be better to serve a meal that did not show them so wealthy. But it was not for her to say.

The commissioners did not dine at the Kirke family table; they remained closeted with David and the elder boys, Sara joining them for dinner. "Have Hannah bring it in to us," she ordered Frances, "for she will make a better showing than Molly would."

Frances wondered if that was because Hannah was the better servant or whether the sight of a Negro maid would give the impression that the Kirkes were wealthy enough to own a slave as well as employing local servants. Perhaps both; Sara's mind ever ran on more than one path at a time.

That left Frances and the younger lads at the table. "Are those men going back to England?" Jarvis asked as they ate.

"No, you hare-brained rascal," said Davey. "They will sleep aboard their ship tonight, but doubt not they will be back, mayhap for several days."

Richard met his mother's eyes. He did not chatter or speculate as his brother and cousins did, but she could read the worry in his look. When the others had finished their meal and got down from the table, he asked her, "Have they come to bring us back to England?"

"No, child. Why should they want us back in England?"

"You said—you told me that because we were loyal to the old king, we would be in great trouble if we went back to England. I thought mayhap they had come here to capture us."

"Nay, Dickon, we are not of such importance as all that. Parliament has more to think of than a widow woman and her young sons. Their business is with your Uncle David."

"But if mine uncle wanted to be in their favour and sell us to them as . . . as servants? Or prisoners?"

"Hush, what folly!"

"I thought they might take me on their ship to work as a

cabin boy. And I would do it, if I had to, but I think Nicholas is too young."

"You are both too young to think of such things." Quietly, Frances chided herself for the times she had confided in the boy, treating him as if he were older than his years. "All will be well. You must not trouble yourself with such thoughts."

Her own questions, like Richard's, were not destined to be answered that night. Sara, David, George, and Philip were closeted late into the evening, talking, and Davey managed to inveigle himself into the conversation, but Frances sent the other boys off to bed and then went to her own chamber.

The commissioners returned in the morning, causing great upheaval as they demanded David produce all his accounts. Two of them began a detailed job of combing through the accounts. While they were about that business, the others went around the community talking to the fishermen, no doubt asking prying questions about how Governor Kirke conducted his business.

"Our people will stand by us," Sara said, more to herself than to Frances. "They are loyal and know that my husband rules this place well."

"That word *loyal* is a shifty word. It seems to change its meaning every month."

"The planters and fishermen here care not what happens in England. Half of them likely think the king is still alive. All they care about is whether things are governed well here and whether they get a fair price for the fish. That is what we offer: good government and good business."

"You place a great deal of faith in your husband, and in people's opinion of him," said Frances. "I hope you are not disappointed."

"David Kirke's not fit to rule!" Peter banged his fist on the table so hard that the man in the fine grey doublet startled as if he had been struck. Meg scurried to the table to refill the gentleman's cup as Peter continued. "He makes no bones of the fact that he's a Cavalier, loyal to the old tyrant Charles, and I don't believe he's sworn no oath to Parliament."

"I do not believe he has been asked to do so yet," said the gentleman.

"But he's a governor, he ought to swear loyalty," Simon put in. Peter had introduced Simon as "my servant" at the start of the interview, but Simon showed no hint of humility in his manner and spoke to the gentleman as boldly as Peter himself did.

Mary whimpered. Meg put the ale jug on the table between the men and withdrew to the corner of the room where her bed was, picking up Mary to nurse her. The wall that Peter had erected to partition off their bedchamber offered a little privacy, but she could still hear everything that was said in the main room of the house. She kept listening to the men's conversation, keen to know if Peter was going to say anything that would make trouble for them.

"And he's an Anglican, near as bad as a Papist, not a true reformed Christian at all," Peter went on. "He reads Sunday services out of the prayer book, he has a big iron cross up on the wall and they all sit facing it on Sundays, and he celebrated Christmas up there in the big house. He allowed the mummers to go around the settlement, with his own sons and servants dressed up and taking part. They came here to my door, though I told 'em we were good Christian people and wanted no part of it, and they showed violence to me!"

There was a pause; it almost sounded as if the gentleman sighed. "This is all very troubling, of course. We want good Christian men in authority. But our commission—well, we are tasked with looking into Governor Kirke's *business* affairs. Whether the fishing business here is well run, whether proper taxes are paid, all of that."

"Aye, he's a shrewd enough businessman, I'll grant that," Peter said. "But look at yon house there, Kirke House, all the fine things they have, the clothes his wife and her sister go about in, the plate and silver they put on their table. D'you think he'd be doing so well off it if he were dealing fairly?"

"And the money he makes off that tavern of his," Simon added. "That's all to his own profit. Every man in the settlement pays him for our beer and wine."

"And it promotes drunkenness," said Peter. "Not that I'm opposed to a man having a drink, for his stomach's sake, as the apostle says, but that tavern is an unruly place. I don't go there no more. 'Tis only good to line Master Kirke's pockets."

"That's Sir David to you," the gentleman corrected.

"Nay, I don't hold with all them Sirs and Ladies—and no more should you, if you're a true Christian. We pulled down the king because no man should have such power. Bowing and curtseying, saying Sir This or Lady That—'tis not according to Scripture. I bow before no one but God."

Peter's bold statement of faith met another little well of silence from the man in the grey doublet. Meg, shifting Mary from one breast to the other, twitched the curtain aside a little to see. If only Peter would be less free with his tongue!

She had expected more trouble from the business with the mummers back at Christmas. Trouble there had been:

Apart from Simon's black eye and Peter's bleeding nose, they had been called before the governor and each fined. But Alfie Bullard, who had started the fight, had been fined the exact same amount, and the matter was closed. On that occasion, too, Peter had started to make fine speeches about what true Christians should and should not do, but the governor had shut him up pretty quickly.

Now the gentleman said only, "I understand your convictions, my good fellow, but my interest is in Governor Kirke's deeds. I have made note of what you say, and I will investigate this matter of his tavern, in particular."

"There's more than that you should investigate," Simon said. "He's a slippery character, our governor, and out to line his own pockets for certes. We'd be grateful to see a better man in his place."

"It is beyond me to decide such things, but I thank you fellows for your time. I have taken enough of it—you have work to be back at." And he was gone, leaving Peter and Simon grumbling as they finished their dinners.

Meg put Mary down by the hearth to crawl about while she cleaned up after the men. This was an easier time of year for her than summer would be, for the fishing had not yet started, and the men were busy mending flakes, stages, and boats, checking their gear and nets, and readying all for the season to come. Until the fish came in, all Meg had to do was cook, clean house, milk the goat, feed the chickens and collect their eggs, do the laundry for Kirke House—all the chores she did year-round—and clear rocks from the garden to ready the soil for spring planting.

When she went later that afternoon to help tend the Kirke House garden, with Mary tightly secured in a sling, she was glad to see Hannah there.

"Did those commission men come to your house?" Hannah asked her.

"One did. I don't recall his name. He was tall, and his clothes were sober colours but very fine cut and cloth."

"They all dress that way—no frippery or bright colours, but they show their wealth in the fabric. I think that one must be Master Sikes, or mayhap 'tis Master Treworgy. What did your husband tell him?"

"Oh, all his complaints, but I do not think the gentleman paid much heed. Peter wanted to talk of how the governor uses the prayer book and keeps Christmas. The gentleman seemed not so much interested in that. He wrote things down, though."

"Aye, they are all writing things down. Three days they have been here now, talking to everyone. My lady is in a swivet about it, for she thinks she'll be turned out of her home and have nowhere to go."

"Where *will* you go? Where will she go, if the governor is sent away?"

"I wish I knew. Anything might happen, I suppose."

Not until late on the fourth evening, dusk falling over the harbour, did Frances find out what would happen. No, she would not be brought back to England in chains, nor would Richard and Nicholas be indentured to work as cabin boys. But David Kirke's luck had finally run out.

He and Sara asked Frances into their chamber. "I am called back to England, to answer charges," David said. "The so-called government have appointed this commission to inquire into our dealings here. They claim I have withheld taxes and revenues, enriched myself and my family rather than paying what is due to the Crown. Though they have torn down the king, they are happy to collect on debts owed to him."

"'Tis all lies, of course," said Sara.

Frances noticed that David did not join in this hearty denial. The man knew his own business and was well aware how many ways one might redirect money to avoid paying revenue, especially to a government of traitors and regicides.

"I will board their ship willingly in the morning," David said. "I would prefer not to leave in chains."

"Of course not." Frances found she was trembling. She wanted to say *What will become of me and my sons?* but she stilled her tongue. They would tell her, and she must accept it, whatever her fate was to be.

"I will go, as well," Sara said. "I will be able to do some good among those who are still our friends in England, while David must answer these trumpery charges."

"Will your sons go with you?"

"Yes," said Sara, but her husband cut her off, something Frances had rarely seen—the two were generally in perfect agreement.

"No. I would not have it so." He looked at his wife, who had opened her mouth to speak again. "Do not gainsay me in this, Sara. Indeed, I would not have you come yourself, but the risk is yours to take. I will not chance my sons in England, in the hands of Cromwell's men. They will stay here. And Frances, I ask you to have the care of them. George is nearly a man grown, of course, but they are all very young still and need a guiding hand."

Frances nodded slowly. She was not, then, to be dragged back to England, nor to be turfed out of house and home. Instead, she was to have the management of six boys and—the household? "What of this house, of your business, of the ships and the men?"

"You need have no care about the fishing, nor the fishing servants," David said. "That is no task for a woman. I suspect they will put another governor in my place, but I will have my brother James come out, if he is permitted, to look to the interests of the Kirke family and see that we are not stripped of all we own. I can entrust some of it to George, but James will oversee it. As for this house, I hope we may keep it and you and the boys go on living here."

"You *must* keep it," Sara said. "I will not have all that we have worked for gone to nothing, to some Puritan they put in our place. We will return and be master and mistress of this plantation again."

"That is my hope," said David Kirke. "I will answer their charges and hope they will send me back here to continue my work. Indeed, while I am over there, England may come to its senses and put the true king on his throne."

"Amen," Frances said; she felt it in her heart like a prayer, that order and monarchy would be restored. But for now, "I will keep your charge and not give up the house unless dragged from it."

There was more talk and packing of trunks and little sleep that night. Shadows grew long; tapers and lamps were lit. George came to his parents' chamber and talked with his father and mother and aunt about how things would be managed. Then the younger boys made such a clamour that they could not be put to bed until everything had been explained.

Davey argued about being left behind and had to be sent from the room to silence him.

Finally, in the grey dawn light, servants carried two trunks down to the boat. David and Sara walked behind them, hand in hand like young lovers leaving the church on their wedding day, stepping into the unknown.

Frances and the lads walked farther behind. The fishermen began to gather down on the shore. Word had travelled; everyone in the settlement somehow knew that the governor was leaving. The men removed their caps as David and Sara passed, and both men and women bowed their heads gravely. She heard them murmur, "God go with you, sir," and, "We wish ye both all the best," and, "We pray you come safe back, sir and madam."

The sun had risen by now, but so had the chill wind off the water. Frances shivered and drew her cloak more tightly around her. The cold, glittering sun danced on the dark waves that stretched out to the horizon. Little Jarvis was crying, but silently. Davey, resigned to his fate, kept a firm grip on his younger brother's shoulders. When they reached the wharf, Sara embraced her sons while David turned to address the ragged group gathered to see them off.

"Thank you for your good wishes, good folk of Avalon! It is my honour to serve as your governor, and I hope to be speedily back in this place. I was a loyal servant of the king when he lived, and I will follow Parliament's direction as long as they are in power, while I pray, as you all do, for the restoration of the true king. Be just, be faithful in your duties, work hard, and all will be well."

"Amen!" cried several voices, as if he had said a prayer. Frances had never thought David was especially loved by the people, but he was respected, and she saw a few of the women wipe tears from the corners of their eyes. One was Meg Taylor, who stood with her little girl on her hip. Beside her, her husband Peter stood tall and straight, with his cap still on his head and the shadow of a smile on his face.

That one is trouble, Frances thought. What had Peter Taylor told the commissioners? Were there others of his same mind, who might be glad to see a new governor?

Then Sara was in front of her, and instead of an embrace, for they had never been the embracing kind of sisters, she put both her hands on Frances's upper arms, gripping her as if to hold her in place.

"I took you in and have shared all with you," Sara said, so quietly none but Frances could hear. "Repay me by being a good caretaker of it all, until I can return."

"You have my word," said Frances. "Farewell. I will pray for your safe return."

"Do so—we have need of all the prayers we can muster." Then Sara turned and was gone, along with her husband, to whatever fate awaited them in London.

CHAPTER SIX

Spring 1652

"It is determined, then," John Treworgy told his wife. "I am to return with all speed to the New Found Land to take up my duties as governor. Will you come with me?"

Patience looked up from her sewing. Her children's cries drifted through the open window on the first warm breeze of April. Maine winters were cold and hard and the spring a welcome delight. What would it be like to move farther north and east, to a rocky island in the midst of the ocean? Had springtime touched that land yet?

She had turned such questions over and over in her mind ever since John's return last autumn. He had gone first to the New Found Land as part of the commission of inquiry, then on to England with Governor Kirke as his prisoner. Also on the voyage to England had been Lady Sara Kirke, whom John described as "a tigress." The commissioners had not been ordered to take her prisoner, but she had insisted on accompanying her husband.

"You are sure that all will be well in Bennett's hands here?" she asked now. Ezekiel Bennett was John's man of business who managed the plantation here in Maine and would, with his own wife, live in their house if the Treworgys went away.

"Perfectly—there is not a man I trust more. I would leave you and the little lads behind only if you felt unequal to the task of moving to a new colony."

"I have settled my mind to it," Patience said. More truthfully, she had prayed for God to settle her mind. She lay awake nights, trying to imagine what this strange, far place might be like, but could form no picture in her mind. Her duty, however, was clear. She took to heart the words of Ruth to Naomi in Scripture: "Whither thou goest, I will go . . . Whither thou diest, I shall die, and there shall I be buried."

Not too soon, she added, as her own prayer. Aloud she said, "We will come with you. I must begin to prepare what we will take with us."

In the end, they took five large trunks—clothing for all weather, for Patience and John and the children and servants, and cloth to make more, for she was unsure how often trade ships would come and what goods they would carry. She brought plate and candles, and ink and paper so that she could go on teaching Josiah his letters. John's Bible, his account book, and two or three other books he thought of value also went into a trunk. Even as the last trunk was closed and packed aboard the carriage that took them to the ship, Patience was convinced she had forgotten something vital, something that could not be bought or made in the New Found Land, something essential to life.

"We will have a good big house to put it all in," John assured her as they watched their trunks stowed aboard. The three servants they were taking, Martha, Isaac, and Solomon, carried a motley assortment of bags and bundles, things their master and mistress might need aboard ship. John had told Patience how he had visited the Kirkes' house in Ferryland and had taken good note of its size, of the great hall and the fine big kitchen, the brewhouse and garden. "We have only to step into it, have our things unpacked, and we will be in our new home."

"Will it have stood empty all through the winter, do you think?"

"No. Lady Kirke left her sons and her sister behind over the winter."

"And they will simply pack up and move out when we get there?"

"I believe they will go back to England—indeed, they may have gone already. Come, 'tis time we were aboard," John said, leading her and the children toward the ship. "All will be well. Trust to God."

God did not protect either Patience or their younger boy, Matthew, from seasickness; they suffered terribly on the voyage, while Josiah, untroubled, followed his similarly fortunate father all about the ship, having to be plucked out of the rigging and restrained from climbing the ship's rails. All this John reported to Patience while she lay moaning in her berth below decks, pausing only when she or Matthew had to vomit into the foul-smelling bucket nearby.

She was well enough to go above deck and look about on the sixth day of the voyage, when either the seas had calmed or her guts become accustomed to the motion. There was little to see: ocean waves all around and a faint line of land in the distant west.

"Tomorrow morning we will see the shores of the New Found Land," John assured her, "and by nightfall we will be in our new home."

He was partly right.

As Hannah brought a dish of eel stew from the hearth, Frances took her seat at the foot of the table, across from her sister with the double row of their sons between them. Throughout the winter, Frances had taken that head seat; she was not sorry to relinquish it. The winter had been a struggle—the usual struggle with the elements and with isolation, but also Frances's own struggle to maintain control over this household of boys and young men. Not to mention the fisherfolk of the settlement, who seemed to believe that with the governor gone they could do as they pleased. More fights had broken out, more incidents of petty theft occurred among the planters and servants than when there had been a governor in residence. George had played at magistrate a bit, but he was not taken seriously. Frances had concentrated her efforts on the household and let the common folk see to themselves.

Six weeks ago, the first English ship into the Pool had brought Sara back, along with news of her husband and plans for the colony. David Kirke was still in prison; he had been cleared of the charge of withholding taxes, but now he was being sued by Cecil Calvert, whose father had once governed the New Found Land plantation, over ownership of the land and business. James Kirke, David's brother, controlled the family's fishing enterprise but had no plans to come out to the New Found Land this year. Both men entrusted Sara to manage the operation.

Sara had inspected everything from the storehouses to the ledgers to her sons' clothing when she arrived. "You have done well, keeping the lads in good order," she told her sister, "and the winter stores are well kept."

"I have done my duty," Frances said.

Sara had spoken as if she had half-expected Frances to burn the house and outbuildings to the ground through sheer carelessness and was mildly surprised to find everything still standing. The tutor they employed for the younger lads had gone back to England before winter set in. Frances had continued the lessons and been well pleased with the progress her own children and Sara's younger boys had made with their reading, writing, and sums. But she knew better than to expect effusive praise from her sister.

Sara soon had teams of men organized to prepare the boats, flakes, and stages for the summer, before the crew of fishing servants she had hired came out from England. Frances was left in charge of the women's work. She had Hannah and Molly clearing ground at the garden, doing what women all over the settlement were doing: picking over the new crop of stones turned up in the thin soil, preparing the ground for planting.

But Frances had no intention of returning to their earlier arrangement, in which Sara was mistress and Frances her humble dependent. She raised the issue one afternoon as

Sara pored over the ledgers.

Sara raised an eyebrow. "You think you should have a larger share of this year's profits because you stayed here over the winter? Because I went to be with my husband, who was unjustly taken prisoner and called to answer for a lot of trumped-up charges?"

Tread carefully, Frances thought; she knew that lifted eyebrow, that tone of Sara's voice. "Not for staying here," she said, "though I could easily have left also, and you might think of what would have happened then. But for the work I did over the winter, the care I took with your household and your sons and supplies. For the months when I was the only adult here to represent your family's interests."

Sara shrugged. "George was here. Should he have an increased share as well?"

"George was a great help to me," Frances said. It was good policy to overstate the case a little—George had given orders to the menservants, and he had not actively impeded her work. "If you are putting aside a portion for him, then I agree he may deserve a larger share. But his work does not erase the work I did. And will continue to do, now that we are two women managing a plantation on our own." She paused, meeting her sister's eyes steadily. "I am not asking for gratitude, only for justice."

"You may as well ask for a crown of rubies and five white swans swimming on the Pool," Sara said, with the ghost of a smile. "I will make a note of it in my accounts. But you would do well to remember—and I have told George the same—that any accounting I make might as well be writ in water. We have no idea what will happen, whether we will get to keep any of what is ours."

George tapped at the door, putting his head inside without waiting for a summons. "Excuse me, Mama. There is a ship coming in. With your leave, I will go down and greet it."

Sara nodded; duties like this she was willing to delegate. She and Frances followed at a more sedate pace. It was a cool May day with a brisk wind. Frances still missed English springs with their warm breezes and riot of blossoms. Here in the New Found Land, sails on the horizon signalled spring long before leaves budded on the trees.

George was not, in fact, the first to welcome whoever was aboard—his mother had taken that privilege for herself by the time the ship had docked. Along with the crew, there was a well-dressed man and woman aboard. Frances recognized the man; so, she knew, did Sara and George. But it was Davey who said aloud, "God's teeth, is it that rascal John Treworgy come back to trouble us again?"

Treworgy stepped ashore. His coming last year had led to David Kirke's removal from office and return to England. If Treworgy had returned and brought—his wife?—then he must be coming to stay.

"Master Treworgy, what an unexpected . . . pleasure," said Sara.

"What brings you to these parts?" George's words almost trod on top of his mother's greeting.

Treworgy looked from Sara to George and then at the other faces around. "I bring word," he began, raising his voice to address not just everyone on the wharf but the planters and servants who had gathered ashore. "Parliament has appointed me as the new governor to replace David Kirke. This is my wife; our children and servants are aboard the ship. Conduct us to the governor's residence, if you please."

Sara smiled and, after a brief pause, extended a hand in greeting to both the Treworgys. "You are welcome to the Pool Plantation," she said. "We were not warned of your coming so have had no chance to make accommodation ready for you, but I am sure we can find a place for you to lay your heads. There is no such house as 'the governor's residence,' only Kirke House, which belongs to me . . . and my sons."

"We have no wish to turn you out of your beds tonight, Lady Sara," Treworgy said. "We had thought you might already have returned to England, but if your departure must be delayed till a suitable passage is found, we will allow you to continue sleeping under our roof."

Now George stepped forward. "Master Treworgy, my family has no intention of leaving Ferryland. This is our home."

"But your father's governorship has been revoked, and he is in prison," Treworgy said. "I am the governor now."

"That may be," Sara said, dragging Treworgy's unwilling eyes back to her face, "but whatever your Parliament says, I am Lady Sara Kirke, and Kirke House is my home. You and your people must find another place to lodge."

"Lady Sara." For the first time, the woman beside John Treworgy spoke. She was young, pale, and fair-haired; she looked meek as milk in her grey Puritan gown and cloak under a high-crowned hat. Everyone seemed startled to hear her speak, including her husband. "I appeal to your kindness as a mother. My children are very young, and we must have a place to shelter. Could we not share the governor's house until . . . suitable arrangements can be made?"

Sara swept the woman with a glance from top to toe. "I know it is a hardship, travelling to a far place with small children. I did the same, when we first came to this land. But what you ask is impossible. With myself and my sister, our sons and our servants, the house is full. You had best sleep aboard your ship tonight. I will discuss with your husband where you might be housed."

The young woman's eyes fell and her head bowed slightly. She did not attempt to answer Sara but left the negotiations to her husband.

Not that there was much negotiation to it. Sara—and George, when his mother allowed him a word—would not brook any suggestion of handing over the house. Frances understood her sister's resistance. Sara could do nothing about the Parliamentary decree that had removed David Kirke from his office and put this Puritan stranger in his place, but she could do something about her house: She could refuse to leave.

The Treworgys retreated, for the moment, in the face of Sara's unshakable determination. The new governor made a half-hearted attempt at a speech to the fisherfolk, telling them that Parliament held the interests of the New Found Land dear to its heart and that he looked forward to leading them through the coming fishing season. Then he and his wife returned to their ship.

Frances guessed that conversation aboard the ship was as lively as the conversation in Kirke House that night, as Sara and her eldest sons discussed the Treworgys' outrageous demand. "The house always has been ours and always will be," declared George. "I remember when we came out, 'twas all abandoned and tumbledown, and Father had it rebuilt to the good solid house it is today."

"How do you remember? Were you not still in petticoats?" Davey probed.

"No, but *you* were still a suckling babe, so you shan't contradict me. I am right, am I not, Mama?"

Frances watched the conversation with interest. She knew Sara and David took great pride in the house, but she had never heard the story of how it came to be theirs. She had always supposed David had had it built for himself.

"It was as good as abandoned," Sara said now. "Governor Calvert was long gone, but his son, Cecil Calvert, appointed another governor who refused to yield up the house until your father made him leave."

"So, much the same case as we are in today," said Frances. "A new governor comes, demands the house, and the occupant refuses to give it up. Will't not end the same way? If Parliament has named a man governor, will they not ensure he gets this house as his due?"

Sara's look was full of scorn. "'Tis not the same case at all. It was not Parliament's word, nor even the king's, that got us this house. It was my husband's own will. And mine is no less than his."

"I've great hopes of this new governor," Peter Taylor said as Meg dished up the evening meal.

"Have you now? What do you think he will do better than Governor Kirke did?"

"He is a true man of God, so I hope he will bring pure religion to our people."

"He is a governor, not a preacher." Meg ladled up her own bowl of pottage and sat down across from Peter.

"Nay, but he says he will have a preacher brought here soon, a true reformed Christian."

"Aye," said Simon, "and the new governor will be Parliament's man, not someone scheming and wishing to have a king back on the throne."

Meg had no reply to this. She did not see that it would make a great deal of difference to folk like herself and Peter whether the governor was the king's man or Parliament's man; the fish had to be caught and made and sold no matter what.

It was of far more interest to her that Simon was back with them, and on a new standing. After living in Peter and Meg's little house for more than a year, he had gone back last winter to Bristol and returned on the first ship of spring. His luck had improved; back in Bristol, his father had died and left him a modest inheritance, enough for Simon to take a wife and return to the New Found Land not as Peter's servant but as a shareman. His wife would come out later in the summer. In the evenings, after preparing the boat and stage for the season, he and Peter were building a small house on the other side of Peter's land. There, Simon and his wife would reside.

With a shareman and three fishing servants hired for the summer, Peter was doing well, as far as the fortunes of small New Found Land planters were measured. Meg loved to look out at their tidy plot of land, her garden, the outbuilding that housed the goat and chickens, and even Simon's new house. With Mary growing fast and the possibility of a new baby on the way, Meg felt content about the future. She and Peter were prospering, regardless of who ruled as governor.

When the meal was cleared, Mary woken from her all-too-short nap, and Peter and Simon gone back to work, Hannah came to the door. As Meg welcomed her, she reflected that if Lady Frances Hopkins went back to England, Hannah would likely go with her, so that Meg would lose her one good friend. She was friendly with the other planters' wives but had made no close ties during her three years in Ferryland. Peter was sure that once Simon's wife came out, the two couples would be as close as family, but Meg reserved judgment on any woman Simon would choose to marry.

"Mistress sent me to ask if you could give us a day's work tomorrow," Hannah said, "cleaning out old Abel Goode's house. Since 'tis a fair big house and has been standing empty over the winter, Lady Sara has a mind to put the new governor and his family there."

"The new governor? In Abel Goode's house?" Meg repeated. Old Abel Goode had died in the autumn, seventy years of age. He had been the oldest settler in the community, there since the days of Lord Baltimore. It was true his place was fair-sized, but there was nothing fine or comfortable about it. It had a big central room like most of the settlers' homes, with a couple of chambers at the back that had once held his brood of children but in recent years had been home to Abel's goats. Once his wife had died and his daughters had married, there had been no woman to keep house. Meg shuddered to think what it would take to clean out the place even for another fishing family to move in there, much less to make it fit for a governor and his wife.

The following morning proved her fears true. Leaving Mary with Sallie Kean, who had six children at home and would gladly look after another in return for a farthing or a small favour, Meg joined Hannah and Molly at the abandoned house. They began by taking a spade to the piles of goat-droppings that had frozen and thawed again over the winter.

"This is not fit for a human to live in," said Molly. "'Tis no shame to keep the animals in the house in bad weather—

me mam and da did it often enough when we were growing up—but you got to keep them penned and clean up after 'em. Looks like old Abel let 'em wander where they pleased, and shit where they pleased as well."

"He was a mad old fellow. Living like this, he could not have been right in his mind," said Hannah.

Meg heaved another spade full of droppings outside the door. "One thing I know is madness—putting the new governor in here, never mind with a wife and children."

"You try telling Lady Sara that," said Hannah. "She is determined not to budge an inch from her house, nor to let this Treworgy and his family over the threshold."

"If 'twere still your mistress in charge at the big house, d'you think she'd have stood so firm, or given in to them?" Meg wondered. Though Lady Frances had been left to manage her sister's affairs in the autumn, most folk kept largely to themselves in winter, doing indoor work and visiting from time to time in one another's houses. Lady Frances had held a feast at the big house on Twelfth Night, and Peter had made his customary complaint about pagan observances and forbade Meg to go, but at least no mummer fights had broken out this year. Apart from the Christmastide and Sunday services at Kirke House, the planters had hardly seen Lady Frances in the cold months.

"Hard to say," said Hannah. "I think she is glad her sister came home in time to deal with this business."

When the filth was shovelled out and the dirt floor swept as clean as it could be, Molly went off to collect hay to strew over it, though the hay, having been cut last autumn, was hardly fresh. "Belike they will want a proper floor put down, wood or even flagstones," Meg mused as she scrubbed at the scarred and stained surface of the table.

"If they stay. This place has not even window-glass; I cannot see folk like the Treworgys biding long here."

In early afternoon, Meg, Hannah, and Molly were joined by three new people, the Treworgy family servants. Martha, the maid, looked about at the room and clucked her tongue in a way that made Meg want to say, *You ought to have seen it four hours ago.* Isaac and Solomon, the menservants, led a string of sailors carrying trunks.

"Lay them along the wall," Hannah directed. "When we have done cleaning, you can find places to put some of your master's goods."

"Is this the bedchamber?" Martha said in a tone of disbelief.

"It has the only bed," Meg replied, "although that could be moved to the larger chamber, if your master wished it." She forbore from mentioning who the residents of the larger chamber had been, though the goat smell still hung in the air.

"And does your service come with the house?" the manservant asked, looking at the three women.

"No, Molly is Lady Sara Kirke's maid, and I work for her sister, Lady Frances Hopkins," Hannah said. "Meg is a planter's wife, hired by the day."

"This will hardly do," Isaac said to Martha.

"Indeed not. I signed on for this journey to be the children's nurse, understanding there would be a housemaid here," Martha replied. "What need will those Kirke women have of them, if they are returning to England? The master could at least look at buying that one," she added with a curt nod at Hannah.

Meg saw how Hannah stiffened at the words. *Buying that one*. "I am contracted to my lady," Hannah said.

"Aye, but mayhap she would be open to an offer," Isaac said. "My master will speak to her. As for the fishwife, she might be hired by the day, until we find a maid. Do you know if any of the fishermen have daughters of an age to go into service?"

There were a few. Clara Kean was sixteen and full of high spirits; over the winter she had borne a child that her mother was raising as her own, a polite fiction that everyone kept quiet about. If a fisherman's son had got her into trouble they would have been married, or as married as they could be without a minister. But as the culprit was George Kirke, there was little that either Clara or her family could do. She might be content to work for the Treworgys, though Eliza Yard, who was fourteen and quiet, seemed more biddable.

"I will make some inquiries, if you please, sir," Meg said. She had no idea how to address the new governor's manservant. "Sir" was probably wrong, but you could never go too far wrong calling men Sir, for they were always proud to take more honours than they had earned. "I take in washing for Lady Sara and Lady Frances," Meg added, "and could do the same for your mistress until she has maids of her own, if she cares to pay me. As for today's work, 'twill be more quickly done, and the house more fitting to bring your master and mistress into, if all hands pitch in together."

"You have a pert tongue in your head," said Martha, but she rolled up her sleeves and set to work, and so did Isaac.

A pert tongue in your head. That was the sort of thing Meg had often heard said of her mother and her sister Lizzie. Meg had been one of the quieter children in their noisy household, and she had married a man who, unlike her father, did not expect his wife to have opinions. She tried the idea on for size now: Was she, Meg Taylor, becoming a woman with a pert tongue?

She kept that tongue under control when she went home. She was late, having sent word to Peter that he must warm his own supper; she stopped by the Keans' house to pick up Mary, who was whinging about having been parted from her mother all day. So Meg came home after the long day's work with a cross baby to a cross husband and his cross shareman and a cold slice of pie for her own supper.

"You should ha' refused to go," was Peter's assessment of her day's work. "Master Treworgy and his wife ought to be moving into the big house. Cleaning out Abel Goode's place for them is folly."

"Then I'd have been hired to clean out Abel's place for the Kirkes to move into instead. 'Tis not as if we can afford to turn down work."

"They should be gone back to England, both those women and their parcel of youngsters. They've no place here now."

"Master Treworgy may be governor, but is't not true that the Kirke family still owns the fishing premises and the fish trade?"

"Aye, so it may be, but they need a man out here to look after it. Can you not quiet that youngster down?"

"She will be well in a minute; I'll nurse her when I've had my own bite to eat." Mary, at two years old, was on the teat still first thing in the morning and last thing before going to sleep at night. At the moment she was gnawing on a hunk of bread softened in water, but it was clear that was not what she wanted, after such a trying day.

Meg had not told Peter that she was expecting another child. He would want a son, of course, but she did not look for much gladness from him at the announcement. She was not certain yet anyway, having missed her courses only twice. If a third month went by, she would share the news.

"Well, I can stand her grizzling no more—I am going out to see what's about. Mayhap they'll need a few more fellows to help unpack and move their things. As long as they've got to sleep in that hovel, we must do what we can to make it suitable," Peter said, putting on a cloak before going out into the chilly evening. Simon followed him.

"Welladay, little one, seems your father changed his tune very quickly, from thinking that I ought not to have helped clean the house for the new governor, to thinking he must do all he can to make them comfortable. But that is his business. This is mine." Meg lifted Mary onto her lap and put her to the breast.

"'Tis exactly like everything we know of David Kirke, to build a tavern but no Sunday meeting house," Patience Treworgy said, buttoning the top button of her husband's doublet for him and smoothing his starched white collar over it.

John laughed. "I'll say naught against the tavern—'tis a bit more civilization than one might expect to find in such a place. As for a meeting house, he is a Church of England man, so you ought to be glad there is no church here. It would have a popish altar, and you would not like that, would you?"

"I would like it better than having Sunday services in Lady Sara Kirke's hall," Patience said. "I have heard they have a great iron cross on the wall, which is popish enough."

"Then 'tis a blessing that there is no church, nor any

minister either. 'Tis easier to teach the people anew than to root out bad habits." He put on his hat and stood before her, spreading his arms wide so she could take in the look of him. "Will I do fair to stand in place of a minister, till one might be brought here?"

"You will, indeed." She tucked a stray lock of hair behind his ear just as Martha brought the two little boys in from the sleeping chamber, dressed in their best clothes.

Nearly two weeks had passed since their arrival, and it had been a trying fortnight. The battle with Lady Sara over occupation of Kirke House had not yet been won, and the hovel in which their family had been placed was barely fit to live in—straw on the floor, unglazed windows covered only with shutters. On their first Sunday, the family had had prayers at home. When John asked, Lady Sara had informed him that the Kirkes usually held a Sunday service at their house for their own household and the planters and their families. "Not all of them attend," she had said. "They are not a very godly folk."

"Perhaps that can be changed," John had told her, and informed her that he would come to her house the next Sunday and lead the service.

"They have been very slack, if not everyone attends," Patience said now, as they headed along a rocky path to the Kirkes' much bigger and finer house with its peaked roof and glazed windows. "At home, or in England, the people could be fined, but I doubt Governor Kirke enforced attendance. And I am surprised Lady Sara agreed to having you take the service."

"I think she is feeling her way carefully, trying to determine how much she can deny me and where she must give in. She is digging her heels in about her ownership of the house and the business, but when it comes to the spiritual well-being of the colony, she is willing to bend. It matters less to her, you see."

"I wonder what form of service they have been accustomed to? Do you think they are still using the prayer book?"

"Undoubtedly they have been, but we will see no hint of a prayer book in there today—she is too canny for that," said John.

He was right. They arrived in the main hall of the house that should be theirs to find the two ladies and their sons sitting on a bench before the hearth, with the serving maids and a few workingmen standing against the wall, hands folded meekly before them. Patience saw no sign of the offending iron cross, though she did note an empty nail in the wall behind where the preacher was to stand.

Another bench stood ready for Patience and her children. Martha, Isaac, and Solomon went to join the servants. As they took their seats, a handful of villagers shuffled in; likely some were coming out of curiosity, to see what kind of service the new governor might lead. There was no prayer book or any other popish foppery, only a simple table at the front of the room, on which John laid down his Bible with a decisive thump. Atop it he placed a book of John Knox's sermons, one of which he intended to read today.

Patience was glad her bench was at a right angle to where her husband stood speaking, for it allowed her to view most of the room. Among those standing by the wall she saw Lady Frances's Negro servant and Lady Sara's young maid. The only other woman she recognized was Meg Taylor, the washerwoman, who carried a child on her hip. She looked small and plain as dishwater next to her husband, who was tall and handsome in a rough-hewn way, with a tumble of dark hair and piercing blue eyes. He had done some work for John already and made himself known as a true Christian who would support their efforts at reform. An ally, or a chancer wanting to ingratiate himself with the new man in power? Time would tell, Patience supposed.

A couple of other fishermen were present with their wives. It was a small settlement, its people and the conditions they lived in as rough as she had expected. Bringing any refinement to this place would be a hard enough job. But, Patience thought as she looked around at the big room with its flagstone floor, it would be a sight easier to civilize Ferryland if she lived in this house.

Midway through the sermon, when John had been reading for half an hour, a child began to whimper at the back of the room. The sound set Matthew off so that he began to cry. "Hush," Patience hissed. "Listen to Papa!" But Matthew continued his whinging.

Patience bundled up Matthew and made her way through the room. The servants and fisherfolk stood aside to let her pass, and she saw Martha move to the bench to sit beside Josiah and keep him in line.

Outside, a chilly wind blew off the water. Matthew wanted to be let down, to toddle around, but he must learn that Sunday service was a time to sit reverently. As he set up another howl, Patience caught the eye of the other woman standing nearby. It was Meg Taylor, her little girl quite content now that she was being allowed to totter around in the grass.

"She must be about two years old, your little one," Patience said.

"Yes, mistress," Meg said, ducking her head. "Yours would be a bit older?"

"Nearly three. They can be a handful at this age, for certes. Is she your first?"

"Aye, mistress." After a pause, she added, "Good day, mistress. I shall take her home now, for she'll not go back in there and be quiet now."

"You ought not to give in to her so."

"She is only a babe, and 'tis a long time for a little one to keep still. You know it yourself," she added, nodding at Matthew.

"Yes, but I will train him to sit quietly in Sunday meeting, and he will learn, as his brother has done already. You must do the same, if you want to raise godly children. I am taking him back inside now, and you had best bring your little one as well."

"I will do so, mistress, in a moment."

Patience carried Matthew back inside, waiting a moment at the door, though Meg made no move to follow. The young woman's face had that mulish stubbornness that was common among the poor, in Patience's experience. She would not openly disagree with her betters but would do as she pleased behind their backs. It gave Patience an inkling of how much work lay ahead if she and John were to try to bring true reform to the folk of Ferryland.

CHAPTER SEVEN

Autumn 1652

The end of the fishing season was always a time of celebration. The dried and salted fish was stacked and stored, ready for shipping across the sea, and trade ships arrived with precious winter supplies that would see the colonists through the long, cold months ahead. Everyone seemed to breathe more freely now that the year's hardest work was over.

Released from her work on the flakes, Meg spent the last day of September working with Hannah in the Kirke House garden. Though she had expanded her own garden over the past two summers, she was still given a share of the Kirkes' produce in exchange for work in their garden. She crouched awkwardly in the turnip bed with her spade; her belly was large now with the new babe. Hannah dug another row of turnips a few feet away, while Mary ran about the edges of the garden, waving her arms at the seagulls perched on the fence and squawking back at them.

"Peter said a ship was sighted off Bois Island," Meg said. "He thinks it may be a trading ship, and I dare hope 'tis, for there's a good many things we need."

"The mistresses said the same, so 'tis like to be true. And all will be glad if it is, as long as there comes no more trouble with it."

Meg felt a pang of worry. While the seasonal round of fishing and making fish had continued undisturbed for the past year, the world of men was unsettled. Governor Kirke gone, and then Lady Kirke back again, and Governor Treworgy and his wife arriving. Then all the wrangling over who was to occupy Kirke House. At the height of the fishing season, when everyone was working hard, those commissioner fellows who had come with Governor Treworgy last summer returned, poking around and asking questions.

Peter had been greatly interested in the return of the commissioners, though they had no questions for him this time. They were looking for old people, people who had been there since the days of Lord Baltimore. There were not many such people left in Ferryland itself, save for Granny Love, who told the other women that the men had questioned her and wrote down every word she said.

"Trouble? Is this to do with the business those men came for over the summer?" Meg asked Hannah now.

"Nay, that were all to do with the big house, how Lady Sara won't give it up to the Treworgys. Seems over in England there's some lord, relative of the fellow who used to be governor here long ago, and he be bringing suit against Sir David. He says the house and land was never Sir David's by right, but that he stole them off this other fellow."

"Oh, is that it? So Governor Treworgy thinks if the Kirkes stole the house in the first place, he can steal it back off them?"

Hannah shrugged. "Something like that. But I don't say it came to much, for the commission men went away again. I hope they will stay away, for we need no more upset."

"Well, there is the ship coming around the point now, and you can see her flags. 'Tis an English vessel, sure enough."

By the time they had finished in the garden, the ship had dropped anchor. Meg hoisted Mary on her hip and headed toward the harbour.

She arrived to find a lively argument in progress, with many of the fishermen and their wives standing in a ring around the combatants as if they were watching a preacher in church, though perhaps with greater attention. In the centre of the ring, on the main wharf, stood Governor Treworgy, Lady Sara Kirke, Master George Kirke, and a man who must be the captain of the newly arrived vessel, all arguing loudly.

Meg could not make out the words, but the tone was unmistakable. She sidled up next to her husband. "What be the matter?" she said.

"The master of the vessel will not unload any supplies until 'tis made clear to him who he is to deal with, and both the governor and Lady Sara do insist they be the one to manage the business."

"But it must be Master Treworgy, must it not? He is governor, and a man."

"Aye, but Lady Sara argues that the business is still in the Kirke family."

And so we will be longer delayed getting our flour and molasses, Meg thought, *while the governor and her ladyship argue about it.*

The quarrel was not settled by the time dusk fell, but Lady Sara unbent enough to invite the governor and the ship's captain to her house to continue negotiating, and so the fishermen and their wives dispersed to their own homes. "As long as we still get our fair share," Aunt Sallie Kean said to Meg as they walked along, "I cannot see why we should care which of the masters makes the gold." Both women snuggled a half-asleep child as they walked; Mary dozed with her fair curls on Meg's shoulder, while Sallie carried the grandson that everyone pretended was her son.

"It matters," Peter said, deigning to join the women's conversation, "because the Kirkes use whatever they earn to line their own pockets and make themselves rich."

"That is what all rich men do," said Sallie's husband, Dick. The Keans were not planters themselves; Dick was Samuel Thomas's shareman, so their winter supplies would depend on what the Thomases earned for their summer's catch.

"Maybe so, but Governor Treworgy is a different cut of governor; he wants to better the whole place, for the advantage of all. He means to build a meeting house for Sunday services next summer."

Dick Kean laughed. "Of all the things we need here, I'd not say a church is top of the reckoning. Governor Kirke did us more good opening a tavern."

"You talk like a fool. The tavern will still be there for you to drown your sorrows, but this harbour needs a place where we can worship God. Without it, we are no better than heathens."

"Look you, I have lived here longer than you, raised my youngsters here," Dick said, "and you call me and my folk heathens because we've no church building? How dare you—"

"Hush now, Dickon," said Sallie, laying her hand on her husband's arm. "'Tis no time for harsh words with a neighbour. The fish is in, the trade ships are coming, and we should all be glad. God give ye good e'en, Meg."

"Good night, indeed," Meg said, wishing she could quell Peter as easily as Sallie Kean seemed to control her husband.

"You must be pleased to have won that battle," Frances said.

She and Sara sat by the hearth fire in the great hall. The maids were supervising as the younger boys went to bed, while the sisters sat and sewed by the warmth of the fire and the last of the daylight slanting through the windows. The *Bonaventure* had sailed for England today, laden with Avalon's salt cod, leaving behind the fishing gear, the barrels of flour and molasses, the bales of cloth, and all the rest of the supplies that would see the colony through another winter.

"I do not think 'twas any great victory." Sara squinted at the shirt she was embroidering for George, a bit of finery for the young man she was fitting him out to be. She and Frances had talked of wanting to send their elder sons to England to further their education and careers, but England was not a safe place for the Kirkes just now. "None of this fuss need have happened at all, had John Treworgy not stuck his nose in."

"Perhaps things will change this winter," Frances said. "It may be by the time ships come again in spring, Parliament will have called the young king home from exile." Surely, she thought, this madness in England could not go on another year? The country must come to its senses, she thought, and put young Charles on the throne. "And then," she added,

"David must surely be set free, and his case settled, so he may come back here restored to the governorship."

"And throw Treworgy and that prim little wife of his out on their ears," Sara said. "Welladay, 'tis pleasant to think on't, even if it is but a dream right now."

Frances felt a twinge of pity for the prim little wife, though she said only, "I am surprised his wife elected to stay. I would have thought she and the children—perhaps her husband as well—would have gone back to New England for the winter."

"'Twould not have surprised me," said Sara. "Before we came here, it was the practice of governors to go back to England for the winter. Some did not even come out here in summer but governed from afar. But my husband has always believed that if this place is to be ruled well, it must be ruled by one who lives here. It seems Treworgy has the same thought."

"He knows if he left, you would find a way to turn him out of even the poor house he has now," Frances said with a chuckle, and Sara did not deny it. "Still, it seems hard for the woman and her children."

"I raised four lads here, and no harm came to any of us," said Sara. "Treworgy has some of the men laying a wooden floor in his house now, so 'twill be more comfortable for winter. And I hear tell he has a glazed window ordered, though he cannot be sure 'twill arrive before winter. The man means to stay."

Sara was right: John Treworgy spent the weeks between the end of the fishery and the first snow making Abel Goode's old house more snug, secure, and comfortable, hiring the services of fishermen who would work for extra goods or coin along with doing their own autumn labour—woodcutting, hunting, repairing their own houses. Hannah reported that Mistress Treworgy was embroidering wall hangings, which would help both to warm and to brighten the place. The Treworgys seemed to have all intentions of lasting out the winter.

Not only were they staying, they intended to continue bringing reformed religion to the colony. All summer, Governor Treworgy had read the Sunday service in the Kirkes' hall for as many people as would gather. But in September a ship from Massachusetts brought a thin, angry-looking man of middle years whom Treworgy introduced as Reverend Bright. He would be wintering in the colony.

"Why do we have to have that streak of bad temper preaching here?" Davey Kirke asked his mother around the Kirke dinner table after the new reverend had preached a sermon full of fire and brimstone and threats of hell. "Are we going to have to listen to the likes of that every Sunday?"

"He is a guest of Master Treworgy," Sara said.

"Threats of burning in hell don't lend to good digestion," Davey said. "At least he's not a bore. Treworgy reads a sermon like he was reading off a list of trade goods."

"List of trade goods'd be a damned sight more interesting," said George, "for that's all to do with making a profit. Much better than all those names from Leviticus or Deuteronomy or the like."

"Mind your language, I pray you, George. We may not be Puritans, but we are not godless in this house," Sara said sharply. "And, indeed, you must set a good example, for come next Sunday, you will be the one reading the service. Not from Master Treworgy's book of sermons, neither, but the proper service from the prayer book."

"What, me? Playing at being preacher? You can't mean it, Mother. If anyone's to do it, give it to Davey. He's got the gift of the gab, at least."

"Gab is not required in order to read the divine service and lead the household in prayer," said Sara. "In the absence of a priest, that duty falls to the man of the house. You will get up there next Sunday and read it properly, and it might not hurt you to study it beforehand."

"You will do very well, George, and this is a good plan, indeed," said Frances. "Shall we put the cross back up on the wall for Sunday morning?"

Sara frowned and shook her head. "Nay, I still have that hidden away safe. If word gets out that we have a cross up as well as using the prayer book, 'twill be one more excuse for Treworgy to make trouble."

"Do he and his pet cleric know you plan to turn them out of the pulpit?" Davey wanted to know, his eyes dancing with delight. That lad, Frances thought, was far too fond of mischief.

"Those who want to hear a Puritan sermon and be told how long they will be tortured in eternal flames may go to Abel Goode's front yard, for all I care," said Sara Kirke. "Master Treworgy can do as he likes—he can build a meeting house overnight, if't pleases him to do so—but he is finished using my hall for his Puritan cant. I will tell him so myself."

"If the service is to be out of doors again, you can go on your own," said Meg. "I'll not stand out in the cold for two hours trying to keep Mary hushed while that preacher goes on and on."

Peter, dressed in his clean shirt and breeches for Sunday, looked as disapproving as she knew he would. But would he drag his pregnant wife and small child out to Sunday service by force? "If anyone asks, say I am not well," Meg added, a concession to his pride. Her back was hurting enough to make the excuse true.

"I'd rather you were with me. 'Tis Lady Sara's folly, denying Reverend Bright the right to preach in her hall—the governor's hall, as it ought to be. 'Tis her fault we must stand out in the cold to worship God."

"That may be," said Meg, "but 'tis no place for a woman with one babe in her belly and another in her arms. You go, so that your governor can see what a good Christian you are."

Peter snorted. "I go to Sunday meeting to worship the Lord, no other reason."

So you tell yourself, Meg thought as the door closed behind him. Peter truly was devout and really did worship with great fervour. But she believed his attendance at meeting had just as much to do with his desire to curry favour with Governor Treworgy.

The other fisherman whose Puritan fervour could be counted on was, of course, their shareman Simon, who was strutting about like a barnyard cock now that the last ship from Bristol had brought his bride. She and Meg shared a name—she was another Margaret, though she went by Peggy—but that was all the two young women had in common. Meg was delighted that Simon and Peggy's little house was completed in time for winter, so they could move in there at once and not seek shelter under Meg and Peter's roof.

"I hope your papa will not be cross with me for saying we cannot go to the service this morning," Meg went on, prattling to Mary who responded by echoing "Papa?" She was too young, Meg told herself, to understand the meaning in her mother's words.

Meg was past hoping for a husband who laughed with her, who was affectionate, who did small kindnesses to make her day easier. Peter Taylor was not that man, and she could not turn him into such a man; now she was relieved if he was only cold and silent. "In faith, I did not have to counterfeit at all," she continued, "for I truly do have a terrible ache in my back. That will be your little brother, wanting to get out. But 'tis too soon for him yet."

By her best guess, the babe was due a few weeks before Christmastide. There would be nearly three years in age between him and Mary. Meg had lost one baby in those three years, so early it had not even quickened; now she was relieved to be so close to her time. November had just come in, with a chilly north wind that blew the remaining yellow leaves from the birch trees, and Meg had grown big enough to feel weary walking about and doing her daily chores.

She set Mary down before the hearth and sat to watch her in the chair she had brought from home as part of her marriage portion—the only proper chair, with a back and arms on it, in their little house, all the other seating being on stools or benches. This was usually Peter's chair, of course, but while he stood outside shivering and listening to Reverend Bright, Meg enjoyed the rare luxury of a comfortable seat.

The pain in her back was bad. The memory of the lost baby flickered across her mind. But that had been so early! She had carried this child for so long, fervently hoping it would be a son, for she thought that would make Peter happy.

She pushed herself to her feet with effort, leaning on the arms of the chair, and opened the door to look outside. The day was raw and windy, and it could be an hour or more before Peter returned from the Sunday service. If the pains continued when he came home, she would send him for the midwife, who would perhaps know something to ease the pain.

By the time Peter returned home, filled with the fruits of righteousness, Meg was lying down on the bed. Peter had made good on his promise to expand the house during the year that Simon had spent sleeping by their hearth, and it was here in the new bedchamber that Meg lay curled up in a little ball. She tried to keep Mary entertained beside her, between the waves of pain. To give Peter credit, he took the matter seriously enough to bring Granny Love within the hour. By that time, Meg was sobbing. It was too hard—the pain knifed into her back, and through it she could feel the stabbing cramps in her stomach. This child wanted to come out.

Granny said the same. "Like it or not, that child is going to be born."

"No! 'Tis too soon!"

"That makes no difference to the brat; they cannot tell the day nor the hour."

"Make it stop," Meg begged, though she knew that was madness. *Make the pain stop. Make the baby stop coming. Unravel time like a piece of badly made weaving. Go back, go back, go back.*

"No going back. You can only go forward. And you will." A different voice, not Granny Love's. Closer, close to her face. A known voice, a loved one. Who was here? The need for her mother, her sister, her Aunt Kat, all sliced through Meg on the next wave of pain, but she knew it was none of them.

Women did not travel from harbour to harbour; women bade farewell to their mothers and sailed away, never to see them again.

"You must hold on, Meg. Granny says 'tis time to push."

She knew, now. She could open her eyes and see Hannah's face close to hers. While the midwife's hands pushed Meg's legs apart, spread her wide so the baby could break her in half, Hannah's hands held tight to Meg's. "Grip as tight as you like. Don't matter if you hurt me. I'll not leave you."

Hannah had been there when Mary was born. She was here now. Perhaps all would be well.

Hannah left the bedchamber carrying the tiny bundle. Peter Taylor sat by his fireplace, drinking a cup of small ale and staring into the flames. It was late now, likely past midnight.

He looked up, his eyes going not to her face but to what she carried. "Dead?" he said.

"Yes. Never took a breath. Too small, too early to live." She paused. "I am sorry," she added. She was sorry, though not for him, particularly.

He shook his head. "'Tis God's will. Nothing could have changed it."

"It was a boy. Would have been a boy."

Again, the young man shook his head. "Mayhap God willed I was not to have a son. Give it to me; I will bury it."

He took the body from her, did not move the shawl it was wrapped in to look at the tiny face. Meg had looked. Though she was lost in pain and anguish, she had asked to see her son's still face before he was taken away.

Peter stood holding the baby for a moment, looking into the flames, then moved toward the door. Hannah had waited for him to ask, but when he did not, and his hand was on the door latch, she said, "Meg is—she will live. 'Twas a hard birth, but Granny Love says she is strong, and the worst is over now."

A moment's silence, then he said, "That is God's will, also."

What would it be like, Hannah wondered, to see everything so simply? God dispensing curses and blessings, even-handed, not to be questioned? Neither to rejoice, nor to struggle and fight against it.

The door opened, and the man carrying the dead child went out into the darkness. *He could have waited till morning*, she thought. *Is he going to dig a grave in the pitch darkness?* Or did he have one dug already, knowing how this would end?

She was alone in the room now, save for the makeshift bed by the fireside where the child Mary had slept through all the tumult. Mary might never know her baby brother had almost existed.

Hannah went over to peer at little Mary, to be certain she was still sleeping peacefully. Then she went back into the bedchamber where Granny Love sat, having given Meg a strong brew of herbs to make her sleep. Back into the chamber where God's will was done.

Patience was trying to teach Josiah his reading while her servant Isaac, assisted by Peter Taylor, nailed in place the wooden boards to cover their dirt floor. Above their heads, her husband was with Simon Tolliver and Solomon, hammering at the roof. Josiah was far more interested in the work the men were doing than in his lesson.

"I could help, Mama! Isaac, can I help? I can hammer a nail!" he bellowed as Patience tried to drag his attention back to the page of Scripture.

Isaac shook his head. "Nay, little master, you will need bigger hands before you can do this kind of work."

"Mama, when will my hands be bigger?"

"Hush! Stop asking questions, Josiah, and attend to your Scripture lesson." Patience pointed back at the page. "God said, let there be . . . What is this word?"

"Light!" Josiah declared triumphantly, and Patience realized she had no idea whether he could read the word or just remembered it from previous recitations of the creation story. Confirming her second guess, Josiah went on, without glancing at the page, "And there was light! Boom! Bang!" The boom and bang accompanied the sound of the men laying another floorboard in place, although it sounded as though God were creating light very loudly.

She would have preferred flagstones. The Kirke House had stone floors, as did some of the better houses back home. But their house in Maine had had wooden plank floors, for pine trees were more abundant and easily worked than stone, and she was grateful for anything other than a straw-covered floor of hard-packed dirt, especially with winter coming on.

When the labourers paused for a cup of ale, Patience allowed Josiah a respite as well. He trotted outside behind Isaac, who was going to the privy, and Patience took a cup of ale herself as she walked over the new-laid boards to inspect them.

"This all looks very well. You should not be long in finishing the rest," she said. "Taylor, I trust your wife is able to launder this week—I have a load of linens for Martha to bring down to her this afternoon."

Peter Taylor looked apologetic. "Nay, mistress, she is not out of bed yet. Likely you'd not heard—'twas only two days ago, Sunday night, that she lost the babe."

"Oh, I am sorry to hear it. I did not think her time was so near."

"No more it was. Her pains started early. The midwife said that was why 'twas born dead. Naught anyone could have done."

"The will of God," Patience said.

"That's what I told my missus," Peter said. "She be taking it hard. We have only the one girl, and she had her heart set on having a boy. It was a boy, as't happens, but never opened his eyes nor drew breath."

Patience knew she herself had been fortunate. Two sons, both born healthy, and she had not had even so much as an early loss. True, she had not conceived another yet, but there was plenty of time. Most women lost a child at birth or in infancy. It could be hard, especially when waiting for God to send a son.

"She lost one before," Peter added, "early on, like. I was wondering, mistress—do you think it could be God's judgment?"

Patience was caught by surprise. *You had better talk to the Reverend Bright about that*, she was about to say. It was strange enough to have such a private talk with any man, much less a fisherman, never mind one so distractingly handsome, with his broad shoulders and his sleeves rolled up to reveal his muscular forearms. It would be better to avoid any occasion of impropriety. Better for her to go back to the table and him to the floor, each to their proper sphere.

But the man was looking to her for guidance. Surely she and John had been sent here to bring true Christianity to these simple people? And his eyes were such a striking blue and filled with such thoughtful concern. *These common folk*, she thought, *feel things quite as deeply as we do, even if they have not the language to express it.*

"Why do you think God may be punishing you?" she asked.

"I know not, mistress. I do my best to be a God-fearing man. I cannot read, but I have a good bit of Scripture off by heart, and I am grateful that the reverend is having proper Sunday services, none of that prayer-book cant. But my wife is more to the mind of most of the folk here. When she thinks of godly things at all, she thinks in the old way. Mayhap 'tis a judgment on her, for not following true faith. Or on myself, for I am the head of the household, and I may not have done all I should to bring her to the light. Or a judgment on this whole place, for being so slow to see the truth." He nodded around. "Even keeping you and the governor here in such a poor lodging—'tis clear to see folks are not following in God's way."

Patience also thought her shabby house was a reflection of the rebellious spirit of the Ferryland people and of the Kirkes in particular. But surely Peter Taylor was thinking too much of himself to imagine that such a common event as the stillbirth of his son was a sign of God's wrath on the whole community.

As if reading her thought, or the doubt in her face, he added, "Henry Sproul's baby died of the croup, back when we just got the fish in. And there's not been a child born alive and healthy here since the spring—just the time you and the governor first come here. I been thinking on it, mistress, and I do think God may be sending us a judgment."

Babies sickened and died, women miscarried or had stillbirths, at all times and in all places, Patience knew. But she also knew that in Scripture, God had sent plagues and curses. Had he not sent a blight on the people of Israel in King David's time? Not to mention the first-born of Egypt? Surely if any people on earth were stiff-necked and stubborn, it was the people of Ferryland, led by Sara Kirke.

"I am only a woman and cannot know the mind of God," Patience said. "You had best talk to Reverend Bright, and to my husband. 'Tis true that God sends hardships to teach and punish us."

"That's my thinking exactly, mistress," Peter said eagerly.

"We have met such opposition here. Having to worship outside in the cold because Lady Kirke will not open her doors to a preacher of the true religion! And now her household going back to their idolatrous worship, parroting the service from the prayer book. Indeed, they are set in their ways. If your wife is of that way of thinking, then you must school her to be more devout. Mayhap the loss of this child will show her the error of her ways."

"Aye, mistress. The Scripture says the husband is head of the wife, and I fear I've not lived up to that as I should. But I will do all I can to make her see that God intends this for a lesson."

The door opened and Isaac came back in, towing Josiah with him. Time for everyone to be back at their tasks. Patience looked at Peter Taylor as he bent to fit another floorboard in place and wondered if she had given him the right counsel. Perhaps she ought to go see poor Meg Taylor herself, bring some of Martha's pork pie and some words of encouragement. It was her duty to help the women of this village, after all. This opportunity was surely sent from God himself.

CHAPTER EIGHT

Spring 1653

The long-awaited first ship to arrive in the spring of 1653 was not an English vessel but a Dutch trading ship. England and the Dutch Republic were at war, but even though the English navy had captured two dozen Dutch vessels trading with the English colony of Barbados last summer, Dutch ships were still coming to the New Found Land to trade with fishermen and settlers. The ship's captain came ashore to pay his respects first to Governor Treworgy and then to Sara Kirke. He spoke English well, but he had little news to share about anything that directly affected the Kirke family.

"England is ruled by this man Cromwell," he said as he drank wine by the hearth in Kirke House. "They say that he dissolved the Parliament, and he is trying to make the country over with himself a king, or something like a king."

Sara nodded; her face gave no hint as to how she felt

about the tidings. Frances's heart sank as she listened to the brief report. Four years now since the king had been murdered and the country seized by rebels, and still there had been no restoration of order. Were the people content with this state of affairs? Had they all turned rebel, or did they live cowering in fear?

Those, of course, were questions Captain Schrijver could not answer. He knew English news as an outsider, knew only what touched his own country and his business. When he was gone, two French ships passed on their way to fish at Plaisance, but their captains did not make port in Ferryland.

Finally, an English ship came into port, carrying supplies sent by James Kirke for the family's plantation, along with word that he had contracted two dozen fishing servants for the summer, to be sent on a later vessel. The captain also brought a letter from James Kirke, addressed to Sara.

"And what news have you of my husband?" Sara demanded. "There is word only from his brother? Does that mean Sir David is still in prison?"

Frances watched how the captain's eyes shifted about the room, how his feet shuffled on the flagstones. "'Tis all in the letter, my lady. Best to hear what your brother-in-law has to say for himself, rather than it be all garbled in my telling."

"Very well then, you may go," said Sara, with the same gesture she used to shoo chickens away from the door.

But when the man was gone, she did not open the letter at once. She sat down, held it in her hand, and stared at it.

"Would you like me to leave?" asked Frances.

"What? No. No, stay by me while I read it." It was the closest thing Frances could imagine to a plea for help from Sara, though it was said flatly, with no spirit animating it.

Frances sat down, a little distance from her on the bench, but still Sara did not open the letter. "It is not good news," she said.

"You'll not know that until you read it."

"'Tis ill news, and you know it. If the news were that my husband was released from prison and coming home soon, the man would have said so. He looked like a messenger bringing word of an enemy invasion to a king, afraid he would have his head cut off for delivering bad tidings." She turned the paper over and over in her hands; she examined the seal. "No, whatever has happened, that fellow did not want to be the one to tell me. Pass me a knife, will you?"

Frances picked up a knife from the table and handed it to Sara, who carefully broke the seal and unfolded the letter.

Sara did not read it aloud; Frances would not have expected that. She saw Sara's eyes widen, heard her sister's sharp gasp. Then Sara closed her eyes and laid the letter on the bench, though she could not have read more than the first few lines. James Kirke had put his most important news first, then.

Sara stood up abruptly, crossed the room with quick, hard steps, and stood by the window, looking out at the harbour. Without turning back to Frances she said, "He is dead."

"Dead? No!" Frances had expected to hear that David was still in prison, or that sentence had been passed and their fortunes would be ruined. He was not even accused of a crime—that case had been settled, and he had been held all this time in a civil case, awaiting a decision in his legal wrangle with Cecil Calvert, Lord Baltimore. But in this new age ruled by Parliament and Oliver Cromwell, who knew what imagined crimes a man might die for?

"Yes, dead. Did you think I would make such a thing up? Or that my husband's brother would tell me for a jest that he is dead?" Sara turned to Frances, her face a mask of angry mockery. "Dead, like the poor king! Is that what you meant to say? That is the only death that ever touched you, is't not? You never mourned your own husband half as much as you mourned poor King Charles—but that is because you never knew what it was to have a man who was the other half of your life, your very self."

She was all bitterness, all spite. Frances hardly heard it but crossed the room to put her arms around Sara. Sara had always been like this, even in the nursery. If she twisted her ankle, she would turn around and shove Frances into a door, just to pass on the pain to someone else. She stiffened, now, in Frances's arms, stood for a moment to allow herself to be comforted, and then stepped back. "Go away. I cannot bear your pity."

Frances moved away from her sister. "Tell me the rest of what James said. How did it happen?"

Sara picked up the paper again, her eyes scanning the lines once more, reading further. "*His trial for Calvert's accusations had long been delayed, one postponement after another,*" she read aloud, "*which is no surprise, so great is the Disorder and Dismay of the courts these days. But it is my thought that the intention was always to hold mye brother long in prison, so that wicked men who covet his lands and his trade could more easily seize all that is his. Nevertheless, the case was fated never to come to trial, for in the Cold of January hee took an Ague, and after a short sickness, was gathered to his Maker. I had last visited him in prison at Christmastide, with many assurances—* Oh, damn the rest. I don't want to read anything about James's assurances. He was there, in London, all the time! Why was he not able to see his brother set free?"

Her voice, on the last word, sounded like a sob. Frances turned away. She had not seen Sara cry since they were children and would not see it today. Nor would she see it later that afternoon, when her two sons and Sara's four were gathered in the hall to hear the news.

By that time, Sara had fully mastered her emotions and stood before her sons, nephews, sister, and servants as solemn as a carved statue. "I have had grave news today about my dearest husband, your father and your lord, the true governor, David Kirke," she said. "To my great sorrow, he has died of an illness while being wickedly imprisoned in London. He died in January, though we are hearing the news of it only today."

Sara's sons did not have their mother's gift of keeping a still face while hearing terrible news. George's jaw dropped and he turned beet red. Philip said, "What? F-father is dead?" and Jarvis burst at once into sobs. Only Davey seemed to remain unmoved, though Frances had always thought him his father's favourite. His gaze, as he watched his mother read his uncle's letter aloud, looked cool and almost calculating.

After she read the letter, Sara excused herself to her bedchamber. Whatever mourning she meant to do, she would do behind that locked door. Frances stayed in the hall with the lads and the servants. While the younger boys, the maids, and the menservants all chattered, seeming to have endless questions about what the master's fate would mean for them, she saw Davey sidle up to George, who sat in his father's chair with his head in his hands.

"Look up, brother. You are the head of the household now, you know," Frances heard Davey say.

George did look up. His face was still red, and tears were in his eyes. "I cannot think of that now."

"But you must. Mother will think of it and expect you to take a man's part."

"Will she?" George echoed. "She seems to have all well in hand."

George was a few months shy of his nineteenth birthday, a man by anyone's measure, except perhaps his mother's. Philip, two years behind him, was quieter, with a persistent stammer that added to his shyness. Philip preferred to work in the shadows, not to be dragged into the light.

Davey was sixteen and looked more ready to don that cloak of manhood than either of his elder brothers did. But Frances doubted that Sara would let any of them fully take the reins of leadership. In order to do that, those reins would have to be pried out of her own hands. Even in grief, Sara was not the sort to give up power.

"So, what have you heard? Do the Kirke women and their sons mean to leave?"

"I'm sure I cannot tell you, Peter. I scrub their linens. Do you think they do be telling their plans to the washerwoman?"

"I'd not have you call yourself that. Indeed, I'd not have you do the work at all. Why should you work for those women, when they defy God's will and the governor's rule? The only good in it is that you gossip with their maid and might hear something of use."

They were outside their house, Peter fixing a shutter while Meg shook out blankets and Mary built a tower out of the small stones Meg had cleared from the garden plot. "I do it because extra coin always comes in useful," Meg said. "I work with Hannah, aye, but you know she is no gossip."

"Yet you and the blackamoor always have plenty to say to each other."

"She is my friend," Meg said simply. "But 'tis not gossip we talk of."

"What else would women's talk be but gossip? And you lower yourself by calling such a one your friend. She is beneath you in every way."

Meg thought of Hannah sitting by her side on that terrible night back in the autumn, holding her hand after the midwife had gone. When she knew that the baby was dead, Meg had cried until she thought she was empty of tears forever. Then Hannah had brought Mary in to her and put the little girl in bed beside her mother, and Meg nestled her face in Mary's curls and thought, *She is all I have now*.

Now she looked again at Mary, who let out a little cry of frustration as her stone tower tumbled to the ground, and thought, *All I have, and perhaps all I will ever have.* Peter had not shown any inclination for swiving since the baby had been stillborn, and Meg was relieved. He lectured her often about the sinfulness of women in general and the sinfulness of Meg Taylor in particular. He said that God would not bless them with a healthy son until she repented and embraced the true reformed faith. *More likely, until you embrace me*, she thought, but said nothing, not wanting to put the thought into his head.

"Whatever you think of Hannah, she has said naught about what her mistress or Lady Sara mean to do," she said now.

"'Tis past time for them women to be gone from here and let Governor Treworgy rule as he ought. This stiff-necked rebellion has gone on long enough."

Stiff-necked rebellion was one of Reverend Bright's favourite phrases—for women, for royalists, for people who used the prayer book, and for Lady Sara and Lady Frances, who still refused to give up Kirke House. But despite the faithful few that gathered at the Treworgys' house to listen to Reverend Bright's lengthy Puritan rants, there were far more planters in Ferryland who would stand by the Kirke women.

The next day was Sunday, and Meg bundled up Mary and brought her along to the new governor's house with Peter for Sunday service. Meg sat on the bench, trying to keep Mary quiet and still with hands folded in her lap, while Master Treworgy read a long Psalm, a prelude to the minister's much longer sermon.

Meg was by no means surprised when Reverend Bright—surely one of the most misnamed of all God's creatures, for his features were darkened with a permanent scowl—began to preach about the wicked Jezebel. He was fond of Jezebel, in a backwards sort of way; he liked to make her the centre of his preaching. "The story of Ahab and Jezebel shows us how wicked, how much against nature it is for a woman to rule a nation. Jezebel was a pagan princess who led Ahab astray! She led all Israel astray! And lo, what was her end? To be thrown out of a window and have her bones licked by the dogs!"

Murmurs of approval from the small group gathered on the benches. Earlier, as winter set in and meeting outside became impossible, the governor had spoken of converting an empty byre into a meeting house. But once the novelty of Reverend Bright's fiery sermons wore off, there were only a handful of folks in Ferryland who favoured that sort of Sunday worship. Apart from the governor's own household, there were Peter and Simon, both of whom brought their wives, and Henry and Sarah Yard with their younger children. The Yards preferred the reformed way of worship, but Meg noted that they did not feel the need to talk loudly about it or try to convert others.

As for the rest of the Ferryland settlers, many still went to Kirke House for prayer-book services. Some folks in the harbour observed Sunday as a true day of rest, with the excuse that as they had no proper building to worship in, God could hardly blame them for not going to church.

So the reformers continued meeting in the governor's house, which was much improved since Abel Goode's time. There it was that Meg sat next to Peter, trying to keep Mary quiet, while Reverend Bright thundered about the unnatural rule of women.

"We saw the same in England, how the monarchy was weakened by evil queens, Bloody Mary and then the wicked harlot Elizabeth. And then it was given over to men who were soft, effeminate, no better than women. God has come down and swept the whole lot of them away and replaced them with strong, God-fearing men! Now, in this far-flung corner of the New World, God has pulled down a wicked governor, but these women have set themselves up in his place. These wicked Jezebels must be pulled down! They must be thrown from the tower, as was Jezebel in the Scriptures, so that the dogs may drink their blood!"

While Peter talked to the men afterwards, Meg soothed Mary, who was always fractious after these long services. Simon's wife, Peggy, glanced over from the conversation she was having with Sarah Yard to frown at Meg and Mary. "That child is most wilful," Peggy said.

"You ought to beat her more," said Sarah. She nodded at her daughter Eliza, who was the Treworgys' new maid, currently collecting the Treworgy children for their dinner. "All mine were beat regularly and never gave me a minute's trouble. Look at my Eliza—you could not ask for a more quiet, obedient lass."

Mistress Treworgy, standing nearby, gave Sarah a gracious nod. "Indeed, I have been most pleased with Eliza. I'm sure 'twas your godly parenting that raised her up so well." Then she looked at Meg, a surprisingly harsh glare for one with such a milk-white face and such soft blue eyes. "I have told you before, you must not be weak with your daughter, Goodwife Taylor. The devil is in little children and must be driven out of them."

Meg bristled. She never felt at ease with women like Peggy Tolliver and Sarah Yard, who seemed to have an answer for everything and far too much advice to give, and she simply did not like Mistress Treworgy. The woman was forever dispensing cautions and rebukes to the planters' wives, and Meg seemed to come in for more than her fair share of such warnings. She gathered Mary in her arms and said, "She is not a wicked child. 'Tis only that she finds the service long."

"That *is* wickedness," retorted Mistress Treworgy. "It is the sign of her fallen nature that belongs to Satan. A child must be broken like a horse to the bit, so her will is in submission to God's law."

A shadow moved, and Peter stood between his wife and daughter on one side and Mistress Treworgy on the other. Nodding like an eager little spaniel, he said, "Yes, 'tis so, mistress—spare the rod and spoil the child. I do try to be firm with her, but a child is so much more in its mother's care. I tell Meg she must be more strict with Mary, to raise her up godly-like."

Meg lowered her eyes, hoping she looked humble. "Of course you are right, husband. I've a good deal to learn yet."

"Pray for guidance and listen to those wiser than you, like godly Mistress Treworgy," said Peter, putting a hand on Meg's back to steer her away. "Thank you, mistress, for taking time to correct my wife."

On the way home, Mary grew drowsy in Meg's arms, and Meg said nothing about Mistress Treworgy's opinions on child-raising. Instead she asked Peter, "Do you think Reverend Bright really means to have Lady Sara and Lady Frances killed?"

"What? Of course not."

"But he said about pushing them out of the tower like in the Bible. He could have them thrown off a roof, or off a bluff into the sea."

"Don't be foolish, woman! He only means to clear them out of Kirke House so Governor Treworgy can move his family in there. There'll be no dogs licking up anyone's blood. Sure, there's few enough dogs round here anyway."

"Henry Yard has hunting hounds," Meg said.

"You're too soft, is what you are, same as you are with the child. The reverend is right—'tis unnatural and wicked, the way them two women have kept control of things round here. Now that Kirke is dead, there's no reason for them to remain."

"There's the lads—they are of an age to take up their father's business."

"If their mother gave in, they would too. The governor and the reverend are having another meeting tonight—just men this time, no women or puling brats—and they are going to rid us of the Kirke women for good."

"Just so long as nobody gets pushed out of a window or eaten up by Henry Yard's hounds," said Meg.

"Trouble is brewing," Frances said at the dinner table on Monday.

"Trouble is always brewing somewhere," said Davey, who did not want to be called Davey anymore, now that his father was dead and he was the one and only David Kirke in the colony. "But need it trouble us?"

"Have you heard rumours, Aunt?" asked George, tearing off another hunk of bread from the loaf and using it to sop up the last of the sauce in his bowl. "I know I have."

"'Tis only servants' talk," Frances admitted, free to discuss it now that Hannah and Molly were out of the room, "but in a place this size, servants' talk is worth listening to. You know that Hannah is friendly with the Taylor woman, whose husband is very devoted to Master Treworgy and Reverend Bright."

"Aye," said Sara, "and what has she heard?"

"That the reverend preached a sermon yesterday about wicked women—"

"That is nothing new," said Davey—David.

"No, but there is more to it this time," George said. "I heard the same thing from Jack Yard, and you know his father is part of the reverend's congregation. And his sister is the Treworgys' maid. But Jack don't go along with their Puritan way of thinking. He told me they are planning something—to remove us from the house by force."

Sara snorted. "I should like to see them try it."

"But they *will* try it, Mother, and they mean to do so. Soon. Mayhap this very night."

"Not tonight—tomorrow night," said Richard quietly.

"What's that, cousin? Are you merely prattling, or do you know something?" George said.

"He is no idle prattler." Frances rose to her son's defence. "What have you heard, Richard?"

"Tomorrow night. The full moon. Will Thomas told me he heard his father talking about it. But his father doesn't approve."

"No more does Jack," George put in. "Most of the planters are with us; only a few are with them."

"They want to attack us now," Sara said, "because of the news of your father's death. They think we will be disheartened. And our summer fishing servants have not yet arrived, so we'll not have enough of our own men to defend us."

"I will gladly draw my sword and cut down any mob that comes at us with sticks and spades," said David with a gleam in his eye.

"This is no time for boys to swagger about," Sara snapped. "They'll not want a fight. And if they do, the muskets will do more good than that fancy sword of yours. But you are right—more of the planters support us than them, and we need to show that." She gave Richard a sharp look; Frances thought it was the first time in four years that Sara had paid more than the most cursory attention to either of her nephews. "How much do you trust this information, Richard?

Tomorrow night, at the full moon? Do you think 'tis sure?"

"Will seemed dead sure of it, my lady aunt."

"We will make other inquiries. George, you talk again with Jack Yard. Frances, see what else you can find out from Hannah, and tell her to get what news she can from the Taylor woman. David, as you have such a gift for worming yourself into people's good graces, talk to the Bullard boys, and the Keans. See would they stand by us, if it comes to a conflict."

"With the best will in the world, Mother." David stood up, grinning at his brothers, cousins, mother, and aunt. "No mob will push the Kirkes out of Kirke House while we have the will to fight!"

The full moon rose on Tuesday night, flooding the sky with silver light. By moonrise, it was common for everyone in Ferryland to be in their houses if not already abed, the last wisps of smoke drifting from chimneys as fires were banked for the night. And, indeed, so it seemed looking out on this night: nothing to be seen but quiet houses, the moon reflected in a path on the water, a few lazy smoke trails etched on the dark blue of the sky.

But the peace was an illusion. David had reported as much, just after sunset. "They are gathered at Treworgy's house," he said. "Eight or ten men. I think they have two guns between them."

Kirke House also had two guns. David had spoken to a few of the planters who had promised to bring their own muskets in support. Frances and Sara watched the windows, waiting for any sign of attack.

"If no one comes to our defence, can we put up enough of a fight?" George wondered. "We've not got a dozen men here, just ourselves and the servants."

"I would avoid bloodshed, if we can," Sara said. "With your father gone, and few friends left to us in England, we could face harsh penalties if we took a life, even in defence of our home."

"If anyone points his weapon at me, I'll fire on him," David said.

Sara glanced out the window. "They are coming," she said.

At first it was not clear who "they" might be, only that the moonlight revealed more than a dozen men snaking their way along the winding paths that led through the village and up to Kirke House. They were coming from the direction of Governor Treworgy's place.

"Give me the gun," Sara said to George.

"What? No. Philip and I will have the muskets."

"You said I would have one!" David protested.

"The three of you can fight over the newer gun," Sara told her sons. "I'll take your father's musket, and I am going out onto the steps, alone, to face down whoever is coming at us. The rest of you stay inside. 'Twill be harder for them to take over the house if you are still inside it."

"Then why are you going out?" Frances said.

"Because of how it looks," Sara said. "You can come with me, if you want, but none of the lads, nor the menservants neither. They have made us out to be two harpies, two wicked women defying the will of men. They will attack women with their words, but they'll think twice before taking a shot at one—or two."

Sara was right; two women defending the house would give the men pause. "I'll come," Frances said. "But just the one gun—I cannot shoot."

From outside, in the cold stillness of the night, the group of men moving toward the house was easier to see. Two of them carried torches; no more were needed in this bright moonlight. Frances thought how easily a torch might be thrown at the roof or through a broken window. That would not serve Treworgy's end—he wanted the house intact. But men in mobs could lose all reason. And Reverend Bright did not care about the house—he wanted to teach these rebellious women a lesson.

"There are so many," Frances whispered to Sara. "David spoke of eight or ten, but there are more than that."

"Aye. I'd not thought so many were against us. And they have more guns than we do." At least four of the men, as they drew closer, looked to be shouldering muskets.

"Look, there is Dick Kean, and Samuel Thomas, and their sons. I had thought we could count on their support. And I see Jack Yard along with his father, though George said Jack could be relied upon. Are they all so easily swayed by that preacher?"

"He does threaten hell's flames for those who disobey—that may be strong persuasion for some," said Sara. "But . . . I am not sure our sons were entirely led astray."

It certainly looked as if they had been. Almost twenty men now approached the house, those not carrying muskets armed with heavy sticks, knives, and even a few pitchforks. And among them were many faces that ought to have been friendly.

Reverend Bright and Master Treworgy marched at the head of the group, and as they approached Kirke House, the men spread themselves around the property. Treworgy stepped forward.

"Lady Sara, Lady Frances. Do not fear. We do not wish harm to either of you."

"Do you not?" Sara said. "You bring a mob with weapons to my doorstep, and tell me not to fear?"

"I desire only what is mine by right as governor of this colony."

"My family's home is not yours by right."

"It is. I have letters from men in Parliament confirming that this house is property of the rightful governor, not of the Kirke family."

"Do you think I care what your Barebones Parliament has to say about it? This is my home."

"Lady Sara, I pray you stand aside and let us take the house."

The expression on John Treworgy's face might almost have been a smile—the smile of one who recognizes a worthy opponent, Frances thought. But there was neither humour nor respect in Reverend Bright's face when he stepped forward to speak.

"Enough bandying words with wicked women! Have no fear, men. Forward, in the name of Christ!"

At his words, more than half the men in the group stepped forward. Frances saw Sara raise the gun to her shoulder. Would she really fire it?

But before she could even put her finger to the lever, most of the men who had moved toward the front of Kirke House turned around, facing their fellows. Two of them had guns, but they were trained on Bright and Treworgy, not on Sara and Frances.

"Enough words. You spoke aright, Reverend," said Samuel Thomas. "'Tis time for you and Master Treworgy to be off home now, and leave the ladies in peace."

"Aye, get on wi' you," said Alf Bullard.

"Don't start a fight—you'll not win it," Dick Kean added.

More of the men were moving now, forming a barrier in front of the steps, standing between the women and the mob, which no longer looked like a mob. Even Henry Yard, who went regularly to the Treworgys' house for Sunday meeting, stood with his sons alongside the men protecting Kirke House. Treworgy and Bright were now flanked by only seven other men: Treworgy's servants Isaac and Solomon, Peter Taylor, Simon Tolliver, and three summer fishermen. They were the true believers, the passion on their faces frightening in the moonlight, but their numbers hardly a threat against so many.

Then the door of the house opened, and young David Kirke stood there with a musket on his shoulder, looking so ready for a fight Frances almost laughed. Behind him came George and Philip. She was not surprised David had won the argument over who would carry the gun. Her own brave Richard was with them as well. Nicholas and Jarvis peered around the door as if they, too, would come out and face down the crowd, but she saw Hannah's hands on their shoulders, pulling them back inside.

David Kirke stood beside Sara. "Come, ye brave fellows! Do you still want to take on my mother, my brothers, and me, and drive us from our home? With all these honest men to take our side and defend our rights?"

The planters, Frances thought, knew which side their bread was buttered on. The Kirkes had brought prosperity to this colony. The lively fishing trade of the Pool Plantation under Kirke leadership had benefited the smaller planters as well, and there was no appetite to drive the Kirkes out.

"Go on home now, Governor Treworgy," Sara said. It was the first time Frances ever remembered hearing her sister call the man *Governor*. Perhaps she felt she could afford to throw him a sop just now. "You go on governing and let us go on with our business—here, in our home."

Treworgy glanced at Bright, who looked fit to burst. But righteous anger was no match for a gang of men that outnumbered his two to one. Frances could not hear what Treworgy said to him, but when the governor turned to address the rest of his ragtag group of men, it was clear he was sending them home. They trudged back down the road one or two at a time.

It was too much, perhaps, when David led the men in a jeering cheer as the attackers retreated. Too much for Bright, anyway. Forgetting whatever dignity was due him as a man of the cloth, he lurched forward, grabbing at the nearest opponent—young Jem Thomas, who still held a pitchfork in his hands. Grappling with the pitchfork as if to wrest it from Jem, Reverend Bright stumbled forward before Jem gave him a good shove, sending him onto his backside in the bushes. To a chorus of laughter, Treworgy helped his pet preacher to his feet.

"A curse upon all of you! You defy God's will and follow the unnatural rule of a woman, and . . . and pray from forbidden popish books, and secretly wish for a king back on the throne. You will be judged for it!" sputtered Bright.

"Aye, and we'll keep right on doing all that, too!" shouted David.

Treworgy turned back as he and the hobbling reverend started down the road. "You will hear more of this, Lady Sara, never you fear."

"No, and never will I fear!" called Sara. To the group of men assembled around her front steps she said, "Well done, good men! To thank you for your service, come along to the tavern, and there will be free beer for everyone. 'Twas a good night's work you have done."

CHAPTER NINE

Spring 1654

The ship that came from England in May of 1654 brought several items from James Kirke for his sister-in-law's plantation: fishing gear, salt, rope, twenty fishing servants, and a tidy young woman who looked so fresh and clean it was hard to believe she had just survived a month-long voyage across the Atlantic. She looked, Frances thought, as if she had been handcrafted and freshly painted within the last week. This was Helen Whittaker, whom James had brought out as a bride for George.

"I don't see why Uncle James couldn't have brought one for me as well," complained David, as he stood with his aunt and mother watching the ship's cargo being unloaded.

"Your time will come," said Sara.

"Belike you will find one in Boston," Philip suggested.

"A prim little Puritan maid, all dressed in grey and ready to train a man out of his sins? Another little Patience Treworgy?

I think not," David said.

Sara was sending David and Philip to Boston this spring, feeling that her sons needed more education and experience of the world than they could get on a New Found Land plantation. While Boston leaned toward Puritanism, it was also stuffed full of wealthy merchants whose true god was Mammon. Sara wanted her lads educated in the pursuit of wealth before they returned to the New Found Land to take up their inheritance.

George had made the same pilgrimage to Boston the summer before; now that he was twenty years of age, Sara had deemed it was time for him to marry. In the normal order of things, a man might wait till he was thirty or older to find the right bride. But Sara wanted George married, and though she had never put her reasons into words, Frances understood. With the elder David Kirke dead, the family needed roots and stability.

Sara had cast all her dice on this colony; she was hanging onto the business, the fishing rooms, the house, like a dog with a rat in its teeth. She, her elder sons, and her brother-in-law James were snared in a number of legal cases over the ownership of the business and the property, some with Cecil Calvert back in England, who still insisted on his family's rights in the land they knew as Avalon, and some with John Treworgy, who was closer at hand.

If the Kirkes were to be established here, to found the dynasty Sara hoped for, then there must be not just sons but grandsons, a new generation of Kirkes. There was already one merrybegot in Ferryland who looked too much like George Kirke for comfort. He was being raised as Clara Kean's younger brother, and Clara was walking out with Alfie

Bullard in a most respectable manner, but still Sara kept a close eye on her sons and hoped for no more such accidents. George needed a good English wife of the right class, to sire sons who would bear the name of Kirke.

So Sara had written to James Kirke in the autumn last year, asking if he could find a suitable bride for George. George himself was less particular in his requirements. And now this young maiden was stepping onto the wharf, smoothing down her skirts and looking around for her husband.

George moved forward, then hesitated and glanced back at his mother, who gave him a stern glare. Frances hid a smile behind her fan. Perhaps now George's wife would give him orders instead, though Frances would not wager much for this young woman's chances if she had to defy her new mother-in-law.

James Kirke himself was along for the voyage, as well as a clergyman to perform the wedding ceremony. The Puritan minister, Reverend Bright, had not opted to spend a second winter in the New Found Land, and no other man of the cloth had settled in the place since. When clergymen came into port, they performed weddings and baptized infants during their brief stay, sometimes marrying the parents of the same infants they were baptizing, since couples often shared a household before a minister could be found to formalize the arrangement. But while such casual encounters might be good enough for the planters and servants, George Kirke's marriage must be solemnized by a proper Anglican priest.

The party that gathered around the Kirkes' table for supper was a large and, for the most part, merry one. George seemed to find Helen agreeable, at least thus far. The bride, the minister, and James Kirke made three people with recent news from England. So there was much to talk of, most strikingly the fact that Oliver Cromwell had been proclaimed Lord Protector.

"He is king in all but name now, and the ceremony was as much like a coronation as you might want to see," James said. "He wore a plain black suit, no robes or crown, but he rode through the street with soldiers marching around him, the mayor of London and the judges and all in the procession."

"Blasphemy!" Frances said. "A country squire to sit on the throne of England and be anointed with the sacred oils?"

"As a matter of fact, there was no anointing, and he wears no crown, neither," said the Reverend Thoroughgood. "Cromwell was asked to take the title of king but turned it down."

"Aye, but that chair he sat on in Westminster Hall looked a deal too close to a throne for my liking," James Kirke said. "He has kingly power, be there a crown on his head or no. Still, he does not seem likely to meddle with our business; Parliament is more concerned about Bermuda's loyalty than that of the New Found Land. As long as the fish keep swimming into your nets, they are not like to trouble you."

"We are well set for another good season of fishing here," Sara said, "and have hopes of expanding our property and enterprises. George has been building a house, and it will be ready to move into after the wedding," she added to Helen.

"Oh, that is very good news, indeed!" said Helen. Frances wondered what this young woman must think of the place she had been brought to. She recalled her own arrival in Ferryland—could it really be five years, now? Though she had to credit her sister for creating a gracious and comfortable home in this wild place, nothing here could compare to the comfort of a proper English town with markets and a church—oh, a church! She thought longingly of the comfort of proper worship, then remembered that such worship was not to be found even in England now.

"And your governor, Treworgy, still hangs on to his position here?" James inquired.

"He makes a show of it, at any rate," said Sara. "He sent his wife and children home last autumn but overwintered here himself and brought them back in the spring, which surprised me—I did not think they would return. He has lands in New England, and I am sure most of his interests would be there."

"He is interested enough to keep tying up the courts in England with his claims to this place," James pointed out. "And is he still troubling you about the house?"

Sara laughed. "After his great attempt to turn us out of the place last year came to nothing, he gave up on that for a while. I do think 'twas his preacher that stirred up most of the trouble. That fellow is gone, good riddance to him. But now that the wife is back, Treworgy has begun complaining again about how poor their house is. Well, he may be happier soon. I have a good mind to let him have this place, if he will drop some of his other claims in return."

There was a moment of stunned silence around the table before George said, "Whatever can you be thinking, Mother? Give Kirke House to the Treworgys? Where will you live?" Though even as those words left his mouth, Frances could see the answer dawning on both George's and Helen's faces.

"Your new house is bigger than this one and has a better situation," Sara said. "I can move there with you and take Jarvis with me. When David and Philip return from Boston, they may join us until they are ready for establishments of their own. There is land enough for all."

Sara had never said a word about giving up Kirke House, even as George was building his new home. He looked frankly horrified, and his bride-to-be looked to him with alarm. Frances could think of nothing but the stunning omission in Sara's tidily made plans.

But she said nothing. She would wait for a private moment with her sister.

Hannah lowered a bucket into the well, watching the rope dance into darkness. Drawing water had always been one of Molly's chores, until Molly had announced last week that she was leaving to be married. Jacob Lane from Renews had made her an offer, and now that a minister had come to the harbour, they wanted to wed as soon as possible; they could move to Jacob's parents' house while he finished building his own. They need not even wait till the fish were in.

Lady Sara had fumed about having one less maidservant while preparing for her son's wedding and the great move. While she tried to hire another, Hannah was doing work that had previously been Molly's.

"Do'ee need a hand with those pails, young maid?"

The voice startled her, not only by its nearness—she had seen no man nearby when she came down the path from kitchen to well—but because it was unfamiliar. It was neither of the Kirkes' menservants, nor any villager she recognized. And none of them would call her "young maid."

She looked up to see the stranger leaning against the fence smoking a pipe. A sturdy, broad-shouldered man about her own age, dressed in a fisherman's tunic and breeches, with a rough homespun cloak over his shoulders against the morning chill. His complexion was as brown, his eyes and hair as dark as her own, and she thought he must be a sailor. The only men she ever saw who looked to have African blood were those who came and went on ships. But if he were, he should be sleeping aboard his ship, not wandering about near Kirke House in the early morning.

"I am used to carrying water," she said. As she spoke, it came to her who he must be. James Kirke had brought out summer fishing servants; they were housed in the old cookhouse not far from Kirke House. The men were expected to fend for themselves, so they rarely came near the big house.

"Aye, I can see you are. No harm meant, maid." His accent was pure Devonshire—English-born, then, she thought, whatever his complexion.

The man lingered. He was stepping out of his place, yet something in his voice, or perhaps the smile that accompanied his words, made her add, "My name is Hannah."

"And mine is Stephen Barstow," he said, touching a hand to his cap. "You serve the Kirkes, then?"

"I serve Lady Frances Hopkins, Lady Sara Kirke's sister."

"Aye. I might well serve her myself. We were told most of us was Lady Sara's servants but four of us was working for her sister, but nobody said which was which. I s'pose the masters—or the mistresses—will sort out what's owed to who at summer's end. As long as I gets my pay."

That was too much talking; he was taking liberties, although Hannah wanted to ask him more. She had not known that Lady Frances was hiring her own fishing servants this season. She pulled up the second bucket, fitted both buckets onto the yoke, and raised it to her shoulders. "Do your work, and you'll have your pay all right. If you've not fished on the New Found Land before, you'll find the summer short but hard."

"Not so hard, if I might see you around now and then."

Now that really was impertinent. He deserved to have her turn and walk away without another word, so she did.

When Sara glanced up from the account books on her desk, Frances sat down on the bench across from her. Better to deal with Sara face to face than to remain standing like a supplicant.

"You always want something when you come to see me here," said Sara.

"Of course I do. And I am sure you know what I want."

"You are doing well for yourself. James remarked on it when I showed him the books. With your own four fishing servants, you will be in an even better position by the end of this season."

"And yet I may be left without a roof over my head."

Sara made a mocking little noise like a sneezing kitten. "Do not make such a great drama of it. You'll not be living in a tilt."

"I may as well, if you give this place to the Treworgys. Do you mean for my sons and me to move into George's house with you?"

Now Sara laughed. "That would be an even greater shock for Helen, d'you not think?"

"'Tis fortunate, then, that none of us wants that to happen. What is your plan for Abel Goode's house, once the Treworgys are out?"

Every move Sara made was carefully planned, moving her family and her enemies around the settlement like pawns on a chessboard, with herself, of course, the queen. Frances had feared she had the former Goode house earmarked for David or Philip. Sara had bought it for a pittance from Abel Goode's heirs and told the Treworgys she was generous not to charge them rent. They had improved it significantly at their own expense.

"Is that what you want? That house?"

"It would suit me well. 'Tis not as big as this place, nor as George's new house, but the boys and I would be well suited there. It will be Richard's when he comes of age, so he will not be left without an inheritance. I would take Hannah with me, of course, and all I would need would be a manservant. Young Rafe will do, if you wish to keep Caleb."

"A manservant and a house. In return for . . . ?"

"In return for all I have done these last five years to add to your holdings and wealth."

"You have done a good deal, especially in letting us use Hannah's labour. But 'tis not enough to add up to the value of a house and land."

"Then I would owe you the rest, to be paid off over however many fishing seasons it may take," Frances said. "Unless you wish to make it a gift."

"A gift." As if it were an unfamiliar word, one Sara had never heard before. "Out of affection, rather than . . ." she waved her hands over the account books before her, "business. Well." She paused. "You shall have the house, if that is what you want. As for the terms, I shall think on that."

"So they be leaving Kirke House after all?"

"So it seems," said Hannah. A fortnight had passed since the arrival of George Kirke's bride, and news of the changes had trickled down from the big house to the fishermen's homes. "Lady Sara will move into Master George's new house, and my lady means to set up on her own in Abel Goode's old house. 'Twill be Master Richard's, when he comes of age."

"Now they can call it Hopkins House, I s'pose." Meg scrubbed at a stubborn stain on a pair of breeches as Hannah spread a petticoat over a bush to dry. Nearby, Mary crouched in the grass, building a doll-sized house out of sticks and stones. "Master Treworgy will think he has won a great victory, getting Kirke House after all this time."

"Aye, no doubt he will." Hannah wrung the water out of another petticoat. "But 'tis nothing to gloat over, to my mind. Kirke House is big, but 'tis old; 'twas built in old Lord Baltimore's time, him as was here before Governor Kirke. There's a deal of repair needed. And with all the work Governor Treworgy has put into Abel Goode's old place these last two years, 'twill be a fine spot for Lady Frances."

"I know. Peter got a good bit of work off them." Peter had been more willing to work on the Treworgys' house than on his own, Meg thought. But then, Governor Treworgy was paying him. And she could not fault him too much. In addition to that work and the fishing, he had managed to expand their own house to add a storeroom alongside the bedchamber. Whatever his shortcomings as a husband, Peter was a hard worker.

Meg tossed the breeches into the basket and took the next pair from the bucking-tub, lifting them out with a stick. "You will move with Lady Frances, then?"

"Aye. She tried to bargain with Lady Sara to give her one of the menservants, but Lady Sara would not go that far. But my ladyship says I am hers, no need to strike a bargain over that. Lady Sara will keep Mistress Durdle on as her cook and hire two maids for the new house."

Meg ran through in her mind the handful of planters and sharemen who had daughters. "There's no one in Ferryland right now who would serve. I suppose the Sprouls' young one, Annie, must be about the right age, but those folks are such poor starvelings, the children are half wild."

"Nay, Lady Sara has been talking to some planter over in Renews about taking his daughters into service."

"That must be the Cottons—belike their two youngest are about fourteen and sixteen, a good age to go into service." Meg herself had been put into service in Aunt Kathryn Guy's house when she was fifteen and had worked there for three years before going home to help with her sister Lizzie's growing brood. Then Peter had come to fish for the summer and courted her. She tried to remember now, six years later, what she had thought of him then, whether she had liked him, thought him handsome, considered he would make a good husband. Or had she only known it was time to marry, to have her own household, and Peter had made the offer?

She said none of this aloud. Instead she said, "I had thought there was a chance that, rather than go with Lady Frances, you might have plans of your own." Twice in the past fortnight she had seen Hannah with one of the fishing servants in the evening, walking and talking along the strand the way courting couples did.

Hannah smiled. "I have had no offer to change my station."

"And if you had one?"

"Ah, who knows? No point cracking eggs before the hens have even laid them, is there? I am near thirty years old; if I am ever to marry and have children, it must be soon. But what have I to bring to a marriage? Or what would a fishing servant have to offer me, come to that?"

"But you admit there is such a man?"

"I can hardly deny it—folk have seen us about. He be a good man but a poor one. As I am a poor woman. So what is there to talk of?"

"But Lady Frances must owe you a good deal, you having come all this way from England and serving her all these years. No doubt she'd be generous, if you was to say you wanted to marry."

"You are getting the horse well ahead of the cart," said Hannah.

Lady Frances has been good, Hannah thought, trudging back up the road toward Kirke House with the basket of laundered clothes on her hip. Good in the way a lady is good to a valued servant: working her hard but not harsh in her demands or her corrections.

Hannah had been paid no coin in the five years since they had landed in the New Found Land, though she had always earned a modest wage back in England. She still had her little bit of savings put away in a strongbox. "'Twould make no sense to pay you money in this country," Lady Frances had said soon after they arrived. "I have little enough of it myself, and they hardly use it here. Everything is on trade and barter. My sister will see you are housed and fed, and when I come into my own fortune again, I will make all right with you."

I will make all right sounded very much as though there would be a sum of money coming to Hannah in time. But of course, Lady Frances had said that when she had expected to be back in England within a year, restored to favour under a new king. Things had fallen out very differently than they had expected.

When Lady Frances had told Hannah she must work on the flakes and serve in the tavern, Hannah had been bold enough to raise the question of payment. "All is being kept in account," her ladyship had said then. "My sister keeps count of what the Kirkes owe to me and of the work you have done. We will be well rewarded for this." That *we* made it clear that their fortunes were bound together, Hannah's to her mistress's.

When Hannah was able to slip away that evening after supper, there was still light in the sky. Stephen had asked her to meet him down at the Pool again, and he was there leaning against a beached pinnace, chatting to another of the fishing servants as Hannah arrived. The other man smiled a knowing smile—he, too, was waiting for a woman.

Stephen was an easy companion for a half-hour's walk along the shore. He had travelled widely and seen much of the world so was rarely short of conversation. "How came you to serve the Kirkes and work ashore this season?" she asked him, when he finished telling her about crewing aboard a voyage to Portugal, where he had narrowly escaped being taken by pirates.

"Truth to tell, I be looking for a place to settle, a place a poor man might have his own few square feet of earth and be beholden to no one," he said. "A man cannot sail forever—at least, I've no wish to. And folk like us will never own anything back in England. I had a look at how things were placed in the Massachusetts colony last summer, when I fished off Cape Cod. A good many folks have settled down there and made a life for themselves."

Hannah was surprised to hear a fisherman talk with such forethought about the future; most fishing servants lived from one season to the next, earning what they could, rarely taking thought beyond that. "And what did you make of that place? Could you see yourself settling there, if you'd a way to get a piece of land?"

Stephen was silent a moment. They had stopped walking and both stood looking at the light of sunset reflected on the water. He bent down, picked up a smooth rock from the beach at their feet, and turned it over and over in his hand. "Not in New England," he said. "The English people there . . . they are become very comfortable with the idea of keeping people bound to service forever. 'Tis not only that they keep slaves. I know there's folk in England own slaves as well; my own mother was a slave as a girl. She was freed at her master's death, which was the least he could do, having got her with child through no will of her own."

Hannah nodded. Stephen had not told her anything of his parentage before, but she knew that among people of mixed English and African blood, cases like those of her own parents—a love match—were far less common than the case of women like Stephen's mother.

Stephen went on. "The idea is creeping up from the Indies, I think, into Virginia and toward New England, that perhaps every man or woman of our complexion is a slave by nature."

Our complexion. Hannah wondered sometimes, after these walks with Stephen, whether he was the first man she had been drawn to simply because he was the first man she had known well who shared the colour of her skin and her African parentage. Was that the tie that bound them? She did not know much of these places he spoke of—the Indies, Virginia, New England. Only names. But she knew the word *slave*, just as she knew that she was freeborn.

"So you came here, hoping to find something better?"

"Aye."

"There are worse places to settle."

"There are, for certes. If I had something to draw me here . . ."

"A piece of land? A house of your own?"

"Yes, either of those . . . or a wife."

To that she said nothing. Talk of marriage between two people who owned nothing but the clothes they stood up in was foolish. Stephen turned the stone over again in his hand, then hurled it out into the sea. The sun had begun to set. They turned toward Kirke House, soon to be Kirke House no longer.

"I've not been idle, or foolish with my wages, these years at sea," Stephen said into the silence. "I have saved a little. I could not buy land, but here in this place, I might be able to be a shareman rather than a servant. I'd have my own roof over my head."

"You've been wise, then, to save for the future." Hannah thought again of her conversations with Lady Frances, of her own long hours of work about the house, the garden, the fishing flakes, the tavern. *What do I have to show for my labour?*

"Careful with that! That box has the governor's good plate in it!" Patience called as the two men hefted the crate with her dishes.

They were not being careless. Indeed, they had been most respectful throughout the whole process of moving, and she was well aware that taking two fishermen from their work so close to the start of the fishing season was a great deal to ask, even when her husband was paying them. But she had waited so long to see her belongings carried to the big house, the *proper* governor's house. She stood vigilant lest some disaster forestall the move.

It was a lovely day, warm with May sunshine. It had been spring already when she left Maine with the two boys and baby Charity, born in the chill of winter. The New Found Land lagged behind New England's seasons, the birch and maple trees only starting to bud. She had been back here for three weeks now, watching winter ebb away again. But they had been three joyful weeks, because of the glad news that Sara Kirke was giving up her house at last.

Josiah and Matthew ran about in front of the house. They were glad to be back here after a winter deprived of the company of their papa. They had run to his arms with cries and shrieks of delight. Patience had greeted her husband more modestly, noticing that another winter had etched a few more lines on his brow and that his hair was showing some grey at the temples. He was nearly forty, almost fifteen years older than she was; she had never thought of the difference as a gap between them until now.

Still, greying or not, he was governor, and Patience was glad to be back. It was good to be the governor's wife. Good to have a purpose. She reminded herself that God had called

John and her to bring true religion to the New Found Land fishermen, although she had known from her first year in the colony that this was an uphill battle.

"Don't you worry, mistress. We'll be as gentle as if you packed the baby in here," said one of the men carrying the box with her precious plate. It was Peter Taylor, giving her a crooked smile that was somehow both saucy and respectful.

John had hired Taylor and his shareman, Simon Tolliver, the two most devout Puritans in the settlement, the men he could trust best. Patience remembered watching Peter Taylor laying plank on her kitchen floor when they had newly arrived in this house. He was not only devout, but young and handsome, and she rewarded him with a brilliant smile as she passed the baby over to Martha. Patience had suddenly decided to walk along with the men to the big house, to see her goods safely stowed.

When all the boxes had been moved to the new house, Patience and Martha began unpacking the set of Dutch tin-glazed plates and all the other kitchen goods. John came in with the men and called for small ale for all of them. "A thirsty morning's work, lads," he said. "Take a cup of ale, with our thanks."

Patience took up a jug of ale and the cups that sat upon the sideboard. Serving the men would be her first act as mistress of the new house.

"Thank ye, ma'am, sir," said Taylor. He wiped sweat from his brow with his forearm before taking the cup from her with a slight nod of his head. He drank, then turned to John. "Good ale, too, sir. From the Kirkes' stores?"

"Nay, hardly!" Patience laughed. She saw John frown slightly at her intrusion into the men's talk, but she went on.

"You must know Lady Sara would take every scrap, stick, and drop of what belonged to her across to the new place. This is a jug of our own that Isaac brought over this morning. 'Twill be grand to have the use of the brewhouse for our own brewing, not to have to do everything in the kitchen."

"Aye, they had it all very neat and to their liking here," Taylor said, looking around the place with a bold eye. To John he said, "Will you keep their tavern open, sir?"

"Oh, I think not. I have never fancied myself a tavern-keeper."

"Indeed not," said Simon. "'Tis one thing for a man to have a cup of ale, brewed by his own good wife, at the end of a hard day of labour. But a tavern promotes spirituous liquors, and drunkenness, and every kind of ungodly behaviour."

"Aye, not the sort of work a Christian governor should be at," added Peter. "We folk look to you, sir—and your good lady—for an example of good Christian behaviour. Which the Kirkes never gave, sir, not in all the time they ruled here."

"That is certainly what we hope for," said John.

"And your lady wife—she gives a fine example of what a righteous woman ought to be." Peter's striking blue eyes looked right into Patience's, as if he could see into her soul and certify that it was pure and holy.

"Indeed, indeed." John seemed suddenly discomfited to have two common fishermen speaking freely in his own kitchen and began herding them toward the door. "Now, with all those boxes packed away, before I settle up with you fellows, there are a few outside chores . . ."

With the men gone, Patience turned back to her tasks. She had been standing without moving ever since she had filled the men's cups, holding the empty ale jug. A pretty thing, that jug, white with blue cherubs on it, almost frivolous in its beauty. She turned it round and round in her hands as if seeing it for the first time. She washed it, dried it, and put it in a prominent position on a shelf above the sideboard. She had brought that jug with her from Maine two years ago and used it often, yet suddenly it seemed something rare and precious, something to handle with care.

CHAPTER TEN

Autumn 1654

From the clothes hung on pegs beside her bed, Frances selected her best silk gown with a pretty embroidered jacket that had been plain when she brought it out from England. She had taken great time and pains to embroider golden flowers all over it during her quiet days here in Ferryland. She would wear it today as a small celebration of her new status as a planter.

Autumn was in the air. The fish was in, salted and dried, and the sack ships had arrived to begin the busy season of autumn trading. All summer, the four fishermen she had hired had worked hard, assisted on shore by Hannah and, to Frances's surprise, by her own sons. Richard had insisted that he take his turn working on the flakes and had made Nicholas do the same. "If this is to be my business," Richard told his mother, "I will know it from the ground up—and Nicky must, also. And we will earn more if we have more hands to share in the work."

"You don't suggest I should learn to split and gut fish also?"

"No, Mama." Then he had grown serious. "But you must learn to keep the account books, as Aunt Sara does. I can teach you. If you have your own land and your own fishing servants, you need to know what comes in and what goes out, to the last penny."

All summer, Frances, her boys, and Hannah worked for the profit of their own household. Their new house, Frances had to admit, had been much improved by John and Patience Treworgy's tenure there, being fitted with glass windows and a good plank floor and divided into three chambers on the first floor, in addition to the upstairs bedchambers. She had no fear of spending the winter there, nor any fear of going hungry during that winter, for the fishing had been good.

Hannah entered the room bearing a washbasin of warmed water and a cloth for Frances to wash her face. She stood by, ready to help with dressing. "Very well, Hannah, lay that there on the table and pass me the green gown, there. 'Tis good to see the end of the season, is't not?"

"Yes, my lady. It has been a good season."

"At least you have not had to serve in the tavern along with the rest of your work."

"True. I've not missed dealing with the men when they're in their cups. The fishermen do complain about the governor closing the tavern, but that's no concern of mine." Hannah laced Frances into the green gown and helped her put on the embroidered jacket. Then, as Frances sat on a stool at her dressing table, Hannah took the comb and began drawing it through her mistress's hair, easing out the snarls and tangles.

"Well, there are many ways to make money. We will find more of them as we go along," said Frances. She did not look down at her hair as Hannah combed it out: she disliked seeing the threads of silver winding through the rich brown colour she had always prized.

"My lady?"

"Yes, Hannah? What is it?"

"Speaking of our fortunes, as you were . . . I have been wanting to ask you something."

"Very well." Perhaps Hannah, busy with so much work, hoped Frances would hire another maid. Frances had already decided to hire both a maid and a manservant if her profit from the summer fishery was good enough. Hannah knew all the planters, their families, and their servants, so would be a good source of recommendations.

But Hannah had something different on her mind. "Forgive me, my lady, but—all the time we have lived here, you have paid me no wages."

"Of course not. I had no income of my own."

"Just so, my lady, I understand. But, now?"

"What need have you of wages? You have your bed here and are well fed. In this country, there is little to spend coin on, even if you had it."

"I beg your pardon, my lady. I am thinking of the future. If I were . . . if I ever wished to leave your service—say, to go back to England, or to marry—then would you settle on me what I am owed, for the time I have served you here? You would be able to do so, now that you have your own income."

Frances was, for a moment, too shocked to speak. Hannah had served her for nearly ten years, and this was the first impertinence she had offered in all that time, but the gall was so great it took Frances's breath away. "It is not your place to pry into my private affairs, nor to make assumptions about my income. I could . . . I could have you beaten, for such saucy talk!"

Hannah's careful face became even more guarded, her eyes dropping to Frances's hair as she pinned it up. "Forgive me, my lady, if the question discomforts you. But I have had the thought—that is, things have fallen out in such a way that I may be thinking of leaving your service. I would need to know what I am owed, before I can make any decision."

"What you are *owed*?" Frances echoed. "Are you a debt-collector? And whence comes this talk of making decisions, as if your fate were your own to command?" She felt at a disadvantage, with Hannah looming over her and Hannah's hands in her hair. She turned around fully to face the maid, heedless of her hairdressing. "You – are – my – servant! I own your labour. You forget your place."

Hannah kept her eyes down. After a moment she said, "But you do not own *me*, my lady."

"Of course I do! I have kept you and fed you all these years, I gave you passage over here. Do you think you could have paid for that yourself? I have treated you as . . . as a member of my family!"

"Am I serving an indenture, then? And if I am, when will it be ended?"

"Ended! Why are you talking like this, Hannah, as if I had hired you like a labourer? Who has put these thoughts into your head?"

"But your husband did hire me, my lady. I was paid a wage, back in England."

"We are not in England now! Stop standing there like a . . . like a painted figure, and come back over here and do my hair. I'll have no prattling of what was done back in England, nor of you demanding a wage like . . . like you were an Englishwoman."

Now Hannah raised her eyes, at last, to meet Frances's. "I am an Englishwoman, my lady. English-born, as you are yourself."

"You know what I mean."

The silence felt long, and Hannah made no move to return to pinning up Frances's hair. "Do you mean that I am your slave?" she said at last.

Of course not, Frances thought. Such an ugly word. She did not think of herself as a slave mistress. But nor could she imagine where Hannah was getting such ideas, demanding wages and talking of going away. "You are my servant," she repeated firmly, "and your duty is to do as I say. Finish fixing my hair, and go back to the kitchen. I will breakfast in half an hour. And there will be no more impertinent talk. Do you understand?"

Hannah's eyes lifted again to meet hers. "I understand perfectly, my lady."

"What on earth could have put such ideas into her head? A Negro servant, talking as if she were free to go where she will!" Frances told the incredible tale to Richard later that day as they walked up to Sara's new house, or rather, to George and Helen's new house, where Sara continued to reign supreme. "Do you think it is because she is friendly with Peter Taylor's wife? Has she been infected by these Leveller ideas?"

"I think not," said Richard. "Taylor may be a Leveller, but not even the Levellers would account a Negro the equal of an

Englishman. That would be madder than saying a woman is the equal of a man. Levellers believe all English men should be equal, which is folly enough, but even they recognize the natural order of things."

"I should hope so."

"No, I would say it is a man who has influenced Hannah to think above her station, but the man is not Peter Taylor." A smile quirked at the corners of his mouth.

"What man? What are you talking of? Is someone courting Hannah?"

"Have you not seen her in the evenings, walking with one of the fishing servants—that man Barstow?"

"One of our own fishermen! He is a Negro also, is he not?"

"I know not. His complexion is swarthy, but he might as easily be a Spaniard, or anything, I suppose. He talks like an Englishman, though."

Frances cursed her own lack of attention. Her maid had been carrying on a dalliance all this time, and she had not even noticed. "Well, I have no intention of letting her go. I will tell her to put a stop to it at once."

"Yes, I think that is wise." Richard looked thoughtful. "Hannah was a good servant when Nicholas and I were lads, but she has been getting above her station these last few years."

"'Tis this accursed country," Frances said. "Nobody knows their proper place, and the lower orders get wrong ideas into their heads. Some of these planters, acting as if they are gentry because they own a single boat and have a scrap of land to grow turnips! But there are not enough merchants and true gentry in this place to keep them in line."

"Are you sure you want to settle here and become a landowner and boat keeper yourself, Mother?"

They stopped walking, having neared New Kirke House, and the look that Richard gave his mother was not the look that accompanied an idle question. He truly wanted her answer.

"I would never have chosen this place to settle," Frances said, "but after five years, things seem no better in England than they were the day I left—worse, if anything. That wicked man Cromwell has set himself up as a false king, or near enough to one. I must have something to pass on to you and your brother. Having our own land and boats is a step toward that. There is no wisdom in spending your whole life pining for what cannot be."

Taking the children into the woods to pick berries had seemed like a fine idea when Patience left the house that morning. The day was sunny, and though it was cool, the wind was light for an autumn day. Everyone about the settlement was busy with the tasks that needed to be done before winter. Men went into the forest to cut firewood or worked on repairs to their houses and outbuildings. Women harvested the gardens, and they, too, went into the woods, usually in groups of two or three with their children in tow, to pick berries.

Berries in abundance—cranberries, raspberries, blueberries—grew around Ferryland; they were the only fruit this stony land seemed to produce. Patience was used to apple trees heavy with fruit as a sign of autumn, but here there were only small, hard, bitter apples. She had heard talk of wild cherries but had seen none. When it came to picking fruit to preserve for winter, berries were the only resort for most New Found Land settlers.

"I can join a party of women and pick berries, mistress," Martha had said when Patience suggested the idea. But Patience had wanted to go herself and thought the boys might enjoy a jaunt into the woods. She ordered Martha to lay aside other chores, gathered up Josiah and Matthew, tucked Charity in a sling, and headed off with two large wooden pails to fill with berries.

Two hours later, they had one pail a quarter full of blueberries. The little boys had first dutifully picked berries, then had pleaded to be allowed to play among the trees, and were now tired and hungry for their dinners. Charity fussed and refused to settle on the blanket where Patience had laid her. It was almost noon, the day was still beautiful, and the bushes were full of berries. But the children had had enough.

"Take them back home," Patience told Martha. "I will stay a little longer and pick—I can gather more if I am not distracted with the children."

"I cannot leave you here alone, ma'am. 'Tis hardly safe."

"You can, indeed, if I tell you to."

"I am sure your husband would not be pleased. What if a wild Indian, or a bear or a wolf, were to come upon you?"

"There are no Indians here," Patience said; all the settlers were fairly certain of that. Native people had once lived on this shore, but they must have long since moved on, for no one in Ferryland had seen one. Her husband had brought wampum beads from Maine, thinking the natives here might use them for trade as the people in New England did, but they lay unused on his desk.

She was less certain about wild animals; there were certainly bears and wolves in the forest. But she was willing to take the risk for a couple of hours to herself, to pick berries in peace and quiet. "What good do you imagine you and the children would be, if any such creature came out of the forest?" she said, challenging Martha. "If the governor questions you, tell him he may come and collect me himself." She had no concern John would come after her; he had gone to Renews for the day.

Martha, grumbling under her breath, took the three children home with her, and Patience spent a happy hour picking berries, enjoying the sight of the fruit piling up in her pail and the thought of the preserves she and Martha would make from them. She was not so isolated, after all—there were woods behind her and on both sides, but she sat in a clearing full of berry bushes, and she could see the trail sloping down to the settlement below and the blue band of sea beyond.

Am I wicked, to want a few hours free of caring for my children, my household? she thought. A woman's duty was to care for husband and children, taking no thought for herself. The pail of berries gave her an excuse. She was not neglecting her family; she was providing for them.

So busy and content was she that a sound from the woods trail behind her made her jump as if she had been slapped. She whipped round, fear clutching at her throat as she thought of the wolf or bear—or the wild man of the forest—who might even now be ready to attack. She almost laughed with relief at the sight of a man, not wild at all but familiar and harmless. Peter Taylor, hauling a cartload of wood.

"Mistress Treworgy! Beg pardon, I'd no wish to fright you. What, are you berry picking all alone?"

"My servant left a few moments ago with the children; they needed to go back for their dinner." Patience wondered why she felt the need to bend the truth, to pretend that Martha and the children had just left. "We'd not picked enough berries to be worth taking back, so I stayed to fill the pail."

He left the cart and moved nearer, looking into her pail. "Aye, you've done well. 'Tis a grand day to be out in the woods."

"A grand day, indeed."

"But 'tis hardly safe for a woman to be alone in the forest. Would you come along with me now, mistress, so I can see you safely back?"

It was a sensible offer to make. And yet it felt momentous, as if everything around her—the breeze, the birds, the grass and trees—were stilled, pausing to wait for her reply.

"Thank you, but I would like to pick till my pail is full."

He held her gaze steadily, not dropping his eyes in deference as he had done before. "I might wait with you. To see that you are safe here. I could help pick, and the work would go faster."

"I . . . that would be very good of you. If you can spare the time." Her heart pounded. Alone in the woods with Peter Taylor? It was perfectly proper of him to offer to see her home, but to linger here? To pick berries together? That did not feel proper at all. She looked down the trail that led toward the settlement, to see if anyone was coming.

Peter had already left his pile of wood and come to sit beside her among the berry bushes, close enough that she could easily have touched him. His hands set busily to searching the bushes for berries. "I am sorry, 'tis women's work, in truth," she said. "You need not pick. Rest from your work, and I will be done soon."

"Nay, 'tis easy enough, and a nice change from chopping down trees. I enjoy blueberry jam as much as anyone, so 'twill be no hardship to pick a few."

His sun-browned hands, the skin hardened and chapped as all the fishermen's hands were from exposure to the cold salt water, looked so strong as they quickly picked berries. She moved the pail so it sat between them, and his fingers brushed hers as he dropped in a handful of berries. She snatched her hand away as if a spark from a fire had landed on it.

"Beg pardon, my lady."

"You should call me mistress, as you usually do—I'm not a lady, not like Lady Sara or Lady Frances. Plain Mistress Treworgy is all I am."

He nodded. "That is as it should be, mistress. I put no stock in lords and ladies, titles and estates. God made all men equal." He paused, his hands still moving as he worked. "Indeed, if the world were truly ordered aright, we would not be mistress and man to each other but plain Peter and . . . Patience."

The sound of his voice saying her name landed like a heavy heartbeat in her breast. She ought to chide him. She ought to leave, right now.

"That is, if we lived in a world according to God's will," he said. "But I know we are far from that. I had hopes, after the war—I thought it might be different. But there are still some men set above others."

"There must be, for good government and order." Taylor was a true and reformed Christian, like herself, but she knew he was of a more radical sort.

"Aye, so I am told. Beg your pardon, mistress, I oughtn't be talking to you of such things."

"I am not so easily shocked."

"Are you not . . . Patience?"

Had he moved closer? She thought he had; he was only inches away. And he had called her by her name again, not as an example of what they might call each other in some Paradise imagined by a radical preacher, but as a bold challenge to propriety.

She saw herself, in her mind's eye, standing up, brushing off her skirts. Heard her own voice saying, *You are taking liberties, Taylor. Remember I am the governor's wife. I would not want to have to speak to my husband about your impertinence.* Imagined picking up the bucket, hefting its solid weight, starting down the path with it.

She did none of those things.

She leaned a fraction closer, heard her own voice—not in her mind, but out loud—saying, "Women are not as easily shocked as you think . . . Peter."

Their names on each other's lips had a power she had not imagined. When she looked into Peter's eyes, called him by name, she was not Mistress Treworgy, not the governor's wife, but only Patience. Patience, who never lived up to her name, who was suddenly impatient for a man's touch.

His mouth came to hers so quickly she had no time to think. For one delicious second, he kissed her and she returned the kiss, her lips parting under his. He was the one who pulled back, both of them wide-eyed. *Predestined*, she thought; *we have no free will after all. This was always going to happen.*

"Forgive me, mistress," he said, his voice rough and harsh, no hint now of the warmth that had tinged it a moment ago. "I should not—forgive me. It was—"

Unforgiveable. She could not say that she forgave him, nor could she pretend to be shocked. She had no words, for none existed in this place and time. Bold and shameless as a kitchen maid with a ploughboy, Patience put her hand on his rough, bearded cheek and drew his face back to hers.

She had only ever kissed her husband before, as was proper. John's kisses were a prelude to the proper, God-ordained act of marriage. She had never imagined that a kiss could stir such desire, such heat. It was as if the spark she had imagined a few moments ago had fallen into the dry grass, and flames were licking up all around them, a swift-moving fire that would leave everything in ashes and ruin.

"Here's Papa coming home with a deal of firewood to keep us warm, and soon you will have your pottage, with a nice piece of pork in it. That'll be grand, won't it?" Meg cooed to her daughter as she moved away from the window and went to the hearth to stir the pottage. She was happy about the pork. Lady Sara had given it to Meg in return for laundering their clothes. Fresh meat was a rare pleasure—most would be salted for use through the winter, but with Peter off in the woods all day, this seemed a good time to treat her family.

"Don't. Like. Pork," Mary said, beating her spoon in a steady drumbeat on the table.

"What a silly goose you are. You have had pork before, and liked it well. Do you want to still be a little baby, only eating mushy pottage and bread soaked in water? You are a big girl, and big girls eat pork and all kinds of good things."

"No. I will *not* like it." Mary's tumble of golden curls, now darkening towards brown, hid a pair of dark blue eyes like her father's that sometimes seemed as stern and serious as his.

She was a clever child who liked to chatter as she played, but she was especially fond of words like *No* and *I will not*.

Meg was grateful Mary saved these refusals for her mother. Peter believed that wilfulness should be beaten out of a child and did not approve of a girl, in particular, saying no when she was told what to do. He had already beaten Mary with a slender birch bough a few times, but it had not made much change in her behaviour.

He was here now, the rush of autumn wind and afternoon sunshine sweeping in as he opened the door. "You are in good time," Meg said, "for your dinner is standing ready."

"And if I were later still, 'twould keep, would it not? 'Tis my business when I come home, and your business to feed me when I do." He hung his cloak on a peg and moved to the fire to warm his hands.

Meg wasted no more breath on him but ladled up three bowls of pottage, each with a chunk of meat in it, then sliced up the bread to go with it. She would have liked to talk while they ate, to tell Peter the little incidents of her day. After baking bread, she had dug turnips and parsnips from their small garden patch, then gone to work along with Hannah in the bigger garden. Hannah seemed troubled, but she had not confided in Meg what the trouble was. She had visited Peggy Tolliver, Simon's wife, and brought her a brew of ginger and peppermint to help with the sickness she was having with her pregnancy. Meg was proud of her effort to be friendly to Peggy, who was not always easy to like. Mary had been a good girl all day, helping to pull parsnips from the garden and playing quietly while Meg cooked the evening meal.

But Meg knew that Peter would dismiss all this as idle prattle. Nor would he share any little tales of his own adventures in the woods. She would have been glad to hear if he had met any of the other men out cutting wood, or even if he had seen a fox or a hare or a bright-red bird. These were the little incidents she remembered her parents talking of at the end of the day, but Peter had no tolerance for such chatter.

Instead, after the meal, he would generally pray a long prayer and recite a Psalm, then give Mary a lecture about how she must be a good girl and obey God. Tonight, however, he pushed away from the table as soon as he was done eating.

"I am going out to chop some of that wood," he said, taking his cloak again.

"Very well," Meg said, clearing the bowls from the table. "No prayers or Scripture today?"

He shot her a glance. "What do you care? You sit like a stone idol through it all, and the youngster squirms and wriggles like a puppy. I doubt either of you gets any good out of it." And he was gone, the door shuddering in its frame behind him.

Mary looked up from under her tangle of curls. "Is Papa angry?"

You mean, more angry than he commonly is? Meg thought but did not say. "Aye, he must be," she said, hoping Mary would not ask a dozen more questions about her father's surly mood. Though Peter had brought back a decent load of wood, he acted as if he had had a bad day. Something must have happened out in the woods to upset him.

Meg had finished tidying the house and put Mary down to bed by the time the ring of the axe fell silent. The sky had already turned to twilight. Even then, Peter did not come into the house. She opened the shutter and looked out to see him walking down the path toward Simon's house. Their long, wrangling conversations about Scripture and politics continued to occupy both men, but it was late tonight for a visit to any neighbour. They would all be up at dawn about their work again.

Meg laid everything out ready for the morning, took off her kirtle and shift, and put on her nightdress, shivering a little before she dived under the heavy quilts that covered their bed. Most nights, Peter fell into a deep sleep, punctuated only by loud snoring. Though Meg longed for more children, she was relieved that Peter rarely reached for her or troubled her in the night—once every few months, perhaps, not more.

He had explained that it was not God's will for them to have more children. Meg was not good enough to be a godly mother to children, especially to the sons Peter wished to have. So she was always in the difficult position of trying to prove herself righteous and good enough to be a mother again, while recognizing that if she ever became good enough to meet his standards, he might start once again with the swiving that she was glad to be shut of.

She had fallen into a fitful sleep by the time she heard the door open, then the latch falling into place. He said nothing to her as he stripped and pulled on his nightshirt, but when he came to the bed, instead of getting in and saying, "Good night, God keep you," as he generally did before sleeping, he stood before her and pulled her to her feet, then lifted her face up to his own and crushed her mouth with a kiss.

She could not remember the last time they had kissed. In that first summer of marriage, perhaps? When they did come together now, it was in darkness, eyes averted, the business managed as quickly as possible. But there was something different in her husband tonight. His hand came to her breast, squeezing it painfully, and then they were on the bed, Peter on top of her with a fierce urgency she had never felt in him before.

She cried out a little, once, with pain, and he slapped her face and said, "Shut your mouth" and went on with it. Quick and hard as if he hated her, hated that he had to do this but somehow could not stop.

When it was over, he rolled away to the wall, his back to her. Instead of the weary relief she felt at other times, Meg felt bruised, though whether in body or spirit she was not sure. She curled up into as small a ball as she could, closed her eyes, and hoped for dreams that would make her forget.

CHAPTER ELEVEN

January 1655

It had been a dreary Christmastide, if you could even call it that, Meg thought. The governor had declared there were to be no celebrations; Christmas was the same as any other day. At New Kirke House there had been prayer-book services, a feast on Christmas Day, games and dancing on Twelfth Night. The Kirkes kept these celebrations to their own household, knowing that Governor Treworgy would not dare touch them directly. But when the Bullard boys tried to organize the other planters' sons to go mummering, Peter had informed the governor, and the Bullards were forced to cancel the mummering and pay a fine they could ill afford.

Now it was the bleak cold of January, with its snows and chills. Two people—Henry Sproul and his wife—died of a fever. Everyone had been afraid sickness would sweep through the community, but there had been no outbreak, perhaps because everyone stayed at home by their own hearths.

In some households, that might have been cozy and comforting. Meg hated the winter days and long nights cooped up indoors with Peter, whose moods were unpredictable. He and Simon had gone on one hunting trip that took them into the woods overnight, and Meg enjoyed more than just the fresh game they brought back—she revelled in being alone in the house with Mary.

Apart from hunting and woodcutting, Peter had one distraction: he and Simon were learning to read the Bible. The Puritan minister who came last summer had begun tutoring them after the fish was in; when he returned to New England in November, Mistress Treworgy had offered to be their teacher. Meg thought this was a good thing—if Peter could read, and somehow managed to get hold of a Bible, it would at least provide some variety to his recitations over the supper table. As it was, they were limited to the Psalms and gospel passages Peter had memorized, which made for a fair degree of repetition.

He had gone this afternoon for another such lesson, leaving Meg to her own work. She was spinning wool while Mary wound the yarn up into balls with a steady, frowning attention. A tap at the door startled her; her nearest neighbour was Peggy Tolliver, but Peggy was now well advanced in her pregnancy and would not be out walking on a cold winter day. Meg was delighted to see Hannah at the door instead.

"Your man is out, is he? I saw him going along the road up to the governor's house," Hannah said as she took off her wrap. "Is he gone checking rabbit snares with the governor and Henry Yard?"

"No, him and Simon are off for another reading lesson,"

Meg said. "Sit down, have some ale and a slice of bread with jam."

"I'll take the ale and thank you, but I've something better than bread." Hannah sat at the table, and Mary, having lost all interest in wool, came toward her to see what she unwrapped from a square of cloth in the pocket of her kirtle.

"Christmas pudding!" Meg exclaimed with delight as the rich smell of dates, figs, and brandy rose from the square of pudding. "Oh, how lovely. Mary, you will like this, for 'tis very sweet."

"I laid aside a slice for you when we had ours—myself and the Kirke House servants—after Twelfth Night," Hannah said. "There's enough for you and Mary both to have some, and have it all gone before your man comes back chiding you about pagan puddings."

Mary laughed along with the two women, without knowing why. Meg would have to remember to tell her that the Christmas pudding was a secret, as keeping secrets from Peter was the only way she could bring any shred of pleasure into their lives. She sang to Mary when they were alone, merry little songs she remembered from her childhood, and played clapping games and skipping games. Mary already understood that her papa would prefer to hear her recite Bible verses and that she should save the songs and games for her mother.

"Tell me all about it, about the folk at the new house and their grand Christmas and what they had to eat," Meg said.

Hannah recited as much as she could recall. How they had cooked a goose so big it barely fit in the fireplace; how Master George Kirke and his new wife had tried to play the hosts, but Lady Sara overrode them at every turn; how young

Master David and Master Philip had returned from Boston full of tales and new games and insisted on dancing. How the younger lads had gotten everyone playing blind man's buff, servants and all.

"A deal of work for you and Mistress Durdle and the Cotton girls," Meg said, "that big goose and all the rest of the food, and cleaning up afterwards."

"'Twas indeed, but at least we were able to have our bit of Christmas merriment, though nobody else could."

"I am sorry Peter do be making so much trouble for everyone else over Christmas. I think him and Simon urge the governor on to be stricter than he would on his own, truth be told."

"No need for you to be sorry. At least the rest of us need not be married to him," Hannah said. She fell quiet after that, and Meg felt, as she often did with Hannah these last few months, that her friend was leaving much unsaid. There was a core of sadness in Hannah she had not known before. In the autumn, when they worked side by side at the laundering or the garden, it was easy to put off such talk, but in the quiet of winter she could not ignore that sadness.

"Mary, you have had your bit of pudding now, and Aunt Hannah and I must have some grown-up talk. She will do her sewing while I spin, and you may take your poppets and go play in my bed."

Mary slid off her chair, grabbed the two much-worn rag dolls that Meg had made for her, and ran for the privacy of the other room. Time without chores was already a rare treat in her young life. Meg sat back at the spinning wheel, and Hannah took from her bag a needle, thread, and a petticoat in want of mending.

"Did you say the governor is gone into the woods?" Meg asked.

"Aye, Henry Yard and his boys were going off to check their snares and thought they might shoot some birds, said they might spend the night in their tilt back in the woods. Sarah Yard told me the governor meant to go along with them. There was a little party of them went off this morning—I thought for certes your man would be with them."

"He never said aught of it, only that he was going up to the big house for the mistress to give him another Scripture lesson." Surely Peter would not go away overnight and not tell her? He had taken no blanket or food for a longer journey, and when she looked behind the door, she saw his gun was still there. So he had not gone on the hunting expedition.

Meg's thoughts turned from her own affairs to Hannah's, but she was unsure how to frame her question. Once, over the summer, Meg had asked her about Stephen Barstow, the fisherman with whom she had seen Hannah walking along the shore. Hannah had said nothing more than that he seemed a kind man, but neither of them had any prospects. Now that the season was over and the fishing servants had shipped back to England, Meg guessed that Hannah missed Stephen, but it felt like prying to ask her directly.

Instead, she asked, "How is it, spending the winter in Lady Frances's new house? Much different, I suppose, from working at old Kirke House."

"Aye, 'tis more work for me in one way, less in another. Her ladyship means to hire a girl to help, but she will put me to work making fish again in summer, so 'twill be no ease for me."

"Hard work, making fish," Meg agreed, thinking of the long hours of summer, the ache in her feet and back standing at the flake, the smell of fish and the chafe of the salt on her skin.

"Hard work for all, but you have something to show for it," Hannah said, a rare note of bitterness in her tone. "Your husband is prospering—he has a shareman, you have chickens and goats, you've added onto your house. The work be hard, but it counts for something."

Until now, Meg had never troubled herself to wonder about the arrangement Lady Frances had with Hannah. For Hannah to have come across the ocean with her mistress suggested either indenture or great loyalty, but if she was indentured, her time must surely soon be served. "And you . . . does your lady pay you no wages?"

"No, and has not since we left England. She gave me to understand that she would reward me for my work once she had control of her own fortune. But she has her fortune now, all right—a house and boat and fishermen of her own."

"And for you . . . ?"

"Nothing." Hannah's needle stabbed quick and fierce into the seams of the petticoat. "In her way of looking at it, I am not even free to leave her service if I wish. She says I owe her for my passage over here and the room and board I have had since then. With all my labour about the house, the fish, the garden, even Governor Kirke's bloody tavern, there is not a penny put aside for me even if I were allowed to go my own way!"

Meg had thought what Hannah was hiding was sadness, but she saw now it was anger. "That hardly seems fair! Did you sign an indenture with her before you left England? For how long?"

Hannah shook her head. "There were no papers. Her

husband paid me wages when we were still in England. When he arranged to ship her out here for safety, she promised she would look after me if I stayed with her. I never asked her what that meant."

"You trusted her."

"I did. Only to find out that she thinks of me as—no reason to dress it up—as her slave."

The word *slave* fell harsh on Meg's ear. She knew that a great many people of Hannah's complexion, people who came from Africa or whose parents had come from there, were held in bondage in other colonies. The few African folks she had ever seen in the New Found Land, apart from Hannah, were sailors or summer fishermen. She had always assumed them to be free men, or perhaps indentured. Hannah told Meg that her own father was a free man in England, and her mother was an Englishwoman. Could a person go from freedom to slavery, without their even knowing?

"But you have served her so well, so faithfully!" Meg found it hard to believe Lady Frances could be so harsh.

"Too well. Too faithfully. I have laboured five years for her in this country and not a thing to show for it—not even the freedom to come and go as I please, which any fisherman's daughter might do if she went into service."

The fire sputtered in the hearth; Meg rose to put another log on it. "Were you . . . did you have a plan to leave her service? Did you want to go away anywhere?"

Hannah's laugh had no humour in it. "Do you mean to ask, did I have an offer of marriage? Not much of a one. Stephen said that he had a little money laid aside, and if I did also, we could talk of marriage. But I told him what Lady Frances said, that I was both penniless and bound to her service. And now he is gone back to England." She sighed. "Tell nobody that I told you this, least of all that husband of yours."

"I would not! But there must be a way out, a way for you to be free and have what is owed to you."

"I see no way. And no benefit in talking of it." Hannah held the mended petticoat up to the light; her neat stitches were so perfect Meg could scarcely see where it had been torn.

They talked of other things, then. When Hannah packed her sewing away, Meg felt restless and offered to walk along with Hannah as far as Lady Frances's house. "'Twill do myself and Mary good to get some fresh air, cold as it is, and on the way back I will stop in and bring a posset to Peggy. She is close to her time now, and the pain in her back is something terrible," Meg added with a smile. Hannah knew what an effort she made to be pleasant to Peggy Tolliver.

Meg was surprised, when she parted from Hannah on the path, to see Simon outside his house chopping firewood. Was the reading lesson over? "Come, Mary," she said. "We will go see Aunt Peggy and Uncle Simon, and then home to make dinner for Papa."

"Will Aunt Peggy have Christmas pudding for me?"

"No, and you must not say you had it. The Christmas pudding is a great secret, between you and me and Aunt Hannah, so you must be very quiet about it."

"Can I say that I was helping to spin?"

"Yes, you may always say that. Little girls must learn to spin and weave and sew. But do not say anything at all, unless Aunt Peggy speaks to you."

"Children must be seen and not heard," Mary said, an adage she was better at reciting than following.

Simon paused his wood chopping as Meg and Mary approached. "Have you come to see my Peggy, then?" he asked. "She's in a terrible way with the bad back today."

"'Twill be a short visit then. I brought some willow bark she can brew up to help with the pain," Meg said, "but I will only leave it and be on my way." She hesitated a moment, then said, "Are you not up at the Treworgys' today learning your letters with the mistress, then?"

"Ah, no, I gave that up long ago, after the first or second lesson," Simon admitted. "God wants every man to know the Scriptures, but it seems He did not give every man the gift of reading. When I tried to learn my letters, they danced and jumped around on the page like flies on a pile of fish guts, so I had to give up trying."

Meg smiled. It was the first thing she had ever heard Simon say that had a hint of either humour or humility in it, and she felt a little thawing toward him. "I have never tried to read myself, but it must be a hard thing to learn, especially for a grown man. Perhaps 'tis easier for children." It was on her lips to say, *Is Peter still learning it, then? Is he up there at the big house all by himself?*

But she did not ask, only took Mary by the hand and went into the house, to offer a balm to the poor sufferer.

Hannah went into the kitchen to begin preparations for the evening meal. She liked the kitchen in Lady Frances's new house; it was smaller than the kitchen at the old Kirke House, but it was all her own, with no Mistress Durdle to order her about. Had it not been for the resentment she had nurtured ever since that conversation with Lady Frances about her wages, Hannah would have been well content in her warm kitchen on this cold January day.

She heard voices in the outer room. Lady Frances was giving orders, to judge by her tone, though Hannah could not make out the words, nor could she tell to whom she was speaking.

She left the kitchen under the pretext of confirming the supper menu and was surprised to see Lady Frances with two thin, pale young people: Elias Sproul and his sister Annie. Looking frightened, clad in threadbare clothes, the two children—they must be fourteen or fifteen, she thought, but the word *children* did not leave her mind—stood a little apart from Lady Frances. As Hannah emerged into the main room, Lady Frances took the girl's arm in a firm grip.

"Ah, there you are, Hannah. I was just coming to the kitchen, to bring Annie to you. I have taken her and her brother on, Annie as maid and Elias as manservant. Come, Elias, I will bring you out to Richard, and he will show you what's to be done." The girl looked frightened enough to run away, but Hannah suspected she lacked the energy or the gumption.

The Sprouls were poor. Henry Sproul had worked for the Kirkes as a fishing servant in the summer and a man of all work the rest of the year and lived with his family in a house that was little more than a tilt. When Henry and his wife took the fever, they had died within a few days of each other. The main feeling in the community had been relief that whatever plague killed them had not spread through the whole settlement; that there were still two Sprouls left, this half-grown boy and girl who looked like they had never eaten a square meal in their lives, had not been much discussed.

"I suppose you know a bit about cooking, helping your mother and all?" Hannah said to Annie when she got her into the kitchen.

The girl nodded, then wiped her eyes and nose with the sleeve of her ragged shift, whether overcome by tears at the mention of her mother or simply rheumy, Hannah could not tell.

"Did Lady Frances tell you much about what work she expected you to do?"

"Help in the kitchen and clean the house. Work in the garden and at the fish in summer." The girl's face was downcast, but she darted a quick glance at Hannah. Her eyes were a blue-grey so pale you could almost see through them, and her untidily braided hair was the colour of damp straw. "She told me to do what you said."

That was good. A new maid would be useful if it was clear that Hannah was in charge of her. "Start chopping those carrots and parsnips," she said. "Do you have anything—any clothes, I mean—that you brought from your home? I am not sure where Lady Frances means to put you to sleep, but you could put your things away before you start work."

"I got no things . . . mistress," the girl said. She left *mistress* hanging, clearly not sure how to address an older woman who was a fellow servant, and a Negro servant at that, but in authority over her.

"You'll call me Hannah." She wondered what the girl would think if she knew she was addressing a servant who was paid nothing, was owed nothing, was not even free to leave of her own will, which presumably Annie Sproul was. Struck by a thought, Hannah added, "What has Lady Frances said she will pay you for your work? Room and board and . . . ?"

It was no business of Hannah's to ask, but Annie would not know that. And she replied promptly enough, "Four pound a year, in coin or in trade goods, for me 'n' Elias together. To be paid in autumn, after the fish is in."

"Well enough. So, her ladyship said nothing about where you're to sleep? There is a little storeroom here off the kitchen . . ." Hannah had been about to say, *We can rig up two beds there for you and your brother*. Then she thought of her own little chamber. It was on the second floor, where the family slept. If the hungry little Sprouls were inclined to thievery, better not have them sleep next to the kitchen and its stores. Though the room off the kitchen was smaller, Hannah felt pleased at the idea of her own space, set apart from the family. It was warmer here, as well. "I mean to move my bed down here," she went on, "and you and Elias can have my room."

"Yes . . . Hannah." Her name so whispered, Hannah hardly heard it.

"Come with me now, I'll show you the room and some bedding. Then you can come back and help me with the vegetables. Master Richard brought home a fine brace of partridges from the woods, so I'll be stewing them for supper."

Four pounds a year between two of them. It was a pittance, but along with bed and board it must have seemed generous to Annie and Elias, who looked as if they might have just sat in their parents' house until they were turned out of it, then lain down on the ground to starve.

If Lady Frances were to offer Hannah two pounds a year—the wage she had earned back in England—she would take it in coin, not in trade goods, and put it away for the future. Indeed, if she had done that since their arrival, Hannah would have ten pounds now. What a start that would be!

Back in the autumn, before Stephen Barstow's ship had sailed back to England, Lady Frances had forbidden Hannah to see him again. Hannah had been able to slip away only once to speak with Stephen, to tell him that she had no wages coming to her, nor even the freedom to leave and make a life of her own.

"She cannot do that," Stephen had insisted. "You've no indenture, no contract binding you to her service for a set time, have you?"

"Nay, nothing ever signed. But then, I cannot read, so what good would it do me?"

"'Tis against the law, to bind a free man or woman to service for life."

"What law? The law in England? But we are not in England." The law in the New Found Land was what the governor said it was, and Hannah had no reason to believe Governor Treworgy would look kindly on her desire to leave her mistress's service. True, he was no great friend to the Kirke women, and he might take Hannah's part just for the pleasure of crossing Lady Frances. But even if she were free to leave, without coin in hand there was nowhere to go. Even Stephen could see that and did not make any romantic promises about taking a penniless bride.

"Best you go your way and forget about me," Hannah told him. "Lady Frances won't hire you on for her crew again next year, now that she knows about us."

"Working for your mistress is not the only work along this shore," Stephen said. "I might come out on one of the fishing vessels for the summer and fish for a ship's master."

Hannah had said nothing to that, only wished him goodbye. She was more fond of him than she had realized, but without any prospects, she could not cling to false hope, nor encourage Stephen to do so.

She turned her thoughts away from Stephen to think of something more pleasant: the partridges, perhaps, swinging plump and promising from the young master's hand. These young Sproul orphans, too, had been brought into the house as a pair, ignorant as shot birds, and she hoped they would have a happier fate. But mostly Hannah wanted their coming to make her own life easier. If service to Lady Frances was all she could look forward to, that service had best be as pleasant as possible.

"Show me now what you have learned since the last lesson," Patience said, sitting as close to the warmth of Peter's body as she dared. They were not alone; no one was ever alone in a house like theirs, especially in winter. From the kitchen she heard the clatter of Martha and Eliza cleaning up from the noon meal. Charity slept in her cradle by the fire. Josiah and Matthew were near the hearth, kneeling in close attention over their carved wooden soldiers, lining them up for mock battles. Josiah, being the older and choosing first, was of course playing as Cromwell and the brave army of Parliament, while Matthew's soldiers must be the hated Cavaliers. Their father often told them stories of the war in far-off England and how God's cause had prevailed over the tyrant king.

The boys, warned to be quiet, played in piercing whispers while Patience bent over the big open Bible with Peter. He and Simon Tolliver had told the minister that they wanted to learn to read Scripture; when the minister left, John suggested that as Patience and the children were staying for the winter, and she was teaching the lads to read and write, she might as well teach two grown men.

"Reading only, I believe," Patience had said. "They said naught of wanting to write."

"Reading is well enough. I believe the common folk should be able to read God's Word," John had said. "Only do not teach them to cipher—'tis no advantage to the merchant, if the fisherman can reckon the value of his own catch."

He laughed, and Patience was assured that this venture had the blessing of God and her husband. There was no reason at all to remember that strange hour back in the autumn, berry picking alone with Peter Taylor. Teaching him to read the Bible would surely make up for any sin that had been committed.

But Simon had given up the effort after two lessons; he said he could not make head nor tail out of black marks on paper. And while Patience and Peter were under John's eye in the house, his eye was not always watchful. Today, with the clear and sunny skies, her husband had strapped on snowshoes and taken their manservant Solomon with him on a hunting trip. He told Patience not to worry if he did not return by dusk; they might spend the night in the Yards' tilt, but he would come home with fresh meat. He had left Isaac to look after the household of women and children.

Patience had the Bible open to Exodus, chapter twenty. "Now, 'tis no good to ask you to read the commandments, for you know them by heart and will recite them from memory," she said. "But look at the page, and tell me can you find Remember the Sabbath day."

Peter bent his head over the page; his dark hair tumbled over his forehand. She clasped one of her hands over the other to stop herself reaching out to brush those curls away from his eyes. His finger moved slowly over the page and she looked at the Bible instead of at his face, but his hands were so long and strong, they stirred the same unruly desires in her.

"There it is." His finger moved beneath the words. "Remember the Sabbath day to keep it holy. Six days shalt thou labour and do all thy work . . ."

"Very good! I can see you truly are reading it. 'Tis good that you have so much Scripture off by heart, but once you can read well, you will be able to open any page of God's Word and find His messages to you."

She remembered her own lessons, her father teaching her the letters and simple words. *Even a girl must learn to read Scripture*, he had told her, *for someday you will be a godly mother and teach your children in turn.*

He had said nothing, of course, about teaching a rough, unlettered fisherman whose dark blue eyes and long, hard body called to her with deadly temptation. But the letters were the same.

Peter's finger kept moving down the page, and he read what he saw there. *Honour thy father and thy mother . . . Thou shalt not kill. Thou shalt not . . .*

Did his voice catch before he said the words "commit adultery"? He looked up; their eyes met.

"You are saying it by heart again. The commandments are no use—you know them too well."

"True enough. When I was a child, our preacher was a great one for memorizing Scripture. But that was only the commandments and the Lord's Prayer. I learned a good deal more later, when I started going to meeting on my own."

"Let me find another passage." Patience took the Bible from him. His hand dropped from the table, not into his own lap but onto her skirt, resting lightly there.

She did not jump or pull away; she kept turning pages. Leviticus, Deuteronomy, the blood-soaked books of the Judges and Kings. He had not touched her since that day on the hillside. He would not dare. She felt blood racing through her body. The pressure of his hand grew firmer, no longer just lying on her skirt, but pressing on her thigh.

"I should apologize to you," he whispered. "For that day. I took liberties. I know 'twas wrong."

She kept turning the pages. Psalms. Yes, plenty of good reading there. "We were both wrong," she said. "We both sinned."

"But the greater fault is mine, is't not? Being a man. For woman is more likely to fall to temptation." His hand was still on her thigh, his eyes locked on hers.

"If you know 'twas a sin, why d'you touch me now?" Her voice a whisper, and surely her little boys, playing at the other end of the great hall, could not hear.

"I cannot help myself."

"None of us can help ourselves. We must pray for strength."

"I do! Oh, I do!" There was real anguish in his voice. "I have prayed so many times over that day, for forgiveness and strength to do right. And now—"

"Here, this is the Psalm I meant you to read!" Her voice came out high, light, hurried. His hand stroked through the heavy homespun wool of her gown. "Do you know this one?"

"I know a good many Psalms." He dragged his eyes from her face, back down to the book, breathing hard as if he had been running.

She pointed at the first words. "It says at the start, *To the chief Musician. A Psalm of David, when Nathan the Prophet came unto him, after he had . . .*"

Peter's finger, tracing the words, stopped. "I thought 'twould be the same as the other words. In the commandment. Commit adultery."

Of course, reading or not, Peter knew the story. "Indeed, 'tis what they did, but here it only says he—"

"*. . . he had gone in to . . . Bathsheba."* He stumbled a little over the name. The lustful king, summoning the wanton woman who had brazenly bathed on her rooftop in sight of the castle.

"Go on," Patience said. His hand was still moving, higher and higher on her thigh. "Go on and read the Psalm," she added.

Again, his other hand rose to trace the words on the page. "*Have mercy on me, O God, according to thy . . . loving . . . kindness?*"

"Yes . . . kindness." His hand was too far up her thigh now. She put her own hand over his, meaning *stop*, but his hand turned toward hers, fingers interlacing.

"*Ac . . . according unto the . . . mull?* Mulli . . ."

"Multitude."

"*The multitude of thy . . . tender mercies? Blot out my . . . trans . . . trans . . .*"

"Transgressions."

"*Blot out my transgressions.*" He turned now, his face dangerously close to hers. "God forgives our sins, Mistress Treworgy. All we folks be conceived in sin, we're too weak to resist. But God forgives, if we're of his elect. He will forgive it all."

Their hands, under the table, still twined. Her children just a few feet away. There was a fault in Peter's theology, but she could not name it.

The main door to the house banged open, and although they were out of the direct line of sight from the door, Patience pulled her hand from Peter's and jumped away from him on the bench as Isaac came in, stamping snow from his feet.

"Mistress." He nodded respectfully to her, gave Peter a curt nod. Isaac could not read and had never shown any interest in it. "'Tis a fine, large day out there. I thought I might take the little lads out for a bit, help me pick up the logs while I cut wood. 'Twill be good for them to get out and run about."

"Oh, yes!" Again, the voice that came out did not sound like her own. "Yes, do take the children, they will like that so much!"

With Isaac and the lads gone, there was only the sleeping baby in her cradle and the voices of the maids on the other side of the kitchen door. The spell was broken now, Patience thought; God had sent Isaac to remove temptation. Having seen the boys out the door, she turned back and crossed the room. She opened her mouth to tell Peter he must go, but he was still tracing words with his fingertip, reading aloud.

"*Behold, I was shapen in . . . iniquity . . . and in sin did my mother . . . conceive me.*" He stood up, moved toward her. "'Tis true, is't not? Every one of us full of iniquity, conceived in sin."

Somehow, his hands were on her waist. *We are given strength to resist temptation*, she wanted to say.

His mouth was hot and firm on hers, his tongue parting her lips. She wanted his hands on her skin, on every part of her body. She meant to pull away but reached in, pulling him closer, pressing her body against his.

Charity whimpered in the cradle. Patience knew she could not commit this sin, not here, with her child sleeping by the hearth and her maids in the kitchen. But if she did not sin, she would surely die.

Trembling with hunger and fear and eagerness, she drew Peter Taylor toward the small chamber her husband used as his study, both stumbling in their eagerness. She locked and bolted the door. The room was dark; it had no window. *Men loved darkness rather than light, because their deeds were evil.*

His busy hands all over now, unlacing her gown, pushing aside the shift. Her hands under his shirt, running over the taut muscles of his belly. He was so strong, so young, so alive. Her breath came faster and faster.

For I acknowledge my transgressions: and my sin is ever before me, was Patience's last thought before she surrendered completely.

CHAPTER TWELVE

Spring 1656

Edward Richard Taylor was born on a chilly, wet day in June, when fog rolled in off the water and summer seemed to have changed its mind about ever arriving. The last fortnight had been warm, and Meg had been glad that, being so near her time, she was spared work on the flakes and in the garden. She had thought that being born in sunshine and warmth would be a good omen for her child.

But when her pains began, the morning was damp, grey, and cold. Peter was already out on the water. Six-year-old Mary grew wide-eyed and frightened when her mother began to cry out. "Go down to the flakes," Meg told Mary through gritted teeth. "Find Aunt Hannah. Tell her Mama needs her."

Mary ran more quickly than she usually did to obey an order, eager to get away from this strange, crying mother.

Hannah would understand, Meg knew. She could collect Granny Love on the way. *It will not be long*, Meg told herself over and over.

Peter would say she should pray. She did not know any prayers that were good for a woman in labour, though she said, *God help me, please, God help me*, over and over through gritted teeth.

If Peter were at home, would he pray for her? Meg used to think her husband was gruff, sometimes cold and indifferent, a hard man but a fair one. But something had changed this last year. Sometimes Meg thought Peter hated her.

This child was born from Peter's hate. He had started demanding Meg's service in bed again but with no shred of tenderness. He seemed disgusted, as if there were something dirty about swiving his own wife. His touch was rough, and he would not look at her afterwards.

Meg braced as another wave of pain washed over. *God help me. It will not be long. God help me. Peter hates me.*

She was no fool. She knew that not all marriages were happy. She knew that the act of mating was joyous for some people, sometimes, and a business to be gotten over with at other times. And sometimes it was violent. She had not thought it could be that way between a man and wife, but sometimes, of late, when Peter took hold of her in bed, it felt as if a stranger had caught her in the woods, pinned her down, and forced himself on her.

And one of those times, back in the autumn, he had planted this seed in her. *God help me. God forgive me. God forgive him.*

Finally, finally the sound of the door, and voices. Mary's high-pitched fear, Hannah's low soothing. The midwife's voice, crackling with age. Who else? Oh, Peggy Tolliver. Where had they picked her up?

"There now, all's well, you're going to have a grand hearty son to give your husband," Peggy said, in what she meant to be a comforting tone, as Granny Love reached up under Meg's skirts to feel how far along she was. "I told the Negro woman to see to the youngsters, Mary and my Tommy—she can bring them all over to the Yards' house so Sarah can watch them. Then I told her to go on again; we don't need her poking her nose in around here."

Meg pulled all her strength together, air into her lungs, power into her voice. "No! Tell Hannah to stay. I need her here."

"Pshaw! What need have you of Lady Frances's servant?"

"*I . . . want . . . Hannah.*" Hannah had been by her side when Mary was born and when she lost the last baby. Would she lose this one? Meg did not know what to hope for. She wanted another baby. But Peter said she was not good enough to be a mother.

Granny Love, straightening from her examination, said to Peggy, "If she wants Hannah, you take the youngsters, and tell Hannah to stay here. A woman in labour should have whoever she wants by her side. She's not got long to go, now."

It will not be long.

God help me.

It will not be long.

Pain, again, the shuddering swell of it. Peggy's shrill voice: "You keep back, I will tell you if we need you. Give me that."

"Hannah!" Meg ground out the word in the trough between waves of pain.

"Here, I brewed you a posset." Hannah's cool voice, a cup held to Meg's lips. Granny Love, saying, "Aye, that will help with the pain, but don't be giving her too much. She needs her strength. Soon be time to push."

Time to push.

Not long.

God help me.

Peter, forgive me.

Back in her kitchen at Lady Frances's house, Hannah filled a pail of cold water to scrub her face and arms. Granny Love had birthed the child; Hannah had taken the baby boy to clean him and wrap him in soft cloths. There was blood on her hands and the smell of the birthing chamber about her.

"Watch out for her ladyship," Annie said, entering the kitchen just as Hannah finished cleaning her hands. "She asked me why you were gone so long and never worked at the fish today. I told her you was helping at Meg Taylor's birthing bed, and she said there wasn't no call for you to be doing that, you're not the midwife."

Hannah sighed. "'Tis not your worry, Annie. Her ladyship will chide me herself, I am sure. Have you done aught with the evening meal?"

"I only just got back in from working at the fish myself."

"No matter. I had the stew cooking on the hearth there all day, and I made the bread before I went out this morning. Help me get it all ready for the table."

Annie set to work quickly. The girl had learned a good deal in her months in the household. She was not a bad worker and was gaining a little spirit, though she was still easily cowed. "The Frenchman is coming tonight," she said as Hannah added a sprinkle of salt to the stew and stirred the pot.

"I thought he might," Hannah said. Monsieur Beliveau was a French merchant who had come to Ferryland to trade. Lady Frances had invited him to dine twice already. Merchants did not usually linger so long, generally sailing away as soon as their business was concluded. But Monsieur Beliveau had been ashore for a fortnight, staying at Kirke House, and it was apparent he was paying court to Lady Frances.

"She'd not marry him, would she? A Frenchman? A Papist?"

"That is not your concern, nor mine. Lady Frances's affairs are her own," Hannah said. She did not want to encourage Annie to gossip.

"No, but what if she were to up and get married and go off to live in some foreign place? She'll take you with her wherever she goes, but me and Elias got to look to ourselves. We could be out on our ears with no work and no place to live."

Annie was probably right. If, after all this time, Lady Frances were minded to take a second husband, even one so outlandish as a Frenchman, she might leave Ferryland. And if that were to happen, she would take Hannah with her. Not because Hannah wanted to go, nor even because Lady Frances needed her so much. But because Lady Frances believed Hannah was her property.

Two years Hannah had lived with that knowledge, turning it over and over in her mind. She had spoken of it to no one since she sent Stephen Barstow away and confided in Meg. Even telling Meg had felt like putting too much trust in another person. But who else in this harbour—in all the world—would care whether Lady Frances's servant was free or enslaved?

When the family was seated for supper, Hannah brought out the dishes, leaving Annie in the kitchen to start cleaning up. She did not trust Annie's skills at serving when Lady Frances had company. Monsieur Beliveau was seated beside her ladyship, a very fine-looking fellow in a blue velvet jerkin, his long greying hair curling about his shoulders. On his first appearance as a guest at Lady Sara Kirke's house, he had excited much attention by appearing with a short, powdered white wig covering his own hair. It was the latest fashion in France, apparently, for men of status to cover their own hair with these wigs. Like most of the servants, Hannah was of the opinion that it was a foolish piece of vanity and much preferred Monsieur Beliveau with his own natural hair. He had quickly conformed to the English custom, and the wig had not been seen for several days.

Also at the table were Lady Frances's sons and one of her nephews, David Kirke. David's elder brother Philip had returned from the brothers' sojourn to Boston and built himself a house on a piece of Kirke family land near Renews, where he was setting himself up as a planter. David, now nineteen years of age, had shown no such inclination for adult pursuits. He had moved into George's household and seemed to have taken up his elder brother's former occupation of flirting—and worse—with servant girls and fishermen's daughters. Lady Frances maintained a soft spot for him nonetheless, although he and Master Richard seemed to rub each other the wrong way and be forever quarrelling.

Master David was witty and kept the table lively with his talk, which was likely why his aunt had invited him to sup with them. As Hannah went back to the kitchen, there was a great burst of laughter at some jest young Master David had made that Monsieur Beliveau had capped with another clever saying. Hannah dished up a bowl of stew for herself. "Go call Elias in," she said to Annie. "He needs to eat, and so do you."

Elias had been fishing in the morning and gutting and splitting cod all afternoon. For all of them, the summer workday was long to take advantage of the light evening hours, and if women left the flakes a little early to prepare a meal for the hungry menfolk, that only meant trading one labour for another. As Hannah looked out the open window, she saw a dozen or more men trudging up from the shore, the day's work done at last. Some of them headed toward the cookhouse where the Kirke and Hopkins families housed their summer fishing servants. Others, planters and their servants, went toward homes where the woman of the house would have a meal ready to lay before them. In an hour or two, everyone would fall into bed, exhausted, to sleep a little before dawn roused them to work again.

Hannah was not in the habit of gossiping with Annie about her betters and did not like to encourage such talk. She did not say aloud what she was thinking: that not one of the folks sitting around Lady Frances's table tonight would understand that ache in the bones, the chafe of salt on the skin, the utter weariness that fell like a heavy cloak on you at day's end. Everyone here lived and died by the fishery, but some never had to dirty their hands with it. Lady Frances's sons took turns working in the boat and on the flake, for Master Richard thought it necessary to learn the business from the ground up, but it was like play for them. They could do it for a few hours and then set it aside, leaving the hard labour to their servants.

There was a noise at the kitchen door; Elias let himself in. He hesitated in the doorway. "Get in here, there's stew for you," Annie said, glancing over her shoulder.

"There's a man out here," Elias said, not to his sister but to Hannah. "Off the ship what came in today. Says he's looking for Hannah."

"For me?" She could only imagine one man who might have come off a ship looking for her by name. Shooing Elias into the kitchen for his supper, she stepped out into the twilight as Stephen Barstow stepped toward her.

"Hannah. Thank God, you are still here."

"Where else d'you think I'd be? I told you I'm not free to leave here."

He had looked so hopeful, so glad to see her. Now, as she reminded him of reality, his face grew sober, and she was sorry to have put out that light in his eyes. "I know it," he said. "You were plain enough with me. I thought I could put you from my mind, and I made no shift to return last summer, thinking 'twas all hopeless."

"You thought aright."

"But you wouldn't leave my mind despite all that, so I signed on to a sack ship making a voyage this way. I had to see you again. To see if—well, if you had any fondness for me, still."

She softened her tone. "'Tis not been easy to put you out of my mind, either. But I told you the truth when I sent you away."

Two years ago, he had taken her in his arms and kissed her. Only twice: once when they spoke about marriage, and once when he said goodbye. She wanted to go to his arms now, but there was no shelter, no safety for her there.

"I know you say there's no way under the law for you to be free of your mistress. I don't know about that. Hard to say what the law is and what it isn't, out here on these shores."

"But whatever the law is, 'tis always on the side of the rich."

"True enough. So, what about . . . outside the law? Would you go without leave? Run away from her?"

"I have thought of it. But I can see no way to do it. I've naught to support myself."

"On your own, sure enough. But, with me?"

"Are you asking me to run away with you?"

He hesitated like a man about to step into the icy waters of the sea. "Yes. Yes, I am. Hannah Peake, will you run away with me?"

Meg lay abed nursing little Edward—Neddy, she had taken to calling him, the same nickname as her father for whom she had named Neddy. Peter had not wanted the baby named after himself, which did not surprise her. He had glanced at the child no more than two or three times since it had been born, and said it would be baptized next time a godly preacher came into the harbour. That was the extent of his interest.

Meg herself could not stop gazing at Edward's perfect little face, his dark eyes and pursed lips, the small button of his nose. "Is he not pretty?" she said to Mary, who sat at the foot of the bed playing with her poppets.

Mary stretched to see that baby. "He looks the same as he did before." She did not say whether that was pretty or not.

Someone knocked at the door. Peggy had been there that morning with a pot of stewed eels, and young Clara Bullard, whose lively company Meg enjoyed far more than Peggy's, had come later with a pork pie and stayed for a visit, agreeing that Neddy was indeed a beautiful baby. None of Meg's neighbours would knock; they let themselves in, knowing she was still in her confinement. "Go answer it," she told Mary, "and be polite to whoever is there."

Mary ran off, happy with the novelty of answering the door. "Mama! 'Tis a lady!"

A lady? Meg tried to picture Lady Frances, Lady Sara, or perhaps Mistress Helen Kirke at her door. When any of the fishermen's wives had a child, the ladies would send a small token with their servants. Hannah had already brought bread from Lady Frances's kitchen, and Lady Sara's maid had come with a brace of ptarmigan. Their duty had been done.

But it was a lady indeed—Mistress Treworgy, the governor's wife—who trailed into the bedroom behind Mary. She wore a sober but well-cut brown woollen gown with a broad collar that looked whiter and cleaner than anything in Meg's whole house. "Goodwife Taylor," she said, "I heard you had been brought to bed of a boy and came to bring you God's blessing."

"Oh, do you carry that about with you?" Meg asked. "God's blessing?"

She could scarce believe her own pertness, and Mistress Treworgy seemed taken aback as well. She settled onto the one stool in the room, though Meg had not invited her to sit. "Any Christian may give God's blessing to another," she said. "I brought a honey cake as well—'tis on the table out there."

"Ah, I thank you. The cake will go down well." Meg stopped herself from saying *Even if the blessing sticks in my throat.* She did not like this prim, tidy woman with her pale eyes and her constant stream of advice about how other women ought to behave and raise their children. But Mistress Treworgy had as yet said nothing offensive, Meg reminded herself, only brought her a cake and said she was coming to give her a blessing.

"Is he a good baby?" Mistress Treworgy asked, peering at Neddy in his blanket.

He is an infant four days old, there's no good nor bad to him, Meg was tempted to answer. She tempered her response to: "I 'low he be as good as he can be. He cries when he's hungry or needs his clouts changed, and he takes the teat with a right good appetite."

"Even the youngest infant has a wayward spirit, you know. It is original sin, the fallen nature in all of us. You must not pick him up every time he wails—you will teach him to have his own way."

"Yes, mistress. Should I hold off nursing him, too? To teach him that life is hard and poor folk must go hungry?"

Mistress Treworgy startled as if she had been pinched. Meg was, again, surprised at her own brazen tongue. She had an uneasy feeling that if she gave saucy answers to Mistress Treworgy, word would get back to Peter, and he would have one more reason to berate her as a bad wife and mother.

"Every child must learn obedience and humility," said the governor's wife. "I will pray for you and your child." She went to her knees and instructed Mary to do the same, though at least Meg, still leaning upon her pillow, was spared having to get down on the floor.

Mistress Treworgy had the decency to pray for the health of the child and the swift recovery of the mother—nothing wrong there. But her prayers, like Peter's, meandered from petition to sermon, giving the impression she was not so much asking the Almighty for blessings as drawing his attention to the shortcomings of others.

"And we beseech thee, Lord, out of the abundance of thy mercies, that since thou hast blessed Margaret Taylor with a son, thou wilt make her worthy to shape him into a godly man. That she will be swift in discipline and train him to patient endurance and longsuffering."

"And bear in mind, Lord, that he is but four days old," Meg interjected as loudly as she dared.

Mistress Treworgy stumbled a bit but went on. "Indeed, Lord, the child is but four days old, yet the sinful nature that is within all of us from the moment of our birth will rise up in him and must be crushed and trampled underfoot that he learn godly humility, and his mother also, that she may learn to curb her sinful ways—"

"In the name of Jesus Christ, Amen!" said Meg. Mistress Treworgy's eyes blinked open, and Mary echoed, "Amen!" and scrambled up from her knees.

"That was very impertinent," said the governor's wife.

"Was it?" Meg was tired, and every part of her body ached. "I'll have no more talk about trampling my poor little baby underfoot, or any such thing, and you can take your blessing with you. Take your cake as well, if I have to pay for it by listening to a sermon."

Mistress Treworgy stood up, her petticoats rustling. "Well, I never heard such talk—and from one in your position! I will—the governor will tell your husband to correct you."

"What goes on between me and my husband is none of your concern," said Meg. To her surprise, the other woman flinched, as if that, more than any of Meg's other tart-tongued words, had struck her to the core. Without another word, Patience Treworgy turned and left the house.

When the door slammed, Meg said, "Mary, go see if she left her cake on the table. I'd love a piece of honey cake."

That night, after darkness had fallen, Patience heard a whistle outside her open window. She saw no one but knew that Peter was nearby, hidden in the trees. They had used this signal before. He knew she was alone tonight; everyone knew when the governor went away.

If she did not come down, he would go away—it had happened before. He would make no fuss, do nothing to bring trouble. Perhaps he even hoped she would not come down. She knew that Peter's sense of guilt, his desire to resist temptation, was as great as hers. They had prayed together for strength to stop sinning.

She was putting on shoes, pulling a shawl around her shoulders, even as she told herself she would not go out. She crept out of her room, past Martha's room, past the larger chamber where the children slept under Ruth's care. Ruth had been hired on a trip to Boston, a good girl from a devout family who came to care for the children when Eliza Yard left to be married. Patience hoped, as she slipped down the stairs, that Ruth slept as soundly as Eliza had. Their menservants slept in a room off the great hall, the better to hear any noise or danger while the master was away.

Out the kitchen door and across the yard to the stand of spruce trees that bordered their property. She could not see Peter, but he whistled again, and then she saw him in the clear moonlight. Three steps, and she was in his arms. For one moment, nothing else mattered.

"You should not have come," she said when she broke away from his kiss.

"I fought with myself, tried not to come. I could not stay away—it has been too long."

Even as they spoke of trying to resist temptation, he pulled up her nightdress, his rough hands stroking, touching, probing. Her breath caught in her throat. They were past the point of turning back, past the point where sin or guilt mattered at all. They had reached the moment when she thought, as she always did, *I would sacrifice heaven for this. I would burn in hell for all eternity, just to know this moment.*

When it was over, he draped her discarded shawl back over her shoulders. "You visited my wife today."

"I thought it only . . . proper." Her breath was still ragged; her heart raced. She was furious at the saucy answers Peter's wife had given her, the woman's spirit of open rebellion. But how could she speak, here and now, of another woman's sin?

"I do not like to think of you being in that house. With her."

"I did not like to go. But 'twould be stranger if I did not." She visited all the planters' wives when they had babies. "We must not—we *must* not—meet like this again," she added.

"Aye, you are right," Peter said wearily. "But I fear we will."

In the crisp moonlight, another kitchen door opened. Another woman slipped outside, glanced around cautiously, and moved toward the shadows of the trees. "I cannot stay long," said Hannah.

"I know. But we must talk, before my ship leaves on the morrow."

"It has all been said before, has't not?"

"Kiss me."

"Kissing changes nothing."

Stephen took her in his arms. Hannah had been thinking of this every moment since he had appeared at the kitchen door two nights ago, but the first minute they had been able to steal was this nighttime meeting. It would profit nothing, yet she could not deny herself this small joy.

"You're sure that changed nothing, are you?" he said with half a grin as the kiss ended.

"Naught that counts in the real world. It don't change my lack of fortune, or yours."

"I told you I've a bit put away. I had some good luck on voyages last year."

Now she did pull back to look at him. "Trading voyages?" Usually sailors would be paid an agreed-upon wage at the end of the voyage; luck rarely entered into it. But there were other kinds of voyages. "You've turned pirate."

His grin was wider now. "You make it sound like I converted to being a Catholic, or a Mohammaden. A man don't turn pirate and stay that way all his life. I'm on an honest merchant ship now, doing an honest job. But last year, aye, I crewed with a ship that sailed on the other side of the law. Better money in it, and I put a bit aside."

"Why did you give it up?"

"They'd no plans to come to the New Found Land. I had to get back here, to tell you I've enough coin for us both, now."

"You'll win me away with your pirate gold?"

"A bit of silver, more like. We'd not be rich, but we needn't starve, neither."

Hannah had few thoughts one way or another about piracy. She did not like to think of Stephen stealing from innocent folk ashore, but ships of one nation often captured those of another and seized their cargo. If poor men could make a little money from rich men's cargo, she'd not weep over it. "It does not change the other matter, though," she said. "Pirate silver or no, my lady'll not let me walk out of her house like a free woman."

"But if you could get away without her knowing, away to some other place, to make a new start?"

"Where d'you mean to go?"

He frowned. "I've not worked that out yet. You know why I don't want to go to the southern colonies. But this land is bloody hard, and 'twould be hard to hide from your mistress here, even if we went to another harbour."

"Back to England, then?"

"I'd never own a piece of land to call my own there. But I'd not care overmuch, if you were safe and we were together."

She was silent, trying to picture it out in her mind. Leaving Lady Frances, heading off into the unknown with this man she had known so briefly—and his ill-gotten silver.

"You are going away tomorrow," she said. "I can hardly stow away aboard your ship."

"Nay, hardly that." He laughed, seeming glad she would even consider it. "But we will put in again here in the autumn, at the end of the fishing season. Mayhap by then you'll have an answer for me."

Off in the distance, deeper in the woods, she thought she

heard voices. A woman's voice, rising to a sharp, gasping cry.

Stephen chuckled. "Some fisherman and his lass, up to the same business we are in the woods tonight, I 'low. But we'll not take it so far as they're doing, not until we've sewed up a plan. I'm not a man to love you and leave you."

"Thank you for that," she said, though part of her wished he had fewer scruples. Should she not have at least one night of pleasure? But he was right, the risk was too great. "I must go back now. My lady will look for me before she goes to bed."

"How much longer will you stay in Ferryland?" Frances asked.

"In truth, *cherie*, my business here is done. I have lingered only to visit longer with you. But that is not good business."

Frances had never imagined herself looking for a second husband. And a Frenchman? A Papist? But Chrétien Beliveau was good-looking, and wealthy, and when she had first met him at her sister's table, he had turned his attention to Frances, even though Sara had been there, full of witty conversation as she always was.

"I should not wish to get in the way of your business. But it has been . . . pleasant to spend this time with you."

"Never fear, this will not be goodbye as you English say it, only *au revoir*. Till we meet again. I return here at summer's end, before I go to spend the winter in Boston. My daughter will join me there. She is a good girl, raised by nuns, but I would wish to have her with me now. We have been too long apart."

Frances knew that Monsieur Beliveau had been widowed ten years, and his only child was this daughter, who was fifteen now. Frances had learned so much about him in the few short hours they had managed to spend together. She could not deny the pleasure in being courted, treated like a woman who could still evoke desire.

"You should run away with me," he said suddenly. "Tomorrow! Come aboard my ship and see the world with me! After Plaisance, we go on to the French colonies at Port Royale and Québec. This English colony should not be all that you see of the New World."

Frances laughed. "It would not be good business for me, either, to leave my plantation in the middle of the fishing season! There is much here for me to manage."

"But your son, your Richard," he pronounced it the French way, *Ree-sharr*, with rolling r's at either end, "he is clever, and very capable. You will leave it all in his hands soon, will you not?"

"Someday. All this is for him, but he is not ready to manage it all yet." As she said it, Frances wondered if that was true. Richard was steady, mature for his nineteen years. "And," she added, "I am no foolish young girl, to run off with a man on a moment's notice."

He laughed—a lovely, deep chuckle that warmed her all over. "Of course not. But, *peut-être*, when I come back, would you consider coming to Boston with me? A little voyage? You have seen nothing in seven years but these same hills, these same forests, this same seashore. And though your New Found Land is beautiful in its way, you know there is much more to the world. Boston is a real town, like you have not seen since leaving England. It is not Paris, nor even London, but there is more than one street, there are markets, there are churches."

"Not my sort of churches, nor yours."

"No. But God will understand, if we were to go to Boston and enjoy it a little, do you not think?"

"I will consider it," said Frances.

He kissed her hand. "That is all I hope for."

CHAPTER THIRTEEN

August 1656

"Now that the governor has brought Reverend Wyvern here, I mean to have the child baptized this Sunday," Peter told Meg. "Simon and Peggy will be godparents. He is six weeks old; 'tis a good time for it."

Meg nodded; there was little for her to do but agree. In the old prayer-book worship form, six weeks after the child's birth, the mother would be churched and welcomed back into the community after her confinement. But Meg's churching would be to tie little Neddy into a sling and go down onto the flakes to return to work, which the midwife had said she should be able to do this Monday. As for Sunday, she was not sure whether Peter would even want her to attend her own son's baptism.

He had been angrier than usual ever since Meg had turned Mistress Treworgy out of the house. Meg was sure he would have beaten her had she not still been in childbed.

Now, he said, "I had thought to ask the governor and his wife if they would do me the honour of standing as godparents, as they did for Eliza and Rafe's babe. But after your behaviour to Mistress Treworgy, I dare not even ask."

"I am tired of hearing about that woman," said Meg. "Why should I listen to Mistress Treworgy tell me how to raise my children and conduct my household?"

Peter's eyes blazed. "You should listen because she's as far above you as the sun is in the sky over us." He pointed up, though the day was overcast; they were outside in the yard while Meg spread the washing out over the bushes.

"I know she is a rich woman and married to the governor."

"You know I care naught for that! Worldly titles, wealth—the Scripture says that's no better than a dung heap. She is above you because she is a godly woman, one who puts the care of her soul above—"

He broke off suddenly, as if the unexpected passion in his voice had choked him. "You'd do well to learn from her, is all," he said, and turned to go back into the house.

Frances and Richard were walking back from New Kirke House, where they had attended the Sunday morning service and stayed for dinner. Nicholas had remained behind to pass a few idle hours with his cousin Jarvis.

"That was a good service. I do think George is becoming better at leading out. He ought to let you read the gospel more often; you did a fine job this morning."

"Thank you, Mother," said Richard.

"And you take it seriously. When David reads, I always

feel he is laughing up his sleeve at God."

Richard laughed. "Now, Mother. Has the morning's worship not put you into a frame of mind for Christian charity?"

As they approached their own house, they met Henry and Sarah Yard and their children coming from the Treworgys' house; some distance behind them trailed the Tollivers, and farther back still, Frances spotted Peter Taylor, with his wife and daughter trotting behind, Meg carrying the new baby. It seemed that by the time the Kirkes had finished their prayer-book service and had a leisurely dinner, the Puritans had only just been released from what was surely an interminable sermon.

Frances opened her gate. Richard had helped young Elias Sproul to build the fence and hang the gate in the spring, so the house stood out even more from the straggling fishermen's shacks that surrounded it. Frances took great pleasure from opening the gate and closing it behind her.

Richard smiled at his mother. "You are pleased with this house, are you not?"

"I am. 'Tis good to have our own place, and I am proud of how our position here has improved. Even so . . ." She sighed.

"Even so, you are thinking about going away," Richard finished.

She gave him a sharp glance. She had said nothing to him of Chrétien Beliveau's proposal, though she had been turning it over and over in her mind in the weeks since the Frenchman's ship had sailed. "You knew?"

Another nicety Richard had added was a bench by the front door of the house; she sat down now, enjoying the view of the harbour as the devout Puritans straggled back from their meeting. Richard sat beside her.

"I thought you might be considering it."

"I have been considering leaving this place ever since we got here. But I never thought I could go away."

"Because you thought only of going back to England, and that door is still closed."

Frances took a deep breath and looked out at the sea. It was a warm day, with a brightness to the veil of clouds that looked as if sunlight might soon break through and blue sky appear. It would be a good day for fishing, but on this one point only, Frances was in agreement with the Puritans: The sacredness of Sunday must be upheld. Most of the fishermen took Sunday as a day of rest—those who did not attend either the Anglican or the Puritan service slept late for once in the week, let their children play outside and the young people stroll along the beach, briefly free from the endless circle of labour.

"You have guessed, then, that I have received an offer," Frances said.

"Aye, from the Frenchman. I heard him say he would return at summer's end, before going to Boston for the winter."

"I have never thought of marrying again," Frances said.

"But if it is your wish . . ."

That is the difficulty, she thought, *knowing what I wish.* She wished to marry handsome and wealthy Chrétien Beliveau, to sail on his ships and live on his properties, free of the hardscrabble soil of this colony and the ever-present smell of codfish. Free of the burden, which her woman's shoulders were not built to carry, of overseeing and managing every part of the business. And yet there was something in that burden that she enjoyed. These last two years, managing her household and plantation, she had felt valuable in a way she had not felt since the days in Newport, when she and William had been at the centre of the king's network of allies and spies, plotting his escape, vital to the royalist cause. This was a different sort of work than she had done as the king's number 47, to be sure, but Frances could not deny that she enjoyed it.

"The French are very civilized," she said now to Richard. A statement that did not in any way answer his last comment, about her own wishes. "They still have a king on the throne and have been good to our young king in his exile. Englishmen who still respect the king have reason to be grateful to France."

"So 'twould be no shame to marry a Frenchman."

"No. And he is a good man. He would be kind to me. All this . . ." She looked around at the house, the garden, the dance of light on the sea beyond it, the boats tied up at rest. "All this is for you and your brother. When you are ready to take it on, there is no more work for me here."

Richard looked so serious; was he eager to be master, no longer ruled by his mother? "I am ready, Mother. I think you ought to go—at least to Boston, for now. When you return, we can talk about the future of the plantation."

She nodded. There was a relief, finally, in having an adult man to help her make a decision. "He is wealthy and has only a daughter," she added. "Instead of marrying a young woman who can give him sons, he wants to marry me. This marriage may benefit you and Nicholas also."

"He may settle everything on his daughter."

"It is possible." She thought of Suzette, this convent-raised French girl she had never seen. "But he has a great deal of wealth and a generous spirit."

"Leave Nicholas here with me," Richard suggested.

"'Twill be good for him. I can spend the winter teaching him more about keeping the accounts and managing the business, things he will need to know."

She had feared that Richard would not want her to go, that he would feel unready to be master. But Richard was eager to take on the challenge, ready to send her off to Boston with the Frenchman.

It was a great relief, Frances told herself. She was proud of Richard. Of course she was.

A week after Neddy's baptism, Governor Treworgy went to St. John's, one of the busiest of the summer fishing stations, on some official business with English captains there. Peter told Meg this in the same breath as he told her he would be repairing the front steps at the Treworgys' house after he came in from fishing.

"Why do they need you? They've two menservants of their own, and a slew of their fishing servants if they want to take a man away from the fish," Meg pointed out.

"'Tis not for you to question the decisions of your betters. If the governor asks for me, I am glad to help."

"Help? Are they not even paying you for this? In the one season of the year when we have a chance to get ahead, you are *helping* the governor out of Christian charity?"

"Christian charity! As if you would know anything about that." And he went out, banging the door behind him, which made Neddy cry out. Mary did not even look up from the sampler she was working at; she was accustomed to her father's anger, and that made Meg sad.

Meg remembered Hannah saying, years ago, *I think your husband is not a good man.* Meg had defended Peter, then, sure there was goodness in him. Now, if someone said that, she would not trouble herself to speak in his defence.

For three days Peter went to work on the steps of the big house at the end of his own long workday; Meg was abed by the time he came in. On the third night she awoke between midnight and dawn and saw that he was not lying beside her. Had he gone out to the privy? She waited, but her husband did not return.

Meg got up, finding her shawl and her shoes by the moonlight that filtered through the shutters. Neddy was asleep in his makeshift cradle and Mary in her small bed. Meg went to the door and stepped out into the cool night, all the while questioning the impulse that sent her out there.

Peter was not in the privy. Peter was nowhere about the place. She looked up at the moon, judging how late it was. Where could her husband be at this hour?

Meg stood outside her house, shivering. After a minute she left the house where her children slept—*only a few moments*, she promised silently, as if they could hear her thoughts—and took the path up toward the Treworgys' house. It was still and silent, as all the houses were at this dark hour.

Then she saw it—someone walking across the garden space behind the governor's house, going from a little outbuilding toward the house itself. A long-skirted person who moved like a woman, like Mistress Treworgy. A woman who walked into the house as if she owned it.

Meg felt coldness spreading through her chest. There was no reason, none at all, for Mistress Treworgy to be out of her house at this hour of night, moving furtively from her own outbuildings to the kitchen door. The only woman out at this hour would be a woman doing something illicit, most likely meeting a lover. And on that thought, Meg saw the lover come out of the small building and move toward the path that led away from the governor's house, down toward where Meg stood in the shadow of a birch tree.

Meg turned toward her house, hurrying to be back inside before Peter saw her. Pieces fell into place in her mind—Peter's doe-eyed admiration of Mistress Treworgy, the way he followed her about like a faithful spaniel. His coldness to Meg, the haughtiness of the governor's wife. Was it possible? The only other possibility was that Peter was dallying with one of the Treworgys' maids, but it was impossible to imagine him having a secret tryst with the matronly, officious Martha or the meek, nervous Ruth.

She was not quick enough to get to the house ahead of him. She heard his footsteps but did not look back.

"What are you doing out here at this hour?"

She turned to face him, waited until he was closer to answer. "I might well ask you the same."

"You might not. What a man does is his own business. What a wife does is her husband's business."

"I'll tell you what I was doing. I woke to go to the privy, found you were gone, and went looking to see if some ill had befallen you."

"Ha! A likely tale. Went sneaking and spying about, more like."

"And what if I did?" She was bold now, having caught him in wrongdoing. "A man who is doing right needn't fear being sneaked and spied upon."

"True enough. So you'll only have seen that I was out on the road. I could not sleep and went to walk about and clear my head."

She could nod, accept that, go back inside and play the good wife. But anger burned in her belly. All the times he had preached and prayed at her, told her she must be a better Christian, that she was not worthy to bring up his children—all the while, he was breaking a commandment.

"Just walking about, was it? Walking to the storehouse behind the governor's garden, while he is away, and sneaking out of it like a thief."

"I am no thief! I—I left something behind when I was working up there and thought I might see if 'twas there."

"Is that so? And the mistress, she was out in the middle of the night helping you look, I suppose? I saw her as well."

His face was easy to read: guilt and anger but no surprise or confusion. So it had not been one of the serving-women, then.

"You scheming, lying little baggage! How dare you accuse me?" His hand moved quickly, slapping her across the face. "That's for your impudence. Never speak to me that way again."

She looked up at him, his face outlined in the moonlight. "You talk plenty to me about a wife's duty to her husband. Seems to me, from the little Scripture I know, a husband's got a good deal fewer duties, but I know one that he does have, and that's to be true to his wife and not go running about with other women."

Now he gripped the front of her shawl, just below her throat, pushing her back against the door. "Never, *never*, speak of this again, d'you hear me? Not to me and not to anyone else. You'll forget what you saw tonight if you value you own skin—and that of your two brats in there."

That silenced her. Until this night, she'd have sworn on her life that while Peter was a hard man, he was also so upright that he would never betray her with another woman. Nor had she imagined he would threaten their children.

But everything had changed. Meg lay mutely in the bed beside this stranger, her husband, and wondered what was to become of her.

On Saturday night, when her work on the flakes was done, Meg washed both Mary and the baby in a tub of water she had heated over the hearth. Neddy cried and squirmed, Mary protested. Peter had gone back down to the shore right after the evening meal; in the long summer light, he and his men could get in a few more hours salting and storing the fish.

"Noooo!" squealed Mary as Meg tried to scrub a week's worth of filth from her skin. Peter would take Mary to Sunday meeting tomorrow, leaving Meg at home with the baby. Neddy had been brought to church for his baptism, but Peter did not trust Meg to keep an infant quiet in the service on an ordinary Sunday. He insisted that Meg try to make Mary look "like a Christian child, not some half-wild creature," as she was old enough to benefit from the service.

Three days had passed since Meg had confronted Peter about Mistress Treworgy. They had not spoken of it since; indeed, they had barely spoken at all. Meg felt as if the print of his hand was still on her cheek where he had slapped her, and the picture of him slipping out of the Treworgys' outbuilding was burned onto her mind just as clearly. She felt suspended in midair, as if she had fallen off a cliff, yet somehow had not yet hit the ground. Something must change, but what?

The door opened and Hannah stood there, looking like she was ready to burst with news. "Have you heard tell what's happening down at the shore?"

Meg loosed her grip on Mary, who smartly stepped away, out of range of the washcloth. "Nay, only the men working at the fish. What else?"

"The ship that came in today from St. John's? There were two women aboard it, and one of them is stood up on Sam Thomas's stagehead, preaching."

"Preaching? A woman?"

"So Master David Kirke told me. He just went down the road telling everyone. He thinks 'tis a great lark. Will you come with me to hear her?"

Meg looked around at the chaos of the room—her wet, half-dressed daughter, her crying baby, the tub of warm water, half of which was splashed on the floor, soaking through the rushes and making a muddy mess. All so that Peter could take his daughter to church in the morning and look like an upright Christian father, while he sat there making eyes at his lover.

"I don't see how a woman could preach a sermon," she said, "or what man would allow her to. But give me a moment to dress Mary and wrap up Neddy, and I'll go along with you."

She had no idea why Hannah, who had always seemed indifferent to preachers and sermons, was suddenly so interested. Perhaps the novelty of a woman doing something no woman could do? With Neddy back in his sling and Mary trotting at her mother's heels, the two women followed the path that led down to the shore, where a small crowd of fishermen and their wives had gathered around the Thomases' stagehead.

A tall woman with dark hair was addressing them, her voice pitched to carry above the sound of waves and seagulls. "You all know God's judgment is coming on those who carry on with drunkenness and gambling and cheating and stealing and lying, all those committing adultery, and all who oppress the poor!" she shouted.

"'Tis the same old tune," Meg whispered to Hannah. "God's judgment on sinners."

"Aye, but it sounds different in a woman's mouth, don't it?"

"Men believe they can rule over other men's consciences—aye, and have power of life and death over them," the woman preacher went on. Though her dress was as plain as any Puritan's, her accent spoke of good breeding and education; this was a woman from a well-off family, Meg thought. "The poor man scrabbles for his crust of bread while the rich man sits in luxury, thinking himself better. The minister stands before the congregation telling them how to pray, as if one man is closer to God than another. 'Tis all blasphemy! Each of us stands before God in our own soul, as simple as if we stood before him clad only in a shift, with no trappings of court or church to cover us up."

Meg saw it in her mind's eye: herself in her petticoat before God's judgment throne. And beside her stood Peter and Mistress Treworgy, both of them in their nightshirts, facing the same judgment.

"Within each one of us, king or Lord Protector or governor, is the Divine Light. God is in everyone, from the highest to the lowest, if we will but see him there. For there is neither east nor west, Jew nor Greek, male nor female, slave nor free, but all of us are one in Christ Jesus. Those are the words of Scripture."

"They are?" Meg said. "I never heard that bit of Scripture before."

"Nor me neither," said Hannah, "but what if 'tis true? Neither man nor woman, slave nor free?"

Meg was not surprised to see Peter and Simon approaching. She was only surprised they hadn't gotten there sooner. "You come down out of there now," Peter called to the woman. "We men be working here, this is no time and place for preaching."

"And preaching is no job for a woman to be at!" Simon added. "The governor is on his way down here. We've sent for him to command you be silent."

"No male nor female, all one in Christ! I do wish to meet your governor and see the Light of God within him, as he may see it in me."

"Blasphemy!" Peter shouted.

"Not fit for a woman to be speaking the Word of God! Shameless!" came another voice—Meg thought it was Dick Kean.

"And Sunday morning's the time for preaching!" someone else shouted.

"Tomorrow morning, come again!" said the woman, her voice rising with an unmistakable note of authority. "Come aboard the *Fair Wind*, and myself and sister Mary will have a word from the Lord for you!" Then, quick as a mouse under a door, she scrambled down the ladder and back toward the small boat where a sailor waited to row her back to the ship.

"They call themselves Quakers," said John Treworgy.

"Quakers?" echoed Patience. She had not been paying the closest of attention to her husband's conversation, her mind being full of other things while her hands were busy mending Josiah's torn breeches. She knew only that there had been a disturbance at the shore earlier in the evening involving some unruly women who had arrived on a ship earlier that day.

"This woman who was pretending to be a preacher," John explained. "'Tis a new sect lately sprung up over in England, even more reformed than the reformers. They are in the habit of becoming so filled with the Spirit of God that they shake as if they were taking a fit. Folk call them Quakers."

"And these . . . Quakers, they allow *women* to preach?"

"They allow anyone to preach. Every Quaker seems to be a preacher, from what I hear. Women, servants, paupers—if they feel moved to it, they just stand up wherever they may be and start making a speech. Several of them have already been arrested in England for irregular preaching, and now 'tis spread to Boston and other ports along these coasts."

"The whole world is running mad," Patience said. She stared out the window with its commanding view of the harbour, the ships in port all flying their brave and colourful flags. Who knew what poisonous ideas were coming ashore in those vessels? Women preachers might be the least of it. "What did you tell them?"

John shrugged. "I did not trouble myself to talk to the woman herself. There are two of them, it seems, one called Hester Biddle and another Mary . . . something. I went to the ship's captain and asked him to use his authority over the women, but it seems he and half his crew have been converted by the women, so he is allowing them to preach aboard his ship tomorrow."

"Can you not stop it? Or at least tell our people not to go hear them?"

"Oh, I am sure Reverend Wyvern will have plenty to say about it; I'll not trouble myself further," John said. "I've enough business to attend to without trying to stop mad-women prating at fishermen. They'll be gone soon enough, at any rate."

"Good riddance." Patience, like John, had more on her mind than women preachers. Earlier in the week, while John was still away in St. John's, she had slipped out at night once again to meet Peter. She had refused to go into the forest—out of doors, she felt too exposed. So they had met in the small outbuilding where the gardening tools were kept.

As always after a tryst, she felt not only guilty but frightened. What if someone had, in fact, seen them and was only waiting to reveal that deadly knowledge? Perhaps one of her own servants had been waiting for John to return home, to tell him of his wife's betrayal. She was sick with worry.

It is the last time, she told herself. She had wrestled with God in prayer, promising Him anything and everything if He would only forgive her and shield her from discovery. She would not only give up Peter, she would fast, she would deny herself any small pleasure. Whatever might wring from God the promise of protection.

The next morning, Hannah told Lady Frances she would not accompany the family to New Kirke House for Sunday service.

"I mean to go hear the Quaker women preach aboard the *Fair Wind*," she said.

"What? You can't mean such foolishness, Hannah."

"I do." Hannah fixed the last of the pins in Lady Frances's hair and handed her mistress her hat. "I want to hear what they have to say."

"Was't not enough, the bit of foolish prattle you heard last night? I'm told the woman made a great spectacle of herself."

"It was enough to make me curious."

She saw Lady Frances draw in her breath as if to say, *I forbid you*, and then check herself. She wondered if Lady Frances had any suspicion that Stephen Barstow had returned briefly to Ferryland. Did she suspect that Hannah was once again trying to find a way to leave her service? Perhaps her mistress felt it best not to be too strict, not to provoke Hannah to rebellion. *And if that is how she feels, that can only benefit me*. If she had ever truly cared what Lady Frances thought about anything, that feeling had been crushed years ago.

"It will go a long time; these ranting, reformed preachers always do. See that you are back here by the time I return from dinner at my sister's house."

Hannah bowed her head. "I will be, my lady, never fear."

This Sunday morning, the cove was even more divided than usual. The Kirkes and Hopkinses were up at New Kirke House for their prayer-book service, and the Puritan faithful trailed up to the governor's house as always. But there was also a group of half a dozen people, Hannah and Meg among them, who boarded the *Fair Wind* and sat among the sailors. There, a different Quaker woman got up to speak about sin, salvation, and this Quaker idea of an inner light that filled every person, both low and high.

Hannah's mind drifted; she noticed that Lady Frances's observation about long sermons was certainly accurate, and she missed the familiar rhythm of the prayer book and its responses. What struck her most was that unlike the gentlewoman who had preached yesterday, this younger Quaker woman spoke with a strong Yorkshire accent, and her speech sounded like that of a poor woman. She glanced from the woman's face to her hands, which flew about as she spoke, as if every word needed a gesture. The hands were as work-roughened as Hannah's own; this preacher was a servant, a poor man's daughter.

When the service was over, the Quaker-converted sailors went back to their posts aboard ship, and the curious residents of Ferryland began to return to shore. Hannah turned to Meg, who was soothing her restless baby. "You go ahead. I want to talk to them. The preachers."

"I can wait for you."

"Nay, you'll want to be back before your man comes out of his church service. No need to make him wroth by knowing you've been here."

"He'll find out soon enough," said Meg with a resigned sigh.

Hannah watched her friend go, thinking how hard Meg's life was, with that stern and bitter man. She had the idea that things had been worse than usual in that household of late, though Meg had not confided in her. But for now, Hannah had her own troubles to think of.

"Could I have a word with you, mistress?" she asked, approaching the woman who had just preached, who had introduced herself as Mary Fisher.

"I am no one's mistress, but we are always glad to talk

with any who are eager for the Word of God. Sister Hester," she added, turning to the woman who had spoken yesterday, "this friend wishes to speak with us."

The other woman sat down beside her fellow preacher. "Indeed, we have come here to bring the word of God's Light to all and to share his word."

"'Tis about the Word of God I want to ask you," Hannah said. "You recited a text when you were preaching yesterday, about there being neither slave nor free in Christ's eyes. Is that Scripture?"

The woman nodded. "'Tis Scripture indeed, from St. Paul's epistle to the Galatians."

Hannah was not sure what a Galatian might be, but she had been turning that phrase over in her mind since last night. "So Scripture says nobody should be kept as a slave?"

Hester looked at Mary, as if unsure which of them should answer this. It was Mary who spoke. "God makes no difference between high and low. I was naught but a scullery maid, but his Light is in me as much as in friend Hester here, though the world would make a difference between us."

"So there is no difference?" Hannah pressed. "Servant and master, slave and free?"

Mary frowned in thought, as if she had not considered this question before. "No difference in God's eyes, but the world makes differences between us. The same text says *neither male nor female*, but God still made us man and woman."

"But you do things a woman is not supposed to do. You preach, you travel about."

"Yes," Hester said. "God makes no distinction when he calls anyone to his work."

"So what of slaves and freemen, then?"

Something in the woman's look softened. "Are you a slave?"

"No!" The word burst more fiercely from Hannah's lips than she had intended. "Neither born, bought, nor sold as a slave. But my mistress thinks I am. She says there is no way to end my indenture to her, even though I never made my mark on no contract. She says I cannot leave her service."

Both women, so sure and confident when preaching, now looked uncertain. "The Scripture says servants must obey their masters but also that masters must treat their servants well," Mary said. She looked to Hester as if hoping the elder woman would have an answer.

"There is a story in the Bible about a slave who ran away," Hester said in her well-bred tones, "and St. Paul told him to go back but told his master to take him back as a brother in Christ, not as a slave."

"I've no wish to be her ladyship's sister. I only want to be free."

"And you've come to us because . . . ?"

Hester let the question hang, and Hannah had to think. Why had she felt driven to seek out the Quaker women? Because of that one verse about slaves and freemen, yes, but also because they were women who were doing something so far outside the realm of what she had always been told was proper. If they could get up and preach to men, could they also use the Scripture to set free someone unjustly bound to slavery?

"I hoped you could help," Hannah said. "Mayhap something from the Scriptures could convince my mistress, or the governor here, to let me have my freedom."

A smile touched the corner of Mary Fisher's mouth.

"I misdoubt your governor will listen to us. Indeed, 'tis more like we will be told to leave, even flogged, as we have been told in other places. But let us talk together about this, and pray over it."

Hannah nodded. A promise to pray about it was less than no use to her. But as she turned to go, Mary Fisher put that work-roughened hand on her arm. "Can you come back this evening? We will have another service before sunset."

"I'll not be given leave to come for a second service," said Hannah. She had one weapon, at least: assurance that those words truly were in the Scriptures. Governor Treworgy made a great noise about following the Bible. Perhaps, armed with those words and what Stephen claimed the law said in England, she might have a case to put before the governor.

Patience knew that the children found Sundays tiresome; it was their sinful nature. The Scriptures said that the Sabbath should be a delight. But Patience remembered childhood, going to meeting in the morning, returning home to a long afternoon when one was not permitted to play, only to listen to Bible readings and prayers.

Apart from trying to keep the children quiet and occupied, Patience usually enjoyed Sundays now, liked the change from daily routine. But today she sympathized with her children; the hours seemed to crawl.

John had plenty to occupy him. He sat on the bench outside their house and talked to the men who came to see him, some to complain about the Quaker women, some to argue that the Quakers had good gospel teaching and should be allowed to stay and say their piece, even if they were women. The windows were open in the midsummer heat, and Patience heard the men's voices drifting in from outdoors as she told the children the tale of Daniel in the lion's den, one of the better Bible stories for keeping their attention.

She had caught Peter's eye in meeting that morning, and he had looked away as always, dropping his eyes respectfully as he sought to keep his unruly daughter quiet. But at that moment, and again when she tried to catch his gaze before he left at the end of the meeting, Patience felt something different in Peter's look. Something closed, shuttered, frightened.

After the Sunday evening meal, John took charge of the boys and their Scripture lesson while Ruth put Charity to bed. Patience, desperate to leave the house, filled a pot with the remains of Martha's stew. Sallie Kean had recently borne her sixth child and was still abed with a fever. Patience thought a visit of Christian kindness would help the sick woman and take her mind off her own troubles.

The Kean woman was grateful for the stew—beef was a rare treat, as most of the settlers could not afford to keep cows or to buy such costly meat from the Kirkes. Patience spent a half-hour amid the chaos of wailing children, prayed for the sick woman, and was on her way back to her own house before the sun dropped toward the horizon.

The road took her past the Taylors' house. Though Peter prided himself on the modest prosperity his hard work had won, Patience saw his home for what it was: a peasant's house, little more than a tilt. She had not only sinned, she had stooped low in sinning, to a man who was far beneath her. Somehow looking at Peter's house made her feel twice as guilty.

Too late she saw the child, little Mary of the tangled hair and dirty face, playing in the yard. Her blue eyes, so like her father's, met Patience's with curiosity. Patience turned to go before the child said anything.

But she had miscalculated—she had been looking in the wrong direction and not seen Meg coming from her henhouse. "Mistress Treworgy!" the woman called in a clear, sharp voice.

She could walk past. She could pretend she had not heard. But something about that tone convinced Patience that if she tried to ignore Meg Taylor, the other woman would chase her up the road, making a spectacle of them both.

She turned back, trying to mould her face into that of a godly woman doing her duty to the poor of the village. "Greetings, goodwife Taylor. Do you need something of me?"

"Do I need something of you? You know well what I need of you, mistress." Now she was standing right in front of Patience, with only a rail fence between them. "I need you to stay well away from my husband."

"Your husband? I've nothing to do with your husband, save that he has done some work for my husband at the house." Patience hoped her voice did not shake or betray the pounding of her heart.

"No? Not when you were giving him them lessons, teaching him to read Scripture? Did you teach him to read the commandment about adultery?"

Those words on the page, and Peter's hand on her skirt, touching her thigh through the fabric. Blood rushed to Patience's cheeks. "I tutored your husband and Tolliver a little, but 'twas not seemly for a woman to teach a man, so I stopped. That was more than a year since. Why are you making trouble about it now?"

"Hard to say. Mayhap because I saw you and Peter leaving the storehouse by your garden in the dark of the night, four nights ago. Were you having a prayer meeting there, I wonder?"

"You—you were sneaking . . . spying? What kind of wife are you? Scurrying about at night when you should have been home with your children!" The words were out before Patience realized she should have denied everything.

"Just as my husband should! Just as you should! Everyone ought to be in their own beds, but not everyone is, it seems."

"Shut your mouth, goodwife Taylor. You know not of what you speak."

"I know very well what I'm talking of, and so do you."

"And what if I do?" She looked Peter's wife up and down with as much dignity as she could manage, given her racing heart and blushing cheeks. "If you tell anyone this tale, and both your husband and I deny it, who in this harbour will believe your word over ours?"

Meg was silent a moment. Patience thought, *There, she will back down; she knows she cannot speak against her betters.* But then the small woman seemed to make herself a little taller and plant her feet firmly on the ground.

"I may be low enough in your eyes, but the same law applies to us both," Meg said. Her voice shook a little, but she went on. "If I tell what I know, d'you think anyone else might say what they've seen? All this time you been sneaking around with my husband, were you so careful you never dropped a single hint? Are you so sure of yourself?"

"This is all bluster." Patience knew her own voice was shaking, too. "There is nothing for anyone to wonder about, and 'twould be your word against mine."

"I'll stand up and call you out in Sunday meeting and see who wants to know the truth."

"Everyone in our meeting knows you are no true Christian. Like as not, they will think you are accusing me to cover up a sin of your own."

"What about *your* husband?"

Patience felt faint but tried to put iron in her spine. "What of him?"

"Anyone can bring their case before the governor. I will tell him the truth as I know it."

"You dare not. I forbid you to speak to my husband!"

Even as she said the words, Patience knew how weak they were. She might be the governor's wife, but she was also the fallen woman, the adulteress.

But the Taylor woman must not—she must *not*—be allowed to carry this tale.

"If you breathe a word of this," Patience hissed at Peter's wife, "I will bring trouble onto your household such as you have never dreamed. Hold your tongue if you want to keep your peace, goodwife Taylor."

CHAPTER FOURTEEN

August 1656

On Sunday evening, Meg laid the table for supper with trembling hands. Peter had been gone all day. Peggy Tolliver told her that after Sunday meeting, Peter and Simon and a few of the fishermen had stayed behind to talk with Reverend Wyvern about getting rid of the Quaker women. Meg listened to Peggy and nodded, not mentioning that she herself had been aboard the Quakers' ship that morning and heard the women speak.

That seemed a long time ago now, though only a few hours had passed. Her confrontation with Mistress Treworgy severed the day in two—severed her life, she thought, for there could be no going back now.

Why was I such a fool? Why did I not keep my mouth shut? she asked herself over and over. The anguish of knowing that her husband was unfaithful was nothing compared to having made an enemy of the governor's wife. Meg's thoughts raced around in her head like her chickens in the yard outside, frantically pecking at regrets and worries.

When she heard Peter at the door, she nearly dropped the bowl in her hands. Had Mistress Treworgy spoken to him? Peter, too, had threatened Meg to keep silent. She had defied him, and for what? What had it gained her?

But when he came in, it was clear this his domestic troubles were far from his thoughts: His complaints were all about the Quakers. "There be two of them," he said, lecturing as he usually did so that Meg was unsure whether he was talking to her or to the four walls. "Not just the one that made a mockery of herself on the stagehead last night; that one's Hester Biddle. The other one, Mary Fisher, is an even more hardened heretic. We went to see the governor today, to see will he order them out of the harbour."

"Surely the governor got more to be worried about than shutting up a couple of women," Meg said.

"His task is to keep order and godly behaviour in this settlement. If you ask me, them two women ought to be in the pillory."

"Nobody's been put in the pillory for nigh on three years," Meg said. "Was the last time when one of the summer fishermen got so drunk he hove a rock through Sam Thomas's glass window?"

"Aye, but that's because the governor is lax in his duty," said Peter. "It should be used a good deal more—the pillory, and the whipping post too, if justice were done."

For adulterers? Meg thought but managed not to say. "I never even saw stocks or pillory till we came here," she said instead. "We got along well enough up in Bristol's Hope without that kind of punishment."

"Oh, aye, the promised land of Bristol's Hope," said Peter, ladling out pottage from the bowl and tearing off a piece of bread. "Up where you came from, 'tis like it says in Scripture—there was no king in Israel, and every man did what was right in his own eyes. There's no governor and no law at all up in Conception Bay."

"I wish I was there now," Meg said, and as she said it, the longing to be there, to see her mother and father and sister again, pierced her like a hook through a fish's mouth. "My mother has never seen her grandchildren, and I've not seen my home for seven years."

"Just as long since I've seen mine. And my mother's not seen her grandchildren neither."

"Yes, but your family is across the ocean!" *And you have never said a word that made me think you cared aught for them*, she did not add. "Mine are only in Musketto Cove, less than a day's sail from here. I heard tell that the Quaker women's ship might be heading to Harbour Grace when they leave here. I want to take the children and go home for a visit."

"Now? In the middle of the fishing? Are you mad, woman?"

I would leave this moment if I could. But there was justice in his objection. No fisherman went anywhere during the fishing season, even if he had the means to travel, unless it was out of absolute necessity. "Later, then. When the fish is in. I'll find a captain who can take me there in the autumn."

"You'd be gone weeks. Who's to keep the house and cook my meals, never mind wasting the money on your passage? Women do not go gallivanting off around the shore, unless they are wicked fools like those Quakers."

"Wanting to visit my mother and sister is hardly the same as travelling the world preaching!"

"'Tis all one—women disobeying husbands, being untrue to their . . . their marriage vows."

She saw the hesitation in his face over the last words. "Untrue to the marriage vows! Well, you'd know about that, wouldn't you?"

Once again she should have held her tongue, but it felt so good to see him recoil at her words. She was sure Mistress Treworgy had not told him about their encounter; he would have mentioned it by now.

"What are marriage boughs?" asked Mary, looking up with that clear-eyed gaze that reminded Meg she was growing up fast. It was not wise to talk in front of her as if she were a baby like Neddy.

"Hold your tongue," Peter said, his words colder than the sea on a winter day. He did not make it clear whether he spoke to Meg or Mary. "And," he added, "you can put any thought of visiting home out of your head—now or ever. You will stay here and do your duty."

On Wednesday, while the men were still out in the boats and the women split and gutted the morning's catch, Hester Biddle walked along the shore announcing there would be a meeting at sunset that evening in Henry Yard's fish store, with preaching and prayer. Meg said nothing when the Quaker woman stopped to speak to her, but later, as she and Hannah were both carrying baskets of fish to the flakes, she asked, "Are you going to that meeting tonight?"

Hannah paused. "I doubt I'd get leave to go. Would you?"

"Not if Peter finds out. What were you talking to the

Quaker women about after the meeting Sunday?"

Hannah set down her basket. "I asked about the Scripture about slaves and free, and whether Quakers believe in keeping slaves."

"They think, like the Levellers do, that all men should be equal," Meg said.

"Aye, but the Levellers take it only so far. All men, but not women. And only Englishmen—they don't say aught about foreigners or Negroes or Indians. But these women, they think the Scripture might go farther. If women can preach, cannot slaves be free?"

Meg almost said *But you are not a slave*, but she stopped herself. Lady Frances treated Hannah as a slave, and if the person who ruled you believed you were bound to them, did that make it so? "Does your mistress know you went to the meeting?"

"She knows I went Sunday but would not give me leave to go again." Hannah paused, and something like fear flickered in her eyes before she went on. "She don't know that I went and talked to the governor yesterday. I told him about that Scripture and told him that if he's the God-fearing man he says he is, he will tell Lady Frances to let me go."

"You did? Lord, that was brave of you," Meg said.

Hannah did not meet Meg's eyes, looking instead at the splayed fish as she laid them out on the flake. "I had to be brave. I've not told you—Stephen came back here."

"He did? When?"

"'Twas a good while ago now, in the spring. He's a bit of money put away from . . . from a voyage that paid well. He asked me would I marry him at the end of summer."

"What did you say?"

"Told him Lady Frances would never let me go. He asked, if she does not, would I run away with him in secret. But I'd be afeared to do that—too great a risk. I thought if I talked to the governor, he might make Lady Frances see sense and let me go willingly."

Meg was in awe of her friend's courage. Then she thought of herself confronting Mistress Treworgy. *Was I brave?* she wondered. She had been chastising herself for being foolish.

"I'm no great one for the Bible, not like the Puritans, but hearing those women's preaching put some courage in me," said Hannah. "If there's no one to stand up for me, I may as well stand up for myself." She paused for a minute, then added, "There's some would say a woman married to a cruel husband has as much right to be free as a servant does from a cruel master."

"There's not many would say that. I doubt even the Quakers would." Meg sighed as she laid one gutted fish after another on the rough wooden platform. "But . . . 'tis gone farther than that now. Peter has . . ." She wanted to tell Hannah, to confide in someone, but the fear of both of them—Peter and Mistress Treworgy—tied her tongue.

"What has he done now?" For all her own troubles, Hannah's concern was written on her face. "Did he—has he got another woman?"

Meg nodded, unable to say the words aloud. Why had she been bold enough to confront both the sinners yet could not tell her friend what Peter had done?

"No need to wonder what Scripture would say about that," said Hannah. "Puritans, Quakers, or Anglicans—they'd all agree that if a man goes off with another woman, he's broken his marriage vow."

"Aye," said Meg. "But it leaves me no better off. When I found out, I told him I wanted to go home, to my parents. He said he would never let me go."

Hannah nodded, and their eyes met as they spread out the fish in the sunshine. Neither of them was free to go where she wished, a common enough fate for women, for wives, for servants. And yet here were these Quaker women sailing around the world, following what they thought was God's call.

"You should go, no matter what he says, if you can find a way to do it," said Hannah.

"And you should go with Stephen if he returns, no matter what Lady Frances or the governor say about it." So easy, Meg thought, for each of them to tell the other what she should do.

That night, when Mary and the baby were both abed, Peter announced that Simon would be coming to visit. "That is well enough then," Meg said, "for I told Sallie Kean I would come over and help clean up her place. She's not better yet from a hard birthing, and with so many other young ones around she needs the help. 'Twill not be long, only an hour or so, but you and Simon will have the place to yourselves for your visit."

Peter looked suspicious, but he would not object to a visit of charity. *Forgive me for the lie, but he's told much worse,* Meg thought as she left the house. She had already gone to Sallie's house to help out before she put her own family's supper on the table, but if Peter did not know that, she would let the lie stand.

The evening was still so warm she had no need even of a cloak to throw over her shoulders, though the sun dipped toward the horizon as she made her way down to the shore. She was surprised to see Hannah there ahead of her, stepping out from the shadow of one of the stages to greet her.

"Did your mistress give you leave to come?" Meg asked, relieved to see Hannah. Though she very much wanted to go to the meeting, she had been nervous of going alone.

Hannah's smile was a wry grin. "No more than your husband did, I'll wager. Likely we'll both be scolded for being here. I told Annie I was going to draw water, though in truth I went walking about in the woods, back where I used to meet with Stephen. I was hoping he'd have come back."

"But no sign of him?"

Hannah shook her head. "Like as not he'll never return. Perhaps it was all talk, or perhaps he wants to return but his ship is not coming back this way after all."

"And you went to the governor to ask for your freedom . . ."

"Aye, I did. And I don't regret it, even if her ladyship beats me for it." There was something new in Hannah's bearing tonight: a sharp edge of determination Meg had not seen before. "Even if Stephen never comes back, I cannot go on serving her forever. I might as well come to a meeting after all, to see what else these mad women have to say."

A tiny trickle of people were going into the Yards' storehouse, so Meg and Hannah followed. It was certainly not a crowd one could hope to be lost in. Everyone would know who had been here tonight, and Meg was sure both she and Hannah would face the consequences. *We could still turn back*, she thought, but they did not.

Inside, they sat on upturned barrels at the back of the store. Close to the front sat the captain and sailors from the *Fair Wind*. In a little circle behind them were Henry and Sarah Yard, their son Jonas and his wife, and a few of the summer fishermen. Were they truly interested in what the Quaker women had to say, or only curious, as Meg was?

She was surprised to see one other familiar face—young Master David Kirke, who sat, as she did, near the back of the group and nodded a greeting to both Meg and Hannah. She could not imagine him being truly devout, but there was a contrary streak in him that might enjoy the oddity of women preachers, especially as Governor Treworgy and Reverend Wyvern were opposed to them.

At first, neither Hester Biddle nor Mary Fisher stood up to preach. They waited for the group of people seated on the deck to grow quiet, and when the quiet was complete, Hester Biddle said, "Friends—for so I call you, so we all are to one another—let us begin." She said a prayer that was shorter and simpler than any Meg had heard before, and then she was silent again.

Mary Fisher explained that they followed no prayer book nor order of service but sat in silence until one of the assembly was moved to speak. Meg wondered how long people would sit quietly like this.

The captain of the *Fair Wind* spoke next, saying that his heart had been touched a few weeks earlier, when the Quakers booked passage aboard his ship and he had first heard them preach. Then Mary Fisher led them in another prayer, and after that Hester Biddle began to speak about how the rich oppressed the poor not only back in England but here in the New World as well, and she said it was a sin, for all were one in the eyes of God.

"Should we sing a Psalm, Mistress Biddle?" Henry Yard asked when she had finished speaking.

"Nay, we do not sing the Psalms. When King David sang them, they came from his heart, but now when people chant them in church, 'tis only a form of words. We say only what we feel from our own hearts," said the woman. "And you're not to call me Mistress Biddle, only plain Hester, for we are all sisters, brothers, and friends in Jesus."

"Aye," said Mary Fisher. "Even were I to speak to your governor, I'd call him Friend John, for no man should be above another."

"But a man should be above a woman!" said David Kirke, and there was a ripple of coarse laughter from the sailors and fishermen, which Hester Biddle quelled with a stern look.

"The husband is head of the wife, as Scripture says, but they are as brother and sister in Christ, equal in the eyes of God. And there is another thing I have thought and prayed on, friends, for one of your number came to me and asked me what the Lord says to us about one Christian holding another in bondage, in slavery."

Meg glanced at Hannah and saw that everyone else in the room was looking at her too. Anyone could guess that she would be the one to raise such a question, since so many Africans were kept as slaves back in England and in the other colonies.

"So, did the Lord say anything to you?" Hannah challenged Hester.

Meg tried to imagine the look on Reverend Wyvern's face if anyone in his congregation, especially a woman, spoke out in meeting in such a way. But Hester took it in stride. "Indeed, after much prayer and meditating on Scripture, he did speak to me. He said that, just as St. Paul told the slave owner Philemon to treat his runaway slave as a brother in Christ, so we are all brothers and sisters, none greater than another. Servants must obey their masters, of course, and anyone serving out an indenture must do it faithfully. But 'tis laid on my heart that one person should never own another or hold them in bondage for life. And though not all Quakers are in agreement on this matter, my friend Mary and I have prayed together, and we are both so convinced that no Christian should own a slave."

"Heresy and blasphemy!"

Meg turned, as everyone else did, to see two men standing in the open doorway of the fish store. The were an unlikely pair: young Richard Hopkins, and beside him the Puritan preacher, Reverend Wyvern. It was the reverend who had spoken. "You women are teaching your own doctrines in place of the law of God!" he added, his reedy voice rising to a high pitch.

"Come in if you want to study God's Word and learn with us," said Mary Fisher. "You are all welcome, friends."

"You are no friends of ours, nor of anyone in this harbour," Richard Hopkins called out, his voice a good deal more powerful than the reverend's. "'Tis not your place to meddle in such business as you are talking of, between husband and wife, between master and servant!"

Hester Biddle had been seated with the others while she spoke, but now she stood up. "I do not try to meddle, young friend. I am only telling my friends here what the Spirit of the Lord has told me."

Meg heard someone else stand up and looked behind her to see Master David Kirke walk slowly toward the intruders with the hint of a lazy smile on his lips. "You are in odd company tonight, cousin," he said to Richard Hopkins. "Making friends with this Puritan? Are you a Parliament man now?"

"You make a mockery of this, as you do of everything," Master Richard shot back. "But these are serious matters. Those of us who disagree in doctrine may still agree on the need to keep order. Servants must obey their masters, wives must obey their husbands, and God never appointed a woman to preach!"

"Amen!" wheezed the reverend.

Others in the fish store were standing now: the captain and his crewmen, Henry Yard and his son. Meg found herself standing too, looking at Richard Hopkins and David Kirke. These two haughty young men, their mothers' wealth evident in their shirts and breeches that were so much finer than the homespun the other men wore. Behind Master Hopkins and the minister she saw Isaac, the Treworgys' manservant, and some of the governor's fishing servants; the young master had not come alone.

"Now, young sir," the ship's captain said to Richard Hopkins, "there's no need to come and sow disorder here. We are only worshipping and listening to these friends preach the gospel."

"This is not gospel!" Master Richard shot back. "The governor has already told you folk that your heresy is not welcome here. I will tell him what sedition has been spoken here tonight!"

"This is my store and my stage, not the governor's!" shouted Henry Yard. "'Tis for me to say who will speak here and who can meet here!"

Hannah grabbed Meg's hand and pulled her farther to the back of the store as the men surged forward. "This will turn ugly," she said. "Get out of the way." Meg saw Sarah Yard and her daughter-in-law doing the same. But Hester Biddle and Mary Fisher did not move from their places even as the fishermen outside tried to push into the store. Did these women believe so much in God's protection, Meg wondered, that they were not afraid of men's flying fists?

Then, just as the first punch was thrown by one of the fishing servants who had come with Richard Hopkins, Hester Biddle raised her hands and shouted. "Stop! Stop this fighting, in the name of Jesus Christ. I command you!"

The two men who were struggling with each other paused long enough for other men to haul them apart. "Brawling like drunkards is not God's will!" the Quaker woman went on. "We will end this meeting and return to our ship and pray for all souls in this harbour. Only let us go in peace, with no more violence."

"Aye, you'll go all right—onto your ship and straight out of this harbour, if you know what is good for you! And we'll have no brawling here!" shouted the reverend, trying to pitch his voice to match Hester's.

Though the two preachers were at odds with one another, their words seemed to calm their followers on both sides. There was grumbling, pushing, and shoving as everyone left the store, but no more fighting. Meg took Hannah's hand, and they made their way through the confusion. When she passed Reverend Wyvern, she could feel his gaze on her as clearly as if he had spoken her name. If she'd had little hope of keeping her disobedience secret from Peter when she arrived, now she had none at all.

That week was a torment for Patience. She wanted to see Peter alone, and she wanted to never see him again. The fact that Peter's wife knew of their sinful alliance ate at her vitals; the fact that she had threatened to tell the governor made Patience's blood turn to ice in her veins. She could concentrate on nothing—not her work, not the boys' lessons, not the endless talk about the Quakers and their meeting that had almost ended in a brawl. None of it touched her.

Patience did not dare leave the house again after her ill-fated visit of kindness to Sallie Kean. She saw no sign of either of the Taylors, but everyone was busy at the fish, and John was often down at the wharves inspecting the work. Peter's wife might have seen and spoken to him there, Patience thought. She was badly frightened on Tuesday evening when Martha mentioned that she had seen Lady Frances Hopkins's Negro maid talking to the governor that day; Patience knew the maid was friendly with Meg Taylor.

"What cause did she have to talk to my husband?" Patience wondered.

"Indeed, ma'am, I've no idea." Martha shrugged. "Whatever it was, they talked a good while, but what would the likes of her have to say to the master?"

What, indeed? Patience could not pry at Martha anymore. She remembered the Taylor woman's words: *All this time you been sneaking around with my husband, were you so careful you never dropped a single hint?* Those stolen nights when Patience had slipped out of her house to meet Peter, had Martha, or Ruth, or the menservants never suspected a thing?

The day after that, Wednesday, John was closeted with the minister for several hours. That was the night the Quakers held their meeting, the one Reverend Wyvern interrupted.

The whole settlement was buzzing with talk of who had attended the meeting, and how it had ended with a fight breaking out.

On Thursday, John went to talk to the captain of the Quaker ship, and when he returned home he had another unexpected visitor—young Richard Hopkins, who also went into John's study and had a long conversation.

Why a second visitor from the Hopkins household? Though the bad blood between the Kirke-Hopkins crowd and the Treworgys had eased somewhat, if Lady Frances knew of something that would discredit the governor—if, for example, she knew his wife to be an adulteress—might she not use that knowledge?

Driven to the limits by curiosity and fear, Patience asked her husband what Richard Hopkins had come about.

"'Tis about this matter of his mother's maid, the Negro woman," John said. "The maid spoke to me herself two days ago, to put her case before me. Now comes young Hopkins to make the argument for his side of the matter, though he knew naught of her coming to speak to me, and I saw no need to tell him. He knew, though, that the maid was at this Quaker meeting last night, and there was talk about slavery and freedom. Richard Hopkins thinks the Quakers have been putting dangerous ideas in her head and wants to be sure the law is on his side."

The planters and their servants often brought their squabbles to John to mediate, which was the proper role of a governor in such a small colony with no magistrates. Many people, though, appealed instead to Sara Kirke or her son George in such matters, as if the Kirkes were still the authority in the settlement. "What is the matter between them?"

Patience asked, still finding it hard to believe this had nothing to do with her own troubles.

"Why, the maid wants to leave her mistress's employ, and Lady Frances will not let her go."

"She is indentured?"

"She claims she never was indentured and is free to leave at any time. Lady Frances claims that because of her long service, and because Lady Frances paid her passage over from England and has kept her in room and board—and, of course, the fact that she is a Negro—she is not free to leave. In other words, Lady Frances views her as indentured for life."

"A slave, then."

"Lady Frances will not put that name to it. But I know not what else to call it, if she can never serve out her indenture or be free to go."

"What will you do?"

"I hope to do nothing but let them find a way through it themselves," John said, folding the paper he was writing on and standing up from his desk. Patience looked at his desk, cluttered as it now was with papers and books, quills and ink and coins and the wampum beads that had never been used to trade with the elusive natives. She never looked at the desk without thinking of herself and Peter coupling on it. The first time.

"'Tis a pretty legal problem, the status of Negro servants," John went on, oblivious to the vivid images his wife was picturing as he tidied the papers on his desk into neat piles. "I have heard of some interesting cases down in the Virginia colony. 'Tis clear that the status of Negroes cannot be the same here in the colonies as it is in England. But of course, Lady Frances's maid was freeborn in England, she is a baptized Christian, and I believe her mother is an Englishwoman, so all that complicates matters. It is a case I would much prefer not to rule on, but I've no wish to antagonize the Kirkes further. If I have to make a ruling, 'twill be unfortunate for the maid."

"Of course, 'twould be folly to rile up the Kirkes for nothing," Patience agreed quickly. She had little interest in the fate of Lady Frances's maid, but this was no time for the Treworgys to be making enemies. Anyone who hated John and learned of the Taylor woman's claims would be eager to use that information. Best to stay on the right side of Lady Frances and Lady Sara. They were still the two most powerful women in the colony, even though it was Patience herself who bore the title of governor's wife.

On Sunday morning, the few and the faithful filed into the hall of the governor's house. Patience stood by her husband's side to greet the worshippers. By now, everyone in the community knew about the Quaker meeting in Henry Yard's fish store a few nights earlier, and knew who had been there. As the Yard family entered, bowing their heads respectfully, Patience hissed in John's ear, "I wonder they dare show their faces."

John nodded to acknowledge her comment but said nothing, turning instead to greet Simon and Peggy Tolliver and their little ones as they entered. Behind them were Peter and Meg Taylor, together with their children, though Meg did not always come to Sunday meeting. Patience remembered the woman's threat, to expose her in front of the meeting. Was that why she had come today?

Goodwife Taylor, who normally kept her eyes downcast around her betters, met Patience's gaze boldly. "Good Sabbath to you, Mistress Treworgy," she said, brazen as brass.

"God be with you," Patience said, keeping her voice steady. *She is going to say something.* A week had passed since their confrontation, but if Peter's wife had lacked boldness to speak before, she now looked as if something had given her courage. She had attended the Quaker meetings; had they stirred her up to speech?

Patience sat through the service with her husband and children in their customary place at the front of the room right before the preacher. John got up, as usual, and opened the service with a prayer before turning the pulpit over to Reverend Wyvern. Patience had never been so aware of the fifteen pairs of eyes behind her as she listened to the preacher rail against the Quakers. "*Unnatural... heretical... disgraceful display.*" She felt sure Peter's wife had not stopped staring at her throughout the whole service; she could feel the other woman's eyes like two white-hot coals pressing into her back.

"Their doctrine is false," the tired old preacher rasped, "and the falsehood in it shows in the detestable practice of allowing women to play-act at being preachers! For women to take on such an unnatural role upsets God's holy order. If a woman can take on the manly role of preaching the gospel, what is to stop her from disobeying her husband, abandoning the care of her children, and committing the sin of adultery?"

There were approving male murmurs from the benches behind Patience. The preacher went on: "I am filled with holy anger to learn that there are people in this very congregation who have gone to suckle poisoned milk from the heretical teats of these women! Any husband who brings his wife to such a meeting, or allows her to attend, is leading her astray, as surely as if he had forced her to commit an unnatural act! And any woman who goes to such a meeting in the ignorance of her husband, or in defiance of his orders, is no better than an adulteress—indeed, she is worse, for she has betrayed God and her husband not just in body but in spirit! If any of you here have debased yourself in such a way, I call on you now to repent!"

He paused. The echo of his last word hung in the still, hot air of the room.

"Repent *now*!" he repeated. "If you have stopped, even once, to listen to these misguided women and their heresy, you must confess and repent before the congregation."

The minister stood with his hand upraised, his brows drawn down in the frown of a father who has caught his child in misbehaviour. Then, from the benches behind, a shuffling of feet as someone stood up. Patience darted a glance over her shoulder. It was Henry Yard.

"You said to repent, sir," the fisherman said in his rough-edged voice. "I told the Quakers they could have their meeting in my storehouse. My missus never went behind my back to hear them, we done it together, like we done everything this thirty year past. We came to the true gospel together, long ago back in England when first we was married, and we never strayed from it, no, not even when we came out here and Master Kirke used to do the service from the prayer book and had that popish cross up on the wall, right there where it used to hang." He pointed at the empty space above the mantel. "Back then, we worshipped in our own house rather than have truck with popish ways. We thanked God when the king was brought down, and we rejoiced when good Master Treworgy came in as our governor and brought a rightly form of worship to this shore."

"Amen," said a few quiet voices; Patience clearly made out Peter's among them. She would know his voice anywhere.

"But to go down on my knees and beg forgiveness for listening to the Quakers, sir, that I will not do," Henry Yard went on, "nor my missus neither. I don't hold 'tis a woman's place to preach like a man, and I don't have no intention of turning Quaker. But there's no harm in hearing the Word, and every preacher might well have some bit of truth to share. Meaning no disrespect, Reverend, but you can't be shaming people and calling 'em sinners for seeking out after truth. That's what our folks fought and died for back in England in the war times, for every man's conscience to be free. 'Tis not your place to tell us what we can or can't think."

"You dare speak so proudly to a minister of the gospel? You dare to tell me what I can and cannot say in the name of God?" railed the reverend.

"Henry be right—you cannot command our consciences! We answer only to God!" That was Sarah Yard; she blurted out her words from her seat. Next to her, her eldest son Jonas added, "I agree wi' Father and Mother, sir. 'Tis not on any preacher to go telling people what they can or can't listen to. Only God can judge."

The minister's face was growing redder by the minute. "God calls on his ministers to name sin when they see it and to guard his sheep against false shepherds! It is the calling of a minister to punish sin in the congregation!"

The murmurs from the benches behind grew louder. Patience darted a glance at John, to see if he would intervene. Outright rebellion from a family as devout and respected as the Yards could be dangerous. Suddenly, without having thought it through beforehand, Patience was on her feet. The room grew quiet again.

"Mistress Treworgy, you have something to say?"

"Yes, Reverend." She took a deep breath and smoothed the bodice of her gown, willing her voice not to shake. Her sons gazed up at her, eyes wide as saucers. "Every word you said here was right, Reverend, about those wicked Quaker women. They are leading people astray, especially leading women to disobey their husbands. That is why I beg your leave to speak, though I am but a weak woman myself."

The reverend's eyes flickered toward John, then back at Patience. "You may speak, Mistress Treworgy."

The shape of what she wanted to say was unrolling like a map in Patience's mind as she spoke. "I cannot pass judgment on Sarah Yard; she went to the meetings with her husband. He is subject to God, and she is subject to him. But I know for certes there is one woman here who went to that meeting alone, against her husband's will."

Patience and Peter had not spoken in private since the Quakers had arrived, but she knew him as well as she knew herself. He would never have allowed it. "You were there yourself, Reverend, and we've all heard the talk of what went on and who was there. So you know that Peter Taylor's wife, Margaret, was at that meeting. I'll vow she was there either secretly without her husband's knowledge, or in open defiance of him." Patience turned and met the other woman's burning gaze. "What should be the penalty for a woman who disobeys her husband in such a way?"

Meg Taylor was standing too now, her eyes fixed on Patience. She was going to say it; she was going to accuse

Patience and Peter of sin in front of the minister and congregation, Patience was sure. But Patience had made the first move in the game and planted the seed of doubt. Anything Peter's wife said now would seem like a petty attempt to lash out at Patience.

She never found out what Meg would have said, for Peter hauled his wife back down to the bench and stood up himself. "Reverend, I only heard tell my wife was gone to that meeting after 'twas done, and I punished her for it with a good beating. But I'll repent of my own sin, of not leading her aright. I've not ruled my home as I should, and I'll ask God's forgiveness."

Now voices clamoured all around. Patience sat down. The minister raised his voice to be heard above everyone. "Peter Taylor, you have done right to confess your sin in not controlling your wife. 'Tis for a husband to deal with his wife's conduct, and you must rule over her at home."

Meg wrenched free of Peter's grasp and jumped up again. "No, sir, 'tis not so! I believe what the Quaker women teach, that everyone, man or woman, has to answer their own conscience before God."

"That is heresy!"

"And no husband should be ruling over his wife's soul, 'specially not when his own soul is far from righteous! When he's no better than a—"

Her words were cut off, stifled by Peter's hand over her mouth. The men murmured approval, but Sarah Yard cried, "Let her speak!"

"Silence!" John bellowed, getting to his feet. "I'll not have a riot in my house, on the sacred day, when we are gathered for worship. Taylor, get your wife and children out of here. I will deal with you later. The rest of you, be still."

As the Taylors left the house, Peter steering Meg toward the door with his hand still over her mouth, the Reverend stepped forward again. "It is the duty of the congregation to punish those who defy the laws of God," he said. "Henry Yard, I call on the governor to levy a fine on you for your disobedience in going to hear those wicked women preach."

There was a grumble from the bench behind Patience that sounded like Sarah Yard saying, "We'll not pay it!" but Reverend Wyvern went on as if he had not heard. "And for a rebellious wife who lies to her husband and defies his orders, what shall her punishment be?"

John, still standing, cleared his throat. "A fine would seem to be fair in that case also, and for the rest, leave it to her husband to punish her." The reverend nodded, but John went on talking, his eyes meeting Patience's. "That is my thought as a man. But 'twas my wife who brought the accusation, and you might say 'tis a woman's matter. What do you think, wife? Does the congregation need to do anything further with this woman, or is't enough to leave correction to her husband?"

"I do think, Governor," the reverend wheezed, "that in such a case—"

John held up a hand. "I asked my wife's opinion and would be glad to hear it, Reverend. She is acquainted with the woman and her husband."

Was there a pause before "and her husband"? The slightest change in John's tone, in the keen eye he turned to Patience? Or was her own guilt making her imagine it?

"A woman should be ruled by her husband, of course," Patience said, again willing her voice not to tremble. "But if she has sinned in public, her punishment should be public as well."

"The pillory!" said the reverend, with pleasure in his tone.

John raised his eyebrows. "We have had little cause enough to use the pillories. It must be, what, two or three years since one was used? I think they have begun to rot."

"If the pillories are rotting from lack of use, people grow careless in their ways," the reverend said. "It is good to remind folk of God's judgment. Indeed, the Quaker women should be in the pillory also!"

"I've no authority over them," said John. "Their captain assures me they will be gone within the week. But for a woman of Ferryland, the wife of one of our planters, it is a different matter." His eyes remained locked on Patience's. "Do you agree, wife?"

Why is he so anxious to have me condemn Peter's wife? Patience could not help feeling John suspected something, that he was toying with her like a cat with a mouse. But if Meg Taylor were publicly shamed in that way, surely nobody would listen to her if she accused Patience of adultery.

"It may be harsh," she said slowly, as if considering the matter carefully, "but if there is a spirit of rebellion in the harbour, surely you will want to make an example, before such dangerous ideas should spread."

John nodded and glanced at Reverend Wyvern. "If you are in agreement, Reverend, I will order it. Peter Taylor's wife shall spend six hours in the pillory next Sunday morning. Now, close this meeting with prayer."

CHAPTER FIFTEEN

August-September 1656

It was almost September, but the August heat had not broken. Leaden-grey clouds hung in the sky, threatening rain that never came, and the air was close and damp as a wet woollen blanket when Hannah went down to the flakes on Tuesday morning with Annie and Elias.

As the women turned the salted fish, Annie nodded out at the waters of the Pool and said to Hannah, "That Quaker ship be in port still. I heard the governor told 'em to begone out of here."

Hannah shrugged. "'Tis no odds to me whether they're here or gone."

Nearly a week had passed since she and Meg had attended the meeting in Henry Yard's store. When Hannah had returned to the safety of her own little room off the kitchen that evening, young Master Richard had stormed in and dragged her before his mother, calling her a disobedient servant for going to the meeting without permission and listening to what he called "rebellious talk" from the Quakers. Lady Frances had forbidden Hannah to go anywhere that was not part of her daily round of duties. The Quakers held no more meetings ashore, even if Hannah had wanted to attend. More importantly, if Stephen were to reappear, she would have no way of meeting him.

She felt as if she were being watched all the time. She would not put it past Lady Frances or Master Richard to have ordered Annie and Elias to keep an eye on her, to make sure she did not run away. Annie was a good soul, if simple, but she was very grateful to Lady Frances for giving her and Elias a job and a home. Who knew what she might be willing to do out of gratitude?

At least they never found out I went to see the governor, Hannah thought with some satisfaction. But little good it had done her. She had explained her situation to Governor Treworgy and asked what her status might be in the eyes of the law. She had even asked him to intervene, to tell Lady Frances she must pay Hannah's wages and let her go. But that had been more than a week ago, and there had been no word from the governor.

Annie was still talking. "And that poor Meg Taylor, think of it! A woman in the pillory! Have you been talking to her since Sunday? She must be broken up in pieces over it all. That husband of hers is a hard man, though a fine lookin' one, I will say."

No, Hannah had not been talking to Meg since Sunday, since the story of her speaking out in meeting and the punishment laid upon her had spread like wildfire around the settlement. She looked now at Peter Taylor's stagehead. His fishing servants were working there, and Peggy Tolliver with them, but there was no sign of Meg. Had he confined her to the house?

Hannah wanted to talk to Meg. They had barely had a chance to speak before the Quaker meeting, when Hannah had finally told Meg about Stephen's return, and Meg had confided in her about Peter's unfaithfulness. Who in this harbour might he be dallying with, Hannah wondered? She wished she could help her friend, but she would only put both herself and Meg in greater danger if she sought her out to talk with her. And the shadow of the pillory loomed large. If they could put a woman there for disobeying her husband, what might they do with a servant who defied her mistress, especially a Negro servant? A woman might have a friend, Hannah thought, but in the end, you had to rely on yourself alone in this world.

"I'd rather they had hauled me out after the meeting and done it at once, if they're going to do such a thing," Meg said to Peter as she slapped a trencher down on the table in front of him on Tuesday evening.

"They could not do it then, and they'll not do it during the week. The governor wants people to watch this, and he won't have them standing around gawking at the pillory on a day when they should be working," said Peter. "It must be done on Sunday. 'Twill be in place of the church service; the reverend means to give his sermon there."

So I will be his illustration, Meg thought. Up there on the platform for all to see, her head and arms bound in the yoke, while he talked about disobedient wives and wicked women. But this waiting was worse than the sentence itself. She was as busy as ever about the house and garden, but Peter had told her she was not needed on the flakes. She knew that was because of the shame, his shame, and their neighbours' wagging tongues. Even when she worked in her own garden, she felt everyone's eyes on her as they passed by. Sarah Yard had paused long enough to say it was a terrible thing, and Clara Bullard said it was shocking and not fit for men to do such things to a woman. But Peggy Tolliver lifted her nose in the air as she walked past, as if it would sully her to even look in Meg's direction.

From the garden, or even from their window—newly done with glass last autumn, a luxury Peter was proud of—she could see the platform with the pillories and the whipping post. Sometimes fishing servants were whipped for slacking or for disobedience, but Meg could not remember seeing a woman in the pillory, and men only rarely. If the stares and murmurs of her neighbours were hard to bear now, what would it be like to stand there for half a day on Sunday when everyone had the leisure to look at her and pass judgment?

"I told you—I warned you. Why would you not listen?" Peter said. He sounded miserable, though Meg knew it was not out of sympathy for her. "What are people saying of me, a man who can control his wife so little she ends up in the pillory?"

"If you are so pressed about it, I'll gladly change places with you," Meg shot back. "Put *you* in the pillory—that's the place for adulterers, is't not? What if I spent my time up there shouting to everyone all that I know? Telling them of your sin, and Mistress High-and-Mighty Treworgy's?"

"You'd not dare. There's not a soul would believe you."

"You must keep Mary away on Sunday. I'll not have her see me like that."

"No fear—I'd not have her know what her mother is."

"What I *am*? Or what the governor and the reverend have decided to name me?" She paused. "You are very cozy with both of them—did you even speak a word for me? Try to talk them out of it?"

"How could I? They think the fault is mine for failing to keep you in line!"

He had certainly tried to keep her in line, beating her both before and after the church service for her disobedience. What he had never tried to do was to defend her. Never spoken a word on her behalf. For years he had been telling her she was a sinner, while he carried on with his own private sin. Now the community had branded her a sinner, and he intended to stand by and watch.

"Hannah, I would speak with you after dinner," said Lady Frances as her servants laid the table.

"Yes, your ladyship." Hannah kept her eyes lowered, her hands busy and efficient as always. *Such a good servant*, Frances thought. Surely that insubordination of hers, asking about wages and whether she could leave Frances's service, had long been forgotten? It had been two years since that troublesome fisherman had paid court to Hannah, and in all that time there had been, until this week, nothing to complain of in her behaviour. Nor had she ever raised the question of wages again. Frances dared to hope that little flare of rebellion was over and Hannah now understood and accepted her place.

But Hannah had gone behind Frances's back to attend a Quaker meeting, and whatever those Quaker women were preaching, it was surely sedition. Frances had heard how Meg, the washerwoman, had stood up in the Puritan meeting and defied her husband, and she and Hannah such great friends. It was all deeply troubling, Frances thought. But the letter she had received today gave her a means to end this folly.

After the meal, Nicholas ran off to hang about the shore with his cousin Jarvis. But Richard lingered. Frances had not yet told him about the letter, but he knew she had received something on the ship that came today, from a trader on his way from Plaisance.

"You had a letter from Monsieur Beliveau?" Richard said now.

She nodded. "He is returning in a fortnight and asks again if I will come away with him to Boston."

"I have things well in hand here, Mother. I can oversee our trade in the autumn and pay the servants their share and take in our winter supplies. You have worked hard these last two years, work not intended for a woman's shoulders to bear."

"And yet, my shoulders are not so weak, are they?"

"No, no, you have borne it well," Richard said hastily. "'Tis only that you deserve a rest. And I want you to know I am well able to step into your shoes."

"If I go away this winter, 'twill be a fair trial for you, to see how you can manage. After all, your aunt and your cousins are here, if you need to turn to anyone for help." She saw the look on his face, and added, "Not David, of course. I know there is no love lost between the two of you, and I'd not suggest you turn to him for advice. But George has grown steady and sensible since his marriage, and your Aunt Sara knows more about managing a plantation than any man ever will. Now, I must speak with Hannah."

"May I stay with you? If I'm to be master of the house, anything touching the servants will be my business as well."

Frances paused, then nodded. It was true; she needed to begin treating him as a man. What had her hard work been for, if not to hand it all over to him? "Come in, Hannah," she bade, hearing the maid's steps at the kitchen door.

When Hannah stood before them both with her hands folded, Frances found it difficult to begin. She could not speak to her servant of Monsieur Beliveau, of how strange it was to have a suitor and a prospect of marriage at her age. Instead, she said, "You have perhaps heard talk that I may be going away for the winter, to Boston, in the company of Monsieur Beliveau. You remember him, I am sure."

"Aye, my lady, I do."

And what do you think of him? Again, that unruly urge to treat Hannah as a confidante. Because who else knew Frances so well, who else could she ask, *Am I being a fool, to dream of being a wife again?* She could ask Sara, of course, but Sara's answer would be too blunt and perhaps one she did not want to hear. She would never lower herself to have such a conversation with a servant, but she could not help wondering what Hannah might think of her choices.

"'Tis true, I will be leaving in a fortnight with Monsieur Beliveau when his ship returns here. You will accompany me and spend the winter serving me in Boston. I will leave Annie here to keep the house."

The briefest of pauses before Hannah said, "No, my lady."

Before Frances could react, Richard shot back. "What do you say? Did you say *No* to my lady mother?"

"I did, sir, and I will again. I am not going to Boston."

"I say you *shall* go with me to Boston, and you are bound to obey me!" Frances said. Her fears had been right: Hannah's rebellious spirit had not been quenched but had smouldered silently all this time, waiting to flare into life. What had fanned the flame? Her lover was long gone; had she taken another? Or was it the Quakers, stirring up rebellion?

"I do not believe I am bound to obey you, my lady—not in this matter. If you go to Boston, I will leave your service."

"This nonsense again!" Richard spat. "Leave my mother's service, as if you were a hireling, free to come and go? You are our family's chattel. You can no more pick up and leave than the boats and the fishing nets can!"

Now Hannah lifted her head, and her eyes met Richard's. "It is not so, sir. I am born free. I . . . I have spoke to the governor of it. I told him that I am no slave and 'tis wrong to hold me bound when I have signed no indenture."

"You—you what? You went to the *governor*?" Richard was on his feet too now, his face colouring with anger, and Frances felt as if something were slipping from between her fingers, as if this quarrel were now between Richard and Hannah and nothing to do with her.

"Hannah, that was very naughty of you," Frances said. "You ought not to have spoken to Governor Treworgy."

"It is far more than naughty, Mother. I know you have a kindness for Hannah for her long service, but you are too gentle with her. This is beyond naughtiness. This calls for punishment."

Hannah turned her eyes from Richard to Frances. "Will you beat me, my lady?"

"No," Frances said quickly, only to stop Richard from saying yes. He would not be sentimental and soft, as a woman would be, as Frances was. She knew he was right, and yet she did not want to see Hannah beaten.

"Go back to the kitchen," Richard ordered, "and do not set another foot outside this house until I give you leave. My mother and I will decide what is to be done with you, but you may make up your mind that when your mistress goes to Boston, you will be aboard that ship with her."

"George Kirke? What did you go to see him for?" Patience asked her husband.

John shot her a sharp glance, and Patience lowered her eyes. She had sounded shrill and demanding, as if she had a right to know who her husband met with and why. Her nerves were on edge, and every unexpected conversation brought back the fear that John had found out about her and Peter. She had to school herself to be a submissive and virtuous wife.

Tossing his hat on the table, John said, "I thought it wise. There's too much unrest in the settlement. This time of year, folks are generally so busy with the fish they've no time for idle talk and troublemaking. But between the Quaker meetings and our Sunday meeting just past, even working dawn till dusk on the flakes is not enough to keep them quiet."

Patience took a deeper breath. This was nothing to do with her. She had been afraid the Kirkes had carried tales about her to John, but he was only troubled by the daily cares of managing the fisherfolk. "So you thought it politic to consult with the Kirkes?"

"Aye. Like it or not, they have as much influence here as I do, or more. Of course, there's no meeting with George Kirke alone—his mother sits at his side like the queen dowager, putting forth her opinions in the most unwomanly way. But they agree the Quakers are causing unrest and that public discipline will send a message about obedience. I told them about Richard Hopkins's request, also."

"Richard Hopkins? What had he to say?"

John sat down and sighed. He looked weary, and Patience hastened to pour him a cup of small ale, which he drank gratefully. "I forgot—that was only this morning, and you were busy with the children's lessons. Young Hopkins came to see me again about this same business of his mother's Negro servant. It seems now she has boldly said that she will leave her mistress's service, though Hopkins says she has no right to go."

"She went to the Quaker meetings also, did she not?"

John nodded. "Aye. They stir up wives to disobey their husbands and servants to defy their masters. We must make an example of these women. 'Twould be a valuable lesson to anyone who thinks to upset the natural order of things."

"So you will make common cause with the Kirkes and Hopkinses, then?"

"There are times we must work together even with our enemies. They may be royalists, but they are as concerned to keep order in the settlement as I am. At least, all of them are save that young scapegrace, David Kirke. D'you know he was consorting with the Quakers too? For no other reason than to stir up trouble, I am sure, for he has not a godly bone in his body. But the rest of the Kirke crowd is in agreement; we will show a united front against Quakers, disobedient wives, and unruly servants."

Patience folded her hands before her and kept her eyes downcast. "You are wise indeed, husband. I hope every woman in the cove—aye, and every man, too—will learn from this."

"A rebellious servant, a wayward wife . . . Now, had we only a third pillory, and an adulteress to put in it, 'twould be a complete warning to all women."

Did his gaze linger on her for a heartbeat too long before he stood up and left the room? No, surely she was imagining it.

On Sunday morning, Annie woke Hannah while it was still dark. "Master Richard says he is taking you now."

Hannah had slept badly. Yesterday, Lady Frances had told that her that she was sentenced to stand alongside Meg in the pillory, as an example to the people. The Quakers were gone; their ship had left Ferryland on Friday. But the good people of the community must still see two women punished for rebellion and disobedience.

"I can spare you this, if you repent," Lady Frances had said, her tone soft and urgent. Master Richard had not been nearby. "I would still take you to Boston with me, if you would only say that you are sorry and have learned your lesson, and will not rebel again."

Hannah had been tempted to say it. To say any form of

words her mistress liked, to spare herself the torment of the pillory. Stephen had not returned; she did not know if or when he would come back for her. If she was bundled aboard a ship to Boston in a fortnight, she might never see him again. He would come back to Ferryland and find her gone.

As she stood looking into Lady Frances's face, so familiar and yet the face of a stranger, Hannah realized that even if Stephen did not return, if he were not in the question at all, she would not go to Boston, nor stay here. She did not want freedom only so that she could marry; she wanted it now for its own sake. She had always been a cautious, practical woman, and the practical thing would be to stay in her mistress's service if she had no better offer. But she was no longer willing to be Lady Frances Hopkins's servant.

"No, my lady," Hannah said. "I have done my best to serve you faithfully for ten years, but you do not own me. And I'll stand by that, even if I must stand in the pillory."

And so, this morning. Annie rousing her with pity in her eyes. Young Master Richard, whose nose she had wiped and whose little wounds she had bandaged when he was a lad, waiting outside with a stern face, his hand gripping her upper arm like a shackle. Lady Frances nowhere to be seen. In the grey morning light, as Richard marched her down the path, she saw the whipping post and the two pillories side by side: One for Meg, and one for Hannah.

In front of the pillories, the governor and his wife stood with the Puritan minister. Hannah lifted her eyes once to meet Governor Treworgy's eyes, thinking of how she had quoted to him: *There is no slave nor free, all are one in Christ Jesus.* Apparently the governor did not care so much what Christ Jesus thought about it.

"You have brought your mother's servant to us, Richard Hopkins," Governor Treworgy said.

"I have. She is disobedient and has threatened to run away."

There was a pause. Nobody spoke, and the sun rose a little higher, golden beams of light spreading across the rocky ground. There was more noise behind; more people were arriving.

Peter Taylor led Meg in the same manner Richard Hopkins had just led Hannah, like a criminal being brought to justice. Hannah's eyes met Meg's for a moment before both women looked back at the ground. Then the governor led Hannah to the pillory, while the reverend led Meg to the other one. Bend the head, raise the arms. The heavy wooden bar settled over Hannah's neck and wrists, and she heard the click of the latch holding it in place.

"Come away, Patience," John said. "We are not condemned to stand here all day as they are."

But I would be, if the truth were known, Patience thought. "You go about your work. I will keep watch, if it pleases you," she said aloud. "Someone should bear witness."

Reverend Wyvern had preached for over an hour, declaiming about the wickedness of women and the boldness of servants who would defy their masters. By the time he had finished speaking, few of the Ferryland settlers remained to witness the punishment of their neighbours.

Young Richard Hopkins had stood for a time watching his mother's maid but turned back for his home before the sermon began. Peggy and Simon Tolliver stood near the Treworgys' servants, and Peggy cried, "Shame! Shame!" a few times, but there were no other voices to take up the call. Henry and Sarah Yard and their family did not appear at all.

Nor was there any sign of Lady Sara Kirke or her son George, for all that Lady Sara generally poked her nose into everything that happened in the cove. But just as Patience thought that, she saw young David Kirke, the third son, strutting along like the cock of the walk as he always did, down the road toward the pillory. So he was his family's representative here this morning, she thought. He went close to the platform, to speak to the two women, though she could not imagine what he might be saying to them.

Patience had seen people in pillories and stocks before—such punishments were common in the righteous community where she had grown up. She had seen woman punished for gossip, for adultery, for disobedience to husbands, for failing to attend church. She had seen women whipped in public. She had never been disturbed by the sight—she had taken it as it was intended, as a warning. *Obey, follow the rules, or the community of believers will make an example of you.*

She had never felt shaken to the core as she did today. *It is because you are like them*, the inner voice of conscience told her. *Indeed, you are worse. If justice were done, you would be there beside them.*

As she looked at the women, Meg Taylor turned her eyes up and met Patience's. Meg, the little fishwife, a half-pagan creature hardly better than an Indian—so Patience had thought of her. Now, looking into her eyes, all Patience could see was a woman like herself. Patience loved Peter; Meg did not. Both of them were married to men they could not love, but only Patience had broken her vows. *And she is the one in the pillory, because of me*, Patience thought. She looked away, unable to bear Meg's eyes.

"So be it," John said. "Reverend, come with me; we will leave my wife here to watch. As she says, she must bear witness." And John, before he turned to go, fixed Patience with a look that shrivelled her soul.

"Well now, Goodwife Taylor. We always thought 'twas your husband's Puritan ways that would get you into trouble. But the Puritans have turned on you, for not being pure enough."

Meg raised her eyes to see young David Kirke's handsome, arrogant face looking down at her. She could not lift her head enough to see him properly. She had been in this position for well over an hour now; her neck, shoulders, and back ached, and there were hours yet to go. She had never in her life had less patience for a rich young man coming to bandy words with her.

"They are punishing me for disobeying my husband," she said between gritted teeth.

"And poor Hannah for wanting to run away from my aunt's service," Master David said.

"Not to run away. To take my leave, as 'tis my right to do." Meg could not turn her head to see Hannah, but she could hear the pain in Hannah's voice.

"Of course. Annie explained it all to me. Nice little thing, Annie. Not the cleverest, but a good heart." He lowered his voice slightly. "She brought your friend to me—Stephen?"

"Stephen is . . . here?" Hannah said, barely above a whisper.

"Yes. He deserted his ship and made friends with the Quakers in Witless Bay, and once he told them of the connection to you, they brought him as far back as Caplin Bay. What odd women those Quakers are! Can't say I am taken with the idea of a woman preacher, but then, I'm not much taken with preachers at all. And while I am taken with women, they're not of the Quaker sort. Still, they wish to help you get free."

He had turned his attention entirely to Hannah now; Meg could see only his arm and hear Hannah's strained voice as she said, "If wishes were fishes, we'd all have a fry."

"How true, how true. But while wishes are not fishes, some of us have a bit more say in what fish we can fry. Stephen would like to take you through the woods trail to Caplin Bay, to join the Quaker ship there. Secretly, of course." Meg saw David Kirke's arm turn as he swung back toward her. "What of you, Meg Taylor? Do you want to run away from your husband? There would be a berth for you aboard the ship as well. The Quaker women feel responsible that their preaching has led to the two of you being in the pillory. Although it seems mild enough. Nobody has thrown rotten fish at you. Not yet, anyway."

"Have you only come to babble?" There was a time Meg would never have thought of speaking to her betters with such spirit, but she felt now that everything was being whittled away from her. She had tried so hard to be a good wife, a good Christian, a good servant. And where had it gotten her?

"I may babble, but I can get you aboard that ship with Hannah and Stephen. The ship is putting into St. John's Harbour before they return to England, so from there you might find a vessel to take you to . . . Cupids, is it?"

Meg was surprised that David Kirke knew anything at all about where she had come from, though she had been his mother's washerwoman for years. But that surprise was swallowed up in the flood of relief at his suggestion.

"Bristol's Hope," she corrected him. "But—you could do that? Get me and my children aboard that ship?"

"The children may be more difficult."

"I'll not go without them." *But I will go*, she realized. If there was a way to get to her parents' home with Mary and Neddy safe in her arms, she would leave Peter. A terrible thing, for a wife to leave her husband. But after an hour in the pillory, it did not seem so terrible.

"I will do what I can." And he was gone, hopping down off the platform, out of her sight. Nobody stood looking at them now save Mistress Treworgy, too far away to hear anything that had been said. Meg made herself meet the other woman's eyes with a steady gaze, and once again it was Patience who looked away first.

She wanted to speak to Hannah, but she would have had to raise her voice to do so and risk Mistress Treworgy hearing them. So she had only her own thoughts to distract from the pain that crept from her neck down through her whole body.

She could not think of a less likely saviour than Lady Sara Kirke's son, who had never shown any particular favour either to herself or to Hannah. But she cared not for his reasons; Meg would climb aboard any ship that offered a chance to get clear of this terrible place.

She shifted her weight from foot to foot, trying to find a position that hurt less. But everything hurt. The sun had fully risen now. There were still more than four hours to go.

By the time the governor's servant came to unlock the pillories, Hannah felt broken in a way that hours of housework and days making fish had never made her feel. Bent at that unnatural angle, her neck and wrists trapped for hours, she felt like a child's poppet that had had some of its pieces torn off. She rubbed her arms, trying to get the feeling back in them, as Isaac opened Meg's pillory.

Richard Hopkins and the Puritan minister had returned. To Meg, the minister said, "I hope you have learned the error of your ways. Go home now. Your husband will deal with you." He looked about as if he expected to see Peter, but there was no sign of him. "On Sunday you will stand before the congregation, confess your sin, and tell the people you have learned the errors of your ways."

He turned to Hannah next. "You are not a part of the congregation of the saints and so none of my concern, except that it is in the interest of all the community that rebellious servants be punished. Your master is here to take you home."

Hannah wanted to talk to Meg about David Kirke's strange offer of help, but there was no time. Richard had a grip on her upper arm again, and she walked silently at his side to Lady Frances's house.

Her mistress was on the doorstep waiting. "Well, Hannah," she said. "It has been a hard day, but I hope you have learned your lesson, and there will be no more talk of running off."

"No, my lady." No more talking about it; that much was certain.

"I am sorry things have had to come to this pass, but I am sure you will do better from now on. However . . ." Lady

Frances shifted her gaze from Hannah's face to Richard's. "My son feels, and I am sure he is right, that your correction is not finished yet. I would not have had you whipped in public, out there in front of the fishermen. Richard will . . . he will do what is necessary."

"He means to whip me?"

"Only a few strokes. So that you will . . . you will not forget this day."

"I am not likely to forget it, my lady."

"No. Well. Richard, see to it." She looked once more at Hannah. Hannah met her mistress's gaze without flinching or looking away. Lady Frances looked hurt, as if she were the one who had stood in the pillory, as if she were about to receive the lash. *She is sorry for herself, not for me*, Hannah thought, and her contempt for the other woman rose up so sharply she had to bite her lip to keep from speaking. After a moment, Lady Frances looked away and turned to go back into the house.

Hannah did not struggle, only stiffened herself against the pain and tried not to cry out as Richard made her take off her kirtle and pull down her shift, and gave her six strokes across her bare back with a birch rod. She would save her strength. If Stephen were truly here and the Quakers willing to take them away—well, she would attempt it. Though if she failed, she would feel this same rod, again and harder.

In all her years in service, she had never been whipped. In her first place, the housekeeper had been in the habit of slapping maids when they made mistakes or were slack in their work. Hannah had learned quickly, earned few slaps, and been glad for the kindlier treatment she received when she went to work for the Hopkins family. Lady Frances did not slap. She had always been a firm but gentle mistress.

Hannah thought of the tales Stephen had told her of Africans held in bondage in the southern colonies. Scores of them on a single plantation and often whipped for the slightest misbehaviour. As Richard brought the rod down for the sixth time, cutting across the bleeding gashes left by his last strokes, she bit her lips to keep from crying out. *I will never live as a slave,* she vowed silently.

When it was over, Annie fluttered around her in the kitchen, close to tears at the sight of Hannah's back. Hannah directed her to the jar of salve. "'Tis a terrible thing, a terrible thing," Annie said as she rubbed the soothing balm into Hannah's wounds. "I never thought the young master could be so cruel. Master David, he says Master Richard is trying to prove himself a man, but why should you suffer for it?"

Master David, Hannah thought. She had seen him flirting with Annie as he did with other maidservants and remembered him saying, *Nice little thing, Annie. Not the cleverest, but a good heart. She brought your friend to me.*

"Your man, he came when you were in that . . . in the pillory," Annie whispered, her lips near Hannah's ear. "He told me he'd wait there for you, and I went and got Master David to talk to him. He's right clever, Master David, and he thought 'twas a terrible thing they did to you and poor Meg. You go lie down now. Her ladyship cannot expect you to serve her supper tonight."

Hannah no longer cared what Lady Frances might or might not expect. And she did not want simple, good-hearted Annie to suffer for her escape. But she could not afford to worry about such things now. Annie must take her own chances and rely on her own wits and luck. *Whatever ill befalls her,* Hannah thought—and a good deal of hardship likely would come Annie's way—*no one will ever try to tell her she is a slave. She has that much over me, at least.*

In her tiny bedchamber, while the family dined, Hannah looked at her few belongings. Her spare kirtle and shift. The few coins she still had saved from back in England, when she had earned a wage. Very little else—she was not a woman to collect possessions. She took her mother's little tin brooch and fastened it inside her kirtle for safety. Her one good, warm shawl. Nothing else to show for all her years here in Ferryland.

While Annie served and the family supped, Hannah moved slowly, with effort, her back burning and all her limbs stiff and sore from the day's punishment. She picked up her bag and went out the kitchen door. After a moment, she heard a soft, whistled note, like a bird call. The signal Stephen had used back in the spring to alert her to his presence.

She should go back inside the house, ignore his call. They were locked in a harbour where almost everyone believed she was Lady Frances's property, where every English ship in port would do either the governor's bidding or the Kirke family's bidding, which in this case would likely be the same. Where the forest stretched dark and forbidding behind them.

The woods trail to Caplin Bay, David Kirke had said, but Hannah's legs ached just walking down the steps from the kitchen door.

She should go back. A known and familiar servitude, even to a mistress who would have her put in the pillory and whipped, was surely better than stepping into the unknown.

And yet. The whistle came again, and Hannah took a step forward, then another. Toward the trees, carrying her bag.

Come what may, I will never live as a slave, she reminded herself.

Just past the garden, between the trees, Stephen was there. Not alone. David Kirke was there, and so was Meg, her baby in a sling, her little girl clinging to David Kirke's back.

Stephen held out his hand, and Hannah, feeling as if she were in a dream, took it. "Hannah, my love," he said. "If we can get to where the Quakers have anchored their ship, they will take us as far as St. John's. Farther, if we wish."

"I'll go," Hannah said, "if I can walk so far."

"If need be, I'll carry you," said Stephen. "Come, we've a good few miles to cover before 'tis dark."

"My wife is gone," Peter said. "And the two youngsters with her."

"She cannot take your children," Patience said. "She's no right to them."

Two days had passed since Peter's wife and Lady Frances's servant had stood in the pillory. Patience and Peter stood on the path that led from the governor's house to the harbour, trying to look as if this were the merest chance encounter between the governor's wife and a fisherman. She knew Peter had been lurking about, hoping to catch her; she knew, also, that his wife had disappeared. For all her own guilt, Patience could not help thinking, *His wife has left him; he is all mine now.* A foolish thought—he could never be hers.

"Meg sent word by one of the Kirke House servants. I know not how they are mixed up in it all, but she said she was going for a visit," Peter said. "Taking the youngsters to her parents up in Bristol's Hope, to get away from the shame of it, she said."

"Peter, we cannot talk like this."

"When will I see you again?"

"You cannot. We cannot. Not . . . after all this." Had Peter's wife spoken to anyone before fleeing Ferryland? Patience felt John's gaze on her all the time now. His voice had an edge when he spoke of adulteresses being pilloried alongside rebellious wives and disobedient servants. The wife and the servant had escaped, but she, Patience, was still here.

"I must see you alone." Peter sounded desperate. "I need—"

"You need to repent of your sins. As do I. Do not come calling for me, even when my husband goes away again."

She turned, back toward her house, forgetting that she had made up an errand to have an excuse to walk past Peter's house. She still carried the little parcel of swaddling blankets for Sallie Kean's child. As she approached the governor's house, John stood outside. Watching her.

"What are the women saying?" he asked.

"The women?"

"You went to see Goodwife Kean. 'Tis been an eventful few days; I thought she might have gossip about it."

"No. No, she is still not well and was sleeping when I arrived, so I did not trouble her." The lie felt awkward, like the parcel she was still carrying. "But Martha says the servants are saying that Lady Frances's maid, and Goodwife Taylor with her children, have run away with the Quakers."

"That is what I heard. But the Quakers were gone before those two women were pilloried, so I don't know the rights of it," John said. "Young Master Hopkins wants me to find the maid and bring her back, but I've not the time to go chasing after runaway women so near the end of the fishing season. 'Tis a wicked tangle, but what can one expect in such a wicked place?" He sighed.

"It is a wicked place, is't not? I thought . . . I truly thought we could do good here. That we could bring the gospel and teach the people true religion and holy living."

Now he looked at her again, that same clear gaze he had given her over and over these last few days. "Our intentions were good," he said. "But unless we take great care, evil may overcome good, rather than the other way round."

"I . . . I hope not."

"I hope not, also. I have a question to ask you, wife."

She clenched her fists in the fabric of her gown, hoping he could not see how she was shaking. "Of course. What is it?"

He hesitated, then said, "You are carrying another child, are you not?"

Now the wave of nausea washed over her; she thought she might faint. He would ask next, *Is it mine?* And she would say that it was, but she could not know for certain. She laid her hands over her belly. "You are right. I've only been sure of it for a few weeks, myself." She braced herself for his next question.

But John only nodded. "I thought so. After so many years a husband and father, I should know the signs. I have made a decision."

She waited, said nothing.

"You will have this child in Maine, as you did when you bore Charity. I will not have you giving birth in this place."

"So . . . we will go home for the winter?"

"We will all go home when the fishing season is done," John said. "I will return next summer, for a time; business will draw me back during the summers as long as I am governor here. But you and the children will stay in Maine from now on. I do not want my sons growing up here, nor my daughter, for that matter. I know you hoped to do good here, but I do not think this land is good for you."

"I am sure you are right, my husband."

He kept that cool, steady gaze on her. She thought he would say something else, but instead he nodded slowly. "You are a dutiful wife, Patience. Do not think I fail to value that." Then he turned and walked into the house, and she followed him.

St. John's Harbour at the beginning of September was filled with ships, their masts thicker than the trees on the surrounding hills. The *Fair Wind* was docking there only briefly before continuing on its journey to England. As the ship dropped anchor, Meg stood on deck holding Neddy, with Mary clinging to her skirt. Hannah and Stephen stood beside her at the rail.

"There must be a ship here that will take me back to Musketto Cove, or somewhere nearby," Meg said, "but i' truth I've no idea how to find one."

"If you'll trust me to help, I will talk to the sailors," Stephen said. "Finding a ship going where I want to go is a thing I've had cause to do many times."

Hannah shot him a quick glance. "Have a care who you talk to," she said.

"Oh, I will be cautious." Stephen put his hand over Hannah's for a moment, a touch of such gentleness that Meg felt her heart turn over. Hannah, like herself, was running away from the cruelties of Ferryland into the unknown, but at least she was with someone who cared for her.

They had had little time to talk since that long, punishing walk through the woods in darkness and their arrival aboard the *Fair Wind* at Caplin Bay the following morning. Their flight had been hasty and hard, and Meg had spent nearly all of her energy trying to quiet Neddy's cries and answer Mary's questions. Now that the ship was in port in the busy fishing station of St. John's, it felt like Meg's first chance in days to draw a good breath.

The Quaker women had taken good care of them, tending to Hannah's terrible wounds from being whipped. The captain had promised his help in getting the fugitives to safety. But Meg could not rest easy until she was in her parents' home in Musketto Cove. Peter would surely follow them in time, to bring back the wayward wife who had fled with his children, and perhaps someday she would have to return with him. But she knew her parents would offer her a safe haven for now. Her greatest fear was that he might stop her from getting to Musketto Cove at all. She guessed that Hannah felt the same fear about Lady Frances and Master Richard Hopkins—they would pursue her if they could.

"If I get passage home, will you and Stephen come with us?" Meg asked Hannah. "I know my parents would welcome you, at least until you know what you will do next."

Hannah shook her head. "'Tis not far enough from Ferryland. I think no place in the New Found Land would be. Governor Treworgy is governor of the whole island, and the Kirke and Hopkins families have dealings everywhere. I'd not be safe anywhere in this land. And Stephen says . . ." She hesitated.

"What does Stephen say?"

"He thinks we are safer back in England. Not only because I will be far from my mistress, but because all up and down the colonies, they are taking Africans for slaves in greater numbers all the time. In all the English colonies. He says even folks born free, as he and I are, are enslaved only for the complexion of their skin."

"And in England . . . are there no slaves there?"

"Some," said Hannah. "Stephen's mother was owned by her master till she won her freedom with his death. But she lives free now, and so do a good many other folks Stephen knows, so he thinks 'tis a safer place for us. He has family there. Perhaps I do still, if my parents are living." Her fingers brushed the little brooch hidden inside her kirtle. "We can make a life there."

What kind of life will it be? Meg wondered. "Peter always said the same thing my parents said, that the great thing about the New Found Land was anyone could be free here, however low his birth was in England. Anyone could tend his own piece of land and fish from his own boat. He said all men were equal here."

Hannah nodded. "So people like to say," she said. "But 'tis not true here, not for folks of our colour. The Quakers think everyone is equal in God's kingdom, and mayhap they're right—but not anyplace on this earth."

"So I'll not see you again."

"No. But don't fear for me. Stephen is a good man, and we will be together."

Meg looked at her daughter, playing with her bedraggled rag poppet on the deck a few feet away, out of earshot. "A good man," she said. "You told me once that Peter was not a good man. You were right, I see now."

"I was," Hannah said. She looked at Meg with her steady gaze. "But you knew that. And you are doing the right thing, going away from him."

"You have been a true friend." Meg thought of Hannah beside her when her babes were born, her calming voice, her steady hands. She reached out for those hands now, and Hannah clasped them in her own. "God go with you."

"Aye, I think he will," Hannah said, "at least as long as I'm travelling with this lot." She nodded toward the two Quaker women, and smiled. "And God go with you, and see you safely home."

CHAPTER SIXTEEN

Spring 1657, Musketto Cove

"When the wind is in the east, 'tis neither good for man nor beast," said Ned Perry, shouldering his way in through the door with a blast of cold east wind, his arms full of wood. "We'll need some fair weather if the lads are ever going to get the boats ready."

"Fair weather will come when it comes," said Meg's mother Nancy as she built up the fire. "Mary, be a good girl and bring me over two little pieces of wood, will you?"

"Yes, Granny." Mary trotted over to Ned, who handed her two sticks which she then ran to the hearth to hand to her grandmother. "When you have done the fire, may I help you make bread?"

Nancy's eyes met Meg's over the child's curls. "She's quick enough to learn, grant her that. She'll be a grand help when you go back home."

"*If* you go back to Ferryland," Ned said. He bristled when Nancy referred to Ferryland as their daughter's home; as far as he was concerned, their house in Musketto Cove would always be Meg's home, the safe harbour she could return to. He would be content to have her and the children stay forever.

Meg knew she was fortunate. Some women ran away from cruel or unfaithful husbands only to be turned away from their parents' doors, told that once the vow was made, they had no home to return to. She had always known that her parents would welcome her back without judgment. They had been appalled at the tale of the pillory and her account of Peter's cruelty and his unfaithfulness. The only thing she had not told them was the name of Peter's lover.

"Your home is here as long as you need it," Ned had told her, though Nancy added, "A man will want the right to his children, though, especially his son. He may come here looking for them and demand you bring them back, though I'd not open the door for him."

Months ago, on the night she left Ferryland, Meg had told David Kirke to pass word to her husband that she was going to stay for a time with her parents. It would give her, at least, something of a respectable reason for going. She suspected Peter would not run after her at once; getting the fish in would be more important to him. But she was surprised the winter had gone past with no sign of him, and no message sent. He was not a man to let his property slip through his fingers, and she was not sure she would have the strength to defy him when he came.

"Belike he's as glad to be shut of me as I am of him," she said now. The children were happy here. Mary loved being doted upon by her grandparents, playing with her cousins, being free from her father's long prayers and beatings. Little Neddy was growing strong, almost ready to start walking.

"That house in Ferryland is yours, not his," Nancy said, a refrain she brought up often. "That was your dowry."

"Aye, but 'tis his now that we are married. The only way I'd ever get it back is if he were dead."

"Not the worst idea in the world, for that louse-ridden cur." Nancy lowered her voice; Mary was surely old enough by now to understand that her mother and her grandparents were speaking ill of her father. "'Tis a hard thing, that a woman cannot hold onto her own property if there's a man in the case. But in order to have what's yours by rights, you may have to make some kind of peace with him."

The door opened again, and one of the fishing servants put his head inside to say, "Master, there's a pinnace coming in."

"Coming in here?" Musketto Cove, tucked between the two large and busy bays of Harbour Grace and Carbonear, was rarely visited by any vessel from the outside. There was no reason to come here except to visit or do business with the Perry family. But today, it seemed, someone had business with them.

The ship was one of the Kirke family pinnaces out of Ferryland, which made Meg's stomach tighten with fear. But the man who climbed out of it was not her husband; it was young David Kirke.

Something in Meg was annoyed to see her father, the grey-haired, experienced planter and sailor, bow his head to this stripling lad just because Kirke's father had had "Sir" in front of his name. "Welcome to Musketto Cove, Master Kirke. What business brings you here?"

"Good day, good fellow. If you are Meg Taylor's father,

I've news for your daughter."

"Aye, come on up to the house, have a cup of ale and tell us what you have to say."

At the table, David Kirke told Meg how things stood in Ferryland. "The governor and his wife left before winter. He says he will be back sometime this year, but 'tis clear he has no more intention of bringing his family back or settling down permanently. I might get the house back off him, if he means to be an absentee governor. But that's not your concern. What I came to tell you is, your husband is gone as well."

"Gone? To New England with the governor?" Surely Peter would not be fool enough to follow Mistress Treworgy back to her husband's home.

"Nay, gone the other way. He took ship for England at the end of the season. He left his shareman, Tolliver, in charge of his house, land, and boat. So if nothing changes, when the fishing starts 'twill be Tolliver running things. My mother questioned whether this was your will, seeing as how the place is yours by rights in your husband's absence, so she charged me to come here, bring you word of your husband's departure, and ask if you are content to have this fellow Tolliver act on your behalf."

"No!" Meg's own vehemence surprised her. "Simon is a steady man, and I am sure he would manage it well, but like any man, he wants to get ahead, and his wife would goad him to it. If Peter is not there to oversee him, I'd fear our house and land might end up being Tolliver's house and land before 'tis all over."

"Then you would return?"

An hour ago, she had been torn. But now, at the thought of Ferryland without Peter, the thought of her own little house, which she had worked so hard for, Meg realized she wanted to go back. It would never be as comfortable as being here surrounded by her parents, her sister and brother and their families, in the warm embrace of Musketto Cove. But the house in Ferryland was *hers* more than it was Peter's, even if the law would not agree. And if Peter returned at the end of the season, or next year? She would have to find a way to deal with him, hard as that might be.

"If you can wait, I will go back with you today," she said. "I would be there as soon as possible, while Tolliver is preparing for the fishing, so he will know who is in charge."

"I like that spirit!" Kirke said with a laugh. "Indeed, I can wait until tomorrow, if you good folk can give me a bed for the night." He glanced over at the children, playing by the hearth. "That cannot be your little one Mary, is it? She's grown half a head taller since we carried her through the woods last summer. Will you come back to Ferryland, Mistress Mary?"

Mary looked puzzled, and Meg feared she would say, *I want to stay with Granny* or *Is Papa there?* But after a moment the child said, "I want to go back to our garden where our own chickens are." She fed her grandmother's chickens daily here in Musketto Cove, but Meg had not realized Mary held onto such a firm memory of their own hens, their own house and garden. It was, after all, Mary's home, just as Musketto Cove had been Meg's.

Master Kirke was invited to dine and stay the night. Ned offered to go along on the morrow to see Meg settled, knowing he could easily find another ship returning to Conception Bay at this time of year. Meg asked what other news there was from Ferryland.

"Not a word about your friend Hannah since you all fled

by night," Master Kirke said. "You'll know more of what became of her than I do. My Aunt Frances was hopping mad. Lucky thing for me that she could never prove I'd had a hand in helping the maid escape."

"Are you one of these Quakers yourself, sir?" Ned asked.

David Kirke laughed. "Nay, I am hardly even worth calling a Christian—far too much of a reprobate to be a Quaker! But I do like to make trouble for those who think themselves high and mighty, whether those be slave owners or cruel husbands. Aunt Frances tried to convince my mother and brother to send a ship to follow after the Quakers, for she believed, rightly enough, that they had something to do with Hannah running off. But Mother told Aunt Frances she'd no coin to waste on chasing a runaway servant, and not long after that my aunt's French merchant came and whisked her off to Boston. She's left Richard to care for her plantation in Ferryland. He is angry at me still, but I don't care a tinker's curse for that."

So, there were changes all round in Ferryland, Meg thought. The governor gone, the Kirke family star rising again, Lady Frances gone. Hannah gone, hopefully to a safe haven with Stephen. And most important of all, Peter gone—for now, at least.

"I'll be ready to go home tomorrow morning," she said.

The bedchamber on the top floor of the rented house in Boston was hot, airless, cloying with the scent of sickness and the herbs used to treat it. In the bed, Chrétien Beauliveau, that large and hearty man, had dwindled to a sketch of himself, drawn against white pillows. Frances and Suzette sat beside him; they had been taking turns nursing him, but now that the doctor had said it would not be long, they both stayed by his side as much as possible.

Frances looked at her husband's pain-lined face. She had known this man little over a year. Part of her could not believe it was ending so soon; the other part told her that a romance that flamed so quickly had always been destined to blaze out just as fast.

They had married in September, soon after arriving in Boston, once sweet little convent-bred Suzette had come from France to join them. The plan had been to take a house in Boston for the winter and to set sail again in the spring, wife and daughter joining Chrétien on his merchant voyages. Eventually they would make a home, perhaps in France, perhaps in New France. All that had still lain in the delicious future, to be talked over during the long winter months.

The fever had come just as winter tapered into spring, felling all three of them, though Suzette and Frances had quickly recovered. With Chrétien, the sickness had lingered for a month. Though he had seemed to Frances such a strong man, his many years at sea had taken a toll on him, and he was nearly fifty years old. Once the sickness settled into his lungs, it was clear that the disease was winning and the man was losing. Fading from them.

His fingers tightened on Frances's. "Look after . . . my Suzette," he said. Not for the first time.

"I swear that I will."

He was a wise man, had called a lawyer long before the fever struck. Death could come so quickly, in so many ways; a man with a dependent daughter, who had recently taken a second wife, must be prudent in making his wishes clear. His considerable wealth was bestowed in such a way that when he died, Suzette would be very rich indeed upon her marriage or majority, and Frances would be more than comfortably provided for. Her lost property in England was dwarfed by what she would receive from this six-month marriage. But that felt like small consolation now.

The maid came to the door with a basin of cool water and a cloth. They had hired a maid upon arriving in Boston, and she was capable enough, but Frances missed how Hannah had known and anticipated her every need, the familiarity of long service. That familiarity had been her downfall in the end, Frances knew. She could not forget that last moment of looking into Hannah's eyes, as Richard took her off to be whipped. Sometimes those dark, angry eyes followed her into her dreams.

She had told Chrétien about Hannah, told him that Richard wanted to send someone to pursue Hannah, to bring her back. But Chrétien had laughed it off. "*Les Africaines*, they are not to be relied on," he said. "You got a good long service out of her; now that she turned rebel, you are better off without her. Hire a little Puritan girl in Boston who will work hard because she believes her God will send her to hell if she is lazy."

Frances was not sure if Rebecca, the maid, had such specific beliefs about work and damnation, but she was a good enough servant and could be easily replaced with another when they left this place. Frances vowed she would never become attached to a maid again.

Rebecca left them, the door clicking shut behind her, and Frances bent forward with the cloth, trying to cool the fever that raged beneath her husband's papery skin. His breathing eased a little; perhaps he was asleep now. It was hard to tell.

Time passed. Suzette got up, went to the privy, came back. "Will he get better, do you think, Maman Frances?"

"It is in God's hands, my dear."

"If he . . . if Papa does not recover, where will we go? Will you send me back to the nuns?" Suzette asked. Her English was good, though her accent was strong.

"Is that what you would like? You could return to the convent in France, if you are happy there, until you are ready to marry."

"I would rather . . . not. May it be that I could stay with you?"

With me. Frances hesitated, not over the idea of keeping Suzette with her, for she was fond of the girl and having a daughter would be a novelty, but at the thought of where she might end up. On an impulse, she had tied her fate to this man she hardly knew; now it seemed she would be thrown back on her own resources. Those resources would be greater, with the fortune Monsieur Beliveau would leave her, but she found it hard to plan for his death as clearly as he had done himself.

"You may go with me, wherever I go. Let us pray that such a decision will not be necessary, that God will spare your father."

They prayed together, Suzette crossing herself in her Papist way, Frances reciting by heart from the prayer book: "O most mighty and merciful God, in this time of grievous sickness, we flee unto thee for succour . . ."

But God did not grant succour. He granted Chrétien a peaceful passing, in his sleep. Suzette had gone to bed, but Frances sat by him, thinking of the strange paths that had led her here. Those paths would leave her husband in a cemetery in Boston, no Catholic priest to give him the rites or say the words at his burial, laid to rest in foreign soil. But he had been an adventurer and a traveller all his life, so perhaps he would not mind. The soul would be home with God, she was sure, regardless of the lack of a priest at his deathbed.

When it was all done—an Anglican funeral service, which was at least better than a Puritan one, and a long meeting with the lawyer to go through the bequests and settlements—Frances sat down to write a letter to her sons. Richard, she knew, enjoyed being master of the plantation in Ferryland. But Nicky was too young to be left entirely to his brother's care. Frances thought she would go back to Ferryland, to meet with Richard and make plans, then take both Nicky and Suzette with her . . . where?

Her central problem had not changed: England was still no home to her as long as Cromwell and Parliament ruled. France, Suzette's homeland, was an unknown land to Frances. Did she have the courage to start over in yet another foreign country?

I could do it. Her French was good; her stepdaughter now owned lands in France that Frances could help her manage, and the true King of England, Charles II, was in exile there. Perhaps, on the basis of her service to the late king, Frances might even find a small place for herself in the court-in-exile. It could be a gracious, elegant kind of life. Certainly a striking difference from the place where she had lived and laboured for the last eight years, from the harsh weather of the New Found Land, its bare, graceless houses, its stony soil, its ever-present salt smell of the sea and codfish. Life there had been hard. Life in France could be easy by comparison.

And yet. She thought of the little house she had made her own. That spot between the sea and the forest where she sometimes felt trapped, but also felt safe. The pride when she went over the accounts and saw the success of her enterprise. She thought of Sara, how the rough edges of their sisterhood were smoothing into a friendly competition, and there was no one else in the world who knew her better.

In France she would be an exile, dependent on others to help before she could build anything of her own, just as she had been when she first arrived in the New Found Land. In Ferryland she had a home, a name, a position. Richard was able to run the fishing business, perhaps, but he was young still and needed a guiding hand, even if he did not think so. Frances could return and be mistress of her own plantation.

Against all that, the smell of fish seemed a small price to pay.

EPILOGUE

Ferryland, July 1660

"Long live the king! Long live the king!"

The summer sun shone down on the gathered fishermen and planters of Ferryland, along with their wives, children, and servants. Everyone had been urged to come to the Sunday morning gathering on the broad expanse in front of New Kirke House, even those who were indifferent churchgoers. Meg stood near the back of the small crowd, chatting to Clara Bullard; Neddy leaned against his mother, clutching her skirts. Mary was a few steps away, chattering into Geordie Kean's ear until both were hushed by a sharp shush and a poke from Geordie's mother.

There was still no minister in Ferryland, and the practice of having separate Sunday services had ended soon after John Treworgy had left for the final time in the spring, though his power had been greatly diminished even before his going. Meg did not always go to services, since the fine for missing them was rarely levied, but she knew they were generally led by George Kirke unless a clergyman was visiting. This morning, though, it was Lady Frances Hopkins who ascended the steps in front of her sister's house to address the gathered settlers.

"Good people of Ferryland," she began, pitching her voice to carry to the fifty or so people standing before her, "I have had news of great import from the ship that arrived yesterday from England. I wish to tell you all, so that we may all rejoice. As you know, early in May Parliament declared that our rightful ruler, Charles the Second, is the true King of England. I received word yesterday that on the twenty-ninth of May, the king arrived in London, where he was welcomed by the people and Parliament and acclaimed as king. After years of rule by the wicked men who murdered King Charles the First, we have a king on the throne again. Long live King Charles!"

From the way she said it, it was clear a response was expected. After a moment, a few of the men called, "Long live the king!"

"God save the king!" Lady Frances shouted.

"God save the king!" the people shouted back, a few more voices with a little more energy this time. Then it was "Long live the king!" again, and Meg found herself joining in.

The idea of a king seemed as distant to her as it had eleven years ago when they had learned that the old king was dead. So many things had happened because of it: Governor Kirke had lost his station, his freedom and his life; the Treworgys had brought their own preachers and their own version of the truth, but failed to bend the people to them; Peter had proven himself unworthy of his Puritan convictions and fled. And somehow all those things had led to Meg in the pillory, then left alone to raise her children. And Hannah in the pillory beside Meg, then gone away to some other life where Meg could only hope she was alive and safe.

Would it all have happened the same, whether the king lived or died? Meg wondered. People like her, she thought, would catch and make fish, till the ground, store away food for winter, raise their children, and help their neighbours, whether one man or another or no man at all sat on the throne in England.

Lady Frances, having heard the cheer she wanted, went on talking. "It has been a long and dark time for England, ruled by those wicked men. We pray for happier and better times ahead, for we are, all of us here in the New Found Land, loyal subjects of the king. We pray the king will soon grant us a new governor for this land, one who worships God, obeys the king, and will lead his people justly. God save the king!" she shouted again, and the people shouted it back.

It was no secret that with Governor Treworgy gone and the royalists back in power, Lady Sara Kirke was sending letters to England asking that her eldest son be given his father's post. George Kirke still lived here in New Kirke House with his mother, his wife, and their children. His younger brother Philip had gone off to start his own plantation at Renews, just as his cousin Richard Hopkins had done in Bay Bulls; Lady Frances had decided she rather liked running her own Ferryland plantation and was not ready to give it over to her sons after all. David Kirke had moved into the governor's house and started his own fishing enterprise. He lived in the house and had reopened his father's tavern, but he seemed to have no interest in governing the colony.

Lady Frances stepped down; George Kirke stepped up, took out the prayer book, and began reading the service for the day. Meg's mind drifted back to the question that tugged at her mind: *Would it all have happened the same?*

She could not guess, at this distance in time, whether Peter might have been a better husband, a more contented settler, if a Puritan governor had not come to stir up his religious fervour. A man who would stray from his wife with one woman might as easily do so with another, even if Patience Treworgy had never set foot on Ferryland's soil. Meg had heard nothing from Peter these four years, but she had continued to manage the household, the two boats, and the fishing servants in his name. Simon Tolliver had made many offers to manage things for her, but Meg had held the line firmly. She had accepted help when she needed it, both from Simon and from her other neighbours, but she made it clear that she was the one in charge as long as Peter was away.

On the way home after service, Mary was as full of questions as her mother, though hers were spoken aloud. "Mama, what does *king* mean? What is a king?"

"The king is . . . a very rich and powerful man, who lives far away in England. He rules over us all."

"How does he rule?"

"Well, he . . . he makes the laws."

"What laws?"

"Er . . . the laws that say nobody can steal, or kill anyone else, or . . . do bad things."

"So nobody will do bad things now that there is a king? Is he like God? God said not to steal or kill." Mary's religious education had become haphazard since her father had gone away, but she remembered the commandments that had been drilled into her in her earliest years.

Meg sighed. "People will always do bad things."

"I'll not do bad things. I'm a *very* good boy," said Neddy, eager to be included in the conversation.

"You are not. You are a very bad boy, and if you disobey Mama, the king will come and chop off your head," said Mary, with a hand motion that suggested chopping the head of a codfish, a thing she had seen often, for she was old enough to help with work on the flakes.

Meg was already walking hand in hand with Neddy; now she reached out and took Mary's hand, swinging both children's hands between hers. "If the two of you quarrel and make trouble with each other, 'tis not the king you need to worry about—it will be Mama who sends you to bed without any supper."

"I *want* to go to bed without supper! I don't want any old pottage!" Neddy said, then after a heartbeat, he added, "But I will eat it if you tell me to, Mama."

Meg laughed aloud at her two children, both so strong-willed and so different from one another. People said it must be hard to raise them without a father, and Meg sighed and tried to look sad, but she secretly believed they were better off than they would have been with Peter in the house spouting Scripture and criticizing every mistake they made.

She paused as they rounded the corner that brought their little house into view. The house had not changed much, save for a second glazed window she had managed to purchase last year, and new shutters she had hired Simon to make. There was a sturdy new chicken coop with a pen for the goats. Perhaps next year, she could get a pig. She had put up most of the new fence herself, though Alf Bullard had set the posts for her in return for Meg caring for Clara's children the odd few times. Her property was not the largest or finest along the shore by any means, but it was tidy, prosperous, and nothing to be ashamed of.

"Why are we stopping? I want to run home!" Mary pulled her hand from Meg's, picked up her skirts, and began to tear along the road toward the house, and Neddy pulled at Meg, wanting to chase his sister but still hold his mother's hand. By the time they reached the door, all three were laughing and out of breath from running.

Meg cut slices of bread and cheese for them to have along with the pottage she had left simmering on the hearth, a bit of salt pork in it, as a Sunday treat. They were just finishing dinner when she heard footsteps outside the door.

Meg thought it might be Peggy Tolliver, perhaps bringing her children to play. She found Peggy easier to get on with since the Treworgys and Peter had gone away; her Puritan principles had eased a little. A Sunday afternoon visit with the Tollivers was commonplace now, and Meg no longer considered Peggy's company a trial.

She was surprised, upon opening the door, to see not her nearest neighbour but young David Kirke. Still "young David" to her, though his father was long dead and he must be about four-and-twenty by now. She had had little to do with the young master since he had aided her and Hannah all those years ago; he travelled often, especially in winter. He had, in fact, been lately in England and returned on the ship that had arrived yesterday, bringing the news that had made Lady Frances so joyful.

"Master Kirke! What can I do for you?"

"'Tis what I can do for you, Meg Taylor. The news of the king's restoration is not the only piece of information I brought back from England. I picked up tales here and there of many folks connected with our people here in Ferryland."

"Hannah? Have you learned anything about where she is?"

He smiled. "No, I did not ask, for I am sure that wherever she is, she would rather that nobody in Ferryland, especially none of our family, knew it."

"I am sure you are right."

"Odd that you would ask about your friend first, when your husband is in England."

"Ships come and go all the time. If Peter wanted to send a message, I would have had it by now."

"And you were in no hurry to send any message to him, were you? But in fact, I do have news of him. I know not if 'twill be welcome or unwelcome."

Meg's throat tightened; she did not know what she wished for. "Whatever news it be, tell me."

He looked around her, at the children still finishing their dinner at the table. Mary was already curious, regarding their well-dressed visitor with wide eyes. "Can you step outside?" he asked Meg.

Meg came out, closed the door behind her. "Is he coming back here? Has he taken another wife?"

"Try once more. Three guesses should take you there."

She waited a heartbeat. "He is dead."

"Yes. In a brawl. It seems your man and a few of his Leveller friends got into a fight with some other men on the Bristol docks because the crowd was celebrating the king's restoration. 'Twas only a small scuffle, and the law did not get involved, but one of the king's men dealt your husband a solid blow to the head. He died that very night."

"Well now. Fighting to the end. If he couldn't die in battle, this would have been the next best thing, I suppose."

"You are not sad."

"No." She could not find a word for what she felt. "Thank you for telling me. 'Tis better to know."

"I did ask around, as I was in Bristol when I heard the news. His brother, whom I got the tale from, knew nothing about Peter having made a will or any such thing. So I suppose this is all yours, and your children's—as it should be."

"Thank you," she said again, and David Kirke turned and left. When he was gone, the door opened and Mary came out. "What did Master Kirke want?"

"Oh, just to tell me some news about . . . someone I once knew," Meg said, ruffling her daughter's curls. She would tell them, of course, when she had time to think. Tell her children that the father Mary dimly remembered and Neddy had no memory of at all had died far away in England.

She tried to feel a twinge of regret for the handsome young fisherman who had courted and wedded her so long ago. But there was nothing left to fan that flame to life. It had been stamped out under Peter's own heel. He had gone away and left her everything she wanted—children, home, plantation, freedom. She could not feel anything but gratitude to God, though she knew it was wicked to thank Him for her husband's untimely death.

She kept her hand on Mary's head as she looked out over the wide waters of the bay, shining in the sun. That broad expanse of blue and silver, the white sails of the ships at rest in the harbour, the rows and rows of codfish drying on the flakes. Her two boats tied up to her wharf. She looked at it all from the step of her own house—her land, her garden, her chickens, her children. Echoing David Kirke's words, she thought, *All mine. Just as it should be.*

AUTHOR'S AFTERWORD

The Kirke and Hopkins families were real people who shaped the fortunes of one of the first major English settlements in Newfoundland: Ferryland, called the Colony of Avalon by its first governor, Lord Baltimore, and renamed the Pool Plantation by Governor David Kirke. Sources differ about the number of sons Sara and David Kirke and Frances and William Hopkins had, along with the names of those sons, but the basic outline of what we know about their lives is represented here as accurately as possible.

Almost all the other characters in this book, except for John Treworgy, Hester Biddle, and Mary Fisher, are products of my own imagination. As has been true for most of history, ordinary, working-class men and women lived and died without leaving much trace in historical records. Occasionally I have used the name of a real person from these records, but the details of people's lives are entirely my own invention, based on what we know about how English settlers in Newfoundland lived in the mid-seventeenth century.

I include a few notes here about specific subjects and people in the story, for those who may be interested in knowing more about the historical background.

The English Civil War: The massive upheaval that occurred in English society during the Civil War (1642–1649) and during the Interregnum period that followed (1649–1660) is often forgotten today. Even the colourful kings of the Stuart dynasty who preceded and followed that period have not received the kind of popularity in fiction, film, and TV that, for example, Henry VIII and the Tudors have, though they certainly deserve it!

More than 140 years before the French shocked the world by cutting off their king's head, the English had done the same thing, only to put that king's son back on the throne after an eleven-year experiment in republican government. The question that sparked the writing of this novel for me was how those cataclysmic events might have appeared to English settlers living an ocean away in Newfoundland, people who still thought of themselves as Englishmen and women.

There is no evidence that Prince Rupert of the Rhine ever visited Newfoundland, but there's also no evidence that he didn't. The idea that he might have slipped away from Portugal, where his fleet was hemmed in by Commonwealth ships in the spring of 1650, and made a visit across the ocean is, of course, fanciful, but if he had come to Ferryland, he likely would have been welcomed by the Kirkes, who were loyal to the Crown. Nonetheless, such a colourful and important character of this time period was too delicious for a fiction writer to ignore, and since so much of his time was spent at sea in the years following his uncle's execution, I thought bringing him briefly to Ferryland was not too great a leap of plausibility.

Frances Hopkins: Writing fiction about real people is in many ways more difficult than writing wholly fictional characters, since I try as much as possible to weave the fictional story into what we know of the real person's life. With Frances Hopkins, this is a challenge. We know almost certainly that she was the wife of William Hopkins, master of Newport Grammar School, who was knighted for his service to King Charles I during the final months of that monarch's life. We know that by November 1648, very shortly after the time when the king was staying in her home or perhaps while he was still there, King Charles himself wrote to David Kirke about the fact that Lady Frances "and her family" were "visiting" Ferryland. We don't know for certain when or where her husband died; King Charles sent William Hopkins a letter in late November 1648, so he may have still been alive at that time. We also don't know for certain how many children the Hopkins family had or what their names or their ultimate fates were, though Peter Pope, whose book *Fish Into Wine* is the best source on the history of Ferryland, suggests two sons named Richard and Nicholas who went on to become planters in different parts of Newfoundland.

Frances's second marriage to a mysterious Frenchman who quickly disappears from the account is a matter of historical record, though I differ (for reasons that would take too long to explain here and are possibly tedious) with Pope's conjecture about who this husband may have been. Like most women from her period in history, Frances left behind only enigmatic traces of her life, leaving plenty of room for a novelist to imagine the rest.

Hannah Peake: Hannah is a fictional character, and we do not have any record of any of the Kirke or Hopkins families employing a Black servant at that time, though it is entirely plausible that they could have. Many Black people, some free and some enslaved, were living and working in England at this time. David Kirke Sr. is on record as having owned and sold an enslaved Black youth named Olivier about twenty-five years before the time of this story, and about 130 years later, John Benger of Ferryland included instructions in his will to free two enslaved adults and three children. For Frances Hopkins to have brought a Black servant to Ferryland in the years between those two records is by no means unlikely.

As for the change in Hannah's status over the course of the story, her fate is similar to that of many Black people in the English colonies during those mid-seventeenth-century years when the practice of chattel slavery was becoming more entrenched and widespread. An individual's status could often be the subject of disagreement, and sometimes of court battles. One instructive case for me in imagining Hannah's trajectory was that of Elizabeth Key, who sued for and won her freedom in Virginia in 1656, the same year in which Hannah's story comes to its crisis in this novel. Like Hannah, Elizabeth was of mixed race, baptized Christian (some English people in those early days believed that Christians could not hold other Christians in slavery), and she argued that her indenture to her master had ended and she should now be free. So while Hannah's story is fictional, it illustrates the real struggles of many Black people at a time when freedom or enslavement could depend on a legal ruling or a master's whim.

The Quakers: The Quaker religion was a very new one in 1656, but already Quaker missionaries, many of them women, were travelling the world sharing their new teachings. Records indicate that one or both of Hester Biddle and Mary Fisher were aboard ships that docked in Newfoundland in 1656 and 1659. There's no evidence that they visited Ferryland, but it was one of the most important settlements and busiest trading ports in Newfoundland at the time and the home of the governor, so they may well have stopped there.

Early Quakers, like Levellers and many of the reforming sects of the time, questioned and defied social hierarchies. It was not until the eighteenth century that Quakers took a defined anti-slavery stance; in the early years, some Quakers spoke out against the slave trade while others owned enslaved people and saw no conflict with their principles. We don't know what Hester Biddle's or Mary Fisher's views on slavery would have been, but Hester Biddle, in particular, was outspoken about the exploitation of the poor by the rich, and Mary Fisher's own humble origins might have inclined her to empathize with enslaved people. I chose to have Hannah confront them directly with the question, because white anti-slavery abolitionists whose names we remember and honour often came to that position after being challenged by Black people whose names may have been forgotten.

Indigenous people in Newfoundland: In many stories about English colonization of the "New World," Indigenous people are silent and absent, an omission I tried to correct in my Cupids Trilogy. This was a concern for me in writing this novel, since in Ferryland at this period, Indigenous people genuinely were silent and absent, with no recorded contact between Ferryland settlers and Beothuk during the years covered by this story.

There is archaeological evidence that some Beothuk visited Ferryland in the sixteenth century, possibly to trade with migratory fishermen or scavenge material from deserted fishing stations, but the little documentary evidence we have suggests they had abandoned the east coast of the Avalon before the start of permanent English settlement. They are mentioned in this story, but only to remark on their absence; newcomers like Patience, coming from New England where settlers were used to contact with the Indigenous population, expected to see them in Newfoundland but did not.

The wampum beads that John Treworgy might have acquired from trading with the Abenaki in Maine and never got to use in Newfoundland are inspired by the discovery of wampum beads at Ferryland in the summer of 2025, while I was writing this book. In the novel, they sit on Treworgy's desk as a quiet reminder of the people who are not far away but choose to keep their distance.

Patience Treworgy: We know that New England merchant John Treworgy, presumably a Puritan since he was favoured by Parliament and given the role, replaced David Kirke Sr. as governor in Ferryland. Whether he was actually a resident governor, whether he brought his wife and family to live there, and indeed who his wife was, are not known. Patience found her way into this novel as a representative of a certain type of woman who upholds the values of a patriarchal religious system even while she herself is oppressed by it.

For the first time since university, I reread Nathaniel Hawthorne's *The Scarlet Letter* while writing this novel and was struck by how very sexless and remote the illicit affair between New England Puritans is in Hawthorne's nineteenth-century novel, set in the seventeenth century. If you think Patience and Peter's relationship owes anything to my desire for a steamier *Scarlet Letter*, you may not be wrong.

Meg and Peter Taylor: Meg is, of course, an authorial shout-out on my part to her parents, Ned and Nancy, two of the main characters in my Cupids Trilogy. She also represents my attempt to imagine how the first generation of English settlers born in Newfoundland might view their homeland and their relationship to their parents' homeland in England. In addition, through Meg, I have tried to pay tribute to the many, many generations of Newfoundland outport women who worked hard to make better lives for themselves and their families under difficult conditions.

While Peter is certainly, as Hannah says, "not a good man," I did not want him to be a simple villain. He is a Leveller, part of a sect of English Protestants who believed in the radical notion of complete social equality—at least, for all white English men. Like Peter himself, most of the Levellers met a bad end, but I felt it important to remind readers that the same religious reformers whom we associate with strict morality, harsh judgment, and a general lack of fun also believed in overthrowing hierarchies, dethroning kings, and creating a more equal society. Nobody is simple, not even the Puritans.

As with any work of historical fiction, I've read widely in researching this book and will not attempt to provide a full bibliography but will mention a few key titles. As noted above, Peter Pope's *Fish Into Wine* (UNC Press, 2004), while it may be a little dense and technical for the casual reader, is the definitive work on English settlement in Newfoundland generally and Ferryland specifically at this period, particularly, as the title implies, on the economics of the codfish trade.

On the situation in England, John Matusiak's book *The Prisoner King: Charles I in Captivity* (The History Press, 2017) was helpful to me in imagining the king as Frances Hopkins would have known him in those last months of his life. Alice Hunt's *Republic: Britain's Revolutionary Decade, 1649–1660* (Faber & Faber, 2024) provided glimpses into both politics and everyday life in Cromwell's England during the Interregnum.

In imagining Hannah's life, I drew on Miranda Kaufman's *The Black Tudors* (OneWorld Publications, 2017) for an overview of the various roles that Black people played in English life at that period, as well as *Black Harbour,* by Xaiver Campbell and Heather Barrett (Boulder Publications, 2023), for an exploration of the traces of Black presence in Newfoundland records over the centuries. *Good Wives, Nasty Wenches, and Anxious Patriarchs* by Kathleen M. Brown (UNC Press, 1996) was helpful in tracing Black women's changing status in Virginia in this period, with some insights that could be applied to other English colonies.

Naomi Baker's book *Voices of Thunder: Radical Religious Women of the Seventeenth Century* (Reaktion Books, 2025) came out while I was working on this novel, and I made use of her chapters on both Hester Biddle and Mary Fisher to lend depth to their brief appearance in this story, as well as to better understand the movement of which they were a part.

As for the real human beings I talked to in addition to reading books, special thanks are due to Dr. Barry Gaulton and Dr. Neil Kennedy, both of Memorial University, for thoughtful conversations about various topics related to my research. As with my last three books, archaeologist and historian William Gilbert gave this manuscript a careful reading and provided context and correction on countless historical details; though my writing has moved beyond his home base of Cupids, he remains an invaluable resource for his expertise on English settlement in seventeenth-century Newfoundland. Many thanks also to Xaiver Campbell for a careful reading of Hannah's chapters with many helpful insights offered. The errors that doubtless remain after consulting with experts are entirely my own.

My first readers—Jennifer Morgan, Lori Savory, Christine Hennebury, and Tina Chaulk—have once again proved their value as sharp-eyed and thoughtful critics as well as enthusiastic supporters. I am grateful for the support of ArtsNL and the Access Copyright Foundation/SK Arts for grants which supported the research and writing of this project.

The team at Breakwater Books, led by the visionary Rebecca Rose, has believed in and supported me across the lifespans of eight books. Breakwater's dedication to bringing books by Newfoundland and Labrador writers to readers across the province and the country is unparalleled. During this project, the stellar teamwork of Rebecca Roberts, Emma Cole, and Oliver Hallett was essential in helping *Beyond the Brightening Sea* reach you, the reader. The thoughtful and sharp-eyed editing provided by Marianne Ward and Leslie

Vryenhoek helped make this a much better book, as did the work of Jeanie MacFarlane.

Finally, thanks to those who have provided more love and support than anyone else: to Don Morgan for helping to make me the writer and human being I am today; to Jason Cole for always being by my side—for better, for worse, for all that—and to Chris and Emma for giving me reasons to believe in the future while I look back at the past. (Yes, Emma, you get thanked twice!)

Trudy Morgan-Cole is the author of seven previous Newfoundland historical novels published by Breakwater Books, most recently the best-selling Cupids Trilogy: *A Roll of the Bones*, *Such Miracles and Mischiefs*, and *A Company of Rogues*. In addition to novels, her other writing includes the play *The Mirror,* about pioneering Newfoundland suffragist Armine Nutting Gosling. Trudy is a retired educator who lives in St. John's with her husband and dog.